RUSSIAN C○
ENEMY SP⟨

To Station Intelligence Chief: Eliminate anyone
who attempts to interfere in our diamond trading
program. The necessary resources and personnel
are approved.

PRIMARY TARGET:

Name: Amanda McClintock, aka Phoenix
Employer: Devereaux, an elusive vigilante
who pursues social justice
Age: 29
Present location: unknown

Amanda McClintock, daughter of deceased
Russian double agent Christopher McClintock, is
a highly skilled covert operative rumored to have
knowledge of the Udarsky Cache, a stockpile of
diamonds that her father systematically stole
from Mother Russia during his years as a spy.
Devereaux has enlisted McClintock to dismantle
the diamond smuggling ring. She is to be
eliminated at all costs.

Dear Reader,

We're thrilled to bring you another exhilarating month of captivating women and explosive action! Our Bombshell heroines will take you for the ride of your life as they come under fire from all directions. With lives at stake and emotions on edge, these women stand and deliver memorable stories that will keep you riveted from cover to cover.

When the going gets tough, feisty Stella Valocchi gets going, in *Stella, Get Your Gun,* by Nancy Bartholomew. Her boyfriend's a lying rat, her uncle's been murdered and her sexy ex is back in town, but trust Stella—compared to last week, things are looking up....

Loyal CIA agent Samantha St. John has been locked up—for treason! With the reluctant help of her wary partner, Sam will hunt for the real traitor—who bears an uncanny resemblance to Sam herself—in *Double-Cross,* by Meredith Fletcher, the latest adventure in the twelve-book ATHENA FORCE continuity series.

Don't miss the twists and turns as a former operative is sucked back into the spy life to right the wrongs done to her family, in author Natalie Dunbar's exciting thriller, *Private Agenda.*

And finally, a secret agent needs a break—but when her final mission goes wrong, she's pushed to the limit and has to take on a rookie partner. Luckily she's still got her deadliest weapon... it's *Killer Instinct,* by Cindy Dees.

When it comes to excitement, we're pulling no punches! Please send me your comments c/o Silhouette Books, 233 Broadway, Suite 1001, New York, NY 10279.

Sincerely,

Natashya Wilson
Associate Senior Editor, Silhouette Bombshell

Please address questions and book requests to:
Silhouette Reader Service
U.S.: 3010 Walden Ave., P.O. Box 1325, Buffalo, NY 14269
Canadian: P.O. Box 609, Fort Erie, Ont. L2A 5X3

CINDY DEES

KILLER INSTINCT

Published by Silhouette Books

America's Publisher of Contemporary Romance

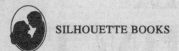 SILHOUETTE BOOKS

ISBN 0-373-51330-5

KILLER INSTINCT

Copyright © 2004 by Cynthia Dees

All rights reserved. Except for use in any review, the reproduction
or utilization of this work in whole or in part in any form by any
electronic, mechanical or other means, now known or hereafter
invented, including xerography, photocopying and recording, or in
any information storage or retrieval system, is forbidden without
the written permission of the editorial office, Silhouette Books,
233 Broadway, New York, NY 10279 U.S.A.

All characters in this book have no existence outside the imagination of
the author and have no relation whatsoever to anyone bearing the same
name or names. They are not even distantly inspired by any individual
known or unknown to the author, and all incidents are pure invention.

This edition published by arrangement with Harlequin Books S.A.

® and TM are trademarks of Harlequin Books S.A., used under license.
Trademarks indicated with ® are registered in the United States Patent
and Trademark Office, the Canadian Trade Marks Office and in other
countries.

Visit Silhouette Books at www.eHarlequin.com

Printed in U.S.A.

CINDY DEES

started flying airplanes while sitting in her dad's lap at age three. She was the only kid in the neighborhood who got a pilot's license before she got a driver's license. After college, she fulfilled a lifelong dream and became a U.S. Air Force pilot. She flew everything from supersonic jets to C-5s, the world's largest cargo airplanes. During her career, she got shot at, met her husband, flew in the Gulf War and amassed a lifetime supply of war stories. After she left flying to have a family, she was lucky enough to fulfill another lifelong dream—writing a book. Little did she imagine that it would win the Golden Heart Contest and sell to Silhouette! She's thrilled to be able to share her dream with you. She'd love to hear what you think of her books at www.cindydees.com or P.O. Box 210, Azle, TX 76098.

To my mother for daring me to write,
my husband for daring me to love and my
daughter for daring me to shoot for the stars.

Chapter 1

New York City

It took her three tense passes by the mouth of the cul-de-sac, but finally, the street was empty of other pedestrians as she approached the alley that was her target. Amanda McClintock slipped into the shadows.

Inky blackness wrapped around her as she peered into the dripping bowels of the city block. Come on, eyes, adapt already. The behemoth just ahead resolved into an overflowing trash Dumpster. Farther ahead, a pair of fire escapes dangled, rusty portcullises of modern decay. Farther still, her goal—Carnegie Hall's backstage entrance—floated in a disembodied pool of light. She eased forward cautiously, every sense on high alert.

It had stopped raining, but the brick walls on either side of her shone greasily. Puddles marked potholes in tired asphalt, and she stepped around them with catlike distaste for water. As she drew near the radius of light, faint echoes of music became audible. It was more a subliminal pulsing than actual sound, but the tempo of her heartbeat increased to match the rhythm vibrating through the air.

Four crumbling cement steps up to the porch. A last check over her shoulder. With quick twists, she unscrewed the single light bulb overhead. The alley went completely black. Slowly, it faded back into view as her eyes adjusted to the dark. She paused until the details took form and checked for any signs of movement. All clear.

She drew in a calming breath that smelled of oil and car exhaust. Releasing the fouled air slowly, she flexed her fingers. Then, with a delicate touch born of experience, she went to work on the lock of the heavy steel door before her. The double-cylinder dead bolt required double tension bars and raking both cylinders simultaneously—a tricky bit of work. She crouched down, her ear inches from the lock as she manipulated the thin metal rods inside its mechanism. A satisfying snick. *Bingo.* She stood up and stowed her picks.

She brushed back her cuff and glanced at the glowing face of her watch. Half a minute ahead of schedule. While she counted to thirty in her head, she searched the darkness of the alley, alert for anything unusual. Still quiet. In a detached corner of her mind, she wondered idly how much Devereaux had paid the security guard who was usually stationed here to be absent from his post. She'd bet it was a bundle. Her employer was obscenely rich and didn't hesitate to pay big to see private justice prevail.

Twenty-eight…Twenty-nine…Thirty.

Time to go. The familiar tingle of adrenaline seeped into her bloodstream and raced across her skin. Her pulse increased sharply, and her body felt light and fast. She pushed the door open and stepped inside.

A fanfare of trumpets resounded arrogantly, heralding the entrance of the violins. The strings wove mesmerizing, snake-charmer's strains, while slowly, implacably, they were overtaken and drowned by the swelling notes of brass horns. Timpani rolled forth and broke over the orchestra like an angry ocean, crashing down and sending powerful echoes across the sea of uplifted faces. Wave after wave of music descended upon the audience, pummeling it in its grandeur. The woman seated at the grand piano seemed lifted from the bench by the sheer force of the sound, compelled to batter the ivory keys. The music swelled louder and louder until the edifice was consumed by it, the very air alive and vibrating. With a final apocalyptic crash, the symphony ended.

Time froze while echoes reverberated in the void. The audience roused itself slowly from its breathless trance and applause thundered.

A dozen rows back from the stage of Carnegie Hall, Taylor Roberts squirmed uneasily in his seat, overwhelmed and unsettled by the performance. He tugged at the black bow tie pinching his neck and shifted his tall frame uncomfortably. Biting back a curse as he banged his knees on the back of the seat before him, he murmured an apology to the patron in the seat and gazed around the auditorium. What in the hell was he supposed to be watching?

It made no sense that his very first field assignment entailed nothing more than sitting in a concert hall watching a Russian debutante pound on a piano. Why would Devereaux pay good money for him to waste his time like this?

The strains of music swelled more loudly inside the building, and the detached corner of Amanda's mind recognized the piece as Tchaikovsky's Piano Concerto no. 1. One of her favorites. Concentrate, you idiot! You've got a job to do. She paused for a moment, forcing herself back into the emotionless state of readiness necessary in her line of work.

She glanced around as the theater's blueprints came alive before her. Orienting herself briefly, she moved off briskly down a corridor and arrived in a few moments at a door bearing a white, handwritten nameplate. In Cyrillic and English lettering was the name Marina Subova.

Show time.

She pulled her silk cuff down over her hand, reached for the doorknob and slipped into the pianist's dressing room. It was spacious and well lit, strewn with clothes, sheet music, full ashtrays and empty cigarette wrappers. Across the room, Amanda spied a man on his hands and knees. His head was hidden under the dressing table, and he was clearly searching for something.

"Ah-ha!" he crowed.

He grabbed something too small for her to see from her vantage point. He backed up awkwardly until his head emerged, then grabbed on to the edge of the dressing table and hauled himself to his feet. Whatever he'd been searching for went into a pants pocket.

His hair was coarse and gray, cut in a short, military style. His shoulders, although massive, stooped heavily, and his spine curved as though he'd carried an enormous weight for far too long. He still easily topped six feet, although in his prime, Amanda recalled he hadn't passed through the seven-foot doorways of her school with much room to spare. Grigorii Kriskin had once been a giant bear of a man. Age might have whittled away much of his bulk, but he was still formidable. She pushed down a tickle of doubt about this mission. And cleared her throat politely.

At the sound, Kriskin whirled around with remarkable agility for his age. His look of caution was replaced by one of pleased surprise as recognition dawned. "Amanda! Amanda McClintock. It is very long since I see you." His English was heavily accented with Russian gutturals. "And what carries you behind stage? You are tired to listen of Marina play, or she not do good tonight?"

"Grisha!" Amanda smiled in feigned surprise. "So, Marina's bear still guards her wherever she goes. Actually, I came back early to beat the crush of fans who will be fighting to get a moment with our star." While she spoke, she eased open the plastic zipper bag concealed in the pocket of her flowing skirt. She palmed the soggy gauze pad inside and stepped toward the man as if to hug him. She held his gaze steadily. Doubt registered in the old man's faded eyes.

Man, he was good. Astonishing that his instincts were still so sharp. He sensed the danger, even though only a long-time acquaintance of the petite, nonthreatening, female persuasion was in the room. As she closed the small distance between them, the old man drew back slightly. To her trained eye, he coiled like a cat preparing to spring. His gaze flickered for the barest instant to his left. A mistake, that. She stepped nimbly to her right, cutting off his escape route, and lunged at him. Lightning fast, her hand shot out and slapped him wetly across the face with the gauze pad.

He jerked his head away and lowered a shoulder to charge. With a growl rumbling in his throat, he rushed her, grabbing her around the waist in a football tackle. The momentum of his onslaught sent them crashing heavily to the floor. He landed on top of her with a thud, knocking the breath out of her. She gasped desperately for air, riveted by the old man's red-rimmed eyes, only a foot from her own, staring at her in unfocused rage.

She squirmed in his rib-cracking grip, trapped under his bruising weight. Suffocating, she managed to wriggle her left hand free. She groped the floor beside her hip with her fingers, searching urgently for the pad she'd dropped.

He jerked his head up sharply, clipping her squarely on the chin. Her jaw slammed shut and a rush of pain blurred her vision. Tasting blood from her badly bitten tongue, she twisted in violent desperation. Yanking for all she was worth, she pulled her entire left arm free. She swept it frantically across the floor. Spots danced in front of her eyes. Her grip on consciousness was slipping. She didn't have much time left to save herself. Where did that damned pad go?

* * *

Taylor's instructions had been to watch for a signal from the pianist to anyone, perhaps someone in the orchestra or in the audience. It sounded like Marina Subova was involved in something shady or even illegal. But what? What could a world-famous concert pianist have gotten herself tangled up in?

The applause finally wound down, and the audience rustled in marked anticipation. His curiosity piqued, Taylor opened his program. Next was a piano solo, one of the pianist's famous variations on a theme. The program explained that Subova's full musical genius was revealed in the subtlety of her improvisations. Tonight she would be playing a variation in A minor. To Taylor, who liked classical music about as much as a trip to the dentist, the piece sounded heavy and depressing. Its melody escaped him for the most part, and occasionally a subtle discord offended his ears. He shifted in his seat and pondered the similarities between modern music and modern art—both were beyond his comprehension and vaguely disturbing somehow.

The improvisation was a huge hit with the audience, and it was several minutes before the crowd quieted enough for the evening's performance to continue. The chubby penguin of a conductor rapped his stand with his baton. After a dramatic pause, he launched the orchestra into a final symphony.

The single breath of the chloroform derivative the old man had inhaled finally took effect, and his grasp around her loosened slightly. Thank God. With a desperate heave, Amanda shoved him off of her. He rolled sideways and rocked back onto his knees, blue-veined hands outstretched. Two gnarled thumbs jabbed for her eyes, and she twisted her entire body aside.

She glimpsed a square of white. And dived for it. With her eyes screwed tightly shut to avoid the old man's gouging fingers, she swung her open hand blindly toward his face. She contacted him squarely across the nose, and he reeled back with a grunt. He got a hand up and grabbed her wrist, holding the drugged gauze away from his face. Amanda strained against him, frozen in a momentary stalemate. Their gazes locked beyond their straining hands.

His eyes were a watery gray and rheumy, his pupils contracted to tiny black points of fury that promised vengeance against this unprovoked attack. A single question raged in their pale depths. *Why?*

She flinched at the sight. This wasn't just some nameless, faceless target. This was a man she'd known since she was a little girl. He had two sons and a half-dozen grandchildren. Had loved his wife fiercely until she died of breast cancer a few years back. He liked to fish. And she was attacking him.

Her hand was slowly forced another millimeter away from his face, and panic hit her. He'd kill her if he got the chance, old friend or not. Of that she had no doubt. Pure survival adrenaline surged in her veins, and she leaned into his powerful wrist. Thankfully, his muscles began to tremble and inexorably began to give way. The pad drew near his face. Abrupt sadness washed across his features. And then, an expression of determination, defiance even, entered his gaze. His jaw rippled powerfully, and a crunching sound came from his mouth as if he'd just shattered a tooth.

Oh, God. No!

Amanda ripped free of his grasp, which suddenly went slack. He jerked in a single head-to-toe spasm, and his face contorted in a rictus of pain. His breath came in a short, rattling gasp. He made a brief choking noise and clutched at his throat. His hands fell away, bent into twisted, useless claws. Amanda reached out and pried his jaws open as his eyes rolled up into his head.

A whoosh of bitter air rushed forth. It smelled of almonds. Cyanide.

He toppled over slowly onto her lap and lay there, motionless. No. No, no, no! Not Grigorii. Panting heavily, she rolled his limp form off of her and scrambled backward on her hands and knees. Panic clawed at her, horror at what had just hap-

pened freezing her brain into immobility. It wasn't supposed
to happen this way. She was supposed to use their acquaintance
to get close to him and knock him out. Then the next team
would come in and carry him away for some drug-assisted
questioning. All neat and clean.

His face was a monstrous shade of red, his lips pulled away
from his teeth in an exaggerated snarl. His eyes stared at nothing. She smelled urine. The acrid odor turned her stomach, and
abruptly, she tore at her skirt. Her pocket. The plastic bag in
her pocket.

She snatched the bag out and slammed it to her mouth just
as she gagged and vomited up the meager contents of her stomach. Cold sweat beaded on her forehead, clammy against her
skin. Shivering violently, she dry heaved again.

She had to get out of here. Away from death. Away from
the body.

She leaned forward and pressed her fingers to Grigorii's neck.
There would be no pulse, but she had to check. He was too good
to screw up killing himself. His skin was already cool to the touch
beneath a scratchy stubble. She yanked her hand away from his
lifeless, rubbery flesh. Acting on instinct, she reached into his
pants pocket and grabbed the object he'd been searching for.

Using the wall for support, she climbed clumsily to her feet.
A stabbing pain in her right ankle announced that she'd twisted
it in their fall. The joint collapsed when she tried to put weight
on it, and streaks of white fury shot up her calf. Now what? She
struggled to form rational thoughts. Finally, belatedly, her training kicked in and her brain began to function. She had to make
it back outside without being caught and then call in someone
to clean up this disaster.

She limped to the door and peered cautiously outside. The
corridor was still deserted, but she'd be noticed for sure if she
bunny-hopped all the way back to the alley. There was no help
for it. She was going to have to walk out of here. She swore
under her breath, but then collected herself. Emotion later. She

supported herself against the wall, using her forearm without conscious thought, so ingrained in her was it to leave no fingerprints. As quickly as she could manage, she hobbled down the hall. By dint of brutal concentration, she suppressed the pain radiating outward in increasing waves from her injured ankle. The journey back to the exit took fully twice as long as her entrance, but her luck held and she encountered no one.

She stepped out into the wet evening and inhaled a long, steadying breath. She forced down the agony one last time. Just a few more seconds and then she could fall apart. After an excruciating descent down the steps and away from the porch, she stopped in a deep shadow and pulled out a radio transmitter. One long, two short and one long beep went out to unseen faces nearby. Her silk evening blouse clung to her shoulder blades, soaked by a film of sweat that had nothing to do with being overwarm. The pain finally overtook her self-control, and she sagged against the cool, damp wall.

In seconds, four shadows rounded the corner into the alley. The first faceless form hissed, "What are you doing here? You were supposed to leave the area immediately."

"Sorry. The target didn't cooperate. I hurt my ankle in the fight."

"How bad is it?"

"My ankle? Bad enough. The mission? Shot to hell."

"What do you mean?"

She nodded at the door behind her. "You'll see."

The shadowy figure was silent for a moment. "I'll call in some backup. Stay here. Someone will come and get you."

She nodded wearily.

"Don't pass out on me, Phoenix. You're going to have to walk out of here under your own power if you don't want to draw attention."

Amanda tried to smile, but it came out a grimace. Where in the world was she going to find the strength to walk one more step on the mass of gelatinous pain that was her ankle?

* * *

Taylor started as his pager began to vibrate in the breast pocket of his tuxedo. He pulled it out, tilting the beeper in the dim theater lighting to read the message that scrolled across its digital face: "Leave now. Walk around the block."

Alarm coursed through him. No one had said anything about his being called out of the concert. He walked swiftly up the aisle to the glaring usher who guarded the exit. "I'm a doctor," he improvised. "There's an emergency."

The usher's scowl eased slightly, and she opened the door enough for him to slip into the lobby. He looked left and right as he stepped outside Carnegie Hall. Nothing appeared out of place. There must be some sort of crisis. But what? He walked all the way around the far side of the concert hall before a low whistle caught his attention. He glanced around at the wet street. Deserted. He veered into the alley on his right. And almost missed the group of shadows huddled against the wall.

"Falcon?"

"Yeah," he whispered back. "What's up?"

"One of our operatives was injured. Get her out of here." The group separated into four shadows carrying a long, lumpy, blanket-wrapped object between them. It appeared quite heavy. In fact, it looked suspiciously like a body. Gut-punching fear slammed into him. Had the woman been killed? Were they about to hand him a corpse?

One of the shadows nodded behind them. "She's back by the porch. Probably will faint if she tries to move on her own—she busted up her ankle pretty good. Sorry to interrupt your social debut, but we've already got our hands full."

The guy sounded thoroughly disgusted. Taylor stepped aside as the men hustled out of the alley and disappeared with their burden. He moved deeper into the murky bowels of the cul-de-sac where the man had indicated. He didn't see her until he was practically on top of her. She was propped up against the wall, one foot held several inches off the ground, her palms pressed against the wet bricks as if she were single-handedly holding up the structure at her back. The shadowed curves of her face were stunning, with an unearthly beauty that was part of the night itself. He stared, thunderstruck. She looked wary as he approached, a fey creature that would bolt at the merest provocation. A need to soothe her washed over him.

"Who are you?" she asked in a low voice.

He missed a mental beat at the British accent, but managed to answer calmly enough, "Apparently, I'm your designated Plan B. How bad are you hurt? Can you move?"

She pushed herself away from the wall. "Let's find out." She took a single step and her right leg collapsed completely.

With a grunt, Taylor caught her as she pitched forward into him. She felt surprisingly fragile, no taller than his shoulder and slender of build. What was someone like her doing working special ops for Devereaux?

A muffled moan escaped her.

"Well, I guess that answers that," he remarked. He bent down and picked up the woman, cradling her in his arms. She made a sound of protest against his chest and he murmured, "Relax. I'll have you out of here in a jiffy." He retraced his steps toward the alley's mouth.

After a moment, she shifted and placed her arms around his neck. The stiffness left her body, and she melted like warm, silky chocolate in his arms. A surge of protectiveness startled him, and he hugged her a little more closely. Down, Tonto. This is business.

They reached the end of the alley and he paused to peer into the street. Empty. No sign of the team that had left only moments before. Wow. He was impressed. He strode to the next corner and eased his companion to the ground. He kept a supporting arm around her, steadying her. She felt like pure sin pressed against him from chest to knee. He hailed several taxis with his free arm before one finally pulled over. The cab's interior light touched her features as she climbed in awkwardly, and Taylor was brought up short. She was younger than he expected. Fair of complexion, with rich, chestnut hair and dark eyes. Gray or possibly green—hard to tell in the lousy light. She was fully as lovely as his first impression, her beauty surreal against the dingy, stained backdrop of a New York taxicab.

The line of white around her tightly compressed lips spurred him to motion, and he slid in beside her. "Where to, fair damsel? Your chariot awaits your command."

She glanced around the cab's interior, and a spark of humor momentarily lit her face. Taylor forced himself not to gawk like a hormonal adolescent. Good God, she was radiant when she smiled. She mumbled the address of a private home in a quiet neighborhood with a brief explanation that a doctor lived there who would treat her and not ask any questions. He relayed the address to the cabbie, then leaned back in his seat and did his damnedest not to stare at his companion.

The taxi pulled away from the curb, and Amanda rested her head against the cushions. She closed her eyes.

It was over.

Now she could think. Feel. The tension she'd held at bay while she was working flooded her. The aftermath was always like this. She reeled with the power of its release. Pent-up emotions seared a path across her soul, leaving it charred and blackened. But there was freedom in the pain. It cauterized her emotions so they could not bleed.

The evening outside glittered like a diamond. Street lamps shone brightly off the wet pavement, and the city looked clean and fresh. As the blocks rolled by, Amanda huddled deeply in the seat, resting her head against the cold glass window of the taxi door. She did her best to ignore the presence of the man beside her. She didn't have the energy to figure out what had happened to her when he'd picked her up. Her sense of being safe and protected was too confusing, too disorienting to grasp just now. She lived in a world alone. Depended on nothing or nobody but herself. The man's help had been an intrusion. She should be grateful for it, she supposed, but for some reason it scared her to death.

She concentrated on blanking her mind and breathing deliberately, on trying to still the violent shaking that was setting in. The throbbing pain in her mouth was growing intolerable, and she felt her shoe becoming tight around her ankle. She needed medical treatment. But she couldn't face anybody quite yet.

Her companion was blessedly silent. She felt his gaze upon her occasionally, but he didn't intrude. Her mind spun in a riot of confused images: an old man's open-mouthed snarl of agony, neon signs flashing on wet pavement, her own frantic heartbeat pounding through her fingertips against dead flesh, headlights rushing toward her out of the blackness.

Her thoughts skipped like a broken record, recycling the events of the evening in an endless screeching cacophony. The encounter with Grigorii passed before her mind's eye over and over in microscopic detail. Eventually, it occurred to her that the aftermath was usually gone in a matter of minutes. She'd replay the job once or twice, dissect and critique her performance, catalog the emotions felt and then file them neatly away. But tonight the aftermath was growing, spreading like a canker, threatening to engulf her. This wasn't how it was supposed to go at all.

A soul-deep terror blossomed in her. Was this what it was like to finally lose one's mind? To burn out completely? *Was she going insane?* She became aware of other feelings. Drenching guilt. Disgust at herself. Disgust at the institution that had demanded this night's work of her. It left a bitter taste of bile in her throat. Her stomach burned like a hot coal was boring its way through her stomach wall into her gut. She suppressed an anguished groan. How could she have taken this job? If she'd known it would end like this, she'd never have agreed to it. Even if Devereaux had sworn that after this one last job she could stand down for a good long rest.

But she hadn't refused.

She'd betrayed a man she'd known since she was a little girl. A man who'd remembered her birthday when her father hadn't. A man who'd been kind to her.

Why? Why did he kill himself rather than let himself be taken?

She'd driven Grigorii to suicide. She was responsible for an old friend's horrible, agonizing death.

Gradually, her mind went blank as shock lowered a blanket of numbness around her. Sensing danger in the encroaching oblivion, she roused herself from her stupor. As the last of her adrenaline wore off, the tremendous drain of the evening's events finally overwhelmed her iron self-control. She looked down at the object, still clutched in her hand, from Grigorii's pocket. A single tear rolled down her cheek and splashed onto an enormous, glittering diamond.

Chapter 2

Nikko Biryayev yawned and rubbed his eyes, which burned and were beginning to blur. He sipped at a tepid mug of coffee by his elbow and grimaced. These were the inglorious moments of his job—the price he paid for a plum assignment like the Russian consulate in New York. He scowled at the sumptuous view outside his window. Too much wealth out there. Too much power. Maybe he'd live long enough to see the whole damned American empire toppled. The thought cheered him. Nikko Biryayev was and always would be a man of the old order.

A knock on his office door interrupted his musings. "Come in," he called.

The night desk clerk stood there, a manila folder in hand. "Sir, NYPD is downstairs. A man carrying a Russian diplomatic passport might have been kidnapped this evening from the dressing room of the pianist, Marina Subova. I've got the dossier on this man."

As the station intelligence chief, something like this fell

squarely under his jurisdiction. Biryayev reached for the folder. "Tell the police I'll be down in a moment." He glanced at the name on the dossier, then looked again. His jaw dropped. Grigorii Kriskin? Everyone from the old KGB days knew that name. He'd been the trusted henchman of Anton Subov—the brilliant chief strategist of the KGB Plans Directorate until the Komityet folded. Kriskin executed many of Subov's diabolical schemes. What was the old warhorse doing in New York? Biryayev would have envisioned Kriskin and Subov sipping cognac and growing gray together in a Crimean dacha. Biryayev pulled a stapled sheaf of papers out of his safe and thumbed through it. He found Marina Subova's name and glanced hastily at the notations beside it regarding surveillance. He tossed the papers back in his safe and grabbed his coat.

Twenty minutes later, Biryayev stood in Subova's dressing room. A team of men dusted the room for fingerprints while a detective beside him delivered a diatribe about bystanders contaminating crime scenes. Biryayev strolled over to the dressing table and unobtrusively pocketed the pianist's silver hairbrush and the microrecorder concealed within it. As soon as he got that recording back to the office, he'd have a better idea of what had happened than the police would ever piece together. Anybody good enough to kidnap Grigorii Kriskin surely would not leave behind evidence for the police. Biryayev exited as soon as he could without arousing suspicion and headed for the consulate.

Amanda roused as their taxi pulled up in front of a gracefully aging brick home. She felt numb all over. Her rescuer leaned over and whispered in her ear as if to speak an endearment. His murmured words were more practical and sent a jolt of apprehension through her. "Our driver's the curious sort. We'll have to put on a show for him. Stay put. I'll be around to help."

She glanced up and met the driver's intent gaze in the rearview mirror. Why hadn't she noticed his interest earlier? She must be in worse shape than she'd realized. Pull yourself together! She grasped to no avail at the bits and pieces of herself.

Her companion opened her door and offered his hand in a gallant gesture. Carefully, she swung her feet out and let him all but bodily lift her out of the cab. As he paid the driver, she watched him curiously. Ebony highlights glinted in his dark brown hair, and he flashed a toothpaste-commercial smile, even and white. As knights in shining armor went, he was doing fine so far.

An odd awareness of him thrummed through her. She felt his tiniest movement, caught every nuance in his expression, startled herself by anticipating the next time his gaze would light upon her. He wore a tuxedo strikingly well. Where had he been, dressed like that, before he'd been called in to help her? He looked as if he'd just stepped out of a fancy casino. He caught her gaze upon him and smiled intimately, as if he knew precisely what she was thinking. It took her aback and sent her heart racing before she remembered they were playing a scene for the driver. Sheesh. She returned the lover's smile in kind.

He held out his arm, and for once, she found herself grateful there was a big, strong man around. She linked her arm through his and leaned on his rock-hard forearm, letting him bear almost her entire weight. He strolled casually up the sidewalk as if totally unaware of her fingers biting into his flesh. She concentrated on matching his even pace, clenching her jaw every time her injured foot made contact with the ground. If only the cab would leave so she could stop! They reached the front porch, and still the driver sat there, infuriatingly counting his money.

Her companion turned toward her and murmured apologetically, "Pardon me for what I'm about to do."

His arms went around her and his mouth lowered toward hers. *Good Lord, he was going to kiss her.* A thrill of excitement raced through her, wildfire running before the wind. It left her trembling in anticipation of she knew not what. His head slanted toward hers, blocking the cab from her view. His lips paused, barely an inch from hers, his breath caressing her cheek like warm velvet. She steeled herself for the invasion of his mouth, but it didn't come. He remained where he was, nearly touching, nearly tasting, nearly possessing her. Anticipation built inside her, and she fought a sudden inclination to lean into him, take the kiss and be done with it.

She could imagine what his mouth would feel like—warm, alive and virile. He'd taste male and musky, perhaps with a hint of Scotch whiskey. He'd be gentle at first, then the kiss would deepen. He'd explore her mouth, and his arms would tighten around her, molding her to him. She'd feel the unyielding strength of his body; she'd sense the tension beginning to build in him, matching her own. Sparks would leap between them, and she'd melt against him. It would be a sensational kiss.

But nothing happened.

She peered up at him. His jaw was tense, and he seemed to be concentrating on whether or not the cab had left. The anticipation whooshed out of her in a rush. So much for that short-lived fantasy. Up close like this, his eyelashes were dark and thick, and his skin had the smoothness of vigorous health about it. His mouth was mobile, expressive. Emminently kissable. Beyond all that, there was steel in him, unbendable self-control.

"Is he gone yet?" Taylor asked in an undertone.

Amanda peeked past his ear. "Pulling out now, the bleeding Peeping Tom."

His lips curved into a grin, although not another muscle twitched. "Gone now?"

"Yes." The syllable was exhaled on a breath of relief.

He straightened. "Well, that was almost fun."

For some bizarre reason, she was disappointed as his arms fell away. She retorted, "Indeed. That was almost lovely. Until you almost got to the part where I almost decided you were getting fresh and almost flattened you."

"I'll keep that in mind the next time I almost consider making advances toward you," he replied wryly.

The cab's red taillights disappeared around a corner. Now that the immediate danger was past, the pain in her ankle came surging back full force. She couldn't stop herself from sagging against the arm of the man beside her.

"Easy does it," he murmured. "Only a few more steps and you'll be inside."

"Not quite. This isn't the house we're headed for."

He looked down at her, startled. "It's not?"

"Certainly not. You wouldn't want that cabbie to know our destination would you?"

"Ah. A misdirection."

Fabulous. They'd sent in a rank amateur to rescue her. A big, strong, gorgeous one, but an amateur, nonetheless. She needed Superman and Devereaux had given her Clark Kent.

"So where are we actually going?"

She pointed. "Three houses down and across the street. The one over there with the awnings and the yellow porch light."

"Can you walk that far?" He sounded doubtful about it.

She shared his doubt, but considered the idea. It would be best if she did walk, in case the neighbors were being nosy. But waves of torment racked her whole body now, and she was starting to feel nauseous. That tipped the scales. She looked up at her rescuer and surprisingly, found herself vaguely embarrassed. "Do you suppose you could…well…?"

A smile crinkled the corners of his light, translucent eyes. "Want a lift?"

"If you don't mind."

He chuckled. "I don't. It'd be my pleasure." He bent down and placed an arm beneath her knees, then stopped abruptly. "This isn't an advance, is it?"

"No. I won't deck you."

"Glad to hear it." He straightened and swept her off her feet. Startled by the quick ease with which he lifted her, her arms went reflexively around his neck. He strode off down the sidewalk, while she registered little things about him. The short hair at the back of his neck was silky soft against her fingers. His cologne was subtle and masculine. His chest was broad and muscular without being chunky—very solid. The hard strength of his arms supported her effortlessly, and his breathing was not increasing noticeably even though he was carrying her and walking at a fast pace.

His eyes were extraordinary. They glittered like ice-blue chrome in the light of the street lamps. His jaw was strong, a little on the square side. Nose—straight. Brow—a smooth plane. All in all, a face with character. Handsome as sin.

She had no more time to observe him because they arrived at Dr. Hammill's front door. After they rang the glowing doorbell there was a lengthy delay, and her companion began to fidget. "Do people show up on this doctor's porch often?" he asked.

She shrugged. "I doubt he bothers to operate a practice during daylight hours." The door cracked open, and she saw the familiar twinkle of bright blue eyes in a wrinkled face. "It's me, Doc Hammill."

The door swung open quickly and they moved inside. Fondly, Amanda inhaled the peppermint smell that always seemed to pervade this house.

"Bring her in here, young man."

Her rescuer followed the doctor's brisk instructions and set Amanda down on an examining table in a tiny office. She almost missed the feel of his strong arms cradling her close. Whoa. *Missing* was not authorized. Not in her line of work.

Dr. Hammill derailed her shocking train of thought. "Hoist that foot on up here, young lady. Let's see what we've got." He peeled off her shoe and cut off her stocking.

She sucked in her breath as gentle fingers probed the swollen joint. She actually had to grab the edge of the table when he rotated her foot slowly. *God, that hurt.*

The doctor glanced up at her. "Now you move it."

She closed her eyes, took several deep breaths and counted backward from ten to one, willing herself to utterly relax and let her mind go blank. In a state of partial self-hypnosis, she separated herself from her lower leg and foot. Observing from a distance, she slowly rotated the ankle, first clockwise, then counterclockwise. She followed the doctor's vaguely heard instructions to point her toe, flex her foot and wiggle her toes. Dr. Hammill's voice registered approval, and she opened her eyes. She blinked while the sense of detachment from her body faded and pain replaced it.

"Well, child, you've sprained your ankle, and substantial swelling has developed. But you'll live," he pronounced. His blue button eyes twinkled. "You may be inclined to slug me for saying this, but the pain is good. It means you probably haven't broken anything. If you had, your foot would tend to be numb and immobile."

"Great," she managed to grit out from behind her clenched teeth.

The doctor stood up. "I'm going to treat your ankle with heat and cold before I wrap it. Let's see if we can bring that swelling down a little."

While her ankle soaked, the doctor looked at her tongue and decreed the cut minor. It would be fine in a couple days. Dr. Hammill kept up a steady stream of small talk the whole time. He'd told her once that he did it so his unorthodox patients wouldn't feel obliged to explain how they'd come by their injuries. She was grateful for the distraction. It was disconcerting having a tall, gorgeous stranger standing like a dark sentinel in the corner, observing her every move and expression with hawklike alertness. She had the uneasy feeling he was reading her in far more detail than she'd like him to. More than once, she almost asked him to leave the room, but then he'd know how uncomfortable he was making her. And that wouldn't do at all.

The doctor made her swallow a couple pills he said were

painkillers. After a few minutes, she started growing unnaturally drowsy and limp. Painkillers. Right. Through an enchanting, rose-hued haze, she watched the doctor nod at her protector, who swooped down on her like the hawk he resembled and lifted her from the table. Her head came to rest on his shoulder, which was ever so comfortable. With mild interest, she watched as he followed the doctor upstairs, down a hall and into a dark bedroom. She could definitely get used to this business of being carried around like a sack of potatoes.

He lowered her onto the bed and she smiled fuzzily. "Thanks for the ride."

Her rescuer flashed her a heart-stopping smile. "Anytime. Sweet dreams."

It felt sinfully delicious to let her eyelids drift closed. Darkness enveloped her.

"Come on, come on," Biryayev groused as the phone rang in his ear. "Pick it up." He'd dialed the home phone number of the junior agent he'd taken under his wing during the past year. He wasn't the type to voluntarily take on a protégé, but when the source of his paycheck spoke, Nikko Biryayev jumped. Grudgingly, but he jumped. Max Ebhardt was his assistant's unfortunate name. Biryayev actually liked him despite his blond good looks. The talented young agent posed no threat to him, since a person of German descent would never progress very far in the Russian power structure. Biryayev could afford to like him. Besides, the kid's expertise with computers could come in handy on this one.

The receiver clicked in Nikko's ear. An annoyed voice grumbled at the other end of the line, "Hello."

"Max. Nikko Biryayev here. I need you at the office right away."

"Now? It's Friday night. It's…midnight, for God's sake. Can't it wait until tomorrow? Or Monday?"

"No, it can't," Biryayev growled. Damned kids. No sense of duty these days. "How soon can you be here?"

A female voice giggled in the background. "Stop it, Candy," Max said away from the receiver. "Uh, I guess I can be there in a half hour."

Biryayev growled, "Make it fifteen minutes. Screw the bimbo on your own time. Right now I need you."

"Fine," Max bit out.

The phone slammed down in Biryayev's ear. He hung up, grinning at the receiver. He took perverse pleasure in messing up Max's love life. The guy's penchant for the ladies was an ongoing source of friction between them.

He was roundly surprised when Max actually did show up in fifteen minutes on the nose. Because he'd been punctual for once, Biryayev cut him some slack and ignored Max's grumbling about bosses with no life of their own messing up everybody else's. The blond agent looked tousled and wore a wrinkled New York Yankees T-shirt that smelled like sex. But he was alert and all business when Biryayev told him what was up.

The two men descended into the bowels of the consulate to the encryption room. Biryayev jerked his head at the lone clerk on duty, who left silently. Biryayev's ears popped as the door sealed into its airtight, soundproof lock. He watched Ebhardt pry the back off the hairbrush and carefully extract a microchip smaller than his thumbnail. The kid loaded the tiny wafer into a special player plugged into a computer console, and typed a series of commands. The machine hummed to life.

Several minutes of silence played, and then the room suddenly reverberated with the booming sound of a hoarse voice. Ebhardt snatched at the volume control and turned it down. Tuneless humming came and went for a couple minutes, then there was the sound of a door opening and a person entering. Biryayev and Ebhardt looked at each other and grinned.

Jackpot.

They listened to Kriskin greet his visitor. Biryayev's eyebrows shot up as a female voice responded. There was a bit of conversation, then a thud and the brief sounds of a struggle.

Several minutes of complete silence followed. The next sounds were faint noises of someone entering the room, then a muffled grunt like a heavy object was being lifted. A door clicked shut and the tape played on in ominous silence.

"Play it again, Max."

This time Biryayev listened for the name Kriskin had uttered. Amanda McClintock. *Amanda McClintock?*

Had the daughter taken up where the father left off? The walls abruptly went bloodred as his gaze blurred with fury, and his eyeballs ached as if they were going to burst out of his head. Rage pulsed in his veins until it became difficult to breathe. The need to put his fist through a wall, to break something, was almost overpowering. He paced the enclosed space like a caged tiger. Oh, he knew Amanda McClintock, all right. The daughter of his archnemesis had the temerity to kidnap one of Russia's most loyal sons? How dare she?

So. The McClintock legacy continued. Very well, then. So would his vengeance. He'd track her down and make her suffer, and then rip her intestines out and wrap them around her eviscerated body. He'd tear her face off. He'd break her neck. He'd...

"You okay, boss? You look a little overheated."

He snarled incoherently, "I'll *kill* the bitch."

Max's eyebrows shot up. "Who? This McClintock woman?"

He whirled around and advanced on Max as if he'd strangle the young Russian. "Find her for me. Tell me where she is so I can obliterate her!"

Max looked taken aback. "Damn! What's got your knickers in such a twist?"

Biryayev stared speculatively at his partner. If Ebhardt was going to help him on this case, he might as well know what he was up against. "Christopher McClintock spied for Mother Russia, and I was his control officer until the bastard turned on me. He stole the whole goddamned Udarsky cache and put a black mark on my flawless record. Russia has a score to settle with the name McClintock."

Max turned around to face a state-of-the-art computer terminal. "Well, uh, okay then. Let's see what we can find." He cracked his knuckles and started typing.

Biryayev hovered restlessly, kibitzing over Max's shoulder as the agent surfed the Internet, extracting secure credit card information, banking documents, even medical records with impunity. "Where'd you learn to do this stuff?" he asked, put off as always by the technology at Max's grasp.

The younger man shrugged. "This is nothing. Just a little garden variety hacking. There's this guy in St. Petersburg—you can't believe the systems he can get into. Scares even me."

After a pregnant pause, a search engine made a match. The printer began to spit forth information on Amanda McClintock. Biryayev snatched up and scanned the sheets of paper almost as quickly as the printer disgorged them. She was the daughter of an art dealer—Biryayev scowled. A lousy art dealer who only managed to stay in business because of handouts from Russia. And the ungrateful bastard turned out to be a double agent. A traitor. Christopher McClintock had betrayed him. The daughter's current age was twenty-nine, her present location unknown. Her primary schooling took place in Scotland, and there was no record of university education. With her father's death, she'd inherited a small estate. Biryayev's gaze narrowed. Really? Or had she, in fact, inherited the fabled Udarsky diamond cache? It was rumored to be worth billions on today's market. He read on greedily. Several years ago, she started turning up in various world capitals. Her appearances were usually linked to the activities of a Devereaux operative code-named Phoenix. "Run the code name Phoenix through our collection of spy dossiers and see what you get," Biryayev directed.

Max did as he was told and a single sheet printed out. Name unknown, location unknown, activities unknown. Physical description unavailable.

"Unavailable, my ass," Biryayev growled. "Get it for me."

The younger Russian shrugged. "That may take some time. I'll need to contact my buddy in St. Petersburg."

"Do it."

Max nodded and turned to the computer screen. He typed out a message and sent it. The electrons flew out into the gargantuan limbo of the Net, waiting to be snatched by Max's contact at some other exit point in the jumble of the information highway. The kid looked up and asked, "So, is she this Phoenix person?"

Biryayev shrugged. "Entirely possible. Her father was a trained covert operative. He could've taught her the tricks of the trade." And the bastard had been crazy enough to do it, too.

Max speculated, "So, she went into the dressing room and took down this Kriskin guy, and then someone else came in and helped her carry him out?"

Biryayev frowned. Kriskin was a large man, not to mention one of the most dangerous unarmed fighters the KGB had ever trained. Even old and out of shape, he'd have been a formidable opponent for a much smaller, weaker female. "Maybe she went into the room first and distracted Kriskin. Then an accomplice came in and took him down," Biryayev postulated.

Max shrugged. "Sounds reasonable." He referred to the computer. "Assuming she's not lying on her driver's license, she's only five foot five and 115 pounds. A hair over fifty kilos. Not very big to be taking out anyone in hand-to-hand combat."

"Print me a picture of her."

The younger agent's fingers clattered on the keyboard. The printer disgorged a black-and-white photo of a quietly beautiful young woman, staring calmly back at the two men. *She had the look of her father about her*. The refined features that spoke of good breeding, the dreamy tilt to her eyes, the romantic shape of her mouth—full of lies. Just like her father.

"Hubba, hubba," Ebhardt commented, grinning.

Biryayev glared. She was the enemy. Like a bloodhound picking up a scent, he hungrily memorized her features. He would find her and eliminate her soon. Very soon. "Is it possible to check the airline passenger lists to Toronto for the next couple days for her name?" he asked.

"No sweat." As Max's fingers flew, he asked, "Why Toronto, boss?"

"It's the next stop on Marina Subova's concert tour. If Amanda McClintock has business to conduct with her, that's where she'll go. If we're lucky, her accomplice will go along, and we can bag them both. I wouldn't mind putting a dent in Devereaux while we're at it."

"Who's he?" Max asked.

Biryayev shrugged. "Nobody knows. References to him started turning up after 9/11. Some sort of rich, reclusive, vigilante type who pokes into delicate situations around the world."

"Whose side is he on?"

Biryayev shrugged. "Hard to tell. He's been a royal pain in the ass to just about everyone at one time or another."

"Criminal?" Max asked.

"If you would call it criminal to seek justice outside the law by whatever means, then yes, this guy's a criminal." As Max started to type into the computer, Biryayev added, "You can check your precious Internet, but he won't show up on it. Devereaux's too cagey for that."

Max quit typing. He asked, "Why would this McClintock woman kidnap or kill Kriskin?"

"Good question. Kriskin's been out of circulation a long time. It's accepted practice to leave retired intelligence agents to their consciences and old age to find what peace they can. I think it's highly unlikely that she was actually after Kriskin. I think he got in her way." Biryayev frowned. "But this Subova girl's been a problem before. Maybe she's gotten herself into trouble again."

Ebhardt frowned. "What kind of trouble could a concert pianist get into with someone like Devereaux?"

"That is a good question, Max. A very good question."

* * *

Taylor awoke to an unpleasant feeling of disorientation. The first thing he saw was an oversize, 1940s-style cabinet radio. Morning sunlight streamed through yellowed venetian blinds into an old-fashioned sitting room. Motes of dust danced in the zebra streaks of light. For a moment he didn't know where he was or how he'd come to be here in this room out of time. And then memory of the previous night returned, of carrying a lovely wounded woman here in his arms. With the memory came a vision of her smile and a hot flood of desire.

A voice murmuring somewhere nearby brought him to his feet. He stretched out the kinks of sleeping on a couch several inches shorter than he was and tracked the voice toward the rear of the house. He met Doc Hammill coming toward him down the narrow hall.

"You're awake. Good. Phone's for you, son. You can take it in the office."

Taylor followed the doctor into the same room where the young woman had been treated last night. An ancient rotary telephone sat on the oak desk. He picked up the receiver. "Hello?"

"Taylor. Harry Trumpman."

His Devereaux contact. "What can I do for you, boss?"

"I'm afraid I have a stupid question for you."

"Shoot."

"What did you do with the lady?"

"You mean from last night?"

"Is there another one I should know about?"

Taylor laughed. "No, sir. There was just the one. Last I saw of her, she was tucked into the good doctor's guest bed and was out cold before her head hit the pillow. She's still sleeping off whatever Doc Hammill gave her. Why?"

"We, uh, don't like to lose track of her. She's been in a…"

Taylor waited while his boss searched for a word.

"…rather *delicate* frame of mind recently. Well, I'm glad that mystery's solved."

"Glad I could help. Anything else I can do for you?"

"Meet me for lunch. Both of you. Say noon at Shecky's Deli down near Fifty-seventh and Fifth Avenue?

"Just a minute." Taylor lifted the receiver away from his mouth. "Doc, is the lady going to be awake by noon?"

Dr. Hammill grinned. "She ought to be waking up any time now."

Taylor pulled the receiver back down to his mouth. "We'll be there at noon."

Amanda stopped at the top of the stairs to watch her rescuer as he paced Doc Hammill's living room. He looked as nervous as an adolescent waiting for his prom date to come downstairs. Like some gorgeous guy had ever waited nervously for her. Between her mad father and the rigid rules of her boarding school, she'd barely spoken to boys in her youth, let alone gone out with them.

He noticed her just then and rushed to the foot of the stairs in a whirlwind of restless energy. "Stay right there," he called.

She blinked in surprise as he bounded up the stairs three at a time. He reached the top, abruptly looming over her. "Dare I ask what you're doing?"

"I'm coming to the assistance of a damsel in distress, of course."

She lifted one eyebrow and asked, "How's that?"

"Your ankle's still killing you, right?"

It was, but she certainly wasn't about to admit it. Her eyebrows came together and she drew breath to deny it, but he cut her off breezily. "You don't have to impress me with your toughness. You did that last night. 'Fess up, now. It's hurting, isn't it?"

"A bit," she answered reluctantly.

"Let me carry you downstairs." Without waiting for her permission, he stepped forward and picked her up.

Desire flared, hot and bright, at the feel of his strong, safe arms around her. Lord, he was pretty. Cover-model material all the way. "I'm going to have to start walking on it sometime, you know," she grumbled.

His voice was low and sexy in her hair. "I know. Although, I rather enjoy hauling you around like a bride."

For a moment, she was too startled by his forwardness to react. Belatedly, she frowned at him. He met her stare head-on, unapologetic. She had to give these American men credit. Their directness had a certain appeal. Even if it was a bit intimidating.

He broke the silence casually. "By the way, if I'm going to keep carrying you around like this, I probably ought to introduce myself. My name is Taylor. Taylor Roberts."

A good name. Strong. It had character. Definitely fit him. "I'm Amanda McClintock," she managed to squeeze out without sounding breathless.

They reached the ground floor and he set her down carefully. "Pleasure to meet you, Amanda."

Doc Hammill bustled out of his office, a welcome distraction. "Don't go running off, young lady. The swelling in your ankle should be down this morning, and I want to tape it before you go tearing around on it again." He herded her into the examining room and forced her to swallow a couple painkillers he swore wouldn't knock her out. Then he taped her ankle and pressed a brown plastic bottle of pills into her hand. She thanked Doc Hammill for his help and hospitality, and they were on their way.

The day was heating up fast, promising a hazy afternoon of brown skies and clammy humidity for New York City. Although the steam heat of late summer had not yet arrived, the air carried a certain oppressive weight. It dulled the usual vivacity of the city's sounds, reducing it all to a methodical repetition of the weekday's weary routine. The streets were relatively unclogged, and the taxi dropped them off in front of Shecky's Deli on time.

Boisterous noise greeted them as a half-dozen employees

shouted good-naturedly at each other behind the counter. Harry Trumpman waved at them from a vinyl booth in the back corner of the crowded restaurant. Good location for a meet. So much background noise no parabolic mike could isolate their conversation and record it. They waded through the line of people waiting for take-out orders and joined him. She couldn't help but admire the way Taylor's broad shoulders cleared a swath through the crowd for her.

Harry waved them into the seat opposite him and said little until the waiter had delivered their sandwiches and left. Then he stared intently at Amanda. She refused to give him the satisfaction of seeing how strung out she really was after last night's disaster, and she met his gaze dead-on.

He asked with quiet significance, "How are you feeling today?"

Like he really cared so long as she got the job done. She answered coolly, "Fine, thank you. Dr. Hammill says my ankle should be as good as new in a few weeks."

Either oblivious to her hostility or unconcerned by it, Harry turned to Taylor. "And how did last night go? Did the pianist signal anyone?"

Taylor shrugged. "Maybe. You might want to have a cryptography expert listen to Subova's improvisations. He may find messages encoded in the music."

Harry raised his brows. "That's an interesting idea. I'll pass it along. Actually, Taylor, that's why I asked you to come along to this meeting. I've decided to bring you in on the full details of the case we're working on regarding Marina Subova."

Amanda stared in undisguised shock. That was *her* case. Why hadn't she been consulted about this? She always worked alone. *Always.* Why in the world would Devereaux bring anyone else in on this one, of all cases? If Taylor messed it up, he could trigger global violence. Literally.

Chapter 3

Taylor leaned forward, all ears. Finally. Now maybe they'd get down to the real reason Devereaux had hired him, not to mention finding out who in the hell had been wrapped up in that blanket last night.

Trumpman spoke in a casual voice just loud enough for Taylor to hear under the discord of restaurant noises. "Recently, a dozen large diamonds have popped up in the United States and Europe. They range in size from eight to twenty carats and are of exceptional quality. Their origins are a mystery. We can find only one correlation between the stones. They appear immediately after Marina Subova performs someplace. We can place six of the buyers at social functions with Subova this year."

Taylor mentally saluted the desk jockey who'd figured out that obscure connection.

Trumpman continued, "We're convinced someone attached to her entourage is smuggling and selling these diamonds. The key question, though, is where in the devil are the stones coming from in the first place? If a large enough number of stones like these were dumped on the world market, it could seriously destabilize diamond prices. There've been more than enough financial shake-ups in the last couple years in the United States. You can understand our employer's concern over this prospect."

Taylor nodded, his face impassive. Years of analyzing hardcore criminals had honed veritable radar in him for a lie. Trumpman wasn't telling him the real reason this diamond smuggling was important to stop.

A ring of truth reentered his boss's voice. "Last night we detained our likeliest suspect, Grigorii Kriskin." Trumpman passed a slightly unfocused picture of a lanky, aging man across the table. Taylor had never seen the face before, but Amanda flinched subtly beside him when she looked over his shoulder at the picture.

Trumpman continued, "He was Marina Subova's bodyguard. Unfortunately, he didn't prove to be very cooperative."

Amanda closed her eyes in acute pain, as if she'd just been stabbed with a sharp object. Now what was that all about? And then there was his boss's odd behavior. Trumpman's body language screamed that he was being evasive. Taylor was careful to keep his expression neutral when he asked, "Just how uncooperative was this guy?"

Trumpman's gaze slid away guiltily, confirming Taylor's suspicion. But then the older man said succinctly, "Kriskin took a suicide pill. Cyanide capsule in a fake tooth. He's dead."

Taylor jolted. "Jesus!"

Amanda recoiled beside him. But it wasn't a movement of surprise. It was a movement of...what? What in the world was going on here? Unseen currents ebbed and flowed thickly around him. The woman beside him stared blankly at the tabletop, revealing nothing of her emotions. He'd worked long enough with criminals to see past the fronts they put up, but he wasn't getting any read whatsoever on her. And that, in and of itself, was telling. If he hadn't glimpsed the lonely, vulnerable person within her last night, there was no way he'd have guessed she existed within the cold professional sitting beside him now.

Trumpman passed Taylor a piece of paper without breaking his narrative. "This list of names, addresses and dates was found in Subova's dressing room. It parallels her concert itinerary. It's a list of the people she'll be staying with during the course of her tour. Apparently, she has a thing against hotels."

"Too much like Bartholomew's," Amanda murmured.

Taylor turned a questioning look on her.

"The boarding school Marina grew up in. Looked like a hotel. Or a warehouse for inconvenient offspring."

The flash of bitterness in Amanda's voice made it a good bet she'd been a warehoused, inconvenient offspring herself. Taylor shifted his attention back to Trumpman.

"Subova's next host is this guy, Gilles Fortesque, in Toronto. Made his millions building automotive prototypes and now runs an import-export conglomerate. You two are going to spend the weekend with him and Subova."

Taylor's eyebrows shot up. How was Trumpman going to pull *that* off?

Trumpman answered his unspoken question. "Amanda will be your entrée to the Fortesque home. You will act as her…escort. Oh, and Marina loves good-looking men."

Taylor glanced over at Amanda and caught a glimpse of some turbulent emotion before her gaze went blank. That had been resentment if he didn't miss his guess. Her control was extraordinary, except momentary chinks in her armor kept flashing. Either she was losing her formidable control, or she was trying to send him a subtle message of some kind. But *what?* His frustration mounted. What the hell was going on here?

"I'm the toy boy?" Taylor asked baldly, in an attempt to punch through the layers of unspoken crap.

Trumpman shrugged. "Basically, yes."

He continued, "I've booked the two of you on a flight this afternoon to Toronto. You'll want to acquaint yourselves with the area before you show up on Fortesque's doorstep."

Not to mention they'd also need to acquaint themselves with each other if they were going to be working as a team on this case. He studied his partner covertly as he picked up his sandwich and took a bite. Without any makeup, in the light of day, her face was unremarkable at a glance. But when he really looked at her, he saw once again how breathtaking she was. Her beauty had an elusive quality that was hard to put a finger on. Like the woman herself. Taylor dragged his attention back to what his boss was saying.

"Any questions, you two?"

Taylor and Amanda both shook their heads in the negative, and Trumpman flashed them a patently false smile. "Then I guess we'd better wind things up and let you two go pack. Your flight leaves in—" he checked his watch "—just over three hours. Taylor, Amanda's the best in the business. You stick by her, and she'll show you the ropes."

Taylor reassessed the young woman beside him. Devereaux's man thought she was the best? That was a hell of a recommendation.

Trumpman added casually, "Amanda, would you stay for a moment? I'd like to have a word with you."

Taylor took the hint and slid out of the booth. "Thanks for lunch, Harry." He threw out a trial balloon. "And thanks for the assignment."

Trumpman threw him a wry look. Now that was an interesting reaction. Thinking hard, Taylor turned and walked out of the deli.

Amanda watched Taylor wend his way through the restaurant. She admired the way his lean waist complemented the width of his shoulders, how his biceps filled out his shirt....

Whoops. She was in grave danger of revealing far too much to her boss if she ogled her new partner openly. She forced her gaze away from Taylor. "What's up, Harry?"

"I have Taylor's dossier if you'd like to see it."

"Let me guess. Hometown boy from Middle America, Ivy League schooling, inspired to be one of the good guys. How many field cases has he run?"

Trumpman shifted uncomfortably. "None."

"None? Does he have any investigative background at all?"

Trumpman frowned. "He's a criminal psychologist—terrific profiler. Has a real knack for getting inside people's heads. We thought this guy might help you to anticipate the smugglers and get ahead of them long enough to nab them."

Amanda ignored the implication that she was slipping, still hung up on another, much more dangerous phrase Trumpman had uttered. *Getting inside people's heads?* Had Taylor been assigned to do that to her? Poke around inside her noggin and figure out what made her tick? Alarmed, she tuned back in to what her boss was saying.

"…our people reported that he was outstanding in his covert-ops training. He's a natural. You may have noticed he's decent looking, too. Should be tempting bait, given your friend's proclivity for the gentlemen."

Amanda stopped an impolite sound from escaping her throat. Decent looking? The guy was a hunk of the first water. She'd practically forgotten to breathe when she'd first seen him last night. She contained her annoyance at her boss and reached with only marginal success for a patient tone of voice. "Look, Harry. I don't like the idea of dragging deadweight around with me. This case is high profile. I need to be able to move fast. You know full well that teams of operatives aren't anywhere near as nimble as solo agents."

"Amanda, I know it's unusual, but I sense a lot of potential in this guy. I need someone like you to bring him along."

Frustration laced her voice. "Then I'll teach him when I get back. The field is not the place to train someone in my line of work. And certainly not on a case like this."

"Amanda, please bear with me."

Harry was shoving Taylor down her throat whether she wanted him or not. Her initial response was to be irate. She clamped down on the sensation. Why would Devereaux suddenly saddle one of its top solo operatives with a partner? An amateur partner at that? "What's going on here, Harry?" she asked abruptly.

He gave her an innocent look. "I'm trying to brief you on your new partner."

"I don't have any choice in this, do I?"

"No, you don't." Trumpman's voice held finality. He sighed and reached into his briefcase. He handed her a small package. Wrapped in plain brown paper, it was about the dimensions of an address book. "Devereaux thought this might help you on the case. No promises, but it's worth a look."

She frowned and took the package but didn't open it. She felt the indent of a bound spine. Definitely a book of some kind. "Right. Well, then. Thanks a lot." Pressing her lips together in a thin line, she slid out of the booth and marched out of Shecky's with as much dignity as her sprained ankle would allow.

Trumpman frowned. He was worried about her. She'd taken Kriskin's death hard. Irritability and displays of emotion—any emotion—weren't her style. Amanda'd been strung out like a high-tension wire for so long, he didn't know how she kept going. Eventually, she had to snap. Burnout was inevitable in her profession. When basically decent, moral people were turned into doers of dirty deeds, even in the name of right, it always caught up with their consciences at some point. He only prayed that when she fell apart, there were enough pieces of her left for Taylor to pick up and bring home.

He rubbed a hand across his eyes. God, he got tired of the game, sometimes. When he'd been younger, he'd thrived on the adrenaline rush. Craved it. But no more. Now it simply brought bone-deep weariness over him. He'd done what Devereaux wanted. He'd forced Taylor upon Amanda, and put them both on this case. He'd argued with his employer against the idea, too, using much the same logic that Amanda had. But Devereaux hadn't budged. The guy was worried about Amanda. She'd been in the field a long time and had been showing cracks around the edges for a couple of cases. It was high time for her to stand down. Except Devereaux insisted she was the only agent for this case, just like he'd insisted on assigning a shrink to her in case she imploded. And Devereaux got what Devereaux wanted.

Trumpman glanced at the tab for lunch and tossed a couple dog-eared bills on the table. Taylor'd catch on. The guy was a sharp cookie. Sharper than folks gave him credit for.

Hell, Amanda and Taylor would probably work out just fine together as partners on this case. He was just getting paranoid in his old age. He half smiled at how impatient Taylor had been when he'd been told his first field assignment was to go to a piano recital. As he stood at the curb hailing a taxi, Trumpman wondered if he himself had ever been that green and eager. Lord, his chosen profession aged a soul fast. Ah, well. Taylor would find that out soon enough.

Amanda took one last look around her hotel room to make sure she hadn't missed anything. Funny how Marina couldn't stand hotels. She didn't like anyplace but hotels. Their sterile impersonality felt safe. No ties, no emotions, no sentimentality. It was an easy matter to empty the closet into her hang-up bag and to toss the contents of the drawers into a suitcase. She loaded her professional gear more carefully, wrapping fragile electronics in socks, and tucking small gadgets into zippered pockets where they wouldn't get lost.

She was still rattled by her loss of composure last night, but she felt alert after a full night of drug-induced sleep. She pushed aside all thought of Grigorii Kriskin's death. Her brief attempt to face her grief and guilt had ripped away the curtain of her control, revealing just how thin a veil it was these days. She wasn't strong enough to go there just yet. Later. Maybe later.

She got to the airport almost two hours before their flight left. She checked her bags and passed through security, then cruised the long terminals, browsing shops and going through the routine motions of checking for a tail. She was standing in a newsstand, glancing at magazines when her internal radar went off. Over there. A blond guy. Young. Dressed sloppily. Too casual. Too inconspicuous. Her heart slammed into her throat. How had someone known to find her here, today, at this time? She was careful not to look back over her shoulder. Who was tailing her? Her mind whirled with possibilities. She'd been on ice for months after her last mission. Nobody'd come after her during that time, and the terrorist cell she'd infiltrated and exposed had been declared dead and gone. Besides, surveillance wasn't that gang's style. They might lob a pipe bomb at her, but they wouldn't bother following her if they knew where she was. She hadn't shown herself to anyone so far on the diamond case. It had all been paperwork chases and electronic trails up to this point. Who, then? Who was that guy back there?

She moved away from the newsstand and headed for a coffee shop and sipped at a mocha latte, barely aware of its scalding heat on her tongue. It had been less than twenty-four hours since Kriskin went down. His superiors probably knew by now there'd been a fight and that he'd disappeared. But nobody should have connected her to him. How in the bloody hell had she been made so fast? Was there a mole at Devereaux?

Harry knew she'd be at the airport today. And Taylor knew. The team who pulled out Kriskin's body knew about Carnegie Hall, but had no idea she'd be leaving this afternoon out of this airport. The only newcomer was Taylor. Was he a plant? She cursed under her breath at Harry for saddling her with this new headache. She finished her latte and threw out the cup on her way back into the stream of passengers rushing down the long corridor.

She walked about a hundred yards, looked up at a gate, and abruptly reversed direction, as if discovering she was headed the wrong way. Careful not to overtly scan the crowd, she glimpsed the blond head and black rucksack. Her palms went clammy. Yup, still there.

Her knees felt wobbly as she walked past him. She was rarely noticed at her work—she could count on one hand the number of times she'd actually been identified and followed in her career. She was the hunter. The stalker. Not the other way around. Her heart pounded at this unfamiliar sensation of being watched. Of being *known*. She didn't bother engaging in the delicate dance of hunter and prey that so often punctuated being tailed. It wasn't worth tipping him off that she was aware of him, and besides, she knew what she needed to know. The blond guy was a pro. With her ankle a mess, she wasn't thrilled at the prospect of going through all sorts of shenanigans to get rid of the surveillance.

She hadn't arranged a signal to Taylor in case something like this happened. Hadn't talked to him about pretending not to know her until they sat down on the airplane. She didn't know what standard covert signals he knew, if any. Did he have any self-defense training at all? How could she have been so careless? She never took it for granted that she'd be able to travel unnoticed. But then, she never worked with a partner, either. Still, that was no excuse.

She found a seat in sight of the security checkpoint Taylor was likely to use and sat down to wait. An hour before their plane was due to depart, she glimpsed his tall form walking up to the metal detectors. A wave of women's heads turned to watch him pass. She had to agree with them. He passed through security, and as Taylor stepped away from the phalanx of guards, she stood up and walked directly into his path. She lurched as he bumped her.

Taylor grabbed her arm to steady her. "There you are. Sorry."

She whispered urgently, "I'm being tailed. Act like you don't know me. Give me a head start and then follow me." It was an incredibly transparent maneuver, but that was the point. If she could interest her follower in Taylor, maybe she could use her partner as bait. She just needed to find a place to spring a trap. For the next couple minutes, she zigzagged in a way that would force Taylor to reveal himself to the tail. If the blond guy was anything short of blind, he'd picked up Taylor by now. She headed for the nearest deserted hallway.

As Taylor passed by the entrance, she hissed, "This way."

He swerved into the passage and raced after her as she darted to a closed door at the end of the hall. She picked the lock quickly and they ducked inside a janitorial storeroom. "Stand here and blatantly peek around the door so the tail will see you," she ordered in a tense whisper. "When a blond chap with a black rucksack passes the hallway, shut the door loudly and head for the back of the room. And for God's sake, get out of the line of fire in case he has a weapon."

Taylor did as he was told, and it was only seconds until he closed the door and turned to run. As he ducked between two tall shelves, a flood of light spilled into the room behind him. A shadow loomed in the door, and she jumped at it. The tail was unbelievably strong. He wrenched in her grasp and managed to get his hands on her neck, but then she got off a short, sharp chop to the side of his head. The guy dropped like a rock.

"You can come out now," she announced.

Taylor stepped out from behind the shelves.

"Help me drag him to the back," she directed as she began to tug on the inert form.

Taylor rushed to the kid's side and, instead of helping her, checked for a pulse. Disbelief vibrated in his voice. "Why in the world did you attack some college kid? What did he do to threaten you?"

Amanda snorted. "When he tried to strangle me, I thought it might be prudent to knock him out."

Taylor didn't say more, but disapproval of her violence glittered in his eyes.

Amanda pursed her lips. "I never said I was in the Girl Scouts. Did you expect me to invite him in for a cup of tea?

Get real. I suppose you think every bad guy wears a raincoat with a suspicious bulge under the armpit, has a three-day growth of beard and talks like Humphrey Bogart, too. This guy was tailing me, all right."

"Look at him! He's just some kid, and you've mugged him." Taylor passed an unsteady hand across his face. "Christ, what kind of delusional paranoid are you?"

Tight-lipped, she said nothing but bent over and searched through the knapsack the guy'd dropped when he went down. Silently, she handed Taylor a computer-generated picture of herself, a Russian diplomatic passport saying the guy's name was Max Ebhardt and two packs of Marlboro cigarettes. Taylor stared in disbelief at the objects in his hands.

"Russians have a thing about Marlboros," she said dispassionately. "I've never been able to figure out if it's because they actually like them or they just like the cowboy in the advertisements."

Taylor opened the passport to examine it. A note of wry apology sounded in his voice. "Says here he's a translator for the Russian United Nations delegation. May I have some salt with that serving of crow?"

She smiled briefly. "Of course."

"What are you going to do with him?"

"Bind and gag him and hope it's a couple hours before anybody finds him. Help me truss him up before he comes around, will you?" Sensing Taylor's chagrin, she added, "Don't beat yourself up too bad. This guy was pretty good. Even I had trouble picking him out at first."

"How long have you been a field agent?" he asked her abruptly.

She looked up from Ebhardt's pack, whose straps she was trying to tear off. "Ten years."

Silent, Taylor took the rucksack from her and yanked at a shoulder strap. It gave way with a loud rip. He handed it to her and grabbed the other strap. In silence, Amanda tied up the Russian agent. She used the guy's belt to secure him to a heavy stack of shelves and gagged him with a piece of cloth torn from the guy's T-shirt. She stood back and surveyed her work. "There. That should hold him for a while."

Taylor took a step toward her and she whirled abruptly. Defensively. Hands up to block or strike. Whoops. Just the partner. She dropped her hands sheepishly. Enough light seeped under the door for her to make out his facial features. He wasn't giving away much with that poker face on.

"Are you all right?" he asked.

"I'm fine," she answered frostily. "He barely laid a hand on me." Her words might be confident, but she couldn't look him in the eyes. Her gaze darted off to one side and then riveted on a spot somewhere in the center of his chest.

Taylor put a finger under her chin and lifted her face gently. She didn't fight him; that would give away too much. He said quietly, "That's not what I meant and you know it."

His palm cupped the side of her head. He lifted his other hand and massaged her scalp. She sighed and closed her eyes. God, that felt good. It would be so easy to sink into the comfort he was offering, to let him soothe away the terrible tension that had built behind her eyes during the chase across La-Guardia. She felt like glass ready to shatter.

Why did someone like Taylor have to come along and offer her a shoulder to lean on at the exact moment she felt weakest? It wasn't fair to have such a temptation dangled in front of her. She couldn't accept his help. As much as she'd like to, giving up control of her emotions was the quickest road to her self-destruction. She had to handle this crisis on her own. She sighed and steeled herself to do what was necessary. And stepped away from his soothing hands. "We'd better go. We'll miss our flight."

Dodging the penetrating look he gave her, she headed for the door. She wished he wouldn't look at her like that. It made her feel like he could read her mind. And that would be disastrous. She paused, her hand on the doorknob, and spoke without looking back at him. "Give me a five-minute head start. Don't acknowledge me in any way until we're seated on the plane. If you're followed, don't get on the plane. I'll do the same. If I don't make the flight, call Harry for instructions."

He replied crisply, "Got it. Oh, and our seats are in the same row. Do you want me to switch so we're not seen together?"

"No. It'd draw too much attention to you. Let's just pretend to meet and strike up a conversation." She made the mistake of glancing over her shoulder at him. Lord, he was gorgeous. "Do you happen to have any self-defense training?"

"Does twelve years of kung fu and five years of Krav Maga count?"

Wow. She should've let him take down the tail. His usefulness just went up a couple notches. She nodded briskly. "Keep your wits about you and don't do anything stupid. And don't assume that, just because we caught this guy, there's not another one out there waiting for you."

She caught a flash of white as he smiled. "I won't make any rash assumptions," he said smoothly.

She frowned. Why did she get the feeling he wasn't talking about being tailed?

She turned and left the storeroom.

Chapter 4

Amanda dropped into her seat beside Taylor, who'd beat her on to the plane. She felt his gaze on her skin almost like a physical caress. Inexplicable heat shot through her. *The case. She was on a case.* The plane taxied and took off before she recovered her cool. But then her resident head doctor asked without warning, "So, what's the plan? How are you going to get us into Fortesque's house? Do you know him?"

So much for her cool. She hated it when shrinks pulled stunts like that, asking questions out of the blue to surprise a person into an honest answer. She spoke below the roar of the engines and was careful to smooth out any ruffles in her voice. "I don't know Fortesque. I know Marina. I'm hoping she'll invite us to his house. Then we'll poke around, try to figure out who's smuggling the diamonds and go from there."

"You know Subova?" he asked in surprise. "How did that happen?"

"We went to the same boarding school in Scotland. We're old friends."

"And Devereaux put you on the case, anyway? Isn't that a conflict of interest?"

She shrugged. "Devereaux is more interested in seeing this case solved than in splitting ethical hairs."

He absorbed that one in silence and then said, "Tell me about Marina."

"You saw her on stage. She performs like that all the time, whether she's sitting at a piano or not."

"Tell me about going to school together."

Amanda sighed. She'd been over this ground with Devereaux's people before. "We both lost our mothers when we were very young, and our fathers found us…awkward. Her father was a government official, and mine was an art dealer who traveled a lot. We got in the way of their careers, and so, off to boarding school," she finished lightly. Taylor no doubt heard the hurt of abandonment behind her words. But she didn't know how to keep it out of her voice. She'd spent most of her childhood scared and alone.

Thankfully, he moved on without pause. "What kind of child was Marina?"

"The class clown. Popular. She had big emotional swings, though. In her dark moods she turned to music. It was almost an obsession with her."

"What obsessed you as a child?" he tossed out casually.

Distant memories washed over her of a shy, serious child who spent much of her time trying to be invisible. The answer was abruptly as clear in her mind as a revelation. "I suppose I was obsessed with pleasing my father." Taylor was cutting way too close to the bone here. "Well, I've certainly run on about myself," she said smoothly. "What obsessed you as a kid?"

He smiled. "I suppose I'm obliged to trade an answer for an answer." He paused for a moment, thinking. "I wanted to do something important with my life. I alternated between wanting to be quarterback of the Chicago Bears and wishing I was James Bond."

"Is that why you chose to work for Devereaux?"

He shrugged. "In part. Besides, the money's good." Then he tossed the ball back into her court, the rotter. "Why did you pick cloaks and daggers?"

Now, there was a question. One she found herself asking more and more frequently. On impulse she answered candidly, "I didn't pick this job. It picked me."

"How's that?"

She had a sneaking suspicion that she had no choice but to answer this guy's questions. Devereaux certainly hadn't put a psychologist on the diamond-smuggling case because he could actually be of any use in solving it. This was an elaborate setup to assess her mental state. Fine. She'd play along. For now. "My father was crazy as a loon. He was convinced Russian secret agents murdered my mother and that they were coming for me next. Whenever I went home on holiday, he taught me all sorts of weird and wacky skills. Everything from handling explosives to hot-wiring cars. After I graduated from Bartholomew's, Devereaux approached me and asked if I'd like to put my…unique education to work. It sounded more interesting than moldering away for four more years in some moth-eaten, stuffed-shirt university."

"How did Devereaux know about your oddball skills?"

She blinked. She remembered asking that question herself. But for the life of her, she couldn't remember the answer anymore. "I'm sure the locals saw my father and me out and about, practicing some surveillance technique or whatnot, and word of it reached Devereaux one way or another."

Taylor asked quietly, "Did you believe your father? Was your life in danger?"

"Believe him? Didn't I just tell you he was mad as a hatter?"

He looked at her steadily, saying nothing.

God, she hated dealing with shrinks. And she wasn't about

to admit to one that a tiny corner of her heart wished her father had been right. "No, I didn't believe my father. I indulged him because he was the only parent I had left."

"How did your mother die?"

"Car accident when I was six."

"Do you remember her?"

She'd been over this ground so many times with so many well-meaning counselors she could scream. "Yes. I have vague, but fond recollections of her. Yes, I dream of her occasionally. No, I don't feel resentment that she isn't here. No, I don't try to replace her in my relationships with others." She glared at Taylor, who returned her look impassively. She could almost see the wheels turning inside that pretty head of his.

"Why are you so sure Devereaux put me on this case to watch you?"

Okay, that shift of topic threw her. "*Did* Devereaux put you on this case to watch me?" she challenged.

"Not that I'm aware of," he answered mildly. Too mildly to be lying, in fact. So. They hadn't told him his real purpose. Then he was as big a patsy as she'd guessed. Somehow that thought was disappointing. Damn Harry to hell and back for saddling her with a psychologist, anyway. How in the world was she supposed to be with Taylor for weeks on end and keep him out of her head? She could hear her father admonishing her in one of his Spy School 101 lectures, "If you succumb to emotion or feeling, you get sloppy. When that happens, you will die. You can only survive if you become a machine."

Right. A machine. She was feeling decidedly unmachinelike at the moment. Restless, she dug in her purse and took out the package Harry'd handed her at lunch. She tore off the wrapping. And stared in shock at the dog-eared leather-bound journal resting in her hands. How in the bloody hell had Devereaux gotten hold of her father's diary? What kind of sick head game was her employer playing with her to give this to her now? How in the world did her father's deranged writings relate to this dia-mond-smuggling case?

A flood of memories rolled over her. Countless times, her father scribbled in a leather notebook just like this one. As his insanity had deepened toward the end, he'd worked on his jour-nals obsessively, for hours at a time. She opened the one in her hands at random and gaped at the date heading the entry. Only a few days before he died. This must have been his last jour-nal. Why hadn't it been in his personal effects when she'd packed up her father's things? And how did it end up with De-vereaux? *Why* did it end up with Devereaux? Alarmed, she began to read.

> …last night I heard the turquoise dragon again. He knows I have his hoard and wants it back. Only by fire shall he have it, the bleeding bastard. Oh, why did I ever succumb to his lure in my greed? I have ruined us all in my efforts to save the world from itself….

Typical of her father's ramblings. She thumbed through the pages and a photograph fluttered out. Before she could retrieve it, Taylor leaned down, blocking the way with his broad shoul-ders. Damn. She watched apprehensively as he picked up the picture and looked at it before he handed it back to her. "That you?" he asked.

She took the yellowed Polaroid photo and stared at it. Mem-ory of that afternoon flooded back as if it were yesterday. She'd been seven. Her father had insisted she help him plant an oak tree behind their home. It had been a sturdy sapling, already twice as tall as her father and as big around as her leg. She'd been worried she'd ruin her new lavender silk dress. Her father'd rambled on about planting the seeds of her security in that tree.

She flipped through the journal, which was nearly filled with her father's spiky, difficult handwriting, but found no other pictures. The pages still smelled faintly of bay rum. Grief pierced her and she closed the book hastily. She'd been seventeen and secretly relieved when he died. He'd been completely delusional by the end. Fortunately, compliments of Daddy dearest, she was very good at setting aside her emotions by the time he had slipped away, consumed by his private demons. Maybe that was part of why she'd taken the job with Devereaux. To carry on her father's work, but sanely. To clear the stain on the family name.

"What's the book?" Taylor asked.

"Something Devereaux said might help me—us—with this case. But I think not."

Thankfully, Taylor was silent for the remainder of the short flight, lost in his own thoughts. She needed most of the time to squash the rioting emotions inside her.

They checked into their hotel suite without incident, and she retreated to her room immediately, ostensibly to take a nap. She spent the time poring over the journal and gleaned nothing but a headache from her father's nearly illegible scrawl. She was glad to set it aside and dress for the evening. It wasn't often she got to go out to swanky restaurants and nightclubs on Devereaux's dollar. When she was sufficiently primped, she called through Taylor's still closed bedroom door, "Come on, Casanova. It's time for your big debut. Let me see."

He stepped out into the suite's living room, reluctantly facing her impatient appraisal. Brilliant. He'd gotten the look just right. He'd moussed his hair into a studied tussle, turned up his collar and nailed a bad-boy, bedroom-eyed look Elvis would have been proud of. Oh, yes. High-class gigolo all the way. She grinned widely.

Taylor scowled in response. "So there's no chance I can get out of being seen in public like this?"

Bloody hell. He was even more uncomfortable with his cover as her lover than she'd anticipated. She was going to kill Harry when she saw him next, and that's all there was to it. She suggested, "Think of it as a disguise."

He continued to look skeptical. Time for emergency measures to thrust him into his role. She stepped near to adjust his black leather tie, surreptitiously gauging his reaction when her perfume hit him. His pupils dilated hard and fast. She smiled lazily into his darkened eyes and murmured, "Can't you pretend to be the slightest bit attracted to me tonight? You're 007 himself. Pretend I'm enslaved by you, and you know it. Use that power. Tantalize me. Romance me. You're gorgeous and sexy and you make me hot beyond belief."

Taylor took a startled step back and cleared his throat. "Uh, right. Sexual attraction."

"Sheesh," she groused, "you don't have to say that like I'm chopped liver."

A reluctant smile curved his mouth. "Sorry. You caught me off guard, there."

"Don't let it happen again," she warned. "Your guard is your last line of defense."

"Is that lesson number one in the *How To Be a Badass Spy Handbook?*" he asked with a faint edge in his voice.

She didn't bother to answer.

They made it all the way through dinner at a trendy restaurant without another slip from him. He kept up the intimate eye contact, the meaningful smiles and undivided attentiveness of a lover. And it damned near stole her breath away. Every time he smiled, her stomach fluttered, and every time he gazed deep into her eyes, her breathing hitched. The way he trailed his fingers across the back of her hand provoked thoughts of doing things with him that made her blush just to contemplate.

No matter how aggravated she might be over her visceral reaction to Taylor, there was no denying it. She was so attracted to him she could hardly see straight. *Of all the rotten luck.* The first man in years she'd been even remotely interested in, and he turned out to be her very off-limits partner. The idea was for him to seduce Marina, not her. Cursing her ill fortune, she continued to flail against the sensual web entangling her. A brush on the arm, a deep look, a secret smile—each added a thread to her discomfort, tangling her more deeply in choking terror. Her entire life was built around the concept of being in complete control of herself, and these raging feelings Taylor provoked were anything but under control.

After the meal, they left the restaurant and proceeded to a hot spot called the Wild Side in the heart of the nightclub district. She had it on good authority from the hotel staff that everybody who was anybody in Toronto congregated there. If Marina had arrived in town, she was bound to be there checking out the local talent. Her old school chum was a barracuda when it came to fast, handsome men. With a glance at Taylor, Amanda smiled grimly to herself. She had a very shiny object to dangle before Marina.

Amanda and Taylor paused just inside the door of the club. It was a circular room with a bar running around the walls in both directions from the front door. The curved bars terminated across the room in an elaborate sound booth. The music was loud and the air was heavy with cigarette smoke and the distinctive, sweet odor of marijuana. This was Marina's kind of place. Rules were broken here.

There was no sign of Marina, however. After one tawny tigress performed a rather lascivious mating dance on Taylor's thigh, Amanda reasserted her claim. She whisked him away for a long, slow dance. He took her in his arms and swung her easily onto the floor, holding her lightly. It was a heady feeling to have all that strength so carefully controlled for her sake. He brushed a strand of hair back from her cheek. His touch was light, but it sent a shiver through her. A single finger curled up and around her ear, coming to rest on the pulse just behind the soft flesh of her earlobe. She drew a shaky breath. Lord, that felt incredible. Electricity flowed from his hand into her body, grounding out low in the pit of her stomach. It disrupted the rhythm of her breathing, leaving her gasping. This was all an act. Just an act. She could do this.

"You come alive under my touch," he murmured. "Where there was only cold gray ash, now there is heat. Fire."

Oh, God. Amanda closed her eyes for a second and let his potency flow over her, ambrosia to her starving soul. She could think of nothing more alluring than to give in to that craving, to glut herself upon the feast he offered.

"Fly to me," he whispered into her hair.

She let go and leaned into him, reveling in his strength. Her head found his shoulder, and he massaged her neck and shoulders while they swayed and flowed with the music. She felt weightless, floating like a butterfly in the wind, letting Taylor carry her away. Just this once, she'd accept what he offered. For a little while she'd let down her guard. She'd be herself. Nothing more, nothing less.

She set aside all her training and reflexes and allowed herself to experience the moment, to exist for pure sensation. She was startled by what it did to her. Dancing in Taylor's arms made her feel feminine. Fragile. The song began to wind down, and regret swamped her that the moment couldn't continue. Very carefully, she memorized how it felt to be free. Then she painstakingly tucked it away in the deepest, safest corner of her mind. She sighed and lifted her head from his shoulder.

"Go give your ankle a break," he remarked practically. "I'll ask around about Marina."

The bubble of the moment burst, leaving a sour, soapy taste in her mouth. So much for the romantic interlude. It had all been an act anyway. She suffered his kissing her fingertips before he drifted away toward a knot of men. Jerk.

Some time later, he walked up to where she was seated at the bar. He had a well-groomed, middle-aged man in tow. Intelligent brown eyes complemented the man's salt-and-pepper hair. Taylor said jauntily, "Amanda, I'd like you to meet Gilles Fortesque. Gilles, allow me to introduce you to a charming and very sexy lady, Amanda McClintock."

With exaggerated flair, Fortesque asked her for a dance.

Gay or French. Or maybe both. Nonetheless, she accepted the invitation. Fortesque turned out to be an inexhaustible dancer. She thought her ankle would explode before the man finally led her off the floor. When they returned to the bar, Taylor handed her a straight shot of vodka wordlessly. She slugged down the fiery liquid with a shudder, praying it would dull the agony shooting up her calf.

Fortesque clapped Taylor on the shoulder, proclaiming, "You must come to my place this weekend. Did you know this little lady knows one Russian on the whole planet, and that Russian is coming to my house tomorrow? What a small world. Really, you must come."

Phone numbers and a scrawled map on a napkin were duly exchanged, and Fortesque wandered off. Amanda kept an eye on him as best she could in the crowded, smoky club. She caught a brief glimpse of him having a short, intense conversation with a dark-haired man wearing funny little wire spectacles. But then the two men smiled and went their separate ways as if they'd been discussing nothing more than the weather. Nonetheless, her internal antenna wiggled and she took a good look at the guy in the spectacles as she and Taylor made their exit. Early to midforties. Olive complexion, thick black hair. Medium build. Mediterranean or Eastern European, maybe.

When she was seated once more in a no-nonsense rental car, away from the club's glitzy magic, thorough annoyance with herself set in. She'd acted like a perfect mush head over Taylor all evening, going all fluttery when he flirted the slightest little bit with her. And for goodness' sake, she'd *told* him to do it! She was annoyed with herself for another reason, too. It wasn't often that she misjudged someone. Taylor was turning out not to be nearly as naive or stupid as she'd expected. In fact, he'd adapted quite well to the situation tonight. While it had made her job easier, there was also danger in his ability to act on his own. She couldn't afford to have him argue with her in a crisis. He would have to be willing to follow her orders instantly and exactly if they were to remain safe. When he'd parked the car in the hotel's garage and killed the ignition, she turned in the seat to face him. "Taylor, I need to tell you rule number three of field operations before learning it gets you killed."

He sighed. "Lay it on me."

She scowled at him. "Don't argue with me if we're in a tight spot, or even if it doesn't look to you like we're in a jam. If I tell you to do something, do it. You can ask questions later, but a second's hesitation can mean the difference between life and death in the field."

Taylor nodded slowly. "I suppose I can live with that."

She had to give him credit. Not all men could or would take orders from a woman. But he'd swallowed that edict without a word of complaint.

The second they stepped into their suite, Amanda kicked off her high-heeled shoes, sighing in relief. She performed a routine sweep for bugs in their rooms. The suite was clear. As she zipped the bug detector back into its case, Taylor asked, "Is somebody trying to kill you?"

"Probably."

He asked reasonably, "Dare I ask who harbors this dark plot against you?"

She responded coolly. "The less you know, the better. I have no intention of getting you involved. You're here to be my stooge and nothing more. If they associate you with me professionally, they'll kill you, too. Your life depends on convincing them how dumb you really are. Fortunately, that shouldn't be too difficult for you to pull off."

"And who is 'they'?" he asked calmly.

Interesting. He didn't rise to the bait when she called him dumb. Chalk up another point for her surprising partner. Belatedly, she answered his question. "The people moving these diamonds are not nice blokes. I've been stepping on some lucrative toes, and they won't take kindly to it when they realize what we're up to."

Taylor retreated silently to his room, frowning. It was hard to gauge how much of Amanda's big talk was paranoia, and how much of it was legitimate. He had no idea how dangerous a case he'd stepped into the middle of. But it was high time to find out. He changed into a black turtleneck and pants, dug out his silent-shutter Leica camera and loaded a roll of high-speed, low-light film into it. He gathered up assorted other gear and stepped out into the hall. He should probably invite Amanda to go with him, but the way she'd been limping, she needed to stay off her ankle tonight. Besides, all he had in mind was a little simple surveillance of the Fortesque estate. Nothing he couldn't handle on his own. He wanted to experience firsthand what it felt like to do Amanda's work. Maybe it would give him a new insight into her state of mind.

An hour later, he contemplated an eight-foot-tall security fence topped by a Y bracket of barbed-wire strands with rolled razor wire nestled in the crook of the Y. There was a conspicuous lack of vegetation touching the fence. Electric, then. Beyond the fence lay a vast, sleeping mansion. Taylor snapped several pictures using a telephoto lens. Nothing remotely dangerous or interesting out here. If this was all there was to it, her work wasn't nearly as exciting or sexy as he'd imagined.

He was almost ready to go back to the car when a sound arrested his attention. A loud noise of crunching gravel ruptured the night's deep silence. Someone was driving up the Fortesque driveway. At this time of night? He watched a white van pull around the circular drive and stop in front of the house. The driver and front-seat passenger got out. As they approached the porch, the double doors swung inward, and a small pool of dim light fell at their feet. So, these nocturnal guests were expected. Okay. Now this was more interesting. His pulse jumped on a surge of adrenaline.

He raced back to the car and grabbed the rope. He ran to a wooded copse even with the house and lassoed a stout branch that overhung the tall security fence. He shimmied up it quickly. His palms burned from the bare nylon, but in moments, he sat astride the branch. He was breathing a lot more heavily than the climb called for. Man, he felt *alive*. He could see where this feeling could get addictive, where someone like Amanda would come back for more and more of it, even if she was cracking up mentally. He inched across the branch and slithered down the trunk of the tree. Pausing long enough to slash away a vertical strip of bark with his pocket knife, he left a white scar on the tree trunk to mark it.

The trees extended to within roughly fifty feet of the front corner of the house. He slowed and crawled the last few yards through the trees. The front door opened again. Three men emerged and he snapped their pictures, his heart pounding double time. If he wasn't mistaken, that was Gilles Fortesque sandwiched between the two visitors. But it was too dark to be certain. They stepped to the back of the van and one of the men tapped on the door. It swung open and a fourth man stepped out, carrying a small leather satchel. The guy from the nightclub with the wire-rimmed spectacles! All four men returned to the house. Power. He was definitely feeling a rush of power. To uncover a secret meeting like this, to be in the know when these guys thought they were getting away with it…yup, it made a person feel kind of invincible. Amanda's sharply worded lessons began to make more sense now. She was used to being the one in control of the situation.

A light went on in a window to the left of the front doors. Wrong angle to see in it from here. Crap. He stepped out of the trees and moved toward the window. The four men stood around a large desk. The satchel was open, and Fortesque bent down, staring intently at whatever lay on top of the case. The Canadian brought a jeweler's loupe to his eye and, using oversize tweezers, lifted a large cut diamond from the table. Taylor snapped a picture. Fortesque put down the first diamond and picked up a second stone to examine. And a third. And a fourth. Holy shit.

As if that shock weren't enough, Taylor practically dropped the camera when, without warning, a pair of guard dogs bounded around the far end of the house and set up a tremendous barking. He frowned when the pair ran away from him toward the back of the house. Perplexed by their behavior, he nonetheless retreated to the woods, watching for a human reaction to the uproar. Amanda could have this part of her job. The sense of impending doom if he got caught sent another, more powerful surge of adrenaline into his blood. The true fight-or-flight adrenaline of someone about to get busted.

A surge of sick dread rolled through him as the rottweilers rounded the end of the house nearest to him. Silent now, they came toward him at a dead run. He dropped any attempt at stealth and sprinted with a speed born of fear. He tore through the trees, heedless of the branches ripping at his face and arms, praying fervently that he wouldn't trip and fall. He reached the fence and saw no sign of the tree he'd originally climbed. Damn! He sprinted along the wire barricade, casting about frantically for the mark he'd left. The dogs were closing in. Twigs snapped beneath their feet close behind him, and he heard the low growls in their throats as they pursued their prey.

Several yards ahead of him, he spied a flash of white. The dogs were almost on him. He put on a last burst of speed and leaped for the lowest branch. In one motion he caught the branch and swung his feet upward, hooking a leg over an adjoining branch. The bark was wet and his hands began to slip. *Christ.* He lurched, clawed at the branch and barely maintained his grip. He pulled himself up and straddled the limb, staring down at the massive creatures jumping at him from below.

Their black sides heaved and their snarls of frustration revealed enormous fangs. Their eyes glowed red in the dark as they clawed at the base of the tree and lunged at him futilely. At 150 pounds apiece, they were the hounds of hell incarnate.

He inched along the limb while the dogs waited below for the slightest fumble. A fall now almost certainly meant serious injury, if not death. He tried not to think about that and concentrated on his agonizing progress across the slippery bark. The branch narrowed, trembling slightly beneath his weight.

He reached the fence. An ominous groaning and subtle cracking sounded under him. Crap. He scooted across the final few feet. The cracking sound was louder now. Frantically, he untied the rope with fumbling fingers. He dropped to the ground on the far side of the fence in grateful exhaustion. Amanda could have this job. He didn't need these sorts of thrills and spills to get his jollies.

The branch above him gave way with a slow rending noise. It touched the wire, and a spray of yellow sparks exploded. He rolled away from the flying sparks, scrambling to his feet. Perspiration soaked and muddy, he slid behind the wheel of the car, releasing the clutch. The car rolled silently down a gentle incline toward the main road. As he neared the pavement, a white van sped by. The same white van that had been parked in front of the house a few minutes ago. On its side, Taylor saw a logo—the letters GFX within the outline of a red rocking horse.

He considered following the van, but decided against it. On such an isolated road at this time of night he'd be spotted immediately, especially since the van was flying like a bat out of hell. Besides, he'd learned what he came here looking for. Amanda was an adrenaline junkie and control freak because of her job, and furthermore, was more than half crazy if she did this sort of stuff voluntarily.

He retraced his route at a much more sedate pace back toward Toronto, driving toward the orange glow in the sky above the city. An insidious satisfaction crept into his gut. He'd done it. It hadn't been pretty, but he'd survived his first surveillance job. Amanda would undoubtedly bust his chops over going alone, but he'd proved the point that he could do it. And he'd learned one last bit about his partner: she got a lot of satisfaction out of winning. Even if winning was measured in grim terms like staying alive or pulling one over on the other guy.

It was nearly 4:30 a.m. when Taylor finally stepped into the hotel's elevator. He leaned back against the wall and closed his eyes as he felt the gentle upward lurch. His muscles ached with fatigue and his eyes burned. The elevator doors slid open with a quiet swish and he roused himself. He plodded down the hallway, regretting that their rooms were at the far end of the hall. He finally reached their suite. And looked down.

He slammed himself sideways against the wall, adrenaline surging. Carefully, he crouched and reached for his ankle knife. The door was ajar.

Chapter 5

Taylor flattened himself against the wall and, with an outstretched arm, nudged the door open an inch more. No reaction. He eased the door farther open and waited again, heart pounding. Nothing. Still crouching, he eased through the opening, pausing just inside with his back to the wall. As his eyes adjusted to the dark, he saw furniture strewn everywhere but no movement. He sidled around the end of the bar, checked behind it, then peered toward the bedrooms. Both doors were wide open. He paused again, listening. Silence.

He slithered down the hall on his belly, hugging the wall. Moonlight streamed through Amanda's window and across the hall into his room. Both were empty. Fear pressed on him like an anvil on his chest. It wasn't just for himself. Near panic surged in his gut at the thought that something might have happened to Amanda. He cautiously approached the enclosed balcony that held the hot tub. Streetlights illuminated the glassed-in area, and it, too, was empty. Taylor straightened, breathing relief, then gasped, lurching through the open doors to the hot tub.

"*Oh, my God.*" He swallowed thickly and nausea rumbled in his gut. Pale in the moonlight, the face of a man floated below the discolored surface of the water. Taylor plunged his hand into the dark water and grabbed the corpse by the hair. The head tilted back awkwardly, and as he lifted it clear, a dark, kidney-colored gash showed beneath the chin from ear to ear. White tendons, cartilage and the fibrous tube of the dead man's trachea protruded grotesquely. With a groan, Taylor let go of the body and convulsed beside the hot tub, retching. What had happened here? Where was Amanda?

He heard a screech of tires and looked up. From the hotel's parking garage below him, a van careened out into the street. Clearly visible on its white side was a red rocking horse. Then Amanda emerged from the parking garage on foot, pistol in hand. She paused to watch the van speed away. With a quick glance around, she pocketed the weapon and darted into a shadow. Relief flooded him in a surge that nearly brought him to his knees. Thank God she was all right. Her figure melted into the darkness and he strained to make her out. It was impossible. He watched for several minutes, hoping to catch a movement, but saw nothing. She was gone.

Amanda pulled the trigger quickly, over and over. She ducked flashes of light as they exploded at her from all sides, lunging first one way, then another. She fired back almost continuously as the attack came at her, wave upon wave of death seeking her. A tremendous explosion of light burst at her from one side, and then there was blackness.

"Drat," she muttered.

She popped another token in the slot, and a deep voice intoned, "Use the Force, Luke."

Amanda sat in the seat of a *Star Wars* video game, watching the entrance to the arcade she'd chosen for her rendezvous with Taylor—assuming he thought to check for a message at the hotel. Dim blue light illuminated her surroundings, and a constant blare of computer-generated noises and sound effects intruded upon her senses. An assortment of young people ranged around the arcade, some lounging casually in front of machines, others writhing at the controls in spasms of body English. A video jukebox along one wall projected rock videos on a large screen. She couldn't hear the music from where she sat, and the frenetic gyrations of the rock stars looked surrealistic and absurd. Another volley of enemy ships sprayed at her from the Death Star, and she methodically picked them off. As her last force shield blew up and her ship was obliterated, she caught sight of Taylor's tall, unmistakable frame, briefly silhouetted as he entered the arcade. Thank God.

While she entered her initials into the machine's list of all-time high scorers, she surreptitiously watched him pause for his eyes to adjust to the light. He moved away from the door slowly, stopping here and there to look at a game. After a minute or two, he stepped to the vending machine where cash was exchanged for the requisite tokens to feed the games. Armed with a pocketful of tokens, Taylor moved past her to a video shooting gallery near the back of the arcade. She watched him pick up a toy rifle and take up a comfortable stance several yards away from a panoramic movie picture of a Canadian lake. Computer generated geese began to flush up onto the screen, and he shot them down with unerring accuracy.

Amanda started as a preadolescent voice spoke abruptly in her ear. "Hey. Are you gonna play or not?"

"No," she said. "I'm done." She climbed out of the seat and moved between the clustered games toward Taylor. She mimicked his progress, stopping here and there to look over a player's shoulder at alien galaxies and advancing monsters.

Taylor put down the rifle, turned and saw her. The flare of relief in his eyes was clear. She had to admit she was glad to see him, too. She restrained a rather surprising impulse to give him a hug. "Nice shooting," she commented.

"Beginner's luck." He shrugged.

"I'm a trained sniper. I'm not dumb enough to buy that line." She looked down at the floor, then back at Taylor. "Are you okay?"

"Me? I'm fine. Are *you* all right? That was a nasty piece of business back there. If I hadn't seen you chase after that van, I'd have been crazy with worry."

"You saw me?" she exclaimed. She felt a funny surge of…something. He'd actually been worried about her?

"Yeah. I must've just missed the fun. I was on the balcony puking my guts out when you left the garage."

She grimaced. The balcony scene hadn't been pretty. "Let's get out of here. Then you can tell me where in the bloody hell you went last night."

They left the arcade, squinting as they stepped outside into the brilliant sunlight. Taylor said, "This way. The car's around the corner."

"You don't still have the same car, do you?" she asked sharply.

"Of course not. I dumped it first thing this morning. Right after I packed up all our stuff and got the hell out of the hotel. Speaking of which, care to tell me why you didn't give me the gun Devereaux had waiting for me at the hotel?"

"You found that, huh?"

"Good thing I did, or we'd have had some tall explaining to do to the authorities."

She grinned. "Like we don't already? There's a dead man in our hotel room." She borrowed a page out of his book and changed subjects sharply to distract him. "Have you had any sleep?"

"Yeah. I snagged a motel room and got a few hours' rest this morning."

"Good. You're going to need it."

He announced as he unlocked her door for her, "I've got an errand to run while we decide what to do next."

She noted the use of the word *we* wryly. The only thing worse than an amateur spy was an amateur spy who thought he knew enough to play in the big leagues. Those thugs in the hotel were almost certainly Russian intelligence, and they were known for taking their games very seriously. More than ever, she was convinced that teaming up with Taylor was a terrible mistake. She'd barely escaped with her own life last night. If Taylor hadn't been lucky enough to be gone when the thugs had broken in, she would not have been able to save his neck. That idea bothered her. And the fact that she was bothered—that bothered her even more.

They rode in silence until he glanced over at her. "So. How did that guy end up floating in the hot tub?"

She shuddered as the events of the previous night rolled across her mind's eye. "Two men broke into our hotel room. They went to your room first, and I heard them there."

The spit of silenced bullets riddling his bed was what had woken her up. She barely managed to dive out of bed before her door burst open and her pillow exploded. As she rolled off the bed, she grabbed the silenced Magnum from under her pillow.

"I made it out of bed before they came to my room and shot it up. I returned fire and they retreated momentarily."

She poked her head up and listened carefully. Silence. Probably still right outside her room. In the moonlight, she saw the doorknob begin to turn slowly. She took careful aim at the wall where she judged the intruder would be standing aside to throw the door open. She exhaled her breath slowly and squeezed the trigger.

"They came back to my room and I shot one of them, in the arm, I think. Then they ran and I heard them ejecting clips from their guns, so I took the opportunity to get out of the room. I headed for the living room first, but they were waiting for me there, so I retreated and came around through the balcony to the living room. Unfortunately, one of them had the same idea."

The plate glass door beside her began to ease open. She

shifted slightly to give herself a clear shot, and a foot came flying around the doorjamb at her with killing speed. She dodged, but not soon enough. She was struck in the left shoulder and thrown backward. Her left arm went completely numb and fell useless to her side. The pistol was jarred loose from her other hand and went clattering away in the darkness.

"One of them joined me on the balcony and we, er, tangled on the porch."

Not wasting time to search for the gun, Amanda lunged forward, slamming into her assailant's thighs with her good shoulder, knocking him off his feet and sending his pistol skittering away, as well. They leaped to their feet to face each other. The area was narrow and dimly lit, leaving little room to maneuver. They each settled into a fighting stance, eyeing their opponent alertly.

Amanda faced the larger man squarely, her right hand held before her. The feeling was only just beginning to return to her left hand. He smiled—a macabre grimace in the halogen-tinted moonlight—anticipating an easy kill of this weak woman.

A student of the art of aikido, Amanda's strength in battle lay in blinding speed and fluid grace. She didn't defeat opponents by overpowering them; rather, she prevailed by bending under attack and snapping back quickly. Opponents had equated sparring with her to wrestling with water. Her assailant lunged, and she slid to the side as the heavier man crashed past her. He slashed her loose nightshirt with a blade he'd held hidden in his left hand.

Taylor interrupted her thoughts. "You didn't get hurt, did you?"

His concern sent a warm rush through her. "No. But it was close. He had a knife."

By her reckoning, this was an even fight now. She had his inevitable underestimation of her on her side, but he had a knife on his. The guy lunged and she sidestepped as he went by, jamming her tingling left elbow in his back to push him forward. At the same time, she hooked a foot in front of his left ankle.

His momentum and her shove sent him heavily against the side of the hot tub. The knife fell from his fingers, and she scooped it up in an instant.

"I suppose he didn't expect me to know how to fight, or perhaps he thought because I was a woman I'd be an easy kill."

The intruder's wind was knocked out of him, and as he pushed away from the side of the spa, he drew a gasping breath. It was his last. She leaped onto his back, grabbing his hair with her left hand and cut his throat. She lurched away from him. She bent down, grabbed his legs and heaved. The body slid into the water.

"At any rate, I managed to get a hold of his knife and use it on him. The other guy ran out into the hallway and I chased him down to the parking garage."

She rounded a large concrete abutment at the bottom of the stairwell just in time to see a white van careen out of the garage. She chased it, straining for a glimpse of the license, but she was only able to make out a red blur on the side of the van as it sped away.

She willed her subconscious to see the red logo clearly, but it remained a frustrating smudge.

"Earth to Amanda, come in, please."

"What? Oh. Where are we going?"

"We're picking up some pictures I took last night. Where were you just then?"

"I was thinking about our visitors. They made one fatal mistake. They burst into your room first and shot up your bed together, then they broke into mine. Next rule, Taylor. Take out all the bad guys at once. If the intruders had split up, each taken one room, and burst in on us simultaneously, we'd both be dead. Assuming you were in your bed where you belonged." She shook her head reprovingly. "Sloppy. The Russians aren't nearly as good as they used to be."

He grimaced wryly. "So. Is last night the first time you've killed a man?"

She whipped her head his way, shocked by the bald question. "Why do you ask?"

"It's the first time I've ever seen a dead person, and it was pretty upsetting to me. I was wondering if you're feeling the same way."

Her defensiveness evaporated. "I try to put it out of my mind and not think about it."

He commented, "If you ever do want to think about it, I'll be here."

Surely he didn't fail to notice that she'd dodged the issue of whether or not she'd killed before. She stared out the window for several moments and then turned all of a sudden to glare at him. "Here's one for you. Why aren't you dead right now? Where were you?"

"I did a little reconnoitering of the Fortesque estate last night. It was an interesting outing." Quickly, he recounted the previous night's discoveries. He'd just finished when they pulled up at a drugstore and Taylor jumped out of the car. "I'll be back in a jiffy."

Fleeing her lecture about working alone, no doubt, she thought sourly. He returned shortly with a couple envelopes of pictures. The photos were surprisingly clear, in spite of being taken in the dead of night from a distance. She pored over the photos of the house and grounds, memorizing each salient feature of architecture, terrain and possible escape.

When she opened the second envelope, she drew a quick breath. One of the thugs from the pictures was floating dead in the hot tub of their hotel room right now. Bile rose in her throat and she passed the photo to Taylor. "That's the guy I killed. I'm not positive, but I think this is the other one who broke into our room," she said, pointing at the other thug flanking the bespectacled man. "I only caught a glimpse of his face as he drove off. He was in a white van."

"Like this?" asked Taylor, passing her a side shot of a white van bearing a red rocking horse and GFX logo.

"Yeah," she breathed, "like that."

They looked at each other, the same question in their eyes. What did Gilles Fortesque have to do with an attempt on their lives? They'd only met the guy last night. Taylor pointed to the bespectacled man frozen by the camera as he stepped out of the van. "Our thugs from the hotel were sticking close to this guy. Like bodyguards. Maybe he's the one who fingered us and not Fortesque."

Amanda examined the face, and after a moment, shook her head. "I don't know him. What business do you suppose he had with Fortesque in the middle of the night? Was he setting us up in case his men didn't get us?"

Taylor thumbed toward the bottom of the pile of pictures. "Take a look at this. I don't think we were the primary reason for his visit to Fortesque." He passed her a picture of the bespectacled man and Fortesque peering at the satchel on the desk.

"What was in the briefcase?" she asked.

"These." Taylor handed her picture after picture of Fortesque examining diamonds.

She sucked in her breath and dug in her purse. And pulled out a tiny velvet pouch. "Did they look like this?" She dumped a diamond the size of the end of her thumb into his hand.

Taylor scrutinized the stone carefully, then picked up a couple photos to compare them to it. "Your rock's in the ten-carat range. But the ones in the pictures are much smaller. Three or four carats at most. But I'd say we've found our connection between Subova's diamonds and Fortesque. And this bespectacled guy."

"And you know about diamond sizing how?"

"Uncle in the jewelry business."

Well, wasn't he just full of surprises? Aloud, she said merely, "Ah. How many diamonds were there?"

"I saw about a half dozen before a pair of guard dogs decided to cut my visit short. There's no telling how many stones were in that satchel. It could have held hundreds."

She quirked an eyebrow at Taylor's reference to the dogs, but he declined to elaborate.

He mused, "Maybe the guy's delivering a batch of diamonds to the smuggler in Subova's entourage by way of Fortesque. At least they're getting smart and using smaller stones."

"Getting smart?" she queried.

"Look what happened when they were passing off twenty-carat diamonds. They attracted a lot of attention, most notably that of our employer. Three-carat diamonds are a dime a dozen, relative to the really big stones. If they'd stuck to passing off smaller stones, nobody would've noticed a thing. Eventually, we'll be able to trace those big stones back to their source. A really beautiful diamond doesn't just appear out of nowhere. It's a work of art, and someone will be unable to resist taking credit for it. Ego always prevails over anonymity in the diamond trade."

She smiled with scant humor. "As it does in so many human endeavors. Just remember, ego will kill you in our line of work."

"Yes, professor. Is that the next rule?"

She scowled while he put the pictures back in the envelopes. He glanced at her. "So. What's the game plan, boss? Do we beard the lion in its den and go to Fortesque's, anyway?"

She shrugged. "We don't have any choice. Our assignment is still to find the conduit for the diamonds in Marina's entourage. I don't know of any way to do that besides arranging to meet her and latch on to the entourage itself. Let's assume for now that Fortesque and Four Eyes were already set to meet and swap diamonds, and it just so happened that Four Eyes sent his thugs to take us out after his meeting with Fortesque. We simply don't have enough history with Fortesque for him to have fingered us. But I have been working on this diamond case for a couple months, and Four Eyes could be aware of me somehow."

"What about the dead guy back at the hotel? Won't the police be looking for us? I left a Do Not Disturb sign on the door, but that'll keep the staff away for only so long."

"They'll honor the sign until they smell him. Since he's submerged in water, an odor will take several days to develop. On top of that, it should take the authorities a while to figure out that the name I checked in under is an alias. They'll chase after Samantha Proust for a good long time. Devereaux is incredibly thorough at creating cover identities. We ought to be out of Canada well before it all gets unraveled."

Taylor grimaced. "How reassuring."

A shudder passed through her, but her voice was steady when she spoke. "I think Fortesque is some sort of go-between with the stones. And I think the attack in the hotel had more to do with the Russian guy in the airport in New York."

Taylor nodded. "Fortesque may not be a threat to us, but the hairs on the back of my neck stand up over his bespectacled guest."

Amanda smiled. "I agree with the hairs on the back of your neck. Let's send a picture of him back to the home office. Maybe Devereaux's computers can attach a name to him. It'd be interesting to know who he works for." After a little searching, they spotted an office supply store. She ran inside, faxed a photograph of the bespectacled man to Trumpman and stepped outside to a pay telephone. Moments later, a pleasant female voice said hello into Amanda's ear.

"Hi, Mrs. Kinney. This is Amanda. Is Uncle Harry in?"

"Just a moment, dear. I'll connect you."

She couldn't remember when she'd started calling Trumpman "Uncle Harry," but it seemed to fit. Plus, it irritated him to death. After a slight buzz indicating the voice-scrambling protection had engaged, Trumpman's voice came on the line. "Well, hi there, Amanda. What can I do for you today?"

"You don't have to sound so blasted cheerful. Two men broke into our hotel room last night and tried to kill us. One of them's dead, and I think I blew a hand off the other one. Taylor's got a picture of the man we think is their boss. I just faxed you a copy of it, and express mailed you the original. We'd like an ID on him."

Trumpman asked tersely, "Who were the intruders?"

"Best guess—Russians, since one of their people tried to follow us out of New York. We have evidence that they're tied into the diamond smuggling, too."

Trumpman was silent for several moments. Finally, he said, "I have to warn you to be careful, Amanda. We're pretty sure Russian intelligence has indeed identified you and is pursuing you with violent intentions."

"Why would they want to stir up trouble with us? The Cold War's over."

"Apparently, they were not amused by Grigorii Kriskin's death."

"Tell them he committed suicide accidentally."

"We already tried. I don't think they believed us."

"What makes you think they have violent intentions toward me?" She didn't like the pregnant pause before Trumpman answered.

"Doc Hammill's dead, Amanda. He was garroted the day after you went to him, and your medical file's missing from his office. M.O. looks Russian." He paused for a moment. "Amanda? Are you there? Amanda?"

In Canada, at the other end of the conversation, the telephone receiver dangled on its cord, spinning slowly, first one way, then back the other.

Chapter 6

Alarmed, Taylor got out of the car and approached Amanda, who was staring at nothing while the phone dangled, useless, before her. He touched her shoulder and she spun around abruptly. He recoiled at the violence of her movement. "Hey. Is everything all right?"

She half laughed, a desperate sound. "No, my dear Taylor, everything is not all right. I am cursed. Everything and everyone I touch turns into something ugly and malignant. I am a bringer of death."

He put his arms around her and dragged her close, offering her shelter. Fine tremors rippled through her. She didn't fight the embrace, and her very lack of resistance was alarming. Something was terribly wrong. He held her close, rocking her and murmuring sounds of comfort and support in her hair while her agony raged around them. After a time, by slow degrees, it began to diminish. When the firestorm had passed, only they remained. He was almost surprised to see they'd sustained no physical injury.

He reached down behind her for the telephone and hung it up. The sound of the receiver settling into its holder seemed to shake Amanda from her nightmare. It was as if the noise signified a door closing in some secret corner of her heart. Her spine straightened and he released her, watching her carefully gather the pieces of her soul and lock them away. Hopefully, her intent was to reassemble them and nurse them back to health, but he feared that was not the case. He followed her to the car and got in silently.

As he turned on the ignition, he glanced over at her. For an instant, her eyes were haunted, and then the mask of her iron self-control fell into place. The act of brutal self-discipline made him shiver. At what cost to her sanity did she maintain that mask? In a moment of insight, he realized he was afraid for her. Afraid to know how much that mask cost her. She stared out the window in silence. Maybe when the smoking ruins of her soul had cooled she'd tell him of her own volition what that phone call had been about. Until then, he had faith she'd implode completely before she'd let him pry out of her what had brought on that crisis.

He drove them back to his motel room and carried in her suitcases while she followed silently. He observed without comment as she unpacked enough items with careful precision to shower and change. He stifled an urge to offer her any further comfort. She'd reject it out of hand. Clearly, she wasn't ready to confront her feelings about whatever had happened. When or if she talked about it, then she'd be able to accept comfort. And whether or not she'd accept it from him—that was another question entirely.

He sat on the edge of the bed and stared at the bathroom door while she showered. He felt so damned helpless not being able to do anything for her. What in the hell was Devereaux thinking, sending someone in her condition out into the field? He knew Devereaux psych-tested operatives like Amanda regularly. In fact, that was what he'd supposedly been hired to do.

When they'd put him into covert-operations training, they'd said it was so he could better understand Devereaux's private army of operators. Which made no sense. They'd hired him precisely because he already understood the minds of shadow operators. He lurched as the obvious truth slammed into him. *It had all been a lie.* He'd been put through twelve weeks of boot camp from hell because *he* was being turned into a Devereaux operative! Holy shit.

Why would Devereaux recruit, train and deploy an operative without that person knowing what or who he or she was? What was so freaking important about this case that they'd dupe him like this? Anger surged in his gut. Who cared what the damned mission was? Nobody used him like that and got away with it. He was outta here. Furious, he surged to his feet—just as the bathroom door opened and Amanda stepped out. She looked up at him, startled.

And another truth broadsided him. *That* was what was so damned important about this case. Not a *what.* A *who.* She was the reason Devereaux had baldly manipulated him. He was here to keep her safe. But God knew, his training wasn't nearly enough to do the job. Unless…

The last piece fell into place. He was here to save her from herself. He sat down heavily on the side of the bed. Son of a bitch. Devereaux had figured that once he met Amanda, he wouldn't be able to turn his back on her. And damned if Devereaux wasn't right. He cursed long and hard under his breath. The bastard had used him.

"Ready to go?" Amanda asked briskly, all business. She wore a red dress, a clingy little thing perfect for a party at a country estate. Reluctantly, he looked up and met her gaze. Her eyes were clear, her face still. Her moment of weakness was gone, her grief ruthlessly suppressed. He admired her inner strength, even if it was terribly destructive to her.

He answered slowly, "Yeah. As ready as I'm ever gonna be. Let's do this."

She slung the strap of her overnight bag over her shoulder. "Remember, no more late-night antics alone. You make sure I'm with you next time."

He grinned. "Can I quote you on that?"

She rolled her eyes and a brief spark of humor lit her face. They checked out of the motel without incident and got in the car. Taylor drove. He glanced over at her and asked casually, "Want to talk about the phone call?"

Her reply was sharp. "No."

What had Trumpman said to her? Whatever it was, she'd bottled it up pretty tightly. Taylor frowned. It was one thing to think about getting inside Amanda's head. But it was another thing altogether to get there. Especially since he wasn't entirely sure he wanted to know what was floating around in this woman's tortured mind.

In the gloaming twilight, they pulled up in front of the brightly lit Fortesque estate, which blazed into the encroaching night. A woman in a black-and-white uniform greeted them. Amanda recoiled as a pair of rottweilers charged the newcomers. A sharp command by the housekeeper called them off, but she could imagine the sort of encounter Taylor must have had with these brutes last night. A grin tugged at the corners of her mouth.

The housekeeper showed them to a spectacularly appointed suite decorated like a medieval Scottish castle. The green-and-blue Campbell tartan and fanned array of swords on the wall reminded her of home. They dropped off their luggage and headed for the pool party, which was already in full swing, to look for Marina Subova. They strolled toward a group of people lounging casually by the large swimming pool, and as they drew near a loud female scream erupted. Out of the corner of her eye, Amanda saw Taylor's hands jerk up. Good. His self-defense mechanisms were sharp. A brunette in an almost nonexistent minidress leaped to her feet and ran toward them. Marina.

"Mashka McClintock! What are you doing here?" the Russian squealed. "Gilles told me he had a surprise for me, but I'd have never guessed this! God, you look good. I heard about your father going mad and all. I tried to call you, but you just disappeared. Is that any way to treat a friend? Really. Well, come sit down and catch me up."

Marina looped an arm around her waist and led her toward the lounge chairs. She spoke in Taylor's general direction, "Would you be a dear and get us—" she turned to complete her sentence and finally looked squarely at Taylor. She broke off midsentence and stopped to stare. "My God, Amanda. Where did you find him? Why do you let him out of bed?"

Amanda laughed, finally getting a word in edgewise. "Oh, him. I found Taylor in New York. Didn't you always tell me how convenient it was to have a man around? Well, you were right. Speaking of which, Taylor, could you scrounge up a pitcher of gin and tonic for us?"

He raised a sardonic eyebrow at Amanda but turned and left without comment.

Marina giggled. "Since when did you get assertive with men? Don't tell me you actually *keep* him! Do you pay him?"

Amanda shrugged. "He's sort of attached right now. He'll drift off when a better offer comes along. At any rate, he's nice to look at and makes a wicked gin and tonic. You'd like him if you got to know him."

Marina scoped out Taylor's retreating backside. "I'm sure I would," she purred.

Taylor returned shortly with drinks, and Marina complained her ear off about the amount of taxes she owed, the lack of good-looking, disease-free heterosexual men in the world and the troll the Russian government had sent to replace her recently deceased bodyguard, who'd died of a heart attack. A dull headache formed behind Amanda's eyes.

The party grew wilder and alcohol flowed freely. A group of people on the far side of the pool took turns snorting lines of cocaine. Taylor shouted in her ear, "Why don't you leave Marina to me for a few minutes and go for a swim? You look like you could use it."

"I don't feel like it," she shouted back over the blaring music.

"Why not? It's a gorgeous evening and the water's warm."

She turned an exasperated gaze at Taylor. "I don't like swimming, all right?"

"Do you know how?"

She glared at him. "Yes, I know how. But that doesn't mean I have to like it."

She didn't like the way he frowned thoughtfully at her. Psychologist that he was, he'd turn her weakness into some multisyllabic Latin diagnosis for sure. Thankfully, he turned his observant gaze on the crowd surging around them. He leaned close and asked, "Is it just me, or am I about to experience my first orgy?"

In the pool, bodies writhed and swayed in a mass of disembodied limbs, pale against the blackness of the water. She put her mouth practically on his ear and replied, "Very possibly. Meanwhile, you're too conspicuous standing there gawking at all the naked people in the pool. Why don't you join them? Oh, and keep an eye on me. I'm going to go talk to Fortesque, and I don't trust this guy."

Taylor shot her a surprised look but stripped down to his bathing trunks and gamely dived into the inky pool. Still in the grip of the first shock of immersion in cold water, he was further shocked when flowing female bodies immediately entangled his, like boa constrictors wrapping around their prey. He wriggled free, only to be entrapped again moments later. He searched for Amanda in the dry-land crowd and caught a glimpse of her red dress retreating from the pool. Fortesque was with her. He appeared to be plying her with a drink of some kind.

A few minutes later he caught sight of her again, laughing freely with their host. Either she ought to get an Academy Award, or Fortesque had some sort of magic touch with women.

Taylor suppressed a sharp reaction to seeing the Canadian hang all over his partner like that.

A pair of hands reaching around his waist from behind to untie his bathing trunks abruptly diverted Taylor's attention. A warm, moist tongue insinuated itself into his ear. He grabbed the hands and turned around. Marina. She stared at him wordlessly. A slow, aggressively sensual smile grew on her face, moving from her slanted eyes to her lips. She reminded him of a tigress stalking. The intensity and personal magnetism revealed in Marina's music were even stronger up close. She freed her hands from his and pressed herself against him. He started as he realized she was nude. The warmth of her flesh was electric in the cool water. Her small, firm breasts rubbed against his naked chest. Marina's cat eyes glowed as she drew his head down toward her. He was intensely, and not particularly pleasantly, aware of her body.

Her lips paused inches from his. "Take me." It was a command, not a request. She kissed him wildly, almost painfully. Somewhere deep in his consciousness, a warning sounded. This woman was not a tigress at all. She was a boa constrictor. She'd wrap herself around him and squeeze for all she was worth, suffocating the breath, and eventually the life, right out of him.

He concentrated on his instinct and emerged from the searing kiss, gasping for air. He said lightly, "You, mademoiselle, are dangerous. You'll drown us both."

"Then let us leave the pool."

With a quick flex of powerful muscles, Taylor popped out on the side of the pool and turned down to speak to Marina, who was still in the water. "Until later, then." He strode away and left her gaping. There was no sign of Amanda or Fortesque anywhere on the pool deck.

He strode through the mansion's semidarkness in search of her while a lurid scene played around him. His nerves jangled. Something was wrong. He could feel it. He made another circuit of the pool and then headed toward the stables, the only place he hadn't checked yet. As he neared the tennis court, he heard a voice coming from the enclosed gazebo beside it. Amanda. Pleading with Fortesque.

He frowned. He didn't doubt that Fortesque was as strong as his bulldog physique suggested, but Amanda should have no trouble taking the Canadian down. The only question was whether or not she could fend off the jerk without doing real damage to him. Taylor stepped into the shadows of the gazebo. Fortesque had Amanda cornered, and Taylor was just in time to see the jerk make a grab for her. She pulled away and cloth ripped as her dress tore down the front. The red fabric gaped open, barely covering her creamy breasts.

Taylor's reflexive fury was accompanied by confusion. Why hadn't she killed the bastard for that? Lord knew she was capable of it. She fended off another lunge, and he wasted no more time pondering the question. He stepped briskly in front of her, facing Fortesque. "Sorry, old chap. I'm afraid undressing this lady is my department."

He turned rapidly, whisked Amanda off her feet and strode away from a dumbfounded Fortesque. Fortunately, their host was fuddled enough by whatever substances he'd been abusing that he could only stand and bluster. Taylor glanced down at Amanda in the moonlight as he strode back to the house.

"Thank God you came," she mumbled. "I couldn't have held off the drugs much longer." And with that, she passed out. She must've been hanging on to consciousness by sheer willpower alone. The woman's self-discipline was phenomenal if she'd successfully overcome the chemical effects of any of the date-rape drugs Fortesque must have slipped in her drink.

As she fell into unconsciousness, he carried her to their room and laid her on the bed. He removed the remains of her dress and stopped cold, staring at the scraps of black silk and lace that passed for her underwear. Lust pounded through him like a rushing freight train. *Stop leering at your partner.* He ripped his gaze away from the sight of her reclining against the crisp white sheets and pulled the blankets over her, not that it did a damn thing to erase the picture of her half-naked from his mind.

He tried to sleep in one of the medieval wooden chairs, but they were hardly made for sitting in, let alone sleeping in. After an hour, he gave up. He crawled in beside Amanda, who was dead to the world, and crashed.

A noise woke him in the wee hours of the morning. The house was finally silent and dark. Amanda mumbled and tossed beside him, trapped in the throes of a nightmare. He touched her shoulder. She didn't wake up, so he propped himself on an elbow and leaned over to shake her. She rolled against him, and for the second time that night, he was confronted with the acute awareness of an unclothed female form pressed intimately against him. He was intensely, pleasantly conscious this time of her soft curves molding to his tense body. "The things I *don't* do for Devereaux," he groaned under his breath.

When she finally settled back into quiet sleep, he disentangled himself and eased her back onto her side of the bed. He stared at the canopy overhead for a very long time.

Amanda gradually gained awareness of her surroundings as layers of unconsciousness peeled away one by one. She blinked against the weak light of dawn, glimpsing the canopy of an ancient bed over her head. How had she gotten back to Scotland? She turned her head and her eyes widened in shock. Taylor was asleep less than a foot from her, so close she could see individual whiskers in the dark stubble that covered his jaw. She eased away from him and his eyes opened, opalescent gray in the pale morning light.

"G'morning," he murmured, his voice rough.

She frowned, groping for speech. "When…where…what happened?"

"We're outside of Toronto at Gilles Fortesque's estate. He spiked your drink last night."

She assimilated that information and tried unsuccessfully to remember the previous evening. She basked for a few moments in the comfort of the warm bed, but one in which she was emphatically not alone. "Did you...did we...?" She stopped in embarrassment.

Taylor smiled. "No, we didn't do anything. I hope you wouldn't forget it if we did."

She smiled back sleepily. But moments later, horror swamped her. "Good Lord, I don't have any clothes on!"

"Whatever," Taylor grumbled unconcernedly. "It's barely 6:00 a.m. Why don't you go back to sleep for a couple more hours? No one will be up around here until at least noon."

Thank God he seemed so uninterested in her state of dress. "I don't remember much about last night. Was it wild?"

He opened one eye and mumbled, "I'm no judge of a wild orgy versus a tame orgy."

She cringed. "I didn't do anything embarrassing, did I?"

He didn't bother to open his eyes. "No. You were shockingly restrained. Should've knocked Fortesque's block off, but you didn't. Remind me to do that when we get up."

Her last thought before she drifted off again was that Taylor could take a number. She'd give Fortesque what he had coming herself.

Later, she regained consciousness abruptly, fully alert, in the manner she usually woke. This time there was no groggy swim toward reality, no vague disorientation. The events of the previous evening were clear in her mind. She ought to kill Gilles Fortesque. Better yet, she should wait until he was surrounded by a big group of his guests and then make a production of forgiving him for his inability to perform sexually last night. She grinned up at the ceiling.

Ouch. Moving her facial muscles sent daggers of pain through her head. Throbbing pain threatened to split her skull in two. She flinched, silently cursing their host. She ought to sympathize with Fortesque's shortcomings in the male-endowment department, too, and suggest in front of everyone that he consider penis-enhancement surgery.

She turned her head with the greatest of caution and saw that the bed's other occupant had departed. Recalling her cozy dawn awakening, she frowned. The remembered sense of security and comfort was completely foreign to her. She didn't need the protection of some man. More to the point, she dared not accept Taylor's protection. As soon as she began to relinquish control of her world, the whole house of cards would tumble down around her. She'd always been on her own, and regardless of whether or not she liked it, with her career she needed it that way. No strings, no commitments. Clean and simple, no emotional baggage.

She didn't need Taylor running around rescuing her like some patronizing knight in shining armor, nor did she need him draining her of knowledge like some blood-sucking vampire so she could be discarded by Devereaux when her usefulness was ended.

God, she hated men.

Chapter 7

At 6:30 p.m. a line of limousines pulled up in front of the estate to carry Marina and the Fortesque guests downtown for a preconcert cocktail party. To Amanda, it looked for all the world like a funeral procession. She and Taylor ended up getting shoved into a limousine with Marina and her entourage. Marina must have engineered the switch because the other passengers in the limo seemed distinctly annoyed with the arrangement.

In fact, the new bodyguard was openly hostile. Hatred poured off the guy in waves that a girl could really start to take personally. He glared at her with unblinking, almost reptilian concentration. Very creepy. Younger than Grigorii, he was still gray haired and barrel chested with advancing age. Probably in his late fifties. About the age her father would have been if he were alive. The bodyguard's face tickled at the edges of recognition. She had the strangest feeling she'd seen him before. But for the life of her, she couldn't place him, even with her photographic recall. Glancing his way now and then, she carefully memorized his features. This was somebody to avoid in the future. For some reason, he seriously disliked her—to the extent that he seemed prepared to take action on it.

Amanda remembered enough of the Russian she'd picked up around Marina as a child to follow the heated argument that developed between Marina and her manager during the limo ride over a piece of sheet music titled "Improvisation in F-Sharp." Marina insisted on changing a chord progression, and the manager was adamant that she must play it exactly as written.

As Marina sulked in silent rebellion, the agent leaned forward. "You know the agreement. If you do not play these pieces exactly as they are given to you, you will be arrested for tax evasion and thrown in prison." He added slyly, "Think of the humiliation to your father."

Amanda gazed out the window, pretending to be bored and uncomprehending. So the Russian government was feeding Marina the "improvisations," was it? Taylor's hunch about encoded messages in the music was looking good. But who were the signals aimed at?

The manager's threat worked. The mutinous expression on Marina's face gave way to sullen acceptance. She laid the music on her knees and practiced the fingering while she hummed to herself. Only when they reached the city did she hand the music back to her manager with a petulant "It sounds like shit."

"Just do it," he snapped.

Amanda was relieved when they finally pulled up before the Hummingbird Centre for the Performing Arts in downtown Toronto. A small crowd of fans greeted Subova as she alighted, and she clung to Taylor's arm as they entered a preconcert cocktail party. Amanda ducked out of the sycophantic gathering and made her way to her seat early. Taylor would have to fend for himself. She couldn't take one more blue-haired dilettante or one more nasty look from that damned bodyguard.

The orchestra had come out on stage to warm up before Taylor was finally ushered to his seat beside her.

He bent down to kiss her cheek and murmured, "Don't ever leave me with that shark friend of yours again. I feel bloody mauled."

She grinned. Her ruffled feathers were getting smoother by the second.

"Ah. There it is. A smile. I knew you had one lurking in there."

She stuck out her tongue at him, then leaned over and murmured in his ear, "About eight rows ahead of us and way left is a man who looks remarkably like Fortesque's bespectacled visitor from Saturday night. Do you recognize him?"

Taylor looked where she indicated. "That's him, all right. What do you suppose he's doing here? Maybe he's the guy Marina's sending signals to."

She shrugged. "Maybe." The concert began, her mind wandered, distracted by Taylor's overwhelming presence beside her. It brought back vivid memories of the previous night. Of waking up plastered against that amazing body of his. She yanked her mind back to business, idly watching her old chum perform. Could the smuggler be Marina herself? Nah. She was too flighty to have done it for this long without being caught. Who, then?

Working theory: the guy in the spectacles wasn't connected to Subova's entourage, but traveled the same itinerary she did. Unbeknownst to her, Marina was playing messages to this guy from someone in the Russian government, probably lining up deals where the bespectacled guy sold diamonds he got from his Russian contact. If her theory was right, the next step was to follow the guy in the glasses.

Max Ebhardt sat at his desk, sorting through a pile of computer printouts on the mysterious figure known only as Devereaux. Even his buddy in St. Petersburg had failed to turn up anything on the guy. Who was this shadow entity and what did he want with Marina Subova?

His phone rang and he picked it up. "Ebhardt here."

Biryayev growled in his ear. "Good evening, comrade. Do you have the information I wanted?"

Max hated the use of the antiquated title "comrade." It made him feel like a Hitler youth. But Biryayev was old school and clung tenaciously to the tattered remnants of the USSR's glory days. It was more than a little pathetic. "Yes, sir. One moment." He flipped on the signal scrambler. "Oh, before I forget. You got an e-mail from Moscow about Fortesque."

"Read it."

Max shuffled the papers on his desk and found the teletype message. "Moscow informs that requested information is highly sensitive—use utmost discretion, etc. etc. Here we go. 'Purchase in progress of military equipment from Gilles Fortesque for transfer to an offshore source. Delivery to be completed at midnight tonight at seller's warehouse in Toronto. Take whatever measures necessary to ensure security and secrecy of transaction.' End of message."

A grunt from his boss. Then, "What have you learned about Devereaux?"

"Not a damn thing. Are you sure this guy even exists?"

"Absolutely. And it's time the bastard was unveiled. Keep on it. I'll be in touch."

Taylor was yawning through the last scheduled piano concerto on the program when Amanda whispered that they must leave the moment the piece was over. Thank God. He nodded and untangled himself in his seat in preparation. When the music ended, he hastily escorted her up the aisle. They slipped out of the auditorium into the nearly deserted lobby of the theater. The audience knew to expect encores, and with the exception of a few worried parents rushing home to pay off babysitters, nobody left during the ensuing applause.

He followed Amanda outside, where she waved at the first taxi in the queue. Bemused, he watched her give the cabdriver fifty dollars U.S. and offer him a hundred more greenbacks if he would swear to wait for them to come back. The cabbie agreed readily. Taylor followed Amanda back to the entrance of the theater, where he stepped in front of her and blocked her path. "I don't mean to sound ignorant here, but what exactly are we doing?"

"We're going to follow our bespectacled friend, of course."

"Of course. And how do you expect the two of us to keep sight of him in this crowd? It would take a dozen agents to tail someone in the stampede out of here after the concert."

"We don't have a dozen agents at our disposal, so we'll just have to make do. You stand at the far left exit and I'll take the one next to it. Those are the two he'll most likely use. Let's just hope we get lucky. Park yourself somewhere inconspicuous to watch the door. Wave at me like you just saw an old friend if he passes you, and make your way outside to our cab. I'll do the same, so don't forget to keep an eye on me, too. Understood?"

"Yes, ma'am," Taylor responded crisply.

Amanda gave him an irritated look and moved off toward her post. He took up his station not far from the ladies' rest room. He should be inconspicuous enough hanging around outside it with the other impatient men who would gather there.

They waited through three encores before the exits were finally thrown open and the crowd began to stream out. Taylor scrutinized so many faces that they all began to blur together, but there was no sign of the man in spectacles. Out of the corner of his eye, he saw Amanda flitting around her exit as if she'd been separated from her date and was searching for him.

Almost three-quarters of the audience had left when Taylor glimpsed Amanda waving and smiling at him as if she'd just spotted him in the crowd. With the advantage of his height, he saw the bespectacled man leave the theater ahead of her. He stepped outside in time to see their quarry cross the street to a dark car and move around to the passenger side. Meanwhile, Amanda was standing at the curb looking around frantically. Their cab had deserted them.

The black car across the street began to pull away as she cursed in frustration. "Bloody hell. We're going to lose him and we'll never pick up a trace of him or his diamonds."

"Maybe not." Taylor picked her up and carried her quickly to the front of the long line waiting for taxis. He pushed aside a couple just stepping up to the open door of a cab and shoved Amanda inside. As the would-be passengers and members of the queue raised their voices, Taylor called out to them before he slammed shut the door of the cab, "My wife is having a miscarriage. I have to get her to a hospital right away. Thank you for your help!"

The cabbie pulled away from the curb and asked, "Which hospital do you want, mister? St. Michael's is the closest one."

Amanda leaned forward. "Do you see that black four-door about a block ahead of us?"

"Yeah," the driver answered cautiously.

"Do whatever you have to not to lose it. There's a hundred dollars in it for you."

The cabbie slowed down and started to pull over. "Now look. You pushed your way into the line and said you had a medical emergency. I'll take you to a hospital if you're sick, lady, but I'm not going to play chase for you. I don't care what you offer to pay me. Got it?"

Amanda leaned farther forward and spoke chillingly. "Buddy, if you don't get this cab moving right now and follow that car, there's gonna be a medical emergency. If I have to, I'll place you under arrest, take your cab and follow that car myself. *If* you happen to survive my driving, I'll see you prosecuted for aiding and abetting a criminal. Or you can get this bucket moving right now and follow that car. But either way, we *are* going to follow it. Got it?"

Taylor restrained his amusement. She did a sensational bad

cop. The driver took one look at her face in his mirror and stomped on the accelerator. The taxi screeched out into the street and hurtled after the retreating sedan. Amanda threw him an exasperated look and moved her eyes in the direction of the cabbie. Ah. He got to be good cop. He nodded fractionally and leaned forward. "Hey! Easy does it, fella. We don't want the bad guys to know we're back here. Just be calm and keep that car in sight. I promise to restrain my partner back here."

The cabdriver glanced at Taylor in relief and slowed down. They drove in silence for several minutes, and finally the guy spoke. "Looks like they're heading for the docks. It's a pretty rough neighborhood down here. Want me to have my dispatcher call the police and get you some backup?" He picked up the mike to his radio helpfully.

Taylor answered quickly. "No, that's okay. You just drive. We'll worry about the neighborhood."

They drove several more blocks before the cabbie spoke again. "Are you two cops?"

Taylor lied easily. "In a manner of speaking. We're federal."

"Government agents, eh? Who is this guy you're chasing?"

"We have reason to believe he's a smuggler."

Amanda elbowed Taylor obviously and threw him a glare to be quiet.

"Wow. A smuggler! I suppose it's drugs? Wait till the missus sees me on the news helping in a drug bust."

Taylor nodded and smiled. "We'll be sure to mention you when we nail this guy. You keep an eye on the news for the next couple days."

"Okay! Hey. It looks like your guy is stopping up ahead."

Amanda spoke. "Pull over and let us out here. Thanks for your help."

"Sure, lady."

They climbed out of the cab, and Amanda folded a hundred-dollar bill and handed it to the driver. "Here. Take your wife out to dinner."

The cabbie took the bill, not bothering to unfold it. He looked Taylor in the eye. "You take care of yourself now, you hear?"

"Will do, pal. Good night."

With a wave, the man drove off.

"Nice job of good cop-bad cop, Taylor."

He blinked at Amanda in surprise. "Was that a compliment I just heard?"

"It was, but if you make a big deal out of it, I'll retract it."

He grinned and remarked in an undertone as they hurried along the sidewalk, "Your secret's safe with me."

"What secret?" she murmured back. "By the way, isn't that our friend up ahead?"

A man in glasses stood on the sidewalk, watching a dark sedan disappear around the corner. He turned and walked away from them. Taylor answered, "That's Four Eyes, all right."

"What's my secret, Taylor?"

"You're capable of being nice. But I swear I won't tell a soul."

Amanda scowled at her partner's foolishness. But then their quarry turned onto a side street. They couldn't lose him!

"Come on!" She took off sprinting for the intersection. Lord, that hurt her ankle. She was grateful to stop and peek cautiously around the corner. Four Eyes stood in front of a lighted doorway, fishing in his pocket. Another man joined him, reaching up to pull a chauffeur's cap lower on his brow. A heavy white cast was prominent on his forearm. She stiffened in recognition. *The guy she'd shot in the wrist at the hotel.* A key glinted under the street lamp, and the bespectacled man let himself into the warehouse. With a quick look around, the second man followed, leaving the street deserted once again.

She and Taylor moved quickly toward the building, circling wide around the same pool of light where the others had stood moments before. A red rocking horse was stenciled on the door. They walked on and ducked around the side of the large building.

The warehouse and its yard stretched all the way to docks behind the building. It was a big, old structure, and the dockyard behind the tall hurricane fence was cluttered. No security system was visible outside the warehouse, but undoubtedly, the building itself had some sort of alarm. A small freighter moored at the dock was lit, and several of its crew could be seen moving around the deck. But all else was quiet.

She crouched, leading Taylor along the fence to a tall stack of wooden packing boxes just inside the fence. She indicated with a hand gesture for him to climb over. He might as well make himself useful out here. He laid his sport coat over the barbed wire, helped her over the fence, and they scrambled down the pile of crates together. She silently cursed her theater dress as it caught on a nail and tore slightly. There was no time to retrieve any cloth fibers. She pointed to the side of the building, and Taylor led the way, darting from shadow to shadow behind stacks of packing materials. He was quick. Enough so that she caught herself being grateful she'd worn flat shoes so she could keep up with him.

He paused behind a pile of wooden pallets, and she took the lead, edging closer to the chest-high concrete loading ramp across the rear of the building. A number of large garage doors opened onto it. It was at the closest of these she gestured. Taylor nodded his understanding. She had to give him credit. So far, he wasn't doing half-bad.

Between them and the warehouse lay one last stretch of open ground. She knelt just short of it and motioned him to come up beside her. She whispered in his ear, "We'll have to run for it across this lighted area. We'll head for the first of those doors and I'll pop the lock. You cover me while I cross."

Taylor nodded.

She frowned. "You do have your gun with you, don't you?"

He removed a silenced Magnum from his pocket. "I even remembered to bring bullets," he whispered back.

His comment almost startled a laugh out of her. Barely in time, she controlled the urge and glared at him instead. "Very funny. Just don't screw up." She pulled her own pistol out of her handbag and secured her skirt above her knees with her belt. "I'll go on the count of three." She took one last look around. No sailors were visible aboard the freighter. "One...two..."

A blaze of light lit the entire loading dock as all of its overhead lighting came to life. *Bugger!* She threw herself flat on the ground and wormed her way back behind a pile of packing material. Fortunately, Taylor was right beside her. With a screech of metal, one of the large doors slid open and several men walked out. They were all burly and dressed in rough clothing. Longshoremen. Their conversation sounded like French, but not quite. Quebecois. From the snatches of intelligible conversation, she gathered that a shipment was bound for the freighter moored behind the warehouse, and these guys were none too pleased at the hour of night they were having to load it.

She looked around for a better vantage point to observe the activity. She sidled off with a gesture to Taylor to follow. They worked their way back around the side of the building. About halfway down was a permanently attached metal ladder leading to the roof. She climbed it quickly with Taylor right behind her. The roof was a large, flat space broken by skylights protruding at even intervals. Light came from one corner, and they moved carefully in that direction. She peered down through the dirty, scratched skylight and made out several men in suits. The group was seated around a table, in a pool of light within the warehouse's cavernous darkness. She heard the murmur of voices, but couldn't make out any of the conversation. She glanced over at Taylor and put her hand behind her ear questioningly. He shook his head in the negative. Damn. After a short search, she found a piece of iron pipe among the scattered debris on the roof and passed it to Taylor. He carefully pried up a corner of the metal sheeting beside the skylight.

Gilles Fortesque's voice floated up to them. "Here's the bill of lading for your employer. I'm sure he'll find everything is in order."

The bespectacled man spoke in a gravelly voice, "I have no doubt of it. Do you include the usual guarantee of performance?"

Fortesque answered quickly, *"Mais certainment."* But of course.

"Do you always speak French when you lie?"

There was a moment of charged silence while Fortesque contemplated whether the question had been a joke or a mortal insult. He chose to chuckle. "Ah, my friend, you must be careful. Your jokes could get you in trouble with someone less blessed with humor than myself."

The bespectacled man stared coldly at Fortesque until the Canadian stopped laughing abruptly and snapped, "You have something for me, I believe."

Four Eyes removed his spectacles, polishing them deliberately with his handkerchief before replying. "Shall we have a look at the merchandise first?"

Stiff jawed, Fortesque led him toward the back of the warehouse. The other men took up places near their respective employers as they moved off into the darkness. Amanda and Taylor followed along on the roof, peering in a skylight that lit up near the middle of the building. Two of Fortesque's men pried open a crate pointed out by Four Eyes. The bespectacled man reached in it and pulled out a Stinger missile launcher. He hefted the antiaircraft weapon to his shoulder expertly, staring down its thick metal length. He turned the piece over, inspected the firing assembly, then gently replaced it in its crate.

He nodded at another crate, which was duly opened. Long rows of automatic rifles gleamed dully. In all, he inspected twelve crates containing a variety of firearms and explosives, enough to equip a small army. Fortesque's men were left to renail crates while the others moved back to the table. Amanda and Taylor retraced their steps across the roof, as well.

Four Eyes laid his briefcase on the table and removed a flannel bundle. He untied the string around it, rolled it out flat, lifted the flap and removed a handful of folded tissue papers.

He opened each one carefully and, one by one, revealed sixty spectacular diamonds. Fortesque scrutinized each stone under a jeweler's loupe and put it back into its tissue-paper nest.

The bespectacled man seemed impatient at the excruciating inspection.

Fortesque glanced up, smiling wickedly. "Just making sure there were no substitutions." He put down his loupe. "Yes, these will do quite nicely. They're as fine as the last batch."

"Mais certainment."

Fortesque threw a sour look at his business associate. "How did your employer acquire so many more of these inconspicuously. He has a private mine, perhaps?"

Four Eyes shrugged noncommittally.

A last pile of paperwork came out, and Amanda and Taylor leaned close to catch the conversation. Abruptly, a dull thud sounded beside her ear, and slivers of wood exploded from the frame of the skylight. *Holy shit.* She dived to her stomach and scrambled around the far side of the raised skylight with Taylor in tow.

He whispered frantically in her ear, "What the hell was that?"

Chapter 8

"What in blue blazes do you think it was?" Amanda whispered in response to Taylor's frantic question. "It was a bullet. There's a sniper on the roof of that building across the street."

Taylor looked at the neighboring warehouse, whose roofline was some fifteen feet higher than the one they lay on, and stated the obvious. "He's got the high ground. We'll never get a shot off at him."

She pointed out, "Our more immediate concern is to get out of here before the gang downstairs hears the commotion and joins the fracas." She thought fast. "The only way we're getting off this roof is to move too quickly for the sniper to target us. We'll split up and run from skylight to skylight. Don't go in a straight line toward the ladder, and don't move at even intervals. If you can get a fix on where the sniper is, shoot back. But at all costs, be unpredictable. And be fast. Got it?"

Taylor nodded grimly at her.

"Let's do it, then." She ran at top speed for the next skylight, and dived for cover as the wood frame exploded beside her. She repeated the maneuver two more times. It was hairy enough making her way across the roof that she was only partially able to keep track of Taylor's progress. At one point he got pinned down badly, and she glimpsed a muzzle-flash across the street. She didn't have a clear shot, but squeezed off a couple rounds to buy Taylor a couple extra seconds to make it across a particularly wide expanse of roof. One final sprint and she lay panting beside him behind the last skylight before the edge of the roof. She eyed the open space, perhaps thirty feet wide. "If we stay low, the sniper won't have a clear shot at us. But we'll have to belly crawl to the ladder. Once you start moving, don't stop for any reason. Just get off this roof. You understand?"

"Yeah. Always create a moving target. Amanda McClintock's rule number forty-two."

She spoke through gritted teeth. "We've probably got less than a fifty percent chance of making it to that ladder in one piece. You can die joking if you want, but I intend to go out fighting. Now get your laughing hide in gear and start crawling."

"Ladies first," he replied gamely.

"Can the macho crap. I'm in charge and I say you go first. I'll cover you until you make it to the ladder, and then you can cover me." She didn't mention the part where, once he was on the ladder, Taylor wouldn't have any angle to shoot at the sniper. She'd be completely undefended for the last bit of her trip across the roof.

He took off crawling with alligator-like power. She had to admit he did a mean low crawl. Almost there. Five more feet and he'd be out of the line of fire. Abruptly, wood splintered around him. Damn. The sniper must have moved. She stood up and fired back rapidly, emptying her first clip. She ejected it and slammed in her spare clip. But in the moment of quiet between barrages, a muted grunt of pain from behind her warned her that Taylor had been hit. Oh, God.

Taylor didn't think he was ever going to reach the ladder.

White-hot pain burned his leg like the limb was being roasted over a blazing fire. So much for all that crap about not feeling bullet wounds right away. He had to keep moving. If he didn't, Amanda would undoubtedly do something heroic and foolish. He would not be responsible for getting her killed. He placed one elbow in front of the other, dragging himself inch by agonizing inch across the endless roof.

Suddenly, he was at the ladder, the metal pipes within reach. He grabbed them and rolled off the roof, swinging himself onto the steel rungs. Moving down a few steps, he felt a rivulet of blood course down his pant leg. He looked up, pistol in hand, and realized too late he couldn't do a damn thing to cover Amanda from here. He popped off a couple shots in the general direction of the opposite roof in hopes that he could at least suppress the bastard's fire until she was clear.

Come on, darlin', he begged silently. He waited an eternity, but there was no sign of her. Crap. A vision of her hit and bleeding flashed through his head. He was on the verge of heading back up to the roof when her feet finally appeared above him. "Hurry, " he called out low.

"You think?" she grunted. "Go on. I'm clear."

He descended awkwardly, as fast as his injured leg would go. Each rung put him further out of the gunman's angle of fire. He was afraid like he'd never been afraid before. Nothing could possibly have prepared him for what it would feel like to be shot at. He was hurt, he didn't know how badly, and suddenly he was vulnerable, defenseless and very damn mortal.

"You okay?" Amanda murmured from above him, following him down so closely she nearly stepped on his hands.

"Dunno. My right thigh's hit. I'm functional for now. Haven't stopped to look at it," he replied, breathing heavily.

"Don't worry about being quiet. Just move as fast as you can. Hopefully the folks inside will think we're some rats scurrying around."

She sounded more disgusted than afraid. Apparently getting

shot at wasn't anything new to her. As the endless ladder stretched away below him, his thoughts raced in a dozen directions at once. How had they been compromised? And who had compromised them? How bad was his leg? Were they going to be able to get away from the warehouse? If he couldn't move, he'd have to convince Amanda to go on without him.

Although it seemed to take forever, in reality it was probably only a matter of seconds before the ground loomed. He dropped the last ten feet or so and rolled onto his side. He felt his leg, and the nature of his wound was instantly apparent. A six-inch-long shard of wood stuck all the way through the outside of his right thigh. A bullet must have struck close to him, shearing off the length of wood and spearing it into his thigh. He used his belt to secure his handkerchief over the entry wound, which felt like the worse injury of the two. Amanda dropped the last few feet to the ground beside him.

"Well, that was fun," he panted raggedly. "What's next, boss?"

"Can you run?"

"Does it matter?"

"Good point. Let's go."

They ran. They headed into the waterfront district with its dark alleys and twisting side streets. Amanda set a killer pace, despite her bad ankle. Their feet hit the ground in unison and they fell into a synchronous rhythm with each other. Abruptly, it didn't matter who was the expert and who was the amateur. Running for their lives together was a great equalizer.

He had no idea how he kept going through the tearing pain, but the choice of agony or death made it possible. Now and then he heard feet slapping the pavement behind them. Someone was definitely chasing them, which was no doubt why Amanda kept pressing on relentlessly. They didn't dare stop until they were in the clear.

After nearly a half hour, he began to stumble, and then to stagger. Pinpoints of light danced before his eyes, and his head floated, detached from his numb and clumsy body. He was vaguely aware when Amanda grabbed his elbow and steered him into an alley just past a bar. She guided him behind a trash Dumpster and propped him against the wall.

"How much farther, boss?" he mumbled.

"You're done. Rest now."

"Hallelujah." He squinted at the circling double images of her. "I have to say this hasn't been the most romantic date I've ever been on, Amanda."

She smiled gently at him. Damn. Was that compassion on her face? No way. Not the ice queen. She murmured, "I don't know about that. This evening has had its romantic possibilities. Like now. Here we are, tucked away in a dark, secluded spot all by ourselves."

He flashed her a weak grin and slurred, "You planning on taking advantage of me?"

She gave him a sexy smile. "You think you're up to it? Why don't you sit down and make yourself comfortable, sailor."

"Thought you'd never ask." He slid slowly down the wall to the ground. His head landed on his chest, and he fell gently onto his side.

A cold knife of fear stabbed Amanda. Taylor had just passed out. From pain or blood loss, she had no idea. Quickly, she loosened the belt around his leg and lifted away the sodden handkerchief. So much blood! Her heart jumped into her throat. An incoherent prayer to several assorted gods raced through the back of her mind. For once, she was glad the light wasn't good enough to see much. She didn't relish seeing Taylor's beautiful body mutilated.

She pulled away the tatters of cloth from the wound on the side of his thigh and saw not the round, blackened hole of a bullet wound, but a long fragment of wood piercing the flesh of his upper thigh. It wasn't imbedded deeply, having penetrated the skin and the heavy muscle of his thigh at an oblique angle. Relief flooded her, so strong it made her light-headed and slightly sick to her stomach. His injury wasn't life-threatening.

It was still bleeding freely, however, and most of Taylor's pant leg was soaked with blood.

Normally, she'd leave the wood in place and seek medical care before she pulled it out. But since the entry and exit wounds were still bleeding heavily, and the likelihood of his seeing a doctor any time soon was nil, she elected to take advantage of his unconsciousness and deal with the injury now. She grasped the fragment firmly and gave a sharp yank. The piece of wood jerked free, and Taylor lurched in a spasm of pain even in his senseless state. A gush of blood spilled out of the ragged wounds, and she slapped her neck scarf and his handkerchief back over them, pressing hard. She held the pressure bandages a long time, until she could no longer feel blood seeping between her fingers, then secured them snugly in place with Taylor's belt.

She tried to rouse him, but with no great success. He opened one eye briefly to glare at her and didn't appear the slightest bit interested in getting up. His eyelid drifted closed. She put her face about twelve inches from his and shook him again. She spoke urgently. "Listen to me. This is very important. Don't move. I'm going to leave you here for a little while, but I'll be back to get you. Just stay put. Do you understand?"

His eyes flickered and the corners of his mouth lifted slightly. "Yes, ma'am."

She scowled and stood up. The man was exasperating even when he was half-dead. She took off his watch, fished in his pocket for his wallet and checked his tanned, strong fingers for any rings. He wore none. Next, she took his gun and spare clips. He didn't need to be robbed just now, and she definitely didn't trust him to use a gun wisely in his condition. She rummaged in the Dumpster beside them for some newspapers and a couple cardboard boxes, which she spread over him. They'd not only hide his tuxedo, but also keep him slightly warmed. Hopefully, the pungent stench of garbage would cover the smell of his blood. She stepped back to survey her work and decided he'd pass for a homeless drunk at a glance. If he got picked up by the police, he could always claim he'd been mugged.

She turned and left the alley, walking calmly along the street as if she strolled this way every evening. There were fewer cat-calls and lewd propositions than she'd expected. She must look worse than she realized. She walked for perhaps a mile before she reached a neighborhood where taxis would venture. Before too terribly long, she managed to hail one. The driver raised his eyebrows when she gave him the address of Fortesque's home and inquired if she had the money to pay the fare. She peeled a hundred-dollar bill off the roll in her shoulder bag, passed it up front and told the guy to step on it.

An hour later, the taxi crunched up the gravel drive to the mansion and a maid let her in. A postconcert pool party was in full swing out back and the house was deserted. She slipped up-stairs avoiding the wild festivities, packed quickly, loaded their bags in the rental car and headed back toward Toronto. What on earth did she think she was doing? Here she was rescuing Taylor, when it was her fondest wish to be rid of him. Wasn't it? Of course it was. He was a huge hindrance to her. She ought to just leave him in that alley. His wound wasn't mortal, and he could look after his own hide. She wasn't responsible for him! She lectured herself on her stupidity all the way back to the waterfront.

She jumped out of the car to collect Taylor and stopped short. Where she had left him, there was only a pile of news-paper and cardboard boxes. Her stomach plummeted to her feet. "Damn!" she burst out, striking her palm against the wall be-side her.

Taylor poked his head out of the Dumpster right next to her. "Looking for me, boss?"

She leaped straight up in the air, and when her heart started beating again, she glared at him. "What are you doing in there?"

"I heard a familiar voice asking about a man and a woman

in evening clothes, and I thought I'd better hide. This was the best I could do."

"Who was it?"

Taylor frowned. "I don't know. I was pretty out of it. It was a man's voice and it sounded close. I knew I was in danger."

"Our sniper must've been asking questions at the bar right around the corner."

"Probably," he agreed. "Uh, boss? Could you help me get out of here? 'Fraid I'm not feeling up to my usual superhuman standards."

With her help, Taylor crawled awkwardly out of the Dumpster and made his unsteady way to the car. She loaded him in quickly and jumped into the driver's seat. They were many miles beyond Toronto before either one of them spoke again.

"Boss?"

"Hmm?" she replied.

"Thanks for coming back to get me."

An odd warmth spread through her. "You're welcome." Lest the moment get too sappy, she added dryly, "If you're truly grateful, roll down the window. You stink to high heaven."

It was nearly daybreak when they reached the U.S. border in Windsor, Ontario. She reached across Taylor's slumbering form to cover his torn and bloody pant leg with his coat. She was grateful he didn't wake as they approached the border guard, who peered in the window politely. Taylor probably couldn't lie for squat under the best of circumstances, and certainly not in his present condition. She told the guard briefly that she was driving because her date was drunk. The guy waved her through with an admonition to be careful. They rolled past the five towering, mirrored cylinders of the Detroit Renaissance Center and joined a smattering of sleepy drivers winding through the sunken expressways of the Motor City.

She drove as though their very lives depended on getting far, far away from Toronto. Exhaustion nipped around the edges of her consciousness, along with something else. Something that kept her foot on the accelerator and her eyes wide open. Fear. Stalking her patiently like the cruel hunter it was. It breathed down her neck, whispering of a narrow escape that might not go her way next time.

She felt Taylor's forehead from time to time, watched for the next rise and fall of his chest to reassure herself that they were both alive. That first bullet had come inches from killing her. They'd been sitting ducks. Damned lucky sitting ducks. She shuddered and drove on.

It was late afternoon before she exited the highway at a cluster of gas stations, fast-food joints and motels. Taylor woke up and groaned in relief.

She grumbled, "I don't see what you're so thrilled about. I'm the one who spent all day smelling you."

He smiled wanly in response.

She turned in at the entrance to a motor lodge and got them a room. While Taylor luxuriated in the shower, she made a quick trip out for first-aid supplies and food. She got back before he finished washing and was sitting cross-legged on one of the double beds, chewing on a piece of barbecued chicken when he emerged from the bathroom. Cole slaw, biscuits, cartons of milk and chocolate pudding rounded out the picnic she'd spread out on the coverlet.

"Let me see your leg," she ordered.

He lifted the edge of the towel wrapped around his hips and showed her the double wounds, which were bleeding again.

She scolded, "Why did you get your scabs wet? You've lost more than enough blood already."

Taylor shrugged. "Sorry. There were still a couple of splinters in it, and I had to dig them out so my leg wouldn't get infected."

Ouch. That sounded painful. She bit back the rest of the lecture and pulled out the gauze and tape she'd bought. She held out the first-aid supplies to him and averted her face as he sat down on the opposite bed, hiked the towel up even farther and proceeded to tape his leg.

"That'll leave an unsightly scar if you don't get a few stitches. Would you like me to set a couple sutures? I've done it before."

He glanced up at her, and his jaw rippled as if his teeth were clenched. "I'm not planning to enter any beauty pageants. I'll take the scar. I've had about enough pain for one day, thanks."

She looked away again hastily. "Remember to slather it in antibiotic cream."

"Taken care of," he bit out. He tore long strips of tape to secure his bandage, and she let out as big a sigh of relief as he did when the job was finally done. Her bed lurched as he sat down on it. She stiffened in surprise, but relaxed when he reached for a piece of chicken.

"So," he asked, "where are we on this case?"

She'd given that a lot of thought during the long drive. "I'd like you to take a look at my father's journal." She rummaged in one of her bags and came back to the bed with the leather diary in hand. "You're a shrink, right?"

He grinned up at her. "Guilty as charged."

"Maybe you can make some sense of my father's writing. It all sounds like wild, meaningless ranting to me."

She handed him the diary, which he thumbed through. He looked up at her, frowning. "Can you actually read this chicken scratching?"

"Yeah. I grew up with it, remember?" She sat down beside him and started to read aloud. Over the next couple hours she read to Taylor while he jotted down occasional notes. It was painstaking work requiring copious amounts of coffee. Eventually, her brain just gave out. She put down the book and rubbed her eyes. "What have we got?" she asked wearily.

He glanced down at his notes. "This was your father's last journal before he died. He wrote it as a legacy to you and was trying to tell you the shortened version of some story. It revolves around some fantasy of him being an international spy with a control officer named Nicky, from whom he took something called Udarsky."

She peered at him from under her hands. "It wasn't a fantasy. He was a spy."

Taylor gaped at her. His expression would have been comical if she wasn't so damned tired. "For whom? Or more importantly, against whom?" he asked incredulously.

"To the best of my knowledge, for the Russians against the British."

He stared. "Your dad was American, wasn't he?"

She nodded. "Yes, and he hated the rigid, imperialist class structure of Europe."

"Your father was a *Communist?* What did he have against the Brits?"

She'd have thought that after so many years of bearing the shame of her father's sins, Taylor's horrified tone of voice wouldn't hurt. But it did. "He wasn't all that passionate about politics. Frankly, he didn't care one way or another who he was spying for or against. For him, it was all about money. My father was an untalented art dealer with expensive tastes and a family to support. The Russians paid him well, so he took the rubles and did what they asked."

"So what does he have to do with this diamond-smuggling investigation?"

She looked up candidly at Taylor, grateful for the compassion in his gaze. "I have no bloody idea." She sighed. "I was hoping you could tell me after you read that thing. Are you ready to get back to work?"

Her father's ramblings got less and less coherent as they neared the end of the book. He ranted repeatedly about something he called the Udarsky cache. Claimed to have found it right under Nicky's unsuspecting nose and brought it out of Russia.

Taylor frowned. "Whatever Udarsky was, Christopher Mc-

Clintock seemed to think it or he was his ticket—and yours—to a life of wealth and ease."

Time for a break to rest her numb brain and burning eyes. She lay on the bed, exhausted.

Taylor stretched out beside her, his body big and warm and disturbingly near. "What's the deal with this oak tree that keeps cropping up? Do you know what he's referring to?"

Grief sliced through Amanda. "Yeah. It's the tree in the picture that came with this journal. He and I planted it when I was seven. Whenever he came home from trips abroad he'd always go straight away to see that tree. I used to wonder if he practiced some weird religious ritual beneath it."

"Were his trips to meet Nicky? To pass over information?"

She frowned. "I don't think so. Nicky was his Russian contact in London. Anything my father learned he passed to Nicky there."

"What kind of spying did your father do?"

"Collected gossip, mostly. Stuff about politicians and the British upper crust who made up his clientele."

"Did your father have any unusual skills like a talent for cryptography or a ham radio hobby that would make him useful to the Russians?"

Amanda frowned. "I don't think so."

"What about photographic analysis? You said he was an art dealer, so he must have been good at looking at visual details."

She stared at him. In all her years of living with the man and the fallout from him, that had never occurred to her. "Wouldn't the Russians have used their own people to do photographic analysis?" she asked.

"Could your dad have had special knowledge of an area that the Russians were interested in? They needed his expertise to tell them what they were looking at, maybe?"

The obvious answer to that pierced Amanda's exhaustion. She propped herself on her elbows, staring at Taylor. She answered slowly, "My grandfather was a missionary to Kyrgyzstan before World War II. My father grew up there. He traveled every inch of that place. Went to some really remote areas. But why would Kyrgyzstan interest the Russians? People in that part of the world still live in yurts and raise yaks. It's hardly a place with huge military significance."

"What the hell's a yurt?" Taylor asked.

"A domed tent made of animal hides or felt. Kirghiz shepherds live in them."

He rolled onto his back beside her and stared at the ceiling for several minutes. Finally, he announced, "I don't see the connection between Kyrgyzstan and diamond smuggling. It's not a place diamonds come from, is it?"

She frowned. "Not to my knowledge. The only thing I know of that comes from Kyrgyzstan is hydroelectric power. They've got a couple huge dams on major rivers."

Her eyes flew open when his hands touched the sides of her head, massaging her scalp. Lord, that felt good. She made the mistake of looking at him. His hands drew her inexorably nearer to the stormy ocean of his gaze. Her breath hitched. Fire ignited within her. It swirled and twisted, grew like a hungry blaze to consume her. His gaze locked on hers, he came closer and paused for a moment, giving her permission to stop this. And then his mouth touched hers.

This man. This moment. It was as if she'd been waiting a lifetime for this single, culminating instant. From this second forward, her life would not be the same. She knew it as certainly as she drew breath. It was a homecoming, a recognition more ancient than time. She *knew* this man, knew the feel of his warm, firm mouth moving gently across hers, knew the taste of him, the scent of him. She sank into that primeval memory and melted into his embrace. Her mouth parted beneath his, and his tongue ran lightly across the smoothness of her teeth. One of his hands went behind her head, and the kiss deepened. His tongue found hers, and she reveled in the velvet roughness of it. He groaned deep in his throat. Elation soared within her. She stretched her emotional wings cautiously, responding experimentally to his kiss. Her hands came to rest upon the hard contours of his chest and began to explore the thrilling mystery of his body. If accepting comfort from Taylor had been freedom, then this was flight.

Harry Trumpman walked into the conference room. It was decorated in shades of bland utilitarian and not quite cheap. It reeked of government. Probably an FBI field office or something similar. He studied the other men in the room. Several of them didn't look FBI. Two of them wore the expensive, old-school suits of…if he had to guess, State Department. One face he recognized from a case Devereaux'd put him on about three years back. High-level CIA. What in the hell was he doing here? Cautiously, Harry sat down at the conference table.

One of the FBI guys spoke first, predictably bellicose. "What do you know about a murder at a ritzy hotel in Toronto a couple days back?"

Harry frowned. "Nothing. Why?"

"What about a shoot-out at a warehouse on the Toronto waterfront last night?"

He looked at the guy and said deadpan, " I didn't know Toronto had a waterfront. I'll be damned. Live and learn."

While the FBI guy scowled, the CIA rep stepped in. Smooth. Professional. "Your boss has a couple operatives poking around, Harry. Care to share what they're investigating?"

"Not particularly. Why?"

"They've bumped into someone we'd prefer they backed off of for now. Are you in contact with your people?"

He wasn't, but he wasn't about to admit that to the people in this room. "I can be."

Mr. CIA pushed a photograph across the table at him. Harry looked down at a swarthy guy with thick, black hair; fortyish in age; wearing a little pair of spectacles perched on his nose. "I need you to do me a favor. Get your people to leave this guy alone."

"Is he yours?" Harry asked.

"No. But we have a vested interest in giving him some room to operate."

That was interesting. "Any objections if my operatives continue to watch him?"

The CIA guy looked Harry in the eye. Too damned sincerely. "Sorry, my friend. You're gonna have to trust me. This guy needs to be completely sterile. We need your people to have no interaction whatsoever. Nothing that could spook him. No contact, no surveillance, *nada*."

"Care to share what you're poking around in?" Harry asked.

The CIA guy shrugged. "Sorry."

Right. He was supposed to lay all his cards on the table while they didn't show him any of theirs. Not bloody likely. "Anything else?" Harry asked sourly.

"No, nothing else. It's good to see you again."

Nothing, his ass. Why would the CIA send in someone that high level to do an errand boy's job? Why the show of interdepartment unity from Uncle Sam? What had Amanda and Taylor stumbled across? Sure as he was sitting there, they'd kicked up one hell of a hornet's nest. Damn, Amanda was good. Two days and she already had the Russians trying to kill her and the U.S. government putting on dog-and-pony shows to back her off.

Taylor tightened his arms gently about Amanda and shifted smoothly, following her down to the mattress. God, he wanted to sink into her, to surround himself with her warmth, her vulnerability. She was sweet and potent, like a fine liqueur. He sipped at her, savoring her complex, elegant flavors. He covered her with enough of his body to offer protection, sanctuary, but not so much as to trap her. One of his hands traveled briefly down her ribs, past her hips, down the length of her thigh to the back of her knee and up again. She shuddered under his fingertips, arching slightly into his touch. Thank God. Her reaction was healthy and normal. Nobody'd done a number on this part of her psyche.

He squeezed his eyes shut in a gut-wrenching battle of lust versus better judgment. Now was not the time. She was just discovering her wings and was not yet ready to fly with him. He marshaled his raging hormones and managed to contain them enough to lift his mouth away from hers. His hand captured one of hers and he twined their fingers together. He propped himself up on one elbow and gazed down at her. "I'm sorry. That was meant to give you comfort. But it's damn hard not to get carried away with you." When Amanda didn't answer, he released her hand and rolled away from her reluctantly. Dammit. He'd pushed too hard.

She sat up and said thoughtfully. "Thanks. For the comfort, I mean. It was…nice."

Startled, his gaze snapped to hers. Her fair skin was rapidly turning bright red.

She looked away hastily and made a production of digging in her suitcase for a change of clothes. "I don't know about you," she mumbled, "but I'm beat. Let's get some sleep."

Taylor awoke many hours later to the sound of water running for a shower and rolled over groggily. Ow! Damn, his leg throbbed like hell. The gray light of predawn gave way to sunrise outside his window, and he turned his wrist in the dim light to read his watch—6:47 a.m. He groaned mentally. He'd slept ten uninterrupted hours, but he still felt like death warmed over. He collapsed back to the mattress and wished fervently for sleep to reclaim him.

He cracked one eye open when Amanda emerged from the bathroom. She was wearing nothing but a large bath towel, and he jolted up onto an elbow. "Well, good morning!"

"Good morning, sleepyhead," she teased back.

He groaned. "Are you always so…perky…at this time of day?"

She grinned. "A decent night's sleep does wonders for me."

"So, where are we off to today, boss?"

She murmured distractedly as she unfolded a map, "I'm not your boss. I'm your partner."

He blinked. Decent of her to acknowledge that. For a while there, he'd wondered.

She traced a highway with one finger toward Mexico and said, "Marina will be playing two more nights in Toronto, then she's on to Rio de Janeiro for a week. We should head there and see if we can pick up the trail of Four Eyes."

He gestured at the map. "Are you suggesting we drive all the way to Rio?"

She rolled her eyes. "Of course not. We'll have to fly at least part of the way if we plan to get there in four days. But the Russians chasing me will be watching the airports. I propose that we drive to Mexico and fly from there to Rio. I assume you don't have a repertoire of false identifications yet, since you don't work for the government?"

He nodded. "That's a good assumption. I've got one passport, and it's in my own name."

"An easy enough problem to fix in Mexico," she replied briskly. "If you're ready to go, we need to get on the road. We've got a long drive, and we need to keep moving if we're going to keep ahead of whoever's trying to kill us."

Chapter 9

Max called Biryayev at home, letting the phone ring insistently until his boss answered it groggily. "Good afternoon, sir. Max Ebhardt here. We have directions from Moscow concerning the message you had me send this morning. You might want to come in and read it."

Biryayev suddenly sounded much more alert. "Is that so? I'll be right in."

Ebhardt was waiting for him when he arrived and handed him the missive silently.

Biryayev read aloud, "'To station intelligence chief. Eliminate anyone who attempts to interfere in our diamond-trading program. All necessary resources and personnel are approved.'" He smiled exultantly at Max. "How do the Americans say it? It's show time!"

Ebhardt's response was dry. "That would be how they say it, sir." Max had never seen true blood lust before, but the look in Biryayev's eyes at the moment must be what the description referred to. It wasn't pleasant to look upon.

Laredo, Texas, looked as tired as Amanda felt. The air was painful to breathe, too hot and dry for human lungs. Stunted bushes along the highway stood torpid and lifeless, covered by a heavy layer of gray dust. As the sun set, it bled slowly across the withered landscape, staining it brilliant red. Cowboy boots, jeans and sweat-stained cowboy hats were the garments of choice; missing only were the jingling spurs and six-shooters to complete the image of the Old West. Taylor drove, following signs to the border. Harassed U.S. border guards, inundated with incoming customs claims, hardly glanced at them as they drove through the no-man's-land between the American and Mexican reception areas. They approached the Mexican border and a uniformed man waved them to a stop. Taylor rolled down the window.

"May I see some identification," the guard said in a bored monotone.

The guard opened the passport of one Alicia Snyder first. He glanced down at the picture, then at Amanda. A brunette wash in her hair and cheek pads matched her to the photograph. "Are you traveling on business or pleasure?"

She leaned across the car, practically lying in Taylor's lap. He shifted uncomfortably and she glanced at him in amusement before she looked out the window at the border guard. She gushed in a syrupy Southern accent, "Most assuredly pleasure. We're on vacation. I just can't wait to visit one of your gorgeous beaches and soak up some sun."

"I see," came the impassive reply. Alicia Snyder's passport was passed back to her.

The guard glanced at Taylor, then opened the remaining passport. He glanced at Taylor a second time and then back down, reading carefully. He closed Taylor's passport, abruptly alert. "If you would pull over there and park your car, I'd like you to step inside for a moment." The guard gestured to a low stucco building behind him.

Taylor glanced at her, alarmed. Her own stomach fell. "Do what he said," she murmured.

As he maneuvered the car into a parking space, he mumbled, "I knew this was a bad idea, trying to make this trip under my own name."

She shrugged. "Keep your wits about you and we'll get out of this somehow. Follow my lead." She walked beside him toward a squat, administrative-looking building, and the sinking feeling in her gut intensified. The guard ushered them into a large room with a row of chairs along one wall and desks scattered across the floor. He motioned for them to sit and disappeared off to their left down a corridor with Taylor's passport in hand. In keeping with her assumed identity, she preened a bit and smiled at a second border guard seated across the room. Taylor took his cue and shrugged, assuming the stance of a casual traveler being patient over an unavoidable delay.

The first guard returned with a man wearing a Mexican military uniform. The officer spoke. "I am Major Ortolo. If both of you would please come with me."

As they headed out of the room the second guard watched them intently. The hairs on the back of her neck stood up in warning as the guy reached for his phone. She had a bad feeling about this. Major Ortolo led them into his office. He gestured them into seats and closed the door, leaving the first guard outside. He sat down at his desk with his back to one of the two windows and she noticed it was nearly full dark outside. He handed Taylor's passport back to him.

"Please do not be alarmed. I am Major Manuel Ramirez di Ortolo. I have been instructed to look for you and detain you so your employer can deliver an urgent message to you. I beg your indulgence while I notify him of your arrival." He made a brief phone call in rapid Spanish.

She was going to kill Harry for scaring her like this. Why

in world didn't he just leave a voice mail for her? She'd have checked it in the next twenty-four hours or so. What could be so urgent that he'd go to these lengths to get in touch with them?

The officer announced, "He'll be here in a few minutes. May I offer you some coffee?"

Taylor and Amanda both nodded. She sipped at a steaming cup of strong, bitter coffee. Crickets were starting to trill outside the window beside her elbow, and she listened to the small talk Taylor kept up with the officer. The niggling feeling at the back of her neck just wouldn't go away.

She caught a tiny movement out of the corner of her eye and glanced up. She started, sloshing hot coffee onto the floor. Through the window behind the major's head was a man's face! In the fraction of a second that took to register, the glass exploded inward. The head and torso of a man pushed through the gap, preceded by the muzzle of a sawed-off shotgun. With a deafening blast, two shells entered Ortolo's back, throwing the major onto his face, sprawled across his desk.

Shock slammed into her, vaulting her from her seat. She leaped toward the window, scooping up a shard of glass from the desktop as she passed it. Grabbing the wrist holding the shotgun, she yanked inward, slicing at the man's throat as he lurched forward into the room.

Thankfully, Taylor lunged at the nonuniformed man who burst through the door. The attacker raised a pistol overhead. "Watch out!" she shouted.

At the last second, Taylor saw the blow coming and dived, absorbing most of its impact with his fall. Nonetheless, he crashed into Ortolo's desk. Amanda's attacker fought back, and she crippled him with a blow to his face with her left elbow. Taylor rolled off the desk and grabbed his attacker's knees, pulling the guy's feet out from under him. Good move. The assailant fell backward into a third man just rushing into the room. Both attackers tumbled to the floor in a swearing heap.

She crouched beneath the windowsill. A second head poked

cautiously through the opening. She stabbed upward, hard and fast, with the shard of glass. A bloodcurdling scream pierced the air, and the head jerked back out of sight. She checked on Taylor and was in time to see a foot lash out from the tangle of bodies beside him. It caught his temple with a sharp blow and laid him out flat. Damn! Before she could leap over the desk and engage his attackers, they disentangled themselves and got to their feet. Both armed. She couldn't take them.

Time to cut losses. She vaulted through the jagged window opening, stopping long enough to glance back into the lighted tableau. Taylor was on his knees, hands clasped behind his neck. The black bore of a pistol was pointed at his head. Another man entered the room. Shock froze her in place. *The bespectacled man.* She turned and dived into the shadows.

She spotted one of her assailants and came up behind him as he crawled feebly for his life. A foot on his back and he collapsed, hands over his wrecked eye, moaning. She searched him frantically, looking for a weapon—any weapon—with which to rescue Taylor. The guy ignored her. Probably going into shock. Her pistol was safely hidden in the trunk of the rental car. This guy must have dropped his shotgun somewhere between here and the window, but she couldn't see it in the dark. He was unarmed except for a knife. Not enough to take on two armed men with a hostage. Dammit! Sick helplessness washed over her. Short of throwing herself into the room in a suicide move, she could only stand by and watch whatever happened to Taylor. Fear and frustration so intense they made her nauseous washed over her.

What did the bespectacled man want with Taylor? She was the one who'd been working on the case. Why hadn't he killed Taylor immediately? As he and his companion goose-stepped Taylor out of the room, she turned and ran, heading for the deepest shadows of the nearest side street.

Taylor shook his head to clear it as Four Eyes spoke to him. The accent was Slavic, but not Russian. "I would speak with you about our deal, agent of the American government. Come with us."

As if he had any choice in the matter with a gun pointed at his head! American government agent, huh? Okay. He would go with that. It was as good a cover as any of his real source of employment. Since he'd never met this guy before, the deal he spoke of must be with Uncle Sam. What would the government want with this guy? He scowled at his captor. "Christ, man! We were waiting for you already. Did you have to be so violent about getting me?"

The guy frowned but did not reply. He and the other man hoisted Taylor to his feet. Whoa. The room spun wildly and his stomach threatened revolt. That blow to his temple must've clocked him worse than he'd thought. The men half supported, half dragged him to a waiting van. While Four Eyes drove, the other guy faced Taylor, pointing an Uzi at him. The weapon's safety was visibly disengaged. Taylor stared warily at the sub-machine gun, praying that one of the many bumps and potholes in the road would not jostle the dirty finger resting casually on the trigger.

"Where are you taking me?" Taylor asked the guard.

The guy jerked his head toward the driver. "He wants to talk with you."

Taylor frowned. Why in the hell would Four Eyes want to talk to an American government agent? Why not just kill him and Amanda? Something was going on here. But as long as that Uzi was pointed at him, there wasn't much he could do about it.

They drove for about an hour, and it all felt like unimproved surfaces. After a short interval of silent travel, as if they drove over grass, the van stopped. His mind racing with a speed born of fear, he reviewed his training on resisting interrogation and concentrated on breathing slowly.

Harry Trumpman walked warily through the open door of the border station and, at the sight of a border guard's body sprawled in the hallway, sprinted for the major's office. He burst through the broken doorway and surveyed the scene in dismay. Shit. He stepped to the desk, moving the major's lifeless arm off of the phone to use it. But then he noticed the bloody windowsill. He glanced outside and made out an inert form on the grass. Dropping the receiver back in its cradle, he raced outside and rolled the injured man onto his back. Harry recoiled at the sight of the guy's mangled eyeball. "Where are the American man and woman?" he demanded.

The man stared balefully at him out of his remaining eye. Harry tried the question again in Spanish, and the man's eyelid flickered. Harry continued in the same language. "Talk and I'll let you live." His voice was hard. "Otherwise, I'll tie your hands behind your back, slit your wrists and let you bleed to death. Slowly. It's a painful way to die."

The guy was sullen. "They're gone."

"Where to?"

Silence.

Harry yanked off the man's belt and secured the poor bastard's hands behind his back. He pulled out his Swiss army knife and held it against the man's wrist. "Where *are* they?" he snarled.

"A farm, fifty, maybe sixty kilometers from here."

"Where?"

"I don't know."

Harry glared menacingly at his captive. "Where is this farm?" he repeated.

"I don't know where it is," the man spit out.

The Swiss army knife made a small vertical cut in the man's right wrist. Harry was careful to avoid any major veins or arteries. The guy began to whimper. The knife made a second vertical cut alongside the first. The man cried out sharply as blood began to run over his fingers. The knife made a third cut. The man babbled hysterically, swearing by assorted saints and on his mother's grave that he didn't know where this farm was. Harry shook his head in disgust. What a mess.

He retraced his steps quickly to the major's office and reached across the dead man once more for the telephone. "Foxtrot requesting phone patch to Alpha."

"One moment, please," the switchboard operator murmured.

A pause and a click. Two rings and a quiet, male voice came across the line. "Yes?"

"Foxtrot here. We've got a problem. Phoenix and Falcon have been snatched and are allegedly being taken to an unknown location, perhaps a farm, fifty to sixty kilometers from this location. I was not able to deliver the message."

A pregnant pause at the other end of the line. "Call in the local authorities and search for them. Turn every stone, Foxtrot. These two are important. *Find them.* Call me back in one hour."

"Right away." Very few crises in Devereaux's affairs rated that urgent tone of voice.

Harry pushed the disconnect button on the major's phone and dialed the local *policia*.

Amanda watched the van pull away and raced in the direction of the retreating taillights. The vehicle with Taylor in it headed away from the downtown area of Nuevo Laredo. She stopped, huffing hard as it disappeared from sight. She took off at a steady run in the same direction, searching for a likely conveyance as she went. About two minutes later, she found what she was searching for. An ancient truck was parked in front of a darkened house, its windows rolled down. A minute under the dashboard, and the crusty old engine sputtered to life. She drove to the next major intersection and stopped. The truck's glove compartment yielded a fortuitous flashlight, and she used it to examine the road. There was one set of fresh tire tracks in the dust. Thank God. She memorized the pattern, then climbed back into the truck, driving another mile or so before stopping again to verify the prints still ran before her.

Stay calm. Keep thinking clearly. Taylor's life depends on it. Though her mind believed the words, for some reason her gut ignored the logic entirely and twisted into apprehensive knots. Time and again she forced down the panic bubbling toward the surface of her mind by repeating the litany over and over. Stay calm. Keep thinking….

The police were on their way. Harry Trumpman stared at the phone, undecided. Arriving at a decision, he picked up the phone quickly before he could change his mind. Thumbing to a coded portion of his address book, he dialed a number he'd only used once before.

After several rings, an adolescent girl's voice answered cheerily. "Hello."

"Good evening. Is your dad at home?" Harry asked.

"He sure is. Just a minute." There was a pause and the sound of laughter in the background.

A man's voice spoke. Harry's CIA contact. "Hello."

"This is Harry Trumpman. I'm sorry to bother you at home, but I've got a bit of a problem. My operatives have apparently been kidnapped in Mexico. I was unable to deliver your message."

"Have you gotten a ransom demand yet?"

"No," Harry bit out.

The CIA man sounded unconcerned. "You probably will soon. Kidnapping and extortion are practically a national pastime down there."

Harry replied, "These kidnappers executed a well-organized, violent attack. I'm convinced local thugs did not do it."

A long pause followed, and Trumpman could almost hear the man's mind assessing damage and considering alternatives. Finally, the contact spoke. "A kidnapping effectively keeps your people under wraps for a couple days. That's probably all our guy needs to do his business and get out of the area. This will work."

That wasn't the point. Harry protested. "Sir, two American citizens have been kidnapped. It's the responsibility of our government to help them."

The man snapped, "It's the responsibility of this government to look out for its national interests."

The bastard. He wasn't going to lift a finger to help Amanda and Taylor. As long as they didn't get in his way, this guy was willing to hang them out to dry.

"By the way, Trumpman, I got a profile on your operatives. Want to explain why you've got a clinical psychologist running around in the field doing wet ops?"

"No comment," Harry growled.

"Look. Give it a few days. If nobody contacts you asking for cash, give me a call and I'll see what I can do."

"My people may not live that long!" Harry exclaimed.

"I'm sorry. That's the best I can do."

"Yeah, well, thanks, anyway." Harry hung up the phone, staring at it in angry disbelief. The cold-hearted son of a bitch. They both knew the Russians had his operatives. Harry snorted. Two days. In two days, the Russians could completely pick a person's brains and fry them with drugs. Uncle Sam was throwing Amanda and Taylor to the wolves.

They forced Taylor to sit in the van for nearly an hour with no explanation. Then the guard threw the van's door open and gestured him out. He got out clumsily, stiff from sitting so long. The jerk jabbed him in the back with an Uzi, shoving him toward a low stucco building in front of them. Taylor assessed his surroundings hastily. A decrepit hacienda, with low-roofed houses and barns arranged in a loose square around a central courtyard. Even in moonlight, the place was a ramshackle ruin. He stumbled and caught himself as the guy behind him poked him again.

"Cut it out," Taylor snapped. "I'm going willingly here."

The jerk laid off with the Uzi, but stayed behind him. Taylor ducked through the low doorway into a filthy room, long abandoned. Four Eyes already sat at the lone table in the main room. A second chair was empty across from him. It was to this Taylor was prodded. A couple more pokes with that damned gun, and he was going to take it from the guard and shove it up his...

The bespectacled man uttered a short, sharp command in some Slavic tongue Taylor didn't recognize. Pokey Man laid off. And then in English, Four Eyes said, "Sit down, my friend. Please forgive my associate's behavior. He is what he is, I am afraid."

Yeah. A moron about to get his ass kicked. Taylor tamped down on his irritation and took the proffered seat. The ancient ruin of a chair creaked beneath his weight.

"Thank you for coming."

"It wasn't like I exactly had any choice in the matter," Taylor grunted.

Four Eyes waved a dismissive hand. "That was all a show for the police. You can claim to have been kidnapped by thugs and the Mexican police will look no further. It was merely a cover."

Taylor raised an eyebrow. "What sort of conversation requires a cover that gets men killed?"

Four Eyes answered earnestly, "I need to get in touch with your employer."

Taylor snorted. "Well, Jesus. Then pick up the phone and call. There's no need to run around killing people for that!"

"It is not that simple. Many people watch my movements at all times. Even contacting you like this required a great deal of planning."

Taylor crossed his arms. "Okay. So here we are. What's your message?"

Amanda laboriously followed the tracks out into the Mexican scrub. Thankfully, once she cleared Nuevo Laredo, the road only crossed a few intersections. The van carrying Taylor took two turns. The first one she spotted relatively easily. The second one had her backtracking for upward of a half hour, but finally, she picked up the tracks once more.

She spotted a cluster of buildings in the distance and slowed cautiously. Easing the rattling, coughing truck forward, she glimpsed what might be a van parked in the middle of the hacienda's courtyard. She stopped her own vehicle and got out since she'd be a hell of a lot quieter approaching on foot. The nearly full moon was low in the sky, but cast enough light to make out a broken-down old ranch that looked as if it had never lived to see a motorized vehicle until tonight.

She froze as a flare of light gave away the position of a man smoking. She squinted and made him out leaning against a porch post, a rifle slung over his shoulder. His cigarette tip flared orange as he sucked at it. Numbskull, she thought derisively. There was nothing like a glowing fag to give away a bloke's position. She dropped to the ground as several shadows emerged from another building, talking low. Crap. Reinforcements. She eased up on to her elbows, peering around a sparse sage bush. Four more men. Weapons over every shoulder and additional holsters on three of them. They walked over to the smoker and had a brief conversation. The disconnected syllables that floated to her sounded Slavic. Four Eyes's men maybe?

Who *was* this guy? He carried around millions in diamonds, made illegal arms deals and had a veritable army of protection. One of the extra guards stayed with the smoker while the other three returned to the building they'd come from.

Crawling, she circled left and approached the guarded building—no doubt where Taylor was being held—from behind. Flat on her belly for the last hundred feet, she eased forward, praying there weren't any scorpions or rattlesnakes out hunting. She watched the building for several minutes. No patrolling guards, apparently. She moved up behind the low house and stood up slowly, peeking in the lone window. The glass was old and wavy, caked with grime. She made out two men sitting at a table. One of them leaned back and crossed his arms. *Taylor.* Thank God he wasn't tied up and beaten or drugged. Yet.

She ducked under the window and moved around to the

other side of it to get a better look at the other man. She caught a flash of reflected light off the guy's face. Glasses. Four Eyes. She couldn't hear what he said to Taylor, but a heavy frown crossed her partner's face. What was going on in there? It didn't look like any interrogation or kidnapper-victim exchange she'd ever seen.

She looked around, considering options. There was a crumbling fireplace at one end of the large room, not far from the table where Taylor and Four Eyes were sitting. On the front walk, facing the porch and its guards, was a larger window. Two doors opened up in the wall to her left. Probably a privy and a bedroom or two. She could go around front and take out the two guards, but the other thugs would probably hear it. Anyway, the others would notice the pair's absence from their post on the porch sooner or later. She could climb up on the roof and listen from the fireplace. Not a bad option. Could be noisy, though, on old adobe tile. Or she could sneak into one of the side rooms. The big drawback to that one was that the windows she'd have to climb through faced the building with the additional guards. Well, no help for it. She sidled around the end of the building on her belly. Her elbows were scratched and raw, but she dug them into the sharp gravel determinedly, inching her body forward. There were a few clumps of grass and a small tumbleweed, but no other cover to speak of. She was a sitting duck if the three guards happened to step outside and look this way.

She eased up under the first window and made out a small bedroom with two pairs of decayed bunk beds. No solid cover, and very little room to move. But then she heard movement in the building next door. It sounded like chairs pushing back. This room would have to do.

Using the dull knife she'd found in the truck, she scored the glazing and rotted wood around a pane of glass and pried it out. She set it on the ground beside her. She moved on to the next pane, looking over her shoulder for movements next door every few seconds. Two panes gone. The fourth pane was long departed already, which left only one more to go. She reached up to cut it out when a door opened. She dropped to the ground. She lay flat and motionless and watched through slitted eyes as one of the thugs stood in the doorway and had a look around. A wisp of cloud drifted across the moon, obscuring the light, and the guy stepped back inside. The door closed.

Her heart pounding, she reached up quickly and freed the last piece of glass. It cracked as she lifted it out and one of the pieces clattered to the ground and shattered. *Crap.* She dived around the back side of the building. Footsteps pounded. She tested the edge of the knife and confirmed with dread that it wouldn't cut butter, let alone human flesh. Options? She looked around fast and made a split-second choice. She scrambled up onto the lip of an ancient rain barrel facing away from the house and jumped. Her fingers caught the edge of the roof. She felt the rotten wood start to break away, but she swung her feet frantically up over her head and landed on her belly on the roof. Blood rushed to her head as she lay there at an uncomfortable angle. She inched backward away from the edge of the roof, praying the structure would hold her weight. She sensed movement directly below and froze as two men crept around the corner, guns drawn.

Please God, let them not look up. She lay perfectly still, trying desperately to make like adobe. The shadows eased past. By slow inches, she pushed up onto her hands and crept across the uneven surface of the roof. Staying below the roofline, she eased across the expanse to the chimney and crouched down beside it. Voices drifted up to her.

Taylor was talking. Something about a message.

Then the bespectacled man's accented baritone floated up. "Tell your employer I will have the stones shortly. They're under production now and I will meet all the specifications."

She frowned. What sort of stones would Devereaux order? To *what* specifications?

Taylor replied, "You're sure about meeting the specs? That's very important."

"Yes, of course. The size was a problem as you know, but a flawless five-centimeter-by-five-centimeter wafer has proven possible."

Amanda grinned to herself. Well done, Taylor.

Taylor spoke again. "Is payment arranged, or do you have any messages about that aspect of the deal, as well?"

Four Eyes was impatient. "No, no. Your employers should still transfer the funds to the offshore account I gave them."

"Very well. Anything else you need to tell my boss?"

Four Eyes answered gruffly. "Actually, we come now to what you need to tell me. What arrangements have been made for my disappearance? What sort of cover have you built for me?"

Taylor's voice floated up. "The arrangements are complete. But other ears are near. I think it best not to discuss any details just now, don't you?"

A growl from the bespectacled man. "The deal was that I'd make contact with you when the diamond wafers were ready and you'd hand over my new identity."

Taylor replied testily, "Well, the wafers aren't in my hand, now, are they? I don't see any merchandise sitting on this table. The deal stands. When the goods are ready for delivery, contact us and we'll take care of you."

Amanda was impressed. She'd never have guessed in a million years that Taylor was such a good liar. And then her attention was diverted by a sound. A vehicle coming up the road. Oh, lord. Please, not more reinforcements.

The conversation broke off abruptly inside. "What's this?" Four Eyes demanded. "Did you bring backup with you?"

Taylor snorted, "How in the hell could I have done that? You're the one who snatched me out of an office at gunpoint. I had no time to call in support."

A new voice, probably one of the guards from the porch. "What do you want us to do?"

"Search my guest and make sure he doesn't have any devices on him."

"What sort of devices?" the guard asked.

Amanda snorted to herself. Must be the same mental giant who lit the cigarette earlier.

Four Eyes answered exasperatedly, "Radios. Homing beacons. Microphones. Transmitters. Anything that might signal his location to his comrades."

Rustling came from inside—no doubt Taylor being stood up and patted down. A door opened and the roof vibrated slightly beneath her. An agitated voice announced, "There's someone out here. Somebody cut out a couple window panes into the back bedroom recently."

"How recently?" Four Eyes asked tersely.

"Within the hour. This asshole has backups out here. We found a truck, too. Piece of shit, but the engine's warm."

A loud crack like a palm on the surface of a table made her jump. "You double-crossed me!" Four Eyes bellowed.

The approaching vehicle downshifted as it drew near. Amanda cursed under breath. And took a deep breath. The shit was about to hit the proverbial fan.

Chapter 10

Amanda watched a late-model sedan reach the edge of the compound. Abruptly, the engine gunned. The car leaped forward, scattering the three men who'd been standing relatively casually, watching its arrival. Amanda saw a single man fly out the driver's door, firing a handgun rapidly. Whoever this maniac was, he had the good sense to dive and roll across the trunk of his car and take cover behind it.

The bespectacled man's guards jumped in all directions, scrambling for cover and positions to shoot from. In the chaos, Amanda saw one of the guards leap around the far end of the building she lay on. Out of sight of all the others. Perfect. As return fire rattled below, she used the noise to race across the roof. She paused for a moment at the edge, lined herself up with the man below and jumped. She landed with both feet planted squarely in the middle of the guy's back. A quick, hard chop to the back of his head with her hand finished off any combat capability the guy had left after she'd flattened him. She snatched his Uzi, flung the shoulder strap on and yanked the guy's pistol out of its holster, tucking it into her waistband at the small of her back. She moved to the corner of the building and peered around it during a volley of fire.

One of Four Eyes's men crouched across the courtyard from her. It wasn't a perfect shot, but it was clear enough. She lifted the Uzi to her shoulder and prayed the weapon's sights were reasonably accurate. The next burst of gunfire exploded, and she squeezed off a single shot in the midst of the chaos. Her target dropped like a stone.

She ducked back behind the building and raced around it. She stopped shy of the other front corner. Crouching low, she had another look at the action before her. Whoever the guy in the car was, he was still pinned behind the vehicle. He appeared to have only a handgun. Outgunned and probably low on ammo, he only popped up sporadically to take a single shot.

A guard lay on the porch not ten feet from her, firing in overlong bursts that raked the side of the car uselessly. She pulled out the pistol, holding it overhead, and stretched out on her belly. Timing her move with the guard leaning on the trigger of his weapon, she rolled out from behind the building and squeezed off two quick shots. The machine gun abruptly went silent.

She rolled back behind the building. A bullet ricocheted off the house, nicking the stucco and peppering her with plaster fragments. Crud. She was made. She jumped up and ran for the back of the house. She tossed the Uzi onto the roof and climbed the rain barrel again, swinging herself back up onto her perch. Odds were these turkeys weren't trained enough to think in three dimensions in a situation like this. At least that was the hope. If she was wrong, she was dead.

The second the firing broke out, the guard bolted from the room, grabbing for his weapon. Four Eyes fumbled frantically at the latches to his briefcase. Taylor had no idea what was inside, but he didn't wait around to find out. He dived across the table and launched himself at his captor. He got his hands around the guy's throat as they crashed to the ground. Four Eyes shoved his fists inside the circle of Taylor's arms and pummeled his elbows painfully. The bastard was stronger than he looked. Rather than let the guy wreck his elbows, Taylor let go of his hold and rolled to the side. He came up onto his feet in one motion and swung at Four Eyes. The guy deflected part of the blow with his forearm but staggered back.

The bespectacled man dived for the briefcase that had skittered across the floor in Taylor's initial attack. Taylor dived after him. Four Eyes rolled, but Taylor hung on grimly until he felt one of the guy's hands slip. He used the opening to slam his fist into the side of the guy's head. Four Eyes went limp beneath him. Taylor shoved to his feet, panting, then crashed to the floor as Four Eyes rolled and used his legs to sweep Taylor's feet out from under him. He landed hard on his shoulder and his left side went numb. The bastard had played possum on him.

Taylor lashed out with his own foot and nailed Four Eyes squarely in the groin. The guy curled up around the blow like a bug, gasping in agony. Taking no chances this time, Taylor rolled out of range and jumped to his feet. Keeping a watchful eye on the man, he leaned down and picked up the guy's briefcase. Taylor snapped it open and grabbed the pistol inside. *What would Amanda do next if she were him?*

Using the barrel of the weapon, Taylor smacked the light bulb in the fixture overhead. It exploded in a tinkling shower of glass. He ducked and raced for the window. Staying low, he risked a glance outside. A lone gunman hid behind the smoking ruins of a car in the middle of the courtyard. One man slumped, motionless, over his gun on the porch directly in front of him. Muzzle-flashes lit up three more positions while he watched. He had a clear shot at one of Four Eyes's gunmen. He crouched beside the door, waited for a burst of gunfire and then spun into the doorway. He located his man and took the shot, just like in his training course. He spun back into the house without waiting to see the results.

Another quick look out the window. Either he'd hit his target or the guy'd moved. Speaking of which, he'd better move, too. Taylor sprinted across the room toward one of the two doors at the far end. He went sprawling headlong as something clamped around his ankle and yanked. *Four Eyes.* Taylor tucked his shoulder, rolled and popped back up on his feet in one fluid movement. Goddammit, that guy was tough to take out. Taylor turned and kicked blindly in the dark with all his strength. He connected with something solid and human and heard a thud.

Taylor turned and raced for the back bedroom. It was darker in here and he paused for a second to let his eyes adjust. His heart slammed against his ribs as a husky shadow loomed outside the window. He froze beside the remains of an old bunk bed. He had no cover to speak of, but if he was perfectly still, maybe the guy wouldn't see him. A fist punched through the rotten wood of the window frame. A pair of shoulders came through the window, the silhouette of a rifle barrel sticking up. Taylor struck with the speed of a cobra. He brought his pistol down on the base of the guy's skull as hard as he could. The body sagged, limp and motionless, draped over the window sill. He plucked the shotgun out of the guy's hands and moved to the doorway, pausing to check the darkened main room for movement. Nothing. He glided into the room, his back against the wall, clearing the space again. Still nothing. Where in the hell was Four Eyes? It had gone quiet outside.

His mind raced. Did that mean all the guards were down, or that whoever was out there trying to rescue him had been taken out? Now what was he supposed to do? Devereaux's training course didn't cover what to do in this situation.

"Taylor?" a voice murmured.

He sagged in relief. "That you, Amanda?" he murmured back.

"Yeah. You clear in there?"

"Four Eyes went down in here somewhere, and may or may not be neutralized."

A flashlight beam swept across the floor from the doorway. Taylor's hackles went up. There was no sign of Four Eyes at all except for a broken pair of spectacles on the floor.

"Is he armed?" Amanda asked tersely.

"I don't think so. He dived for his briefcase, but I got the pistol out of it."

She called out low over her shoulder, "Harry, do a perimeter check. There's one hostile on the move, probably unarmed. But don't take any chances."

"Harry Trumpman?" Taylor repeated in disbelief.

"The very same," Amanda replied. "You can come out now, by the way. All the other hostiles are down."

Taylor pushed away from the wall. His legs felt like limp noodles. Jesus H. Christ. His heart was pounding like a jack-hammer. He moved to the front door and out on to the porch. Amanda stood there, an Uzi slung over her shoulder as casually as a handbag, a pistol gripped in her right hand. He stepped forward and wrapped her, weapons and all, in a bear hug. Her arms came up around him and she returned the embrace fiercely. They stood in the silence and dark like that for several seconds.

She mumbled, "We need to help Harry check the perimeter and mop up this mess."

"You're right," he sighed into her hair.

Their arms fell away from each other, and suddenly the night air felt cold. Taylor shivered briefly and bent down to pluck the Uzi from the dead hands of the guard sprawled on the porch beside him.

"That thing's got to be about out of ammo," she commented. "He laid on the trigger like a movie star in a bad war flick."

He grinned at her. "Yeah, but the bad guys won't know it's low on lead, and I feel better having it. It's been one of *those* kind of nights, you know?"

She grinned back. "Why, yes. Yes, I do know."

* * *

But she wasn't grinning the next day as she stood on broiling tarmac, as two American military planes taxied up to a cluster of people through waves of shimmering heat. The pair of turboprop King Airs parked side by side and the engines shut down. Silence, broken only by the sound of the wind brushing through the grass, settled once more. The planes were plain white with a thin black stripe for trim. They looked like generic-brand groceries. Air Force, then.

A phalanx of U.S. government agents flanked her, and Taylor stood some thirty feet away, surrounded by his own cadre of guards. The two of them weren't under arrest, compliments of Devereaux's string pulling, and the fact that they'd acted purely in self-defense in killing and maiming the goons last night.

Four Eyes had gotten away.

Not that this was the biggest problem on her list at the moment. A search of the bodies revealed that the dead men were all Eastern European in origin. And none of them had shown up on Devereaux's computer file of government agents. They'd been private operators. Mob. What were *they* doing tangled up in this mess? Her head fairly ached with the possibilities.

And then there was the U.S. government. Harry made it clear that Uncle Sam hadn't been interested in mounting any sort of search for her and Taylor right away. While kidnappings and cash ransoms were common down here, Harry'd indicated that there was much more to Uncle Sam's reticence than unconcern over a garden-variety kidnapping. Not to mention these FBI types, or whatever they were, had spent the past twelve hours carefully keeping her and Taylor completely apart. They were about as subtle as bulls in a china shop about their maneuvering. Why did they care if she and her partner talked or not? She snorted. Clearly, it was imperative that she and Taylor compare notes, and soon.

To that end, she tapped the arm of the agent beside her. "Pardon me, but I'd like to say goodbye to my partner."

The guy's gaze darted to his buddies. "Uh, that won't be possible, ma'am."

"Why not? He's standing right over there. All I want to do is walk over and thank him for saving my neck. It's not like we're going to trade national security secrets."

That remark got an interesting flicker out of her guard's collective gazes. Holy cow. National security? She blinked innocently. "Come along with me. You can monitor everything we say."

The agent still hesitated.

"Aw, come on," she cajoled, batting her eyelashes shamelessly.

The guard looked at his companions. One of them shrugged fractionally and nodded. "Okay," he said heavily. "But no funny business."

"Sheesh," she groused. "You're treating us like we're some kind of criminals. We're the ones who got attacked and kidnapped, here." She shook her head and strode toward Taylor, her hands jammed in her pockets. She palmed the scrap of paper she'd scribbled upon earlier and stuffed into her jeans.

He turned as she approached and his ice-blue gaze locked on her. The poor guy looked roundly confused over what was going on around them. She knew the feeling. She held out her hand, and he stared at it blankly for a second. Then he reached out and grabbed it in his big, warm grip. His gaze snapped up to hers, abruptly alert.

She said quietly, "Thanks for everything. You saved my life and I'm grateful."

He replied smoothly, "I think you saved mine a couple times more than I did yours. It was a pleasure working with you." His hand fell away, taking the tiny square of paper with it. Their respective phalanxes of guards closed in around them once more, effectively isolating them from each other, even though they only stood a few feet apart.

"See now, guys," Amanda commented, "that wasn't so bad."

As her guards scowled, a man in a suit got off one of the

King Airs. The way everyone's shoulders straightened, she gathered this guy was the big cheese. He carried himself with authority. He stopped in front of her and Taylor and shot them both a withering stare. She refrained from laughing. Like she was supposed to be intimidated by this guy?

He said darkly, "The two of you have interfered in matters far beyond your comprehension."

She chuckled to herself. Yup. That was her and Taylor. Too stupid to understand what time of day it was.

"We asked Devereaux to take you off this case, yet you continued to pursue it."

No matter that they'd never received the message. In good faith, Harry enlisted Major Ortolo to detain them so he could deliver it. But that didn't count, apparently.

"As American citizens, I'm ordering you on behalf of your government," the man paused for dramatic effect, "to cease and desist this operation. Do you two understand?"

She nodded dutifully and did her best to paint a contrite look on her face. Good thing she was a Brit. She was so going to enjoy shoving this fiasco down this jerk's throat some day.

"Very well, then. Miss McClintock, an airplane is waiting to take you to New York, and Mr. Roberts, you may join me on the plane bound for Washington, D.C. Taking you home is the least we can do to compensate you for your troubles down here."

She barely managed not to roll her eyes. It was also the only way to guarantee splitting up the two of them. She paused on the top step of her plane and looked over at Taylor, who was just getting ready to duck into his ride home. He nodded once at her, his expression grim.

Taylor stood at a pay phone outside a convenience store a few blocks from Andrews Air Force Base and dialed the long series of numbers on Amanda's piece of paper. This phone didn't have its phone book anymore, so he couldn't look up the country code, but he was pretty sure his call was going somewhere in Europe. A long pause and a ring sounded in his ear. Yup, definitely not an American phone. He stuck a finger in his nonphone ear to block out the car noises behind him as a female voice spoke in rapid German. He'd only had a year of the language in college, and he fumbled for words. *"Sprechen sie Englisch?"* he asked.

"Of course." She switched into smooth English. "What may I do for you today, sir?"

"A friend gave me this number. I need to get in touch with her."

"And what is your friend's name?"

"Amanda McClintock."

"Ah, yes. She is a client of our service. One moment, please, while I connect you."

An offshore answering service, huh? Pretty slick. His ex-partner was nothing if not prepared for all contingencies. As a faint buzzing commenced in his ear, he frowned. That sounded for all the world like the line was being scanned for taps. Some answering service.

Another woman's voice came on the line. "To whom am I speaking?" she asked briskly.

"My name's Taylor Roberts."

"Yes, Mr. Roberts. I have a message for you from Miss McClintock. It says to meet her at the Ocean Breeze Resort in Acapulco at your earliest convenience should you be interested in continuing to pursue your mutual objective. She will be waiting for you."

Damn, Amanda was good.

"Thanks," he said into the phone. "By the way, where are you located?"

"Berne, Switzerland, sir."

"Danke schön," he murmured.

"Bitte schön," the woman replied.

He hung up and climbed back into the waiting cab. "Dulles Airport," he told the driver.

* * *

Taylor arrived in Acapulco that evening, tired and in need of a good meal. He cleared customs and headed for a cabstand, where he requested transportation to the Ocean Breeze Resort. The attendant pointed to a garish lime-green Jeep parked along the curb ahead. Taylor gathered from the man's jumbled English that the Jeep belonged to the hotel. What kind of weird establishment was Amanda sending him to? The vivid hue of the Jeep was almost painful to look at, and the driver was wearing a equally loud tropical-print shirt. But when he identified himself to the driver, the man was exceptionally courteous and responded in flawless English, "Ah, Mr. Roberts. We've been expecting you. Your cabana is ready and waiting."

The guy loaded Taylor's bags as he climbed into the unconventional vehicle. They drove for some time, winding ever higher up into the mountains surrounding Acapulco Bay. The lights of the city lay hundreds of feet below, hugging the crescent curve of the shoreline, and the water deepened in hue from navy to black as the moon began to rise. When they'd wound their way nearly to the pinnacle of the cliffs overlooking the city, the Jeep turned into a lushly foliaged, unmarked drive. Two bellboys rushed out to fetch his bags while the driver led him into a sumptuous lobby. The sound of bubbling fountains danced lightly on the night air.

The concierge greeted Taylor politely and offered to escort him to his cottage, which, it turned out, was already paid for and waiting for him. He followed the concierge outside and down a flagstone path. They passed under arched arbors supporting sweet-smelling hibiscus and bougainvillea and walked by fountains graced with whimsical statues. At the far edge of the spectacular tropical garden, the concierge showed him into a private bungalow perched on the edge of the cliff. The bellboys were already there, unpacking his belongings, hanging them neatly in closets and folding them into drawers. He walked through the cabana and out the plate glass doors to his private terrace. Jasmine and roses scented the evening air, and fresh-cut water lilics floated invitingly in his private swimming pool.

"Would you like breakfast served out here in the morning, sir?"

Taylor turned to the concierge. "That would be perfect. Say, around ten o'clock?"

"Fine. And will you be taking a meal this evening?"

"Yes. I don't care what it is—something light, whatever the chef recommends."

"Is there anything else we may do for you, sir?"

"No. You've been more than kind." Taylor dug into his pocket for his wallet, and the concierge hastily intervened.

"No, no sir. That is not necessary. Your host has already compensated the staff most generously. We have been instructed to see to your every need. It is our pleasure."

He should have anticipated that. With a polite nod, the concierge turned and left, taking the bellboys with him.

A dip in the swimming pool sounded perfect to wake him up and clear his head after the past couple days' exhausting events. He changed into swim trunks and checked his leg. It was healing nicely from the puncture wounds. He had a couple bruises and was sore as hell from the fight with Four Eyes last night, but nothing that a few laps in the pool couldn't work out.

The cool water was bracing after the long hours he'd spent all day folded into airplane seats. As he gazed down at the city lights reflecting off the ocean, the moon rose over the bay. Floating there all alone in his private pool, it seemed as if Mother Nature were putting on this show just for him. It felt odd to be alone. For what seemed like a lifetime, he'd been with Amanda around the clock, travelling and living with her under the most intimate conditions. She'd been a part of his every waking breath, a player in his every thought. And then she'd been ripped away from him without warning by the U.S. government. It was like having his arm amputated. A vital part of him was missing. He kept expecting to turn around and see her there, and every time she was not, it was a new disappointment. He missed the quiet confidence she exuded. With her beside him he'd felt like he could do anything. She'd been a guardian angel one step behind him who could rescue him from any situation he got tangled up in.

What was up with those government agents' weird behavior last night and today, anyway? They acted as if he and Amanda had barged in on a matter of national security. He froze, his attention riveted on that thought. Had they done exactly that? But how? What could a diamond-smuggling operation have to do with national security? Several other countries' economies would no doubt take a hit if the diamond market toppled, but the U.S. and its strategic interests wouldn't be all that directly affected. So why were everyone's knickers in such a twist to keep him and Amanda apart? And what had Four Eyes meant by "diamond wafers"? What the hell were those good for? Some high-tech defense application?

He floated there for a long while, thinking, but no answers came. The moon climbed overhead, shrinking from a throbbing yellow globe to a hard white ball bathing him in cold light. He climbed out of the pool, shivering in the evening's settling chill. He toweled off quickly and padded through the bungalow in the dark to the bathroom and a steamy shower. As he was dressing, dinner arrived. He yelled to the busboy to lay it out in the living room. Taylor walked out of the bedroom. And stopped in the doorway.

On the opposite side of a cloth-covered table bearing several silver-covered dishes sat Amanda, sipping a glass of white wine. She was dressed in a white linen dress, crisp and cool like the night air and as beautiful as one of the rare and fragile orchids gracing his garden. A smile spread across his face. Damn, it was good to see her.

Amanda looked up when Taylor entered the room. As always, she felt a momentary shock at how strongly his presence affected her. She'd wanted to keep this meeting all business, but her whole body tingled with awareness of him. She returned his stare, savoring being near him once more. It had been lonely without him today. Who'd have guessed she'd miss his teasing and wry humor as much as she had? She'd missed his warmth and concern for her, too. Her father had been the last and only person ever to show her such affection before he completely lost his marbles.

Taylor's voice was rich with pleasure as he greeted her. "Amanda."

She couldn't help but smile back. "Taylor."

"I missed you."

How could three such simple little words have such a powerful effect on her? They reverberated through her entire being like thunder. *He'd missed her.* Slow joy spread through her, like honey dripping in a warm golden stream to bathe her in its sweetness. She came to her feet, drawn forward to meet him in the middle of the spacious room. The shadowed lamplight blurred in a dreamlike haze around her. Only Taylor stood out in sharp, clear focus, his beautiful smile welcoming her. He held out his arms, and it was the most natural thing in the world for her to walk into them.

She reveled in the solid bulwark of his body, which surrounded her, protected her and warmed her. Her ear pressed against his chest, absorbing the familiar, comforting sound of his heart. His hands massaged her back lightly and he buried his face in her hair. She rejoiced in the sense of belonging he gave her. Her eyelids drifted closed, and she let go of all the tension in her neck and shoulders. If she could have purred, she would have. She tilted her head back to look up at him, and Taylor's large, warm palm was there immediately, supporting and caressing the back of her neck. His breath brushed against her temple. "Did you miss me?" he murmured.

"Mm-hmm." Her mouth curved into a lazy smile.

His thumb traced the soft fullness of her lower lip. She opened her eyes and looked up at him. His blue eyes were almost black with an emotion she'd never seen in them before. He was serious, intent, his concentration on her total. He lowered his head toward hers.

His mouth stopped only inches away from hers. "May I?" His voice was a husky half whisper.

Her whispered reply came, unbidden, from the bottom of her soul. "But of course."

Chapter 11

It was a reunion of souls. Warmth and wine, friend and colleague, they blended and became simply man and woman. The kiss deepened and they drank of one another, feasting upon the joy of their discovery. Eventually Amanda took a breath as Taylor lifted his mouth from hers. He lifted her in his arms and she felt as light as dandelion fluff. The room spun slowly in a kaleidoscope of passion-tinted hues. Mouths and tongues fused again in a heated dance that spiraled ever faster around them, leaving her dizzy and gasping for breath. Taylor strode to the sofa and carried her down to it, following after her. She sunk into the soft cushions, covered by his big, warm body.

She gripped his shoulders with desperate intensity as the limits of her universe stretched and expanded to encompass this realm of sensation. To hell with living like a machine. It was a stupid idea, anyway. And then the second part of her father's axiom popped into her head. She tensed.

Taylor lifted his head immediately. "What is it?"

She shook her head. "Something my father used to say. He used to tell me that to stay alive I had to become a machine. I had to live without feeling, or else my emotions would be used against me as a weapon."

Taylor sighed. He pressed up and away from her and shifted to sitting on the couch beside her. His arm came around her shoulders and he tucked her against his side. He was silent for a moment and then asked, "What happened to your mother? Was she really killed in a car accident?"

She blinked at the shift of topic. "As far as I know."

A pause. "Not to be insensitive to your loss, but based on your father's opinion of the danger of emotions, is there any chance it wasn't an accident and your mother was actually murdered? He was a spy, after all. What if he was discovered and somebody took out your mother to get at him? Maybe your father wasn't so paranoid, after all."

She blinked, stunned at Taylor's logic.

"Is the loss of his beloved wife what sent him over the edge into madness?"

She nodded.

He said slowly, "So somewhere deep in your mind, you believe that your parents' love for each other cost you both of them. No wonder you want nothing to do with love."

His words shocked her into utter stillness. *No.* She shunned love because her work required total concentration. Because emotions distracted a person. Because she traveled constantly and had no stability in her life. *Because she was afraid of it.*

Taylor remarked into the vacuum of her dismay, "There's nothing wrong with you bottling up emotions you perceived as dangerous. It was a perfectly logical response to your loss."

She frowned. "But if I can't love, I'm broken."

Taylor sighed. "Amanda, Amanda. You're not broken. Rejecting emotion was a predictable, normal self-defense mechanism. You just didn't give it up when it outgrew its usefulness."

"I don't know. The past week I've gotten the feeling I'm outgrowing the notion pretty fast."

He grinned and said lightly, "I'm a pretty lovable guy, huh?"

She rolled her eyes. "Don't you go and cop a big, macho attitude on me, Romeo."

He laughed. "Not a chance. You'd kick my butt and hand it to me on a platter."

She pushed up against his chest. "Speaking of platters, your dinner's getting cold."

He dropped a kiss on the end of her nose and stood up, escorting her to the table. She lifted the lids off the plates while he poured wine. Moonlight streamed in the window and a warm breeze fluttered the gauze curtains. A soul-deep relaxation came over her, the sort of unwinding she hadn't experienced in years. Taylor sat down across from her. He took a bite of supper and sighed in pleasure. "This is delicious. What kind of fish is it?"

She smiled. "It's sea bass. They call it *corvina* down here." She joined him in consuming the delicately flavored fish.

They were lingering over a desert of sumptuous mocha mousse when she finally asked, "So, Taylor. Why did you come down here?"

He paused, no doubt considering the multiple layers within her question. "First, if you needed me, I wasn't going to let you down."

The glow that had been building through supper expanded even more within her.

He continued, "Second, we got tangled up in the middle of something huge, and Devereaux got bullied into pulling us out of it. That makes me real curious. I hate not knowing what's happening or why. Third and most important, someone tried to kill you and we don't know who it was. That person is still out there. I'm worried about you."

She savored the idea that he was worried about her. "What do you propose we do about all of the above?" she asked.

He responded with a question of his own. "What are the options?"

"Well, we could bag it all, take my pension from Devereaux and go live somewhere comfortable and remote for the rest of our days."

He shook his head in the negative. "I don't like the idea of leaving someone out there on the loose who's gunning for you."

She continued, "Well, we could drop the case like everyone wants us to and go on to the next project Devereaux has for us. Or we can ignore what everyone's telling us and press on with this investigation. The downside of that is we'll be on our own. We'll likely get little or no assistance from Devereaux and no protection from our government."

He said dryly, "I don't think our government was planning on protecting us much, anyway. From what Harry said, I gather Uncle Sam was prepared to let us rot in Mexico for a good long time before they came to the rescue. I say we press on."

She looked at him intently. "Are you sure about this? It could get dangerous."

He shrugged. "We've already been followed, shot at and kidnapped. How much more dangerous could it get?"

She answered with the voice of long experience. "A lot more dangerous. If I've learned one thing in this business, it's that just when you think things have gotten as bad as they can possibly get, they can always get worse."

"Fair enough. But I'm still game. I still want answers to my questions."

"Like what?" she asked.

"Well, obviously, I want to know what the deal with the diamonds is. Why's the U.S. government protecting Four Eyes, whom we know to be a diamond smuggler and arms dealer? Who's he working for? And who's trying to kill you? Are the two related? Why did Devereaux drop your father's journal into the mix, and what's the connection with it to everything? Why did he go to so much trouble to get me on this case, when you and I both know I'm not even the slightest bit qualified to be out here in the field?"

"Don't sell yourself short, Taylor. You've done remarkably well given how little experience you have. But you are right. We do have to rectify your lack of preparation for this before we go any further. I refuse to endanger your life needlessly. I'd like to beef up your basic skills a bit more. Get you comfortable with sharpshooting and make sure you're well versed in infiltration and escape. The training course Devereaux puts his people through is good, but I have a suspicion this case is going to demand more of both of us than a basic black-ops course covers."

In point of fact, it was his *mind-set* she was most concerned about, and not his technical skills. She needed him ready, willing and able to commit violence at the drop of a hat if it was required.

He frowned. "It's not like we've got a world of time on our hands, here, or the facilities to practice black-ops work."

She shrugged. "I've already covered the facilities bit. As for time, tomorrow is soon enough to get started on your advanced training."

He pushed back from the table. "Care to step outside and enjoy the evening air?"

She smiled and rose to join him. "I'd love to."

They strolled outside and went to lean on the rail at the far edge of the terrace. The view at their feet was spectacular, and the sweet scent of honeysuckle perfumed the air. She murmured, "In a setting like this, it seems ridiculous to consider going back into the trenches and picking up this case."

He looked down at her earnestly. "Yes, but do you really want to live in a gilded cage, always in fear for your life?"

She sighed. "No. You're right. We need to put this mess to rest once and for all."

They stood there for several minutes in silence. Crickets and frogs fought to be loudest in the dark, and she let their chorus wash over her. Taylor broke the silence by asking quietly, "Who is Devereaux, exactly?"

"As far as I know, Devereaux is a private citizen with great wealth and power. After terrorism reared its ugly head in a big way, my guess is he decided that legitimate governments weren't going to be able to fight fire with fire. He struck out on his own to combat what he perceives as the evils threatening the world today."

"Is he one of the good guys?"

She shrugged. "It depends on how you'd label meeting force with force. He takes the fight to bad guys, most certainly, but his methods aren't lily-white and pure by any means. I have no idea what his other operatives are up to. For all I know, they could be out there assassinating world leaders. He keeps his operatives totally separate as a rule. That's part of why I was so surprised when you were brought onto this case with me."

"What do you know about Devereaux personally?"

"Nothing. The few folks I know who've ever spoken to Devereaux use the term 'he.' He shrouds himself in mystery. Probably is so rich he has to be invisible—otherwise he'd be the target of every tabloid, political cause, business venture and quack out there."

"Will he come after us if we pursue this case on our own?"

She shook her head. "He put us on it in the first place. I'm sure he'll help us as much as he's able to, depending on how closely the U.S. government is watching him."

"So all we have to worry about is whoever's trying to kill you and whoever's going to want to stop us from finding the source of Four Eyes's diamonds."

She replied, "I'd agree with that assessment."

"Just out of curiosity," he asked, "why did *you* come down here? What's your motive in pursuing this investigation?"

"You mean besides wanting to know why in the bloody hell Devereaux dropped my father's diary in my lap?" she asked dryly.

"There is that," he replied equally dryly.

"After this case, Devereaux was going to stand me down. He thought I was losing the edge. I suppose I'm out to prove that I'm not crazy and I can still get the job done."

"Are you crazy?" Taylor asked matter-of-factly.

Her gaze snapped to his. "You're the shrink. You tell me."

He was silent a long time, and her heart pounded as she waited for his answer. Suddenly, it was important to her to know what he thought. More to the point, to know that he thought she was okay. Why did his opinion matter so much to her? It shouldn't.

Finally, he turned his head and gazed at her steadily, his expression giving away nothing. "It doesn't matter what I think. You're determined to see this case through or you'd never have passed me that phone number."

Her expectations deflated. Psychobabble double-talk. He wasn't going to give her a straight answer. Damn him. "Tell me something, Taylor. Do you think you have it in you to kill someone in cold blood?"

He jerked. "Why would you ask me something like that?"

Why would she, indeed? Maybe she had an impulse to hurt him, to punish him for withholding his opinion of her state of mind. "It may come down to that in this investigation. I need to know if you'll have what it takes when the chips are down."

"Killing in self-defense is one thing. I did that back at the hacienda without thinking twice about it. The bastards were shooting at us and it was kill or be killed. Not a hard choice. But cutting someone down in cold blood—I don't see us needing to do that."

She replied quietly, "I'm warning you, it's a choice you're going to end up having to face. Sooner or later, you're going to come up against a pro who's out to kill you, and you're going to have to make a preemptive strike. If you hesitate in that moment, you're a dead man. Mark my words."

"So noted," he bit out.

A tense silence settled around them.

She sighed. "Promise me one thing."

"What?"

"If you discover you don't have the stomach for this kind of work, you'll quit. Be honest with yourself and with me, and walk away before you get us both killed."

He nodded decisively. "Deal. So, what do we do first?"

She laughed with scant humor. "Relax. Getting you up to speed isn't going to happen overnight. I'll see you tomorrow at, say, one o'clock? I've got a few errands to take care of in the morning."

"I'll be here."

"Until tomorrow, then." She went into the second bedroom, and closed the door.

At one o'clock sharp the next afternoon, Amanda returned to their suite. At her orders, Taylor picked out a half-dozen different shirts and followed her to the parking lot with them. They rode in a bright green Jeep to a high-rise apartment building in an affluent district of Acapulco. A short, dapper man answered the door when she rang, his aging face lighting up with a grin for her. "Come in. Come in. It has been a long time, *querida*." After a hug for her, the man led them into his living room and served them glasses of iced tea damp with condensation.

She chatted with the man for a few moments about his family and the current number of grandchildren, and then she got down to business. "Xavier, I need not one, but two favors from you today."

"Anything for the daughter of the man who saved my life many times."

She reached into her purse and pulled out an eight-by-ten photograph of Four Eyes. "We need to know everything you can find out about this man. His name, who he works for, what he's involved in, where he is now, what brand of cigarette he smokes...everything."

Xavier took the photo and studied it closely. "I shall digitally enhance it somewhat to remove the graininess from being enlarged, and then I shall see what I can learn. And what is your second request, my dear?"

She smiled. "This one is much easier. My friend Taylor, here, has urgent business abroad of a delicate nature. He needs to be able to travel discreetly. Can you help him with some identification?"

"When were you planning on leaving?" Xavier asked.

"Not for several weeks. Even though our business is urgent, we have about a year's worth of training to do first, and three to four weeks is about as little time as I can condense it into."

An hour later Xavier had photographed Taylor in a variety of wigs, makeup and prosthetics to alter his appearance. The lime Jeep was waiting for them when they emerged into the bright afternoon, this time with all their luggage stowed in the back of it. She gave the driver an address, and in ten minutes, they pulled up beside a used but solid Land Rover in a parking garage. A quick exchange of suitcases into the new car, a hefty tip to the Jeep driver and she and Taylor were on their way.

It was after midnight when she turned off the marginally improved dirt road onto an even smaller dirt track. Tall grass rubbed the bottom of their vehicle, and deep potholes made for slow, bone-jarring progress.

Taylor peered ahead dubiously. "This looks pretty deserted. Are you sure you know where you're going?"

She grinned at him. "Yes. And that's the idea. We'll have plenty of privacy."

The track made several switchbacks as it climbed the side of a steep hill. They rounded a last turn and the track petered out in a small meadow at the summit of the mountain. A sprawling structure that had once been white stood in the center of the grassy expanse. The walls of a long building faced them. Neatly centered in its side was a rusty iron gate. She angled the Land Rover through the partially open gate and stopped inside a square area overgrown with tall weeds. The courtyard was surrounded by a continuous one-story structure. Directly opposite the gate they had driven through, a two-storied facade belonging to a small chapel broke the tiled roofline of the place. They drove to the left side of the enclosure and pulled up beside the covered walkway that lined the entire courtyard.

Taylor commented, "This place looks like a convent."

She smiled as she climbed out of the vehicle. "Good guess. It was a monastery. The local Catholic parish still owns it, but it's been deserted for years. It didn't take much persuading to get the local priest to lease it to a couple artists for the summer. What's better, the locals think it's haunted. A *bandito* and his gang raided here something like sixty years ago and massacred all the monks for a supposed treasure horde. Nobody ever comes near the place, according to the padre."

"No kidding?" he remarked. "I always wanted to sleep with a ghost."

She led him to a heavy wooden door under the walkway and unlocked a shiny new padlock, which looked wildly out of place on the ancient cast-iron hasp. The door squeaked open and they stepped a few feet into the room. She lit a kerosene lamp the padre had told her would be waiting on a table just inside the door. The man had been as good as his word.

Taylor made a face as he looked around. "Let me guess. No electricity."

"No running water, either," she announced cheerfully.

He opened his mouth to speak, but rather than let him start complaining, she led him through a makeshift sitting room to a long hallway with monks' cells off either side of it. The first two had been sparsely furnished into bedrooms. After they deposited their bags on the beds, she showed him the outbuildings by lantern light. When they stepped inside the cookhouse, which was still in surprisingly good shape, Taylor stared in surprise. Supplies for several weeks were stacked neatly on shelves along the wall.

He looked sharply at her. "When did you arrange all this? Surely the padre didn't pull all of this together today."

"This is the contingency I mentioned last night. I made some phone calls two days ago before we were flown out of Mexico. I figured you'd want to continue with the case, and I knew you'd need the additional training."

Taylor frowned. "Am I really that predictable?"

She grinned. "Don't knock it. I have a special appreciation for orderly minds." After her father in his final years, Taylor could have no idea just how fervently she meant that. She headed back for the living quarters. "How about if I show you the rest tomorrow? I'm beat."

"Great idea," he agreed.

She waded across the dew-covered courtyard, and headed directly for bed. The windowless cell cum bedroom was pitch black, and only the faint sound of chirping crickets reached her. She lay there, completely relaxed, and was not aware that she had fallen asleep until she woke many hours later to a loud creaking noise accompanied by cursing. Curious, she got up, dressed and stepped out into the main courtyard. Bright sunlight assaulted her eyes, but squinting hard, she made out Taylor working on a large, rusty well pump. The handle was moving ever so slowly, each down stroke accompanied by an enormous squeak of protest from the ancient well. She strolled over to observe the epic struggle between man and pump.

Taylor straightened and wiped perspiration off his forehead. "Well, don't just stand there. Grab on and help me!"

She grasped the handle above his hands, and between them, the accumulated rust slowly relinquished its hold It felt good to be out in the morning sunshine, watching it glint off the sable highlights in his hair. Their combined effort was eventually rewarded with a trickle of rusty water into the stone basin beside the well. Several minutes more of vigorous pumping finally saw a clear, cold stream of water pouring forth.

Amanda had just put a bucket under the spout when a golden streak came tearing out of one of the buildings toward them. She dropped to the ground, rolled and captured the racing creature in a single blur of motion.

A furious, yowling cat struggled in her arms. Scratches sprung up all over her arms before she got the blasted creature by the scruff of the neck. She glared up at Taylor over the feline's squirming head. "In the first place, help me subdue this damned beast before he mauls me to death. And in the second place, why in the bloody hell didn't you react to the threat when he came tearing at us? At a minimum you should have assumed some sort of defensive stance. Didn't you say you had some martial arts training?"

"It was a cat," he stated flatly. "I didn't perceive it as a threat—therefore, I didn't react as if it was one."

She stood up, holding the furious animal well away from her body. Carefully, she let it go. It took off in a baleful streak of yellow lightning. "Bad guys disguise threats all the time. You've got to learn to react to the attack itself, not to what the weapon looks like. I've seen pencils that were poison dart guns and fountain pens that were pistols."

He scowled. "I've seen my share of spy movies. I'm fully aware that all kinds of nasties can be disguised as innocent-looking stuff."

"This isn't Hollywood. Our necks are on the line here."

"I get it already," he grumbled. "Next time, I nail the cat. Can we move on to something else?"

She scowled. "By all means. Follow me."

Thus began three miserable weeks for both of them. Amanda drove Taylor from the minute they woke up in the morning until he collapsed of exhaustion each night. She pummeled him in hand-to-hand combat, hiked him up and down mountainsides blindfolded, made him fire rifles until she thought she'd permanently go deaf—even with ear protection—and made him learn so much information it felt as if she was pointing a fire hose at him and demanding he drink from it. She rode him constantly to pay attention to the details, anticipate possible complications and to think, think, think.

And all the while, his charismatic presence bombarded her.

All that sweaty brawn couldn't help but have its effect on her. But it was his mind that drew her in. He was smart. Really smart. A quick learner with a ready sense of humor and a way of cutting straight to the heart of a matter. He had a basic decency about him, an honesty that went soul-deep. He was a good person. So unlike most of the people she came across in her line of work. The insidious attraction she'd had for him since the beginning wormed its way even deeper into her psyche, until it became an act of conscious effort to maintain a professional distance from him. She probably drove the poor guy even harder because of it. But good sport that he was, he bucked up under it all and came through like a champ.

And after a couple weeks of sheer misery and grinding frustration for them both, it all started to come together. He started to hold his own when they fought, his shots formed tight clusters on the targets and she started to nod in approval rather than critique his every move. One night after a late supper, she said quietly, "Let's take a walk."

He groaned and stood up.

She laughed and retorted, "Not that kind of walk. I'm talking about a stroll. For pleasure. To see the stars."

"Ah." He grinned. "Well, in that case, I'd love to."

The sky glittered with so many points of light that they defied counting. An entire universe was displayed before them. It made her feel infinitesimally small and as vast as the night at the same time. She shivered and was startled when Taylor looped his arm around her shoulders, drawing her close to his warmth. Even though she'd driven him mercilessly the past few weeks, a real camaraderie had developed between them as he came to understand her world and became a part of it.

"You're ready," she announced quietly.

He froze. "As in ready to go catch us a diamond smuggler?"

"Well, I thought we'd start with something a little less ambitious than that. My father would have called it giving you your sea legs."

"What did you have in mind?"

"Before we left Mexico, Harry Trumpman gave me a manila envelope. Made a show of doing it in front of the federal agents."

"Ah, yes. Now that you mention it, I remember it."

She explained, "Devereaux gave you and me another assignment, no doubt to convince Uncle Sam that you and I were off the diamond case. It's straightforward—a small-time drug dealer needs to be shut down. He's supplying the son of an influential businessmen, and Devereaux's repaying a favor. I thought we could do the job together."

"Sounds easy enough," he remarked.

After the crazy stuff she'd taught him about explosives and assassinations and international espionage, stopping a small-time thug probably did sound like a piece of cake. "Great," she said brightly. "We'll leave first thing in the morning. Oh, and there's one other thing."

He grimaced as if he knew he wasn't going to like whatever came next. "What's that?" he asked cautiously.

She took a deep breath and plunged in. "From here on out, I think we'd be better off keeping our relationship strictly professional. It's going to get pretty hairy over the next few weeks, and I think we both need to keep our minds focused strictly on the case."

"No deal," he responded bluntly.

She froze in turn. "I beg your pardon?"

"I said no deal. We're allowed to define our relationship however we see fit, and I choose to leave open the possibility of there being more than work to it."

"But," she sputtered, "but, we're going to be together around the clock!"

He grinned. "Yup. Lots of opportunity for us to get to know each other even better."

"But the distraction…"

"Darlin', I've wanted to go to bed with you *bad* for the last month, and I'd lay odds the same thing's been on your mind. But it hasn't stopped us from training like maniacs or concentrating when it was required, now, has it?"

She spluttered, too speechless to even form words. Finally, belatedly, she found her voice. "Taylor!" She threw up her hands. "Why can't you just be happy with what we have now?"

He answered her question succinctly. "Because I want more. I want it all. With you."

Chapter 12

Amanda was waiting at the table when Taylor joined her for breakfast the next morning. No matter what he said, she was determined to keep their relationship strictly professional. Staying emotionally detached had kept her alive this long, and she wasn't about to change her ways at this late date. He'd just have to deal with it.

She watched him pick up the manila envelope by his plate and turn it over. He opened the flap and pulled out a dozen photographs of a Caucasian man. The envelope also included a single sheet of typed paper. She'd already memorized the terse summary of aliases the target used, his address, the license plate numbers on all three of his late-model luxury cars and several favorite hangouts where he practiced his main occupations of drug dealing and pimping, with the occasional mugging-for-hire thrown in.

Taylor looked up from the page. "All the instructions say is to stop him. What exactly are we supposed to do? Apprehend this guy and turn him over to the Mexican police?"

"This guy would likely be able to buy off someone in the legal system and go back to his old ways. Our task is to stop him from selling any more drugs. Ever. What do you think would be an effective means to that end?"

Taylor snorted. "We could always kill him."

She answered calmly, "True. Is that what you suggest we do?"

"What?" Taylor lurched in his seat. He scowled at her and growled, "Don't mess around with me like that. You about gave me heart failure."

"What makes you think I'm messing around?"

His gaze snapped to hers.

"Look, Taylor. Our instructions are to stop this guy. If that's the only way you can come up with to do it, then that's what we'll have to do."

"Ah." Understanding dawned in his expression. "I need to think outside the box."

God, he was a quick study. She sat back while the wheels turned in his formidable brain.

"I've got it," he announced. "We'll leave him a message. Literally."

She listened with amusement as he outlined his plan. It was clever, unexpected and definitely could work. "Okay. What supplies will we need?"

He rattled off a list of items, all of which they had on hand.

"Contingencies?" she quizzed next. "What could go wrong?"

Taylor came up with a number of ways his plan could go off track and how to combat each. He finished with, "Worst-case scenario, we get into some sort of shoot-out with him and any security types he has and we end up killing him."

"Are you okay with that?" she asked.

He shrugged. "Based on the information here, this guy would get life in prison if the Mexican courts got ahold of him. Death isn't a whole lot worse sentence than that from what I hear. If he attacks us and we have to defend ourselves, so be it."

Much better. Taylor was infinitely more decisive on the subject of violence than he had been a few short weeks ago. They might just stand a chance of staying alive if he kept this sharp edge in the field. "Let's do it, then," she said simply.

During the trip to Mexico City, where the target lived, they worked out the details of the surveillance they'd set up and the gear they'd need to secure. Fortunately, she already had procured a veritable arsenal of weapons for Taylor's training, so that wasn't an issue. They stopped at the first tourist information center they found in Mexico City, and she purchased a map. The target's home turned out to be a high-rise apartment building in a decent neighborhood near the business district. Taylor parked the Land Rover across the street from the entrance and they watched it for a while. Well-dressed residents passed through the glass doors, held for them by a solicitous doorman. That guy might pose a problem. Taylor came up with several ways to get past the doorman.

After getting a feel for the guy's home, they found a clean but moderately priced hotel nearby. The kind of place where a pair of American tourists wouldn't stick out. She stood back while Taylor checked in, using one of his new passports. He sailed through passing off his false identification to the desk clerk. Nicely done.

As suppertime approached, they strolled back to the target's neighborhood. They ate dinner in a café, eavesdropping on conversations and watching traffic patterns out the window. She watched Taylor absorb the feel of the city, the smells and sounds, the way people carried themselves, the way status was differentiated between classes of citizens, how people addressed strangers, anything that might help him to act and think like a native. By the time they left the restaurant, she was startled to see that he'd already blended himself into the landscape. Either she was an amazing teacher or he was a phenomenal student.

They took a taxi back to the hotel and changed into dark clothing. She and Taylor spent the night camped out in the Land Rover waiting for their target to make an appearance coming or going from his home. It was grindingly dull. So much for the glory and sex appeal of being spies.

They settled down to watching the building daily, learning the routine of the place, the rhythms and habits of its residents. They rented a new car every day or two and soon were able to recognize dozens of the building's tenants. One man in particular was interesting. The guy was almost Taylor's height and of similar build, and he always entered and left the building alone. He came home from work each evening near the end of the day watchman's shift. The man usually wore a distinctive raincoat, and never failed to wear a hat. With a little makeup and similar clothing, Taylor could pass for the guy at a glance.

A week into the project, Amanda quizzed Taylor over breakfast on what they knew.

He listed off the salient facts. "Security is tighter than meets the naked eye. A camera looks down on the entrance to the building. After midnight, a uniformed security guard strolls through the lobby exactly once every hour and talks briefly with the doorman, who sits inside the locked lobby and reads all night. No napping on the job for him."

She nodded. "Any adjustments required to our plan?"

"We may have to change the timing a bit, but that's about it."

"Are we ready to go, then?" she asked.

He nodded. "We just need to get the van and we're all set." He'd already found and bought a raincoat and hat that matched those of the resident who looked like him.

Their eyes met in silent understanding as she returned the nod. And a realization hit her. They'd become a team.

Taylor was too nervous to sleep, but he did stretch out on his bed for a few hours while Amanda caught a nap. How she could be so calm about tonight, he had no idea. Too wired to lie still any longer, he got up and stuffed the pockets of his rain-coat with all the gear he'd need. Next, he went to work with stage makeup to turn himself into the resident they'd picked. There. He was ready to go. From here on out it would be a wait-ing game. Their target brought prostitutes home with him about half the time. He'd brought girls home with him the past three nights in a row, so maybe they'd get lucky tonight and he'd be alone. A guy had to get a little sleep, after all. If not, they'd try again tomorrow night or the next night or the next.

At midnight, he woke Amanda. She was so calm it bordered on irritating. He asked her, "Can't you pretend to be at least a tiny bit tense about tonight?"

She smiled, amused. "Sorry. This isn't dangerous enough to spike my adrenaline. Besides, it's your show. I'm just along for the ride."

To bail him out if he got in over his head. This was his final exam and they both knew it. They'd worked their tails off for the past three weeks to bring him up to speed on covert ops, and tonight was the culmination of it all. He could do this, dam-mit.

He drove to the target's apartment building and parked their rented delivery van around back. Taylor pulled on the coat and hat that completed his disguise. Amanda adjusted her brunette wig and nodded to him. She looked like a reasonably respect-able woman, the kind that the guy Taylor was impersonating might bring home with him. The night was muggy, uncomfort-ably warm. Sweat rolled down his back, and he prayed his makeup wasn't running down his face in similar fashion.

"Is my face still in place?" he murmured to Amanda.

She glanced over at him critically. "Yup. Looks fine."

"How do women do this makeup thing all the time? Don't you live in constant fear of it coming off?" he groused.

Amanda grinned completely without sympathy. "Welcome to my world, big guy."

They walked around the block, approaching the building

from the same direction the tall resident usually did. Taylor strode up to the entrance confidently, and the doorman got up drowsily to murmur a greeting and let him in. Taylor tilted his head so his hat would throw a deep shadow across his face and stepped into the lobby. Holding his breath that the doorman wouldn't remark on Amanda, they waited for an elevator. Thankfully, the guy was discreet.

It they'd timed it right, the night watchman ought to be a couple minutes from beginning his rounds. The digital floor elevator to their left indicated that the lift had just been called to the basement. That would be the security guard coming up now. Damn. He was running a few minutes early. Come on, come on. Where was their elevator? It ought to be here by now.

The elevator to their left dinged. Shit. The door began to slide open.

Whoosh. Their own elevator door opened in front of them. Taylor stepped in before the thing was half open, shielding Amanda from the guard's view with his body. He saw a blur of gray uniform out of the corner of his eye. Keep walking, buddy. Don't look. The door slid closed. Taylor breathed a sigh of relief. The first hurdle passed.

They rode up a few floors and got off, punching a floor button that would send the elevator to the top of the building before it returned to the lobby. They moved quickly and quietly down a stairwell to the service area in the basement. First things first. Set up their escape. Taylor checked his watch. They had about fifteen minutes before the security guard was due to return to his office beside the elevator bank in the basement. They had to be done with their business down here and gone well before then. And the punctual bastard had gone off schedule. Who knew when he'd actually be back now?

He murmured to Amanda as he pulled on surgical gloves, "Should we bag this for tonight? The guard's running early."

She shrugged. "Your call."

Damn. He knew she was going to say that. Vividly aware

that he was being graded, he cursed himself for showing a moment of weakness to her. "Let's press ahead. If we back out now, we'll have to develop a whole new approach to getting into the building, and that'll take more time than I'm willing to spend on this op."

She nodded. "That's reasonable. If the objective were more important, we'd probably wait for another day."

He pulled out tools and a spool of wire from his coat pockets and quickly rewired the security system on the emergency exit door. The system was designed to keep people outside from getting in and not the reverse, so it was a relatively simple task to run a parallel circuit from the inside that would fool the system into thinking the door was still closed. Amanda watched impassively, only observing as they'd agreed she'd do on this mission. He finished the job and glanced up at her for approval of his work.

She nodded crisply. "If you ever get tired of being a shrink, you'd make a fine electrician."

He grinned. Hurdle two down. Seven minutes gone. Time to get out of here.

He stepped back and took a few precious seconds to make sure his wires ran tight against the door frame. Someone would have to look very carefully to notice the tampering with the system. Now on to the primary objective. Butterflies erupted in his stomach. He could do this. He'd been trained by the best. Man, he could use a trip to the toilet right about now. He walked quickly to the stairs with Amanda right behind. She still looked as cool as a cucumber. More sweat trickled down his back. He definitely had to work on that Zen thing she did where she set aside all her emotions.

He was huffing when they reached the sixth floor, where their target lived. And it damn certain wasn't because he was out of shape. Nerves, dammit. He took several deep breaths, bringing his pulse back almost to its resting rate before he proceeded. Calm. Think calm. Yeah, right. More like, don't pee in your pants. Dry. Think dry....

Blessing the silent crepe treads Amanda had put on a pair of shoes for him, he made his way to the target's apartment. He signaled her to keep a lookout while he checked out the door. She nodded and turned to face down the hall. He knelt and peered under the doorjamb. No light. Next, he ran a sensitive electronic device similar to the one Amanda had used to sweep for bugs around the edges of the entire frame. Nothing. No electromagnetic alarm. He then inserted a hair-thin glass fiber between the door and the frame and ran it slowly and gently all around the door. The sensitive filament encountered nothing but the regular locks and the door hinges. No pressure alarm. Last, he inserted a fiber-optic tube into the door frame and connected it to an electronic meter. No photoelectric beams around the door. No motion detectors.

This guy was either very confident or very stupid. The most conservative scenario was the former, which led Taylor to the premise that this guy was well protected from the other side of that door, probably armed and combat trained himself at a minimum. Taylor adjusted his thinking on taking the guy down in a fight accordingly. He'd go in with his weapon drawn and the safety off. He checked his watch. They'd been inside twenty minutes. They had to get out of the building during the next cycle of the security guard away from his desk. That left them about thirty minutes to pull off the job and get back downstairs.

He bent down and went to work on the locks. The regular lock in the doorknob was a breeze, but the security dead bolt was a bitch. He nearly gave up on the damned thing at least a half-dozen times, but each time at the very last second, he'd hear another tumbler click into place. The dull, metallic noise sounded painfully loud in the silent hallway. Finally, he was done. Seventeen minutes. *Christ.* He'd seen Amanda do locks like that in a minute flat. At least she'd had the good grace not to fidget while he'd wrestled with it.

He yanked his mind back to business. Now was the moment for total concentration. He took a calming breath and reached for the doorknob. It turned under his hand. Hurdle three. Amanda looked up and down the hallway one more time and nodded to him.

He pulled the silenced pistol out of his pocket and pushed open the door with a shaky hand. Lord, his adrenaline was pumping hard. He felt like he could sprint up Mount Everest with energy to spare. He willed his pulse to slow. Amanda gestured for him to lead the way.

He gestured back that he'd clear the front rooms first, and then they'd head for the bedrooms. She flashed him a thumbs-up and a quick smile. The unexpected encouragement from her gave him just the morale boost he needed. Damn, she was good. She knew exactly what he needed before he did. But then, she'd done this sort of thing before.

The apartment was dark, except for a red glow to his right. A huge aquarium stood against the far wall of the living room and the color emanated from it. A dim red light bulb shone steadily in the back of the tank, no doubt from its heater. It made the tank look disturbingly like it was filled with blood.

Concentrate, dammit. The apartment building only had four floor layouts, and he identified the correct one while he gave his eyes a moment to adjust to the dark. Two bedrooms down the hall in front of him. The first bedroom door was open. He eased up to it and lunged inside, pistol in front of him, sweeping his gaze and his aim left and right. *Empty.*

He approached the other bedroom door with Amanda on his heels. It was closed. Catlike, he approached it. Amanda's hand touched his back, lightly, giving both of them a reference to the other one's position in case a fight should break out. He'd swear he felt her fingers tremble the slightest bit. Adrenaline hitting her, too, was it? About damned time.

He eased the door open silently. Directly across from him was a large bed. It had white sheets, and the covers were in a pile on the floor at the foot of the bed. The target was asleep, sprawled on his back, naked. Hairy bastard. A thick pillow propped up the target's head, and Taylor saw the guy's face clearly in the streetlight seeping through the curtains. There was no mistaking the dissipated, pugnacious features. The guy snored gently. Timing his steps with the target's noisy exhalations, Taylor glided up to the bed. With extraordinary care, he removed a six-inch-square piece of adhesive paper from his pocket. He'd prepared it earlier with a note made of letters cut from magazines. It read, "Stop dealing drugs, or next time this will be a bullet in your head." Taylor peeled the protective coating off the back of the paper. The faint rustling of the waxed paper made him freeze. He counted to ten, but the guy's snoring continued without interruption.

Taylor lowered the paper by infinitesimal degrees until it rested, featherlike, on the target's hairy chest. The dry epoxy compound coating the back of the paper would hold it there securely until the target ripped it off. Painfully.

Taylor eased his hand away from the man's sleeping form. His gaze happened to fall on the clock on the guy's nightstand. Six minutes until the security guard was due to make his rounds. And that assumed the guy was on time and not early again. Damn.

The snoring stopped.

Taylor froze. He stood still for what seemed like forever, but his silent count told him it was less than a minute. The target shifted slightly, then settled once more into heavy breathing. Amanda's finger's tugged lightly on his belt, and then he felt her ease backward. Taylor followed her, moving as slowly as he'd entered until he reached the doorway. He closed the door carefully behind him, then turned to follow Amanda stealthily through the apartment. But something caught his eye. The red light in the back of the aquarium was blinking.

Shit. A silent alarm. He knew it as surely as he was breathing. He broke for the door, snagging Amanda's arm as he leaped past her. She picked up immediately that something was terribly wrong and sprinted for the door beside him. He paused only long enough to ease the door shut behind them and then uttered a single terse word. "Run."

They took off down the hall toward the fire escape. It was a good hundred feet in front of them. The elevator dinged behind them, announcing its arrival. Crap. He put on an extra burst of speed he didn't even know he had. Amanda dived for the door beside him and they slammed through it side by side. "Go ahead while I block it," he panted. She hesitated and he bit out, "Go!"

He took out the spool of wire and stomped on one side of it hard. It squashed somewhat. He jumped on it again until it deformed into a rough wedge.

Excited male voices erupted in the hallway. Damn. They were headed this way. Fast.

He jammed the makeshift doorstop in place, slamming it with his heel until it dug into the rubber floor mat in front of the door. The voices were almost opposite him now. He turned and took the first stairwell in a single leap. He fell, rolled and was on his feet again in one move. Another leap down the next stairwell and the next. He was punishing his ankles and knees, but he didn't care. He didn't need a firefight trapped in a stairwell with bullets ricocheting all over the damned place.

He heard scraping above him. The doorstop was giving way. Any second now he'd hear the metallic ping of lead on metal. One more flight to go. He burst through the door into the basement and skidded to a halt nose to nose with the bore of a pistol. It felt as if his heart stopped beating. He looked up. Amanda's cold gaze met his. The pistol yanked up and away.

"Let's go," she bit out.

"You think?" he retorted.

He caught the fleeting grin that touched her face as they raced for the boiler room. Taylor threw his coat and hat into the trash incinerator and jumped for the exit while the fabric flared up behind him. Amanda already had the outside exit open and waiting. He helped her finish frantically stripping the wires off the door. Since they were made, it was better to leave no evidence of any kind behind. He yanked out the last wire, and an earsplitting bell erupted over his head. Taylor jumped half out of his skin.

He sprinted after Amanda, tearing through the inky dark of the alley by feel and desperate instinct. He careened around the corner and saw her leaping into the driver's seat of their getaway van—one of hundreds of plain white delivery vans that plied the streets of Mexico City. While he flung himself into the passenger seat, she started the engine and pulled out into the street sedately. No way would he have been able to restrain himself from flooring the damn thing.

He wiped off his makeup, and Amanda pulled off her wig. He bundled the remaining bits of their disguises and used gear into a plastic grocery bag. Amanda drove until they were well away from the area, and then pulled over by a garbage can on a dark street. He tossed the grocery bag in the trash and got back in the car.

"Are we clear?" he asked as he climbed back into the van.

She answered tersely, "If we've got a tail, they're better than I am."

He grinned. "Then I highly doubt we're being followed."

"Where to now, James?" she asked in a cheesy British accent thicker than her usual one.

"Home," he said fervently.

"Do you mean the monastery or Indiana?"

Her question stung him like the snap of a rubber band. He glared at her. "Do you honestly think that just because we had a close call back there I'm going to quit on you?"

She glanced over at him. "That was a dicey scene. It could have gone real bad real fast."

"But it didn't," he retorted. "The training and skills you taught me saved my neck. Yeah, it was close. But it was also a success."

"Barely," she grumbled.

He sighed. "Save the postmortem until tomorrow, will you?

I'm coming off the adrenaline rush and I feel like a ton of bricks just landed on me."

She nodded sagely. "I know the feeling well."

He rested his head against the back of the seat, torn by conflicting emotions. He had a sick feeling in the pit of his stomach, like the one time he'd ever shot a deer as a kid. Yet, at the same time, he felt exhilarated. Amanda was right. It wasn't that hard to actually do this kind of work with the proper training and frame of mind. Maybe the two of them weren't so very different, after all. Maybe all people had a capacity for breaking rules lurking somewhere deep inside them, waiting to come out. He couldn't very well condemn her for doing things that he, too, had done now. The sick feeling crept back, but he forced it down. The mission, dammit, the mission.

Amanda was grateful to turn over the driving to Taylor several hours later. It seemed that she'd just laid her head back when he touched her shoulder, both waking her up and informing her she'd fallen asleep. They switched seats, and she took over for the last leg of the trip back to the monastery. The sun was high in the morning sky, and the dry mountain air was heating up fast.

She glanced over at Taylor. He'd handled himself well last night, all things considered. His catch of the blinking aquarium light was inspired. Her head ached faintly to think of what a fiasco the mission could have turned into had he not seen the silent alarm. She slowed down, peering carefully along the margins of the road for the nearly invisible dirt track that led up to the monastery. She turned onto it. The grass was faintly crushed as if someone had been up here recently. The padre must have brought the food she'd asked for. Enough for another couple weeks. The time they'd need to plan their next move. She guided the Land Rover wearily up the mountain. Now that the night's adrenaline was thoroughly burned off, all she felt was dog tired. She stepped out into the overgrown courtyard gratefully and stretched while Taylor did the same.

Funny. Something didn't feel right.

She froze, her senses on high alert, trying to pinpoint what was wrong.

Silence. There were no birds. At all.

And that smell. Faint decay. Almost like rotting meat. The smell didn't belong here. Any carcasses of wild animals would be consumed by the circling flocks of vultures long before they rotted. She looked up. Speaking of which, why were so many vultures cruising overhead and none of them landing, or at least perched on the roof of the chapel waiting for the humans to get away from their kill? She eased to her left, sidling toward their living quarters. A big, silent shape eased off to the right. Taylor. Good man. He'd picked up on her intuition, or maybe had the same reaction himself. He plastered himself beside the door to their makeshift gym for a moment and then disappeared inside low and fast.

She opened the door to their living quarters. There was an almost subliminal staleness to the air, but no actual scent that she could put her finger on. She raced on quiet feet to the bedrooms. Crouching, she eased the door of her room open. Nothing. Darting across the hall, she dived and rolled into Taylor's room. Nothing. She stood up, and one by one, cleared all the old monk's cells. Working her way methodically around the compound, she met Taylor at the chapel after he cleared his side of the monastery.

"What the hell's going on?" he murmured.

"You tell me," she murmured back.

"It's too damned quiet. And what's that smell? Did we leave something out in the kitchen?"

She shook her head. "I buttoned it up myself. The only meat in there is dried or canned."

"Well, the smell's coming from somewhere in this immediate vicinity," he announced.

She nodded in agreement. She stepped a few feet forward and stopped to sniff the still air. "I think it's coming from over that way." She pointed toward the well in the center of the compound. She set off through the tall grass, stopping every few seconds to track the scent. And then she saw it.

"Oh, God," she breathed, dropping to the ground and plastering herself on her belly.

Taylor dived to the ground at her side. "Threat?" he bit out.

"There." She pointed in front of their noses. About three feet away, a fly landed on one glassy, dead eye of the irascible orange tomcat who'd been their reluctant roommate. The creature's back arched in an unnatural death spasm, even his tail curled over his back, scorpion-like. All the cat's claws were fully extended. Taylor reached out.

"Don't touch it," she warned sharply.

He jerked his hand back.

"Look at how he's lying," she said.

Taylor eased himself a few inches off the ground to get a better look. He dropped back flat beside her. "Jesus," he breathed.

"How recent?" she asked tersely.

"The cat emptied his bowels in the seizure that preceded his death, and the pile's not dry yet. I'd say a few hours at most," he answered. "Maybe within the hour. Are you thinking what I'm thinking?" he asked.

She replied grimly. "I am if you're thinking nerve gas. Sarin, maybe."

"Damn," he grunted, "I was hoping you'd say something else."

Someone had found them here. Someone with nerve gas and a desire to kill them. Someone who was probably still nearby, given how recently the cat had died. Her brain scrambled futilely for some idea of who the assailant might be.

"We gotta get outta here, Amanda. Now."

He was right. They didn't have time to lie here, staring at a dead cat. "All our critical gear's already in the car," she murmured. "Let's crawl over to it and gun our way out of here. Do you want to drive or shoot?"

He grinned briefly. "I better drive. You're the best damned shooter I've ever seen."

She couldn't spare time to be pleased by the compliment right now, but she filed it away for later. "Let's go."

They belly crawled over to the Land Rover. A nod to each other underneath it and they eased upright, climbing into the vehicle quietly. She eased a pair of pistols and three of the four rifles out of their bags. She laid the spares on the floor of the Land Rover and propped the barrel of an AK-47 semiautomatic assault rifle out the window. It was modified to hold an extended clip and fully loaded, which it was, could fire two hundred rounds before needing a reload. She met Taylor's gaze and was fiercely glad to see only determination in his crystalline gaze. Thank God he wasn't buckling in fear.

Taylor started the car. He drove around the well and slowly approached the gate. "Hang on, baby. Here we go," he growled as he stomped on the gas.

The Land Rover shot forward, flying through the gate like a bullet. It went airborne as it hit a rut and flung her up into the air. She slammed down hard, jarring her whole body. She barely managed to hang on to the rifle. And then a rattling sound from her right. Machine gun fire. The metallic tear of bullets through the skin of the car. She pivoted and returned fire, spraying the whole section of woods just outside the monastery's entrance. Another rut. They sailed through the air. And slammed back down to the ground. She fired again. A burst of return fire and she adjusted her aim to the left. Maybe a second shooter, or she'd misjudged the first round of hostile fire. Either way, she raked the second position with a hail of lead. Taylor careened around the first turn down the mountain, and the rattle of gunfire stopped. The Land Rover began to slow.

"Gun it," Amanda shouted. "They'll follow us!"

Taylor slammed the accelerator down, and they flew down the mountain at a suicidal pace, even by her standards. How he managed to wrestle two tons of bucking, sliding machine down the mountain without flipping it over was beyond her. But soon, they shot out onto the main road.

"Go right," she commanded as they reached the first intersection. Taylor screeched around the corner, pointing the Land Rover toward the village. Of course, they were leaving behind a plume of dust that guaranteed their pursuers would follow them accurately, but she had an idea. She watched tensely behind them as Taylor kept the pedal to the metal and they flew away from their would-be killers. His mad rush down the mountain seemed to have bought them some time. That and their attackers would have to uncover their vehicle before they could give chase.

"Where to?" Taylor asked as they approached a cluster of ramshackle stucco buildings.

"The auto shop. It's ahead on the right," she directed.

It was hard to miss. A dozen cars and trucks in various states of disrepair were parked haphazardly around it. Taylor pulled up and cut the engine. Amanda jumped out, purse in hand. A young man stepped outside, wiping his hands on a blue paper towel. Just the guy she was looking for. The owner's son. If anybody in town was going to have a fast car, it was this kid.

In Spanish she said, "I need to rent a car. The fastest one in town."

"No cars for rent here, lady," the kid replied, surly.

"Wanna bet?" she asked smoothly. She opened her purse and took out a fat wad of American greenbacks. The kid's eyes bulged as she thumbed through the stack of hundred-dollar bills. "Two thousand dollars for the car for two days."

"Three grand," the kid countered. "For one day."

"Done," she answered promptly. She peeled off the money and tucked the rest back in her pocket. She held out her free hand. "Keys."

The kid fished in his pocket and tossed her a set. "Silver Porsche Carrera. Around back. Don't look like much, but she's the fastest thing this side of the border."

"Thanks." She stuffed the wad of bills into his hand and called to Taylor, "Let's go!"

They grabbed their bags and raced behind the shop. The Porsche did look like it had run the Paris-Dakar road rally a few times. They managed to cram their gear into the back, and Taylor took the wheel. She climbed in to the passenger seat while he jackknifed his long legs into the car.

"Time to go," she urged.

"You got it, partner," Taylor replied, grinning.

"You're having fun?" she asked in surprise.

His grin broadened. "Didn't you know driving a fast sports car gives a guy a hard-on?"

She lifted an eyebrow. "No, I didn't. I only knew they were the next best thing to a turbo-powered vibrator."

Taylor laughed as he turned the ignition. The motor rumbled to life, growling hungrily for speed. "Oh, yeah," he commented. "This baby will fly."

"It better. Our lives depend on it."

He pulled out of the parking lot. "Where to?"

"East. You drive while I make a phone call. Oh, and keep an eye out for a couple guys in a late-model SUV driving fast."

"Our attackers?" Taylor asked. "Why an SUV?"

"Sarin is sensitive to extreme heat. Direct sunlight would heat it up too much, so it would have to be inside a vehicle, probably one with air conditioning. Canisters of nerve gas and a couple machine guns would take a fair bit of room, too, not to mention you wouldn't want to be seen driving around with those kind of toys slung in the back of a truck."

He guided the car out of town. "Makes sense. Are these guys likely to follow us?"

She shrugged. "Probably. But I highly doubt they can match the speed of this car. We'll lose them in a couple hours. Long before we reach the coast and lose ourselves among the tourists."

She punched out a phone number from memory and prayed there was cell phone coverage in this remote area. It was scratchy, but the call went through. A female voice picked up the line. When Amanda identified herself and asked for Xavier, the woman said nastily, "You have caused my father a great deal of trouble."

But then the old man's voice came on the line.

"What's up?" she asked. "What do you have for us on the guy in the picture I gave you?"

Xavier answered with unaccustomed nervousness, "That picture has turned out to be—how do you say it?—a hot potato. I am afraid I have stirred up a hornet's nest."

"Talk to me," she urged. "Someone just tried to kill us and we're running for our lives here."

"As am I, *querida,*" he murmured.

She waited in grim silence for the rest of it.

"I can get you what you need to know of this man. But it comes with a price. A high one."

Foreboding rolled over her. "How high?" she asked.

"I can get you the information you need from a source of mine. However, he needs a favor done first. There's a man in Cozumel he needs killed."

"Killed! We don't do that sort of thing," she exclaimed.

"I am sorry. That is his price."

Desperation clawed at her. She had to know who was after her, and she knew, *knew,* the man in the spectacles was the key to it. "Isn't there someone else you can talk to? Someone else who knows who this guy is?" she asked urgently.

Xavier answered regretfully. "The fact that nobody knows of or will speak about this man is informative. His very anonymity tells me he is dangerous and powerful in the extreme. Be careful if you would tangle with him, Amanda."

She laughed without humor. "That's the idea. I need to find out who he is so I can get out of his way."

"Then you must pay the price my source demands."

She was silent for several seconds. "I'm not saying I'll do it, but who does he want killed?"

The car swerved as Taylor jerked spasmodically. Hell, she'd be rattled too if she heard him say something like that.

"His name is Maldonado."

"Viktor Maldonado?" she asked in disbelief.

"You know him?" Xavier replied in surprise.

"Of course. He controls practically every drop of oil that leaves Mexico. Word has it he's as corrupt as they come."

"Word is right," Xavier commented sourly.

"His security has to be outrageous," she speculated.

"Oh, it is. The standard techniques for assassination have all failed on him. He wears head-to-toe body armor at all times, surrounds himself with a mob of the best mercenaries money can buy, and he all but owns the Mexican police."

"And your source thinks we can take him out?"

"No. But I do," Xavier answered quietly.

"We'll have to think about this," she told him.

"Time is short, Amanda. My contact is very nervous."

She answered grimly, "We'll be in touch."

Chapter 13

Amanda stared at the moonlit waves lapping gently upon the wide strip of white beach. She buried her toes in the still warm sand and looked down at Taylor, stretched out beside her on a blanket. There was nothing like a good moral crisis to ruin a perfectly beautiful evening. "What are you thinking?" she asked him.

Taylor half smiled. "Aren't I the one who's supposed to ask that question?"

"Not this time." She wasn't about to let him duck answering her. "Should we do the job?"

He shrugged. "I'm sure that between us we could pull it off."

"That's not the issue and you know it," she snapped.

He sat up, his big shoulders blocking the moon hanging low on the horizon. "No, it isn't," he answered evenly. "The issue is whether or not to kill someone else to save your life."

She stared at him in frustration. "So? What do you think?"

"It doesn't matter what I think. I'm not the one whose neck

is on the line. You're going to have to make this decision by yourself. What do *you* think?"

She threw up her hands in exasperation. "Stop doing that answer-a-question-with-a-question psychologist thing with me! If I decide to go ahead with it, will you help me or bail out on the job?"

He looked keenly at her, his eye sockets fathomless black caverns in his shadowed face. He looked like a mask of death. She shuddered, blinking away the image. "Amanda, I decided a long time ago that I wouldn't abandon you, regardless of what happened. I haven't changed my mind."

A flood of old emotions rushed over her. The crushing loneliness after her mother died, the creeping helplessness of watching her father slip away from her into his own private hell. The agony of standing on the steps of her boarding school, watching her father drive away into the gray rain, knowing in her heart that he was never coming back. Her heart welcomed Taylor's words, but her mind doubted his sincerity. "Does that mean you'll help me with the job?" she challenged.

"It means that I won't leave no matter what decision you make. Whether I do or don't agree with what you do is irrelevant. I'm in this with you for the long haul."

A nonanswer in the current context, but maybe enough. A lot more than enough in the larger sense. But still, her disquiet remained. She realized she'd been hoping he'd lose the stomach for descending into her world. That he'd take the high ground. Tell her flatly not to even consider killing Maldonado. Disappointment coursed through her. She stood up abruptly and slogged through the sand to their hotel. The night air was cooling off fast, and a chill danced across her skin.

It was done. Taylor's corruption was complete. She had led a decent man into lawlessness. She had to give him credit for coming up with a clever way to avoid actually hurting his victim in Mexico City, but he'd stepped across the line. At her prodding, he'd gone to a mental place where he'd seriously consider taking another human being's life. She'd made him a criminal. She'd never allowed herself to call it that before, but crime it was. Why, in all the jobs she'd done for Devereaux, had she never seen it for what it was? The revelation struck her like a physical blow.

How could this one man's noncommittal attitude about her current dilemma bring remorse to her when all those reprehensible acts in her past could not? *Because Taylor's eyes had become a silver-blue mirror reflecting the emptiness in her own soul.* She stopped in her tracks. Had *she* taught him that coldness? She closed her eyes, her father's harsh code filling her mind. Be hard. Do not feel. Survive at all costs. But a corner of her heart rebelled. Was the price of survival too high?

She squelched the feeling and took several deep breaths, concentrating on blanking her mind of all thought. She resumed walking toward the hotel, her mental balance precariously restored. Pleading a headache, she retired early, unable to bear the strain of hiding her ravaged emotions from Taylor's discerning eyes any longer.

Taylor looked up from breakfast as Amanda came into the room, red faced and panting. His gut churned with apprehension. He had to let her fight her way through this choice alone. "Work anything out on your run?" he asked casually.

"I decided I like being alive."

"That's a start," he commented. In fact, it was much more than that. Time was, when he first met her, he wasn't sure she did want to live. "Any other revelations?"

"I was wondering if there's another solution, like your note on that guy's chest. Something that might stop Maldonado without my having to kill him."

He nodded thoughtfully. "It's worth a try. Did you have anything in mind?"

"Not yet. I thought I'd set up surveillance on him and see what I can come up with. Maybe he's got a weakness somewhere."

He asked quietly, "Need any help?"

Her smile unfolded like a flower, grateful for the touch of the sun. "Absolutely."

Their gazes met in warm communication. She'd passed the test on her own and he'd acknowledged her breakthrough. He reached across the table and squeezed her hand. She returned the pressure.

Breaking the spell of the moment, she said briskly, "We'd better get to work, then, partner."

Damn, it felt good to hear her call him that.

Maldonado was easy to find. The guy flashed his wealth and power all over Cancun, where he had a winter home. That, and he never went out without a veritable army of security. The phalanx of thugs around their target made Amanda nervous. She had a bad feeling about messing with this guy. But her neck was on the line here. She pressed past her intuition, searching for some chink in this guy's armor where she could get a hook into him and make him stop his illegal activities. Without killing him, of course. Had she still been operating alone, she might have seriously considered taking up the offer from Xavier's contact. But when she thought about looking Taylor in the eye after she took a contract for cold-blooded murder—there was nothing to think about. She could never face him if she did something like that. Unfortunately, she needed the contact's information if they were going to pick up the trail of diamonds again.

They'd been following Maldonado for about a week when, for a second time, she found herself lying on the roof of an apartment building across the street from the Hotel Coronado. It was an outrageously swanky resort, rumored to run a high-stakes, illegal casino operation that was politely ignored by the very well-compensated local police.

"What's he's doing in there, do you suppose?" Taylor murmured.

She glanced over at him, relishing the heat of his hard body against hers. "I'd guess gambling. But I expect we'd do well to find out for certain," she replied.

"There," Taylor announced. "He's coming out."

She glanced at her watch. Same time as last week. He'd arrived in the hotel at about 8:00 p.m. and stayed till 1:00 a.m. sharp. She put the binoculars to her eyes, tweaking the focus to bring the hotel entrance into view. And lurched violently. A man, one of Maldonado's thugs, was staring straight back at her through a pair of his own binoculars. She watched in horror as he said something and pointed up at their position. She swore and barked, "We've been made!"

Taylor jumped up, yanking her to her feet. "Plan B?" he grunted as he took off running.

"Oh, yeah," she ground out as she sprinted beside him.

They raced past the stairwell leading down from the roof and headed for the back of the building. They slammed clips onto the climbing harnesses they already wore and, as one, leaped off the side of the building. She fell for a good thirty feet before the brake on her rope engaged, yanking her down against the side of the building. She flipped over and rappelled downward with a low, zinging hum of nylon rope on metal. Taking huge, multistory leaps way outside the boundaries of safety, her feet hit the ground a split second after Taylor's. She ripped the clip off her harness and turned to run for her life. And came face-to-face with a pair of Uzi machine guns and two seriously pissed-off-looking bodyguards. She flailed her arms for a moment, screeching to an abrupt halt beside Taylor.

A man in a gray wool suit walked forward out of the shadows behind the two thugs. *Maldonado.* He said in Spanish, "Perhaps you would like to tell me why you've been following me. Give me a good story," he purred, "or you won't walk out of this alley alive."

Oh, Lord. Taylor didn't speak more than a few words of Spanish. It was up to her to save their skins. She thought fast. "We're photojournalists. We've been trying to get a story on you."

"Who do you work for?" Maldonado demanded around a fat, smelly cigar.

"We're freelancers. We'll sell whatever we get to the highest bidder."

"What's a story on me going for these days?"

She answered shortly, "With candid photos, a hundred thousand U.S."

His eyebrows shot up. "And why would a simple businessman like me be of such interest to the media?"

"Not to the media. To the public. You're rich, you're powerful and everyone knows you're above the law. The common people want to experience a little piece of your life, even if it's only through a few pictures."

"What newspaper wants this story?"

She rattled off the names of several tabloids popular in Mexico and Central America. Maldonado considered her and her cover story for a moment. Finally, he walked right up to her and blew a fetid breath of smoke in her face. She felt Taylor coil beside her and she silently willed him not to do anything suicidal.

The Mexican growled, "Here's a story for you, you paparazzi bitch. If any of my men ever see you again, let alone anywhere near me, they're going to kill you and your friend. And then they're going to kill every last member of both your families and everyone who's ever known either of you. I will erase you and any memory of you both completely off this earth. *Capisce?*"

The evil power radiating off the man was palpable. She had no doubt whatsoever that he was fully capable of doing exactly what he'd threatened. Ignoring the weak feeling in her knees and steeling her nerve, she glared back at him and snarled, "I *capisce,* you arrogant son of a bitch. Now you *capisce* this. If anything bad happens to me or my partner, the international press will have a bloody field day with the information we've already sent them about you. You'll be lit up so bright you won't be able to see, let alone carry on with the illegal shit you're mired in."

Maldonado yanked the cigar out of his mouth and shoved his face within inches of hers. She all but gagged at the rancid odor of his breath. Spit speckled her cheeks as he snarled, "Don't fuck with me or my operations. I'll bury you. You'll disappear forever. I'll cause you so much pain you won't be human anymore. You won't even know to wish for death, I'll mess you up so bad."

He pivoted on one Italian-leather-clad heel and stomped away, jerking his head at his goons as he stormed past them. She watched the trio swagger into the night, confident they'd scared her and Taylor completely off. Silence fell in the alley. Amanda released a slow breath.

"I gather he wasn't inquiring as to the state of our health?" Taylor asked dryly.

"That would be correct," she replied equally dryly. She felt sick to her stomach. "Not only did he threaten to kill us, but he also threatened every member of our families and all our friends."

Taylor's gaze registered shock, and then something else. Slow, simmering fury.

She said, "I don't have any close, living relatives, or many friends for that matter. But if I were you, I might make a few phone calls and tell your loved ones to be careful for a few months." The rage in Taylor's gaze heated up another notch. Crud. She really didn't need him doing anything stupid just now. She added, "One thing's for sure. That guy has got to go down."

"Amanda," Taylor warned. "You know not to get tangled up in vendettas. Remember? No emotion. Let's pull back from this guy. There must be another route to find out who Four Eyes is."

She glared at him. "Aren't you the guy who believes in always doing the right thing?"

"Yes," he answered cautiously.

"Emotion or no emotion, my gut's telling me that Maldonado stinks a whole lot worse than his cigars."

"So, then you're going ahead with your plan? Calmly and rationally?" he asked.

She answered without hesitation. "Absolutely."

They shifted to long-range surveillance on Maldonado, strictly high-tech, telescopic work. There was no need to buy trouble with the guy's goon squad. Their big break came exactly one week later. Amanda had picked the lock on a vacant office in the building next to the Hotel Coronado. Its windows faced the bigger hotel. It took them most of the afternoon to set up the equipment that had arrived by express courier that morning. She shuddered at the cost of it all, but any price tag was worth it to take out the bastard.

Sure enough, at 8:00 p.m. sharp, Maldonado's entourage pulled up in front of the hotel. Taylor pointed the heat-sensing scope at the man as he stepped out of his limo. Amanda confirmed through binoculars that the image on the TV monitor beside her was their target.

"You've got a good lock," she murmured. "Now, let's see where he goes."

Taylor tracked the human-size blob through the lobby of the hotel as his scope looked through the hotel walls like they were cellophane. Maldonado and a group of other blobs got into an elevator. Taylor tracked its rapid, nonstop progress all the way up to the penthouse. All the blobs got out. Several other blobs milled around in the room, but when Maldonado walked in, a half-dozen blobs broke off and seated themselves around a table.

"Can you tell what they're doing?" she asked.

"Let me tighten down the signal," Taylor muttered.

She watched on the monitor as the heat seeker zoomed in on the table. The men were doing something with their hands. After a perplexed moment, she laughed. "They're playing cards!"

"Poker, to be precise," Taylor added. "Maldonado is seated facing the window."

She asked, "What are the odds that old Viktor plays poker here every Friday night?"

Taylor grinned. "I'd say pretty good. This is the third week in a row he's come here at the exact same time on the exact same night." A thoughtful pause. "Odds are he and his poker buddies sit in the same seats, too. Card players are a superstitious bunch."

They spent most of the next week hashing out the details of her scheme based on the theory that Maldonado played poker every Friday night, sitting in the same seat. The next Friday found them back in their empty office, waiting for Maldonado again. Sure enough, he arrived at the stroke of 8:00 p.m. and went straight up to his penthouse poker game. Amanda watched with deep satisfaction as he sat down in the same seat he had the week before. "It's a go," she exulted.

They left first thing the next Wednesday, paying cash for two bus tickets to Mexico City. The trip back across the country took considerably longer than it had in the sturdy Porsche, and it was late afternoon when they arrived at their destination. There was a certain risk to returning to the lion's den, but it was also probably the last place whoever was after them would look right now. They bought a bag of carryout enchiladas and grabbed a room at the nearest cheap motel, registering under two of the IDs Xavier had whipped up for them. Amanda stretched out on the bed beside Taylor and thumbed through a telephone book.

"This one looks good," she announced.

He leaned down beside her and looked where she pointed.

"It's an old Catholic hospital. The part of town it's in was prosperous thirty years ago but is running down fast. I doubt they've updated any of their equipment since the place was new."

"Perfect," he murmured in her ear. A shiver whisked down her spine. Lord, he had a powerful effect on her. He could convince a girl to walk away from diamonds and criminals and never look back if he put his mind to it.

"What say we turn in and get an early start tomorrow?" he asked.

Abruptly, the idea of crawling into the same bed with him made her jumpy. She hadn't thought twice about it when he checked in to the single room earlier. It was less conspicuous for a man and woman to travel as a couple. But now… "Uh, sure."

She lay under the covers in the dark, as tight as a high-tension wire. She lay as far away from him as possible, perching on the very edge of the bed. But still his warmth crept around her, beckoning her to its solace.

"You okay?" he asked out of the dark.

She jumped, startled. "Uh, yeah. Fine. Why?"

"I can feel your tension all the way over here. Do you need a back rub or something to help you relax?"

Oh, God. The thought of his hands all over her—it made her pulse jump violently. "No!" Blast. She could feel his smile even though it was pitch-black in the room.

"I don't bite, you know." Challenge wove subtly through his seemingly innocent comment. He was calling her a coward.

Her eyes narrowed. She flipped over on to her stomach. "Fine," she huffed. "Give me the damn back rub."

He chuckled and she felt him sit up. She started when his warm hands touched the bare flesh of her back, sliding under her baggy T-shirt. His touch was as potent as brandy in her blood, sending a rush of heat to her head as his fingers glided upward. He kneaded the knots at the base of her neck, stripping out the tension and leaving her as soft as pudding. Man, that felt good. His hands eased down her spine, releasing the pressure built up there and all but knocking her out. A delicious languor spread outward from his palms, and she felt like she might melt right into the mattress.

"Better?" he murmured.

"If I could purr, I would," she groaned.

A quiet chuckle.

She tensed briefly as his hands slid over her buttocks. But

when he began to work his way down her left leg, she sighed in bliss and gave in to his massage. He worked his way back up the other leg, and by the time he slid over her rear end again to finish up with her back once more, she didn't have the will left to care, let alone react.

Taylor felt when Amanda slipped from a state of total relaxation into sleep. He stretched out beside her and listened to the light, easy sound of her breathing. She'd come a long way since they first met. Whether or not she was ready to take the next step and make love with him was anybody's guess. He'd just keep going slow and let her take the lead when the time came. Damn, it was hard to restrain himself. He wanted her so bad he ached sometimes. He felt an urge to toss and turn, but forced himself to lie still lest he disturb her. Sometime during the night, he finally fell asleep.

Amanda rented a van and bought worker's overalls the next morning. The decals declaring them to be a medical-equipment repair company took a little doing, but by midafternoon, their cover was firmly in place. The timing was perfect. The staff at the hospital would be nearing the end of their shift and be tired and inattentive. A brief flash of ID badges and the two of them sailed past the overworked hospital staff. They followed an elderly nun's directions and headed down a hall toward the X-ray department. An equally brief explanation to the X-ray technician that they were here to do scheduled maintenance, and the two of them were left alone with an X-ray machine.

"How's it look?" she asked.

Taylor gave the machine a once-over and looked up at her, grinning. "Perfect. It's about forty years old. Big, old, high-dose unit. I can't believe anyone still uses these things. One X ray from this equals about thirty X rays from a new machine."

She shrugged. "You use what you've got when you're poor." She shuffled through a stack of schematics she'd pulled off the Internet until she found a close match. "Put on one of those," she directed, nodding at a couple lead-lined aprons hanging on hooks. Donning one herself, she carefully dismantled the machine, exposing the essential components. The X-ray generator weighed close to a hundred pounds and was big and awkward. But with a lot of sweat and a little swearing, she and Taylor wrestled it free. They laid a lead apron in the large trunk they'd brought with them and lifted the machine inside. Another lead apron on top, and they closed the whole thing up.

Amanda stepped out into the hall to make sure the coast was clear. When she waved Taylor out, he lifted the trunk onto his shoulder. Thank God for him. She'd have given herself a hernia if she tried to lift that thing. They headed toward the loading dock at the rear of the hospital. She stayed with the trunk while he walked swiftly to the van and pulled it around back. The whole maneuver took less than an hour, and they were on their way back to Cancun.

"Was it just me," he remarked as they hit the highway out of town, "or was that too easy?"

She laughed. "Don't sneer at good luck. Everybody's entitled to a little of it now and then."

They made good time back across the Mexican peninsula, arriving shortly after midnight with their prize. Maldonado's poker game was the following evening. They didn't have much time to spare.

Early Friday afternoon, they used the last set of pristine IDs Xavier had worked up for them to check into the Hotel Coronado. Taylor and a bellhop lifted the trunk out of the van and wheeled it across the lobby. To the inquiring look of the manager, Amanda replied, "Scuba gear."

The guy smiled and nodded, turning back to his work.

As soon as they got to their room, she opened the trunk and checked on the X-ray machine. It seemed to have weathered the trip upstairs well. While Taylor transferred the supply of tools and gear they'd bought that morning from his suitcase to the trunk, she made a reconnoitering sortie to the top floor of the hotel. The first thing she noticed when she stepped off the elevator and looked down the long hallway was the complete absence of Do Not Disturb signs, room-service trays on floors or newspapers outside doors. The concierge had been lying. Entire floor sold out, her eye. She'd bet the whole floor was unoccupied. Compliments of Maldonado and his security staff.

She made her way to the far north end of the hallway and paced off sixty feet. She stood in front of room 1814. If her calculations were correct, this room was directly under part of the penthouse where the poker table stood. She pressed her ear to the door, listening for any sounds from inside. Nothing. Using a credit-card-shaped, magnetized pass key hooked to a hand-held computer, she electronically picked the room's lock. A green light over the lock flashed, and she clicked the door open. She stepped inside. The room was devoid of any signs of human habitation. Better yet, there was a thick layer of dust over everything. This room hadn't been rented out or cleaned in weeks. Probably wouldn't be until Maldonado left Cancun.

After checking the hallway and finding it deserted, she taped the latch so the door wouldn't lock behind her when she left the room. She put a dab of metallic gold paint on the tiny green light over the key card slot that indicated the door was unlocked. The enamel blended in with the brass fixture, and at a glance, nobody'd ever know the door was rigged. Time to get back to Taylor and start the next phase of the operation. They had a boatload to do before tonight's poker game.

She retraced her steps back down to their room. Taylor was ready and waiting for her. Together, they carried the trunk out of their room. Lord, all that lead was heavy. They passed on the first elevator, which had hotel guests in it. The next elevator that arrived was empty and they wrestled the trunk inside. Its doors slid open at the top floor. A quick check. The hallway was still deserted. They stepped out and made their way to room 1814 as fast as they could. Huffing, Amanda hauled her end of the trunk into the room and set it down gratefully. She pulled the tape off the door latch and let out her breath. So far so good.

"Let's get hopping," she told Taylor. "It's five o'clock already."

He grinned and handed her a white polyester jumpsuit. "Hop into this," he retorted. She donned the suit, used in clean rooms for the computer-manufacturing industry. She grimaced as she tucked her hair into the matching shower cap. At least Taylor looked nearly as silly in his cap as she must. She pulled on a pair of surgical gloves, snapping them into place while Taylor did the same. Thus fortified against leaving fiber evidence for the police, they got to work.

She unpacked their gear and spread it out on one of the two double beds while Taylor rewrapped the lead aprons around the X-ray machine. She picked up a pair of large handles attached to powerful suction cups and passed them to Taylor. He pushed back the curtains and attached the handles to the window while she fished out a pair of putty knives. Working together, they peeled away the caulking that held the plate glass in place. A dozen bolts unscrewed, and Taylor was able to lift the sheet of glass out of the window frame. A stiff breeze swirled into the room as he leaned the glass carefully against the wall.

The wind was a harbinger of how tricky the next bit of the operation was going to be. Grimly, she stuffed the curtains behind furniture to keep them from flying in her face. While Taylor tied a long rope around the base of the toilet and looped it around the legs of both bed frames, she strapped into a mountain climber's harness. He passed her the end of the safety line and she attached a carabiner to it and knotted the rope around the oval metal clip. Taylor donned a pair of leather gloves, grabbed the safety rope and sat down on the floor just beneath the window. He braced his feet against the wall and nodded up at her.

She threw a coil of rope over her shoulder and stepped up onto the windowsill. The wind tore at her, and she steadied herself against the frame at her back. The ocean pounded far below and she did her best to ignore the spectacular drop. Gripping the safety rope attached to her waist, she leaned outward against it, craning her neck to look up. A windowsill loomed directly overhead. She prayed it was the correct one as she shook out the rope from her shoulder and gripped the rubber-coated grappling hook attached to its end. She swung the heavy hook in a couple big, slow circles and then tossed it upward. It missed, and clattered down the wall beside her. Crud. She held her breath and waited for a response from inside the penthouse suite. Nothing. She counted to sixty. Either nobody was inside yet, or nobody'd heard her. She tried again. This time the hook caught on the steel lip of the window ledge. She yanked hard on the line to test it. It felt secure. She hooked herself to the second rope.

"Here I go," she murmured toward her feet.

Taylor's reply floated up to her, "Be careful."

Yeah, right. She took a deep breath, and transferred her body weight gently to the new rope. She thought she felt a small slip in the grappling hook and froze, her feet dangling in space. She made the mistake of looking down. The ground spun in a slow circle beneath her, beckoning her to a messy end. She willed her heart not to beat so fast, but for once, it failed to co-operate. Praying the lurch had only been the rope stretching, she reached up and grasped the line over her head. The rubberized palms of her climbing gloves gripped the slick nylon, and she hauled herself an arm's length higher. It wasn't far to the window ledge overhead, just a few arm lengths. But each time she released one hand to reach higher, her heart constricted sharply. Finally, she reached up and felt a metal lip. Grabbing on with both hands, she hauled herself up the last few inches. There was a dicey moment when she had to hang by one hand and tie off her climbing harness with the other. A temporary slip knot, and then she was able to release the ledge and use both hands to secure herself more firmly. Mountain climbing never had been her favorite pastime.

She took off her gloves and stuffed them in a zipper pocket. Reaching up once more, her fingertips touched cool, smooth glass. The penthouse window. The wind gusted, swirling even more strongly near the top of the tall building. She twisted slightly, first to the left, then back to the right. She felt slightly nauseous. Concentrating fiercely, she pulled out a thin, black rubber hose with a tiny, wide-angle camera attached to it. She'd gotten the camera from a surgical-supply house—it was used for photographing people's colons. She grinned briefly at the irony. She planned to send something much worse than this camera up Viktor Maldonado's arse tonight.

Earlier, Taylor had cut a ring in a suction cup and glued it around the camera's lens. The diameter of the whole thing was slightly less than two inches. She smeared a little spit on the suction cup, being careful to keep it off the lens of the camera, then reached over her head and pushed the suction cup against the bottom of the window glass. She peered through the eyepiece at her end of the hose. A darkened room sprawled in wide-angle distortion before her. Perfect.

She put a length of clear, high-strength tape across the back of the camera, attaching it more firmly to the corner of the window. She untied her climbing harness and descended carefully, letting out the length of rubber hose as she went. She taped it down to the side of the building with lengths of duct tape she peeled off the thigh of her suit. When her feet finally touched the window ledge of their room, a giant surge of relief washed through her. And then strong arms swept around her, pulling her inside. To safety. She huddled against Taylor's heat, soaking up the feel of him. Eventually, he loosened his grip enough for her to slide down his body until her feet touched the carpeted floor. A shudder of need passed through her. But it was more than just his body that called to her. It was the whole devastating package.

Abruptly, she realized her knees were shaking. From that blistering embrace or the relief of being back on solid ground, she had no idea. But she was happy to stand back while Taylor reached outside to flip the hook free. She jumped aside as he pulled sharply on the line and the grappling hook sailed through the window, narrowly missing her.

"Watch it!" she protested laughingly. "I didn't just risk my neck out there for you to go and kill me while I'm standing in a perfectly safe hotel room!"

"Sorry. How's the optic scope working?" he asked.

"Have a look for yourself."

She passed him the end of the black tube and he peered through the telescope-like lens. "Perfect. I've got a straight-on view of Viktor's chair. You did great."

She arched one eyebrow. "Did you expect anything less?"

He laughed at her, "Now who's copping the macho attitude?"

She stuck out her tongue at him as he picked up the scope again. He took a few measurements using a tiny red laser beam in the camera for reference, then he measured a commensurate distance on the ceiling of their room. "If I'm right, that X I just made marks the spot where Viktor's poker chair will sit tonight."

"You better be right," she said with abrupt seriousness. "This plan doesn't have any room in it for error."

"Never fear, darlin'," he drawled, "we'll nail this bastard."

She passed him a hand saw that he used to cut a hole roughly two feet in diameter around the X on the ceiling. She fetched towels from the bathroom that he wrapped around the electric drill they'd brought. He was just climbing onto a chair under the hole when the door burst open.

Amanda started violently and Taylor nearly fell off the chair as he lurched. The maid was just as startled and they all stared at each other. Taylor began to laugh and the maid joined him. The woman laughingly fired a scolding spate of Spanish at them to the effect that they were making a mess when she was supposed to be cleaning this room. Amanda replied in Spanish that they were testing for asbestos contamination and this room should be left alone for several days or else the woman could catch a fatal lung infection. The maid retreated hastily.

As the door closed behind the woman, Amanda sat down heavily on the edge of the bed. "Lord, that was close."

"What was she doing here?" Taylor asked.

"Apparently these rooms are getting ready to be occupied."

"Viktor's leaving town, is he?"

He couldn't! Not after they'd done all this work to nail him. The setup was perfect. They'd never get another shot at the guy like this. She answered Taylor grimly, "Let's pray he doesn't leave until after we hit him tonight."

Taylor matched her grim expression. Then he asked, "What did you tell the maid?" His frown turned into a grin when she translated for him. "Great cover story."

She retorted, "Well, you've got to admit, we look like alien invaders in these getups."

He stepped over to her and pulled her to her feet. "I dunno. I think you're too cute for an alien." He dropped a light kiss on her lips and then stepped away, climbing back onto his chair.

A ripple of intense pleasure started at the back of her neck and ripped through her, making her shiver with its passing.

"Hand me the drill, will you?" he asked.

Numbly, she handed him the tool.

Taylor grinned to himself as he put the scope to one eye. Then he carefully drilled up through the floor of the penthouse. Too far under the table. But he had a good reference point now. He switched to a circular bit that would take out a two-inch circle of flooring. He adjusted the position of the drill and drilled a second hole. He was careful to just break the surface of the floorboard and not rip through the layer of plush carpeting under Maldonado's seat. A neat disk of wood came away with the drill bit. Perfect.

Next, he bolted a crisscrossing sling of flat steel bands to the steel floor beams. Then came the hard part. He and Amanda donned lead aprons and lifted the X-ray machine out of the trunk. Every muscle straining, he climbed onto the chair and lifted the machine with Amanda helping from below. He managed to wedge a corner of it into the waiting sling. Some of its weight lifted off his shoulders. Whew. He settled the apparatus more securely in the nest of steel bands, then turned it to align it with the hole in the ceiling. He climbed down from the chair. Lord, his neck hurt. Hefting that much awkward weight overhead was a bitch. He sat down on the bed, and started when soft hands settled on his shoulders. He savored the massage Amanda gave him, not so much because it eased his cramping neck muscles, which it did, but because of the milestone it represented. She was voluntarily touching him in a way meant to give him pleasure. Son of a gun.

Finally, he sighed and stood up. "Hold that thought. When we're done here, I could use another one of those."

She moved away from him nervously and went to work using a glass cutter to take a small notch out of the upper corner of the plate-glass windowpane. Using the suction cup handles, Taylor lifted the heavy sheet of glass back into place while Amanda routed the black rubber hose from their hidden camera through the notch. He held the window in place against the buffeting force of the wind while she put in a couple screws to secure the glass. He finished installing the rest of the screws and then caulked the whole thing. Then he ran an extension cord up to the X-ray machine and plugged it in. Now for the acid test. He turned it on. It made a low hum. Outstanding. He turned it off and climbed down out of the crawl space. They were ready to go.

He and Amanda spent the next half hour cleaning up and putting all the debris into the trunk. He stripped off his clean-suit by the door and checked the hallway. Clear. The maids must be done cleaning these rooms. He carted the now-light trunk to the elevator. A quick trip down to the hotel's garbage incinerator, and the scraps from their labor went into the flames.

He got in the elevator and pushed the button for the eight-

eenth floor. But it stopped at the lobby. The doors opened and
his heart skipped a beat at the sight before him. Two of Maldonado's goons stood right in the middle of the lobby, talking
to each other. If either one of them happened to look up, he'd
be smack dab in the middle of their line of sight. *Crap.* He dared
not make any sudden movements. He stood there, frozen, for
the eternity it took a couple to step into the elevator with him
and the door to close. Maldonado's men never looked up.
Christ, that had been close.

The couple got off at the twelfth floor and he rode the rest
of the way up to eighteen. He sprinted for their room, and the
door opened before he came to a full stop. Amanda'd been
keeping watch for him through the peephole. The door latched
behind him and he checked his watch. Six-thirty. He slipped
his clean-suit back on. One last bit of work to do. Standing on
the chair, he lifted the circular piece of ceiling material he'd
sawed out earlier and slid it into the ceiling space, perched beside the hole. He attached a half-dozen inch-long brass strips
to its back side. All he'd have to do when it was time was lower
the Sheetrock into place. The brass pieces would catch the
edges of the hole and hold the ceiling where it belonged.

He climbed up into the crawl space one last time. Amanda
passed him a lead apron, which he draped double thick between
himself and the X-ray machine. The lights went off below.
Now all they had to do was wait and hope that Maldonado
showed up.

The trick would be to deliver just enough radiation to make
Maldonado good and sick without killing him. Amanda's plan
was to irradiate the bastard enough to cause him a lifetime of
health woes, serious enough for him to end his career and spend
the rest of his days in and out of hospitals. She wouldn't murder the guy, just permanently incapacitate him. Hopefully that
would satisfy Xavier's contact enough for the source to spill
the information on Four Eyes. The guy's exact instructions
were to take Maldonado out. To remove him from the business

and crime scene permanently. Clearly the guy's intent had been for them to kill him. They'd just have to convince the client that doing the job this way ultimately accomplished the same goal. It kept all their hands clean of murder, and more to the point, it would appease her newly forming conscience.

When she'd suddenly developed an aversion to taking out a bad guy who was getting in her way, she had no idea. They'd had to go through an awful lot of extra effort to do the job this way instead of just putting a bullet between the bastard's eyes. But the thought of looking into Taylor's eyes, of seeing the disappointment in them if she took the easy way out and killed this guy—she just couldn't do it. For some reason, she wanted Taylor to approve of her. To be proud of her. Hell, she wanted to be proud of herself.

The sweet part of the plan was that Viktor wouldn't get sick right away. And when symptoms did show up, they'd look like a case of acute food poisoning. The odds of a local hospital checking him immediately for radiation poisoning were slim at best. By the time he got a correct diagnosis, the two of them would be long gone from here, back on track to find out where those damned diamonds were coming from and why everyone associated with them seemed to want her dead.

His watch crawled toward eight o'clock. Through the scope, he watched waiters set up a buffet in the penthouse and a bartender take his place. At about seven-thirty, the other poker players began to arrive. At 8:03 on the nose, Maldonado strode into the room. Even shortened and broadened absurdly by the wide-angle lens, there was no mistaking the guy's arrogant profile. Taylor breathed a sigh of relief when Maldonado took his usual chair. However, the bastard was lounging farther back than Taylor had counted on. He debated with himself whether to proceed or to wait a little longer. He decided to wait.

Ten minutes later, Maldonado looked at his cards and laid them down, then hitched his chair closer to the table. There! Maldonado was in the perfect position. Taylor waited for a burst of laughter from overhead, and under cover of the noise, flipped on the switch. These first few moments were the most critical. The low hum from the machine mustn't be noticed. Taylor watched carefully through the scope, but no one reacted. None of the bodyguards moved from their lounging positions around the room. He started his stopwatch.

As the minutes dragged by, Taylor ran the calculations again in his mind. He needed to deliver between three and four hundred rads of radiation. This machine would take about two hours to achieve a three-hundred-rad exposure level, taking into account the guy's chair and the scattering of the X-ray beam, which was eighteen inches away from its target instead of the usual inch or so in a hospital. The clock had been running for one hour and ten minutes when Maldonado excused himself from the table. Taylor swore silently and turned off the machine. Don't let the bastard start barfing yet.

Maldonado returned a couple minutes later, obligingly returned to his seat and assumed just the right position. Taylor turned the machine back on. When his stopwatch read two hours and thirty minutes, he turned it off. Maldonado had just embarked upon a long and sick retirement.

Taylor eased himself out of the crawl space, pulling the circle of Sheetrock back into place overhead. Amanda passed up a little pot of spackling, which he spread around the seam. Dabbing at the wet compound with a paintbrush, he textured it to match the ceiling. It wasn't a perfect patch, but it would escape a casual inspection. By the time anyone was seriously looking for it, he and Amanda would be on another continent.

He cleaned up the last bit of dust on the carpet while Amanda stepped to the window. She jerked sharply on the black hose, disconnecting the suction cup from the window above. She used a pocketknife to cut through the hose close to the notch in the window and shove the tail out through the small hole. The camera snaked downward into the darkness.

A bit more caulking, and the notch in the window was sealed.

Again, not perfect, but it would pass a casual inspection. Amanda nodded at him, and they stripped off their clean-suits by the door, wadding them into a big shoulder bag she carried. He scratched the spot of gold paint off the door lock with his fingernail and followed her quickly and quietly down the hall.

They returned to their room just long enough to don a set of disguises. Once their appearances were altered into that of an aging couple who could pass by Maldonado's men unrecognized, they cleaned their room meticulously, wiped it for fingerprints and walked out. It was shockingly easy to stroll past the phalanx of security. Retired tourists were a dime a dozen, and no one gave them a second glance. They headed out to the beach, and Amanda unobtrusively picked up the thin, black tube of the camera and slipped it in her purse.

They crossed into Belize without incident. They holed up for the night in a cockroach-infested rattrap that passed for a hotel in Belize City. The next morning they boarded a disreputable-looking plane bound for Caracas, Venezuela, where Xavier had told them to go after they killed Maldonado.

Neither Belize City nor Caracas was high on the list of garden destinations for American tourists these days. With Taylor's dark hair and Amanda's fluent Spanish, they were able to blend in with the locals without too much trouble. They'd checked into a hotel and finished eating a miserable room-service meal that evening before Taylor began to feel the tension of the past couple days drain away. They'd made it. He didn't know whether to be exhilarated or just plain tired.

He looked up at Amanda. "Now what?"

She met his gaze squarely and said quietly, "Let's go to bed."

Chapter 14

Amanda did her damnedest not to flinch as fire leaped in Taylor's eyes. No doubt about it, he'd caught her meaning. She wanted this. She was ready for it. And besides, this was Taylor she was talking about making love with, not the handful of awkward boys she'd tried uncomfortable sex with in her school days. Thankfully, he didn't say anything. She didn't think she'd have the courage to go through with it if he insisted on psychoanalyzing her reasons for her decision. He just nodded and turned out the lights. And when the safety of the darkness had enveloped them both, she knew it would be all right.

His big shadow moved toward her slowly in the dark, and his hands were light upon her shoulders. He slipped his fingers into her hair, massaging her scalp gently, and she was lost. Pleasure uncurled within her at his touch. His lips brushed the side of her neck. Oh, yes. That felt lovely. She let her head fall back to give Taylor better access to her sensitive flesh. His lips touched her neck again, resting on the pulse leaping wildly at the base of her throat. She exhaled on a sigh that was half a moan, and his arms tightened around her waist.

She reveled in the sensation of pressing against him from her toenails to the part in her hair. Tonight, she could crawl all over his gorgeous body like she'd been dying to for weeks. The relief of finally feeding that need made her feel like sobbing. She peeled off his shirt. His pants followed, along with the rest of his clothes. How her clothes disappeared, she wasn't quite certain, but she definitely didn't care. She only knew she wanted to be naked and sweaty with him. Right now.

She ran her hands over his chest and felt his heart jump beneath her palms. Her own body responded wildly, suddenly bathed in moist desire. She dragged his head down to hers, kissing him with all the need that had built up in her since that night they'd first met. He met her head-on, his tongue wet and hot, swirling inside her mouth. He groaned and she arched up into him, voracious for more. Their teeth clacked together in their careless rush, but she didn't care. She sucked on his tongue, pulling it into her mouth rhythmically, mimicking the sex act she craved like a bad addiction.

Taylor backed her up toward the bed, breaking her fall with a knee beside her. And then he loomed over her, big and hard and hot. She ran her nails down the length of his throbbing flesh and he grabbed her wrist and pulled it away. She laughed up at him and he growled in response as he quickly slipped on a condom.

She reached for him again, tugging him down to her, and this time he didn't resist. His weight was glorious, pressing her deep into the mattress. She felt a sheen of sweat on his back as he ground his hips against her, teasing her with the hard slide of flesh against her pulsing core. She undulated up into him, coaxing him to come inside her, but he slid down her body maddeningly and took her breast into his mouth. She lurched up off the mattress as lightning zinged to every region of her body and wrapped her legs around his hips.

That did it. He surged up over her and thrust into her, impaling her in a single stroke. She cried out at the exquisite sensation of being stretched not quite to the point of pain with his burning fullness. He began to retreat, but she surged upward, sucking him back down with her greedily. With a chuckle that was half a growl he drove into her again. She shuddered in an excess of pleasure that rolled over her like a Mack truck. Again he pressed deep within her, and again, she gasped in amazement. She could feel him reaching for some shred of restraint, but she wanted no part of it. She wrapped her arms and legs around him and pulled him to her very core, rocking her hips in an irresistible rhythm as old as time. He needed no further invitation. His mouth captured hers hungrily, and he plunged his tongue inside in rhythm with his body as they feasted greedily upon each other.

He buried his face in the crook of her neck, and she hung on for dear life as they rode out the storm they'd made together. It towered around them, a raging hurricane of heat and friction and delirious pleasure. It consumed her entirely, building to a pitch so intense she almost passed out from it. As she spasmed uncontrollably around him, Taylor shuddered and joined her with a groan dredged from the bottom of his soul.

She fell back to the bed, drenched in sweat and satiation so overpowering she thought she might die. They spiraled downward slowly, their breathing ragged, their bodies spent. Taylor rolled over and pulled Amanda across his chest, holding her close, while they both struggled for breath. Words like *shattering* and *liberating* floated, disconnected, through her mind, but she could find no real words to describe her reaction to what had just happened between them. Gradually, she became aware of his mouth moving warmly against her skin. It traced a lazy path from her ear to her temple. She felt his smile against her flesh.

He began all over to make love to her, but this time so slowly and sweetly she knew she was going to die. And for the first time in her life, peace flowed through her.

* * *

"Okay, Xavier, we met our end of the bargain—now it's your contact's turn."

Taylor rolled over lazily and listened while Amanda repeated what sounded like a phone number. His muscles were weak with the residual languor of the greatest night of sex he'd ever had as he looked over at the bedside clock. Almost noon.

He watched her punch out another phone number and reached over to stroke the naked flesh of the small of her back. She smiled at him over the receiver, and the expression went all the way to the back of her eyes. Thank God. He'd been briefly worried last night that the wild abandon of their initial sex would put her off it for good. Lord knew it had overwhelmed him, and he hadn't brought any big emotional baggage to the experience.

Amanda spoke in English. "A mutual friend suggested I call this number." A pause. "Yes, he is still breathing, but he is finished. Let's just say he had an unfortunate exposure to a disease that cannot be cured." Another pause, and then she snapped, "There was no requirement that he die instantaneously, and I assure you he will be incapacitated for the remainder of his life. I don't have time to sit around waiting for him to die—it could be a while. But he will never do business again. Will that satisfy you?"

How had the person at the other end responded to that? He watched Amanda listen in silence for some time to whatever the reaction was, her face showing nothing but intent concentration. Then she said shortly, "Got it." She hung up the phone.

"Well?" he demanded.

"We're meeting him tomorrow night. He says he's got the goods on Four Eyes."

"Is this guy legit?" Taylor asked.

She shrugged. "I suspect he won't double-cross us now that we've demonstrated a willingness to harm someone."

Taylor frowned.

"Oh, don't go all worried and analytical on me," she responded lightly. "I have no intention of turning into a killer for hire. You and I both know Maldonado was long overdue for a comeuppance. And if we can get the information we need, we might just stand a chance of staying alive long enough to have a repeat of last night."

He had to grin at that one. It was a blatant manipulation, but he indulged her and allowed himself to be distracted. "You're alive, now, aren't you?" he asked leadingly.

A slow smile spread across her face. "I am at that, now, aren't I?"

It was nearly dark the next evening when they finally crawled out of bed and into the shower. They got dressed and had a light supper across the street from their hotel. Taylor hailed them a cab while Amanda watched discreetly for tails. The pistol holstered under his left arm felt strange, but no way was he going into this meeting without one. He had a second pistol strapped to his right ankle, and he knew Amanda had one in her purse. They jumped in the taxi and pulled away from the curb, Amanda's attention still focused outside.

"We're clean," she announced.

He let out a relieved breath. He hadn't realized how accustomed he'd gotten to functioning as though his every move was being watched. Apparently, he'd embraced Amanda's rule number one of healthy paranoia without noticing it. The squalor of downtown gave way to more prosperous neighborhoods, and their cab began to look downright shabby compared to the ostentatious wealth lining the streets.

He'd picked up enough Spanish to understand when Amanda leaned forward and asked the driver, "How much farther?"

"Not far. One kilometer," the guy replied.

"Stop here," Amanda ordered. The guy pulled over underneath a giant mimosa tree, its feathery fronds casting an umbrella of shifting shadow. Something deep in Taylor's gut was relieved that they hadn't just driven up to their contact's home as proud as you please. His intuition screamed that this was a meeting they should approach with caution.

As Amanda counted out bolivars for the driver from the mixed currency wad in her purse, Taylor noted movement down the street. In fact, several movements. "We've got company," he murmured.

She straightened, nodding fractionally. "Let's take a walk."

The back of his neck tingled. *They were so being watched.* They neared the gated entrance to a grand estate, and a man stepped out of the shadows with an easy swagger. He held back a jacket far enough to reveal a leather holster at his hip and uttered a short greeting in Spanish that was clearly some sort of a challenge.

Amanda replied fluidly. Whatever she said, the guy relaxed and nodded politely.

They walked past the guard, and Taylor felt the moment when the guy turned away from them and went back to wherever he'd come from.

"Private security," Amanda muttered.

The estate they'd just passed was far from the most impressive in this area. All of the houses here must have similar setups. "If our contact's this rich, why didn't he just hire someone to knock off Maldonado?" he replied under his breath.

"Good question. Let's ask it when we get there."

Based on how the house numbers were increasing, they had about a half mile to go. They walked in silence for a couple minutes, and then he asked quietly, "If this is such a safe neighborhood, why do I feel so damned uneasy?"

"I don't know," she responded, "but I'm feeling itchy, too."

Their steps slowed a bit as they peered into the darkness around them. Rolling lawns stretched away into black nothingness behind tall iron fences. The occasional brick wall crowded the sidewalk, and trees towered everywhere. Streetlights were sparse, coming mostly from decorative lamps at the gates to driveways. They walked a bit farther, and the feeling of being watched began to bother him once more. But this time, no pugnacious guard sauntered out and made himself known.

"I don't like this," Amanda mumbled.

Out of the corner of his eye, he caught her hand drifting to her purse. Casually, he unbuttoned his sport coat for quick access to his pistol. Tension thrummed through him.

"Look relaxed," Amanda murmured.

"Look sharp," he retorted.

She grinned up at him. And all hell broke loose. Four men leaped out of the shadows, weapons drawn, shouting for them to freeze. Taylor dived to the right while Amanda leaped left. Their assailants yelled and rushed. He kept rolling, past a tree trunk and out into the street. As his shoulder slammed into asphalt, he ripped his pistol clear. A dull thud beside his right ear. The bastards were shooting at them! Silenced weapons. He took aim over the top of his head as he completed the roll onto his stomach. Before he landed flat, he pulled the trigger. A sharp cry, and one of the men went down, holding his leg.

A loud report from his left. Amanda. She was functional, then. Another man down. Damn, she was a good shot. He leaped to his feet and zigzagged across the street, drawing thankfully inaccurate fire. He dived for a clump of tall bushes, crashing through the stiff branches with a rending of fabric. Rolling to a crouch, he braced his pistol in front of him. A black shape dived behind a car about thirty feet down the street on the same side as him. Taylor looked around frantically.

He holstered his pistol and reached up, jumping for a branch overhead. He swung up into a tree and crouched in the crook next to the trunk. He pulled his pistol again and took stock. No more attackers were forthcoming. One man lay still on the sidewalk across the street and another lay on the ground, grimly wrapping a cloth around his leg. The third guy was being stealthy behind a car and there was no sign of the fourth man. No sign of Amanda, either. If he had to guess, she'd bolted into the yard across the street and gone cross-country. Probably had the fourth guy in tow.

Nothing he could do for her at the moment. Their unsilenced weapons would no doubt draw a police response in a matter of minutes. He didn't have all night to sit up here and play hide-and-seek with the turkey behind the car. He thought fast. The pistol in his hand was loaded with Teflon-coated bullets. But the smaller pistol in his ankle holster carried explosive rounds. He'd get one shot at this; the muzzle-flash would give away his position. He readied himself to jump down and pulled out the small revolver. He took aim at the lower rear end of the car the thug was using for cover and squeezed off three quick shots at the vehicle's gas tank.

A blinding explosion rocked him, slamming him out of the tree. He fell heavily onto his left shoulder, knocking the wind out of him. He forced himself to his feet while he dragged air into his shocked lungs. Come on, body. *Move.* A scream from the far side of the ball of flames announced that he'd incapacitated his attacker.

He briefly considered crossing the street and following after Amanda, but that would bring him into view of the two downed men. Just because they were lying on the ground didn't mean they couldn't shoot him. There was nothing like a good possum act.

He faded back into the shadows. Dodging from one pocket of black to another, he made his way down the street. Sirens screamed in the distance, and lights were popping on everywhere up and down the street. Screw this. He jumped up onto the brick wall beside him and dived into the yard behind it. He sprinted across the smooth lawn, making his way behind a sprawling stucco house. A quick trip over the fence and into another property. This place had a pair of barking dogs, but trained killers they were not. The pair of German shepherds followed him as he raced across their territory, leaping and barking as if this were a great game. Two more estates traversed, and he slowed down to catch his breath. Fortunately, all the commotion in the street seemed to have drawn the private security guards out to the streetside gates. There were a few motion-activated spotlights to dodge, but he jogged, mostly unhindered, toward their original destination.

He crouched inside a wrought-iron fence, across the street from the address they'd been given. Their contact lived in a blond, brick colonial mansion resting in a copse of big old trees. A lawn rose gently to its walls and rose beds dotted the expanse. Nice place. Well back from the street. A few lights on. Apparently the fiasco down the road hadn't alarmed anyone inside. He looked up and down the street. A couple security guards were visible and a police car raced past.

He considered his options for getting across the street unnoticed. None. Well, if he couldn't hide, he'd blend in. He approached the driveway of the estate he was hiding inside. A guard hovered just inside the gate, his nose all but pressed against the iron bars in an attempt to see what was going on down the street. Taylor pulled his gun. It was ridiculously easy to creep up behind the idiot and clock him across the base of the skull with his pistol butt. He took off his ruined sport coat, stripped the guard's jacket off and shrugged into it. It was way small and there was no way he could zip it, so he pushed it back to reveal his holster. Quickly, he moved over to a digital control pad for the front gate. Crap. Now what?

He pushed the big, round button beside the number pad. The big gates began to swing open. Praise the Lord. He strolled into the street. Stopped to look toward the cluster of sirens. Moved further across the street as if to get a better vantage point. And then he was on the other side and melted into the shadows. He found a thick clump of bushes beside the fence and flung the jacket up over the iron spikes topping it. He climbed over the fence awkwardly and dropped to the ground on the far side. The coat hung up on the spikes when he tried to tug it loose. No help for it. He left it hanging where it was.

He stuck to the shadows of the trees as far as he could, and then he dropped to his belly. There was enough cover between the beds of roses for him to make his way toward the house unseen. It was slow going, though. Slow enough for him to have time to wonder where in the hell Amanda was. Was she all right? Had she gotten away from the fourth attacker? Who were those guys, anyway? As he dragged himself foot by foot toward the mansion, one thought crystallized in his mind. He was keeping this appointment come hell or high water. He was going to find out who was managing to stay on their heels like this.

Amanda crouched in the bushes by the street, mere yards from one of their attackers. The guy groaned periodically and clutched at his leg wound. Must have hit his femur to be in that much pain. She'd love nothing more than to step out and ask him a few pointed questions about whom he worked for and why he was chasing her, but that would be asking for trouble on her part.

Instead she held her position, watching the burning car and waiting for the emergency response that would be forthcoming any minute. Shooting out that car's gas tank had been an inspired ploy by Taylor. She'd been surprised when she caught the muzzle-flash out of the tree. Good thinking to go vertical.

After her initial dive off the sidewalk, she'd fired a single, lucky shot that dropped one of their attackers cold. Then she'd climbed the fence behind her and taken off running, praying Taylor was still up. Footsteps pounded behind her, and she headed for some shrubbery, dodging in and out of shadows as she tried to lose her pursuer. Then a stroke of luck. She stumbled on the edge of a hole where someone had dug up something big like a tree. She dived into it, curling up in a ball and clawing at the soft dirt, sending cascades of it over herself. Heavy breathing passed by. She stayed put, though. He'd circle back when he lost sight of her. Sure enough, about a minute later, someone passed by again more slowly. A quiet curse. *Uttered in Russian.* Her heart slammed into her throat.

She counted to a hundred and then climbed out of her hole. Dirt trickled down the back of her neck, but she didn't have time to shake it out of her hair or clothes. Moving with catlike stealth, she'd eased back toward the point of the attack. Who *were* these Russians? Why were they so determined to kill her? And how in the bloody hell were they managing to stay one step behind her and Taylor?

A fire truck pulled up, blocking her view of the burning car. She resisted an urge to shrink back deeper into the shadows as two police cars pulled up seconds later and four officers jumped out. One of them raced over to the two downed Russians. He shouted for a medic and then turned to the Russian with the leg wound. Then, blessedly, the policeman asked who the guy was. Amanda strained to hear the man's answer.

"Nikko Biryayev. Russian State Security."

Russian government? Shock rooted her feet to the ground. No way. What did they want with her? Were they tied into the diamonds somehow? The Venezuelan police officer had a good look at the guy's identification and seemed satisfied with it, so he must be for real. She waited until an ambulance crew tried to move the Russian. Under the cover of his moaning pain, she slipped away in the dark.

Thoughtfully, she made her way across a half-dozen estates, dodging on autopilot the various security guards, lights and dogs she encountered. The guy who'd followed her at La-Guardia had been Russian government, too. What was the link? Were they trying to track down the smugglers, too, or was there a more sinister connection? Were they part of the diamond-smuggling operation?

She stopped at the top of a gentle hill, crouched in the shadows of a stately beige Georgian mansion. The contact's house. She checked her watch. They'd been jumped nearly a half hour ago. *Where was Taylor?* Gad, she hated it when they got split up like this. What she wouldn't give to be wired with microphones and radios right about now. But wires would undoubtedly freak out their contact if they were searched. Speaking of which, they were due for their meeting in about five minutes. C'mon, Taylor. Show up.

She waited, more worried than she was willing to admit, for fifteen more minutes. She'd begun to consider going to the meeting alone when, without warning, a hand clapped over her mouth. She jolted violently and grabbed the hand preparatory to ripping its thumb off. A voice whispered in her ear, "Hi, honey, I'm home."

She sagged in relief and turned in Taylor's arms, throwing her arms around his neck. "Thank God you're safe," she murmured. She inhaled his wonderful, reassuring scent as he crushed her in a warm, safe hug. Regretfully, she lifted her head off his shoulder.

"Yeah, I know. We've got to go," he murmured. "So, who were those bastards?"

"Russian," she bit out. "Government."

He stared at her, mirroring her shock. "What the hell do they want with us?"

She shrugged. "One bad guy at a time. Let's find out who Four Eyes is first, and then we'll worry about what burr's up the Russians' butts."

She felt Taylor's silent chuckle. "Front door or back?" he murmured.

"Front," she breathed. They stood up and she brushed herself off as best she could. She still felt little balls of dirt down the back of her shirt, but there was no help for it. She picked a few stray leaves off Taylor, and the two of them strolled around to the front porch as if they owned the place. He rang the doorbell.

A gray-haired man opened the door cautiously. He lurched in momentary surprise, but composed himself almost instantly. "You must be Xavier's friends," the man said smoothly. "Come in, come in."

Amanda frowned mentally. He hadn't expected them to show up on his porch. Why not? He was the one who set up the meeting…. *He'd sold them out.* This guy was the reason Russian agents had just jumped them.

"Why, thank you," she said graciously and glided inside. She didn't look at Taylor, but she felt when the same conclusion hit him. He stiffened for one furious millisecond, and then it was gone. Smooth as silk, he followed her inside. God, he was good.

Their host led them into an elegant sitting room, dimly lit by a single small lamp in a far corner. She noted their host took a seat with his back to the light, casting his face in deep shadow. Fine. If he wanted to be all spooky and mysterious it was no skin off her nose. She wasn't leaving here tonight until she knew everything there was to know about Four Eyes. She took a seat beside Taylor on an antique, and highly uncomfortable, couch.

Their host spoke English, but with a melodic Spanish accent. "Thank you for coming here this evening. The matter of which you wish to speak is most delicate."

She refrained from rolling her eyes. Whatever. The guy'd just pronounced himself a rank amateur. They always got carried away in the drama of the moment. She replied dryly, "Thank you for seeing us on such short notice. It was very kind of you."

"So tell me," the man said lightly, "how is it you managed to penetrate the impenetrable security of Viktor Maldonado?"

She had no intention of giving away any trade secrets to this jerk. She replied with a polite smile, "And why is it you were so hot and bothered to see him dead?"

Their host leaned back in his chair, displeased. At least he caught the hint. She wouldn't reveal her secrets, and he wouldn't reveal his.

"Did you see the evening news tonight?" she asked into the deepening silence.

The man's frown eased. "Yes. There was a bit about one of the richest men in Mexico being hospitalized. Apparently doctors are puzzled over why he's so ill. He's been flown to the United States for treatment."

Amanda shrugged. "There is no cure for his condition. He will be gravely ill until he dies. He is no longer a viable business entity of any kind."

"I wanted him dead."

"You needed him out of your way for business purposes, and this way you don't have blood on your hands. Besides, this way he'll suffer—a lot—before he dies."

Fierce satisfaction gleamed in their host's black gaze.

She leaned forward. "I believe you have some information for us."

The man stood up and moved to a desk across the room. He pulled a key ring out of his pocket and unlocked a deep desk drawer. He reached inside to spin the lock on a small safe, and pulled a manila envelope out of it. He handed it to Amanda as he walked past her and sat down once more.

She opened it and pulled out a sheaf of handwritten notes. On top was a faxed copy of the photograph she'd given Xavier. She translated the Spanish aloud for Taylor. "His name is Alexii Brodin. He comes from a city called…Udarsky in Kyrgyzstan, goes by the nickname Kirgy. Age forty-five, rap sheet a mile long all over Eastern Europe. Racketeering, smuggling, drug running, weapons trading, theft, bribery, murder, the works." She frowned as she read on. "He's attached to the Russian Mafia."

Taylor interrupted. "The Mafia? As in mostly ex-KGB, now controls Russia like Al Capone did Chicago? That Mafia?"

"The very same," their host replied. "Of that there is no doubt."

She flipped to the last page. "It says here he's getting protection from someone big, because he was able to move freely through the United States recently, *after* he was identified by the FBI." She looked up at their host. "Is the Russian Mafia that connected inside the FBI?"

The man's gaze was sharp. "I highly doubt it. I think your friend owns someone high up elsewhere in your government."

She glanced down at the notes. "It says here he was last seen in Mexico. Do you know where he is now?"

Their host leaned back in his seat. She didn't like the look on his face. The arrogant prick was going to try to extort something else from them beyond the Maldonado job.

Sure enough, the guy steepled his fingers and said slowly, "I might."

She surged up off the couch and across the room before the guy could blink. She jumped on him, planting a knee in his groin and grabbing his throat, pinching off the veins on either side of his trachea. She shoved her face within inches of his. "Here's the way the rest of this conversation's going to go. You're going to tell me exactly what I want to know, and I'll let you live. One wrong answer and you die. Got it?"

The guy's panicked gaze met hers, and he nodded as much as he was able to with her hand jammed up under his chin.

"Where is Brodin now?"

"I don't know," the guy croaked.

She tightened her fingers, cutting off the guy's air. His eyes were getting bloodshot.

"But I know where he's going to be," the man choked out frantically.

Amanda eased off slightly on the pressure. "Keep talking."

"He's flying into Caracas within a few days to do a business deal."

"What sort of deal?" she demanded.

"I don't know. But it's huge. Drawing in a lot of big players."

"When?"

"I don't know." The guy didn't wait for her to choke him again before he rushed on. "But I can give you advance notice of when he's due in. Maybe six hours."

"Make it twelve," she snarled, "and I might let you live."

"Okay, okay. Twelve hours," the guy whined.

She gave him the phone number of her answering service and made him repeat it back to her until she was sure he'd remember it, even in his terrified state. Then she said, "Next question. Why did you sell us out to the Russian government? Why not tell Brodin?"

The guy stared in dismay. "I didn't—"

She cut off the rest of the air he'd have used to finish that lie. "I don't care if you want to take over Brodin's business, or sleep with his wife, or just screw him over. But if you so much as breathe a word to him about what you've told us, or you ever try to double-cross me again in any way, I'll tell Brodin myself that you ratted him out."

A spreading, warm wetness at her knee told her he got the point just fine. Man, this Brodin character really had this guy scared. Truth be told, Brodin had her a little spooked. If only she knew why he was so determined to kill her—him and the Russian government. She stood up and saw Taylor standing behind her with his pistol drawn.

"Please," the guy babbled, "if you try to kill Brodin, do not fail. Otherwise, he will know he's got a leak, and he'll come after me and my family. I implore you. Don't miss."

She answered coolly, "I never miss." She held out a hand. "Give me your car keys."

The guy fished in his pocket for the key ring he'd used earlier. The keys rattled musically as he passed them to her with a trembling hand. She said lightly, "Don't bother reporting it stolen. I'll have it returned to you when we're through with it."

She tied the guy to the chair with his necktie, then scooped up the envelope and the notes on Brodin. Taylor fell in beside her and they made their way quickly to the back of the house, being careful to touch nothing that would pick up a fingerprint. They found the garage through a mudroom attached to the kitchen. Taylor slid behind the wheel of the late-model Mercedes while Amanda activated an automatic garage door opener on the driver's visor. The big door rattled up. Taylor backed out and turned around, pointing the car down the driveway. The front gate opened automatically as they approached it. They rolled out into the street and away into the darkness. They burned almost a half tank's worth of gas before they were dead certain they hadn't been followed from the guy's house. It was well after midnight when they finally drew near their hotel.

"Let's ditch the car here," she announced. "We can walk the rest of the way back."

Taylor nodded and turned into a narrow side street. It was dark and seedy. They climbed out of the car, and a gang of potentially unpleasant young men closed off the entrance of the alley and began to stroll toward them. She cursed under her breath.

Taylor grinned down at her. "Watch this." He picked up his pace and strode right at the gang. The thugs were a bit taken aback, but closed ranks quickly. Crud. The last thing she needed right now was a gang rumble. Too many other thoughts were racing around in her mind demanding consideration. "Anyone speak English?" Taylor asked casually.

"Yeah," one of the toughs spoke up.

"Here. Catch." Taylor tossed him the car keys. "Go have fun."

The guy looked down at the keys and then up at the gleaming black Mercedes behind them. "Are you kidding?" he squeaked. Amanda grinned as the tough-guy mask fell away and revealed a teenage kid in the middle of a dream come true.

Taylor laughed. "Nope. It's hotter than a house fire, but it's all yours."

As the gang caught the gist of what he'd done, disbelieving smiles broke out. They parted ranks to let her and Taylor pass through. There was a brief whispered exchange, and the one who spoke English put a hand on her arm. She tensed to fight. "Hey, lady. Some suits was asking around if anyone had seen a man and a woman looking like you. They was showing pictures. One of my boys says you was in the picture."

"Is that so?" she replied. "What did these guys look like? Were they Russian?"

A kid spoke up in Spanish. "Nah. Not Russian. They stank of U.S.A. all the way."

"DEA?" she asked. They were by far the most common U.S. law enforcement presence in this neck of the woods.

"If they were, they ain't the regulars," one of the other boys retorted.

She nodded slowly. "Thanks for the heads-up." She murmured to Taylor, "They say some Americans were flashing around pictures of us a while ago."

They walked back toward their hotel, alert for anyone following them. She murmured, "Let's go back to that café across from the hotel and see who's hanging around."

"Good idea," Taylor replied. "Besides, I'm hungry."

She laughed. "How can you think of food at a time like this?"

He laughed back at her. "How can you not? With all that running around and threatening people we did tonight, I've really worked up an appetite."

It took them only minutes to pick out the Americans watching the hotel. The pair sat at a bar just inside the hotel lobby. Big plate-glass windows opened out onto the street from the cocktail club so the guys could watch outside, too. As a stakeout spot went it wasn't bad. The men were decent at what they did, but they just didn't blend into the local scenery.

"FBI, do you suppose?" she asked Taylor.

He studied the pair. "I don't think so. I did a lot of work with FBI agents when I was counseling convicts, and those two don't seem...blue-collar enough. FBI types work hard and get their hands dirty. Those two over there look like they'd rather be sitting in an air-conditioned room pecking at a computer."

She agreed with his assessment. The Americans looked faintly uncomfortable in the bar, nursing drinks long gone warm and watery. She frowned. "Do you remember Marina Subova's itinerary? I thought she was in Europe right now, not Venezuela."

Taylor nodded. "She's in Germany until tomorrow, then Switzerland for a week."

"Then what's Brodin doing here? Does that shoot down

your theory of him getting delivery messages for diamonds from her music?"

Taylor stared at her thoughtfully. "I still think I was right about that. However, Marina's manager threatened her with tax-evasion charges if she didn't play the music. That would mean the Russian government was using Brodin, not the Russian Mafia. Was our contact tonight wrong about Brodin's employer?"

Amanda shook her head sharply in the negative. "I was looking the guy in the eye and he was scared to death. He told the truth. Brodin's Mafia."

"So the Russian government was making convenient use of a Mob thug for some purpose," Taylor stated.

"But what? Surely Mother Russia doesn't need shipments of small arms and explosives. It's got warehouses full of that kind of stuff."

Taylor shrugged. "Are they supplying terrorists, or someone they don't want Russian equipment to show up in the hands of?"

"Russian military gear is so widely available on the black market already, a little more wouldn't be remotely noticeable. They've got to be using Brodin for something else."

"Something attached to diamonds?" Taylor asked.

She nodded slowly. "It's the only element in this whole puzzle that's consistent. Starting with Devereaux's involvement in this case, to gemstone diamonds showing up around Marina Subova, to the arms trades by Brodin."

Taylor leaned forward abruptly. "No offense, but why in hell did Devereaux put you on this case to begin with? You were seriously overdue to stand down. Why did you, in your mental and emotional state, get sent after a handful of diamonds? Sure, the stones were big, but why would Devereaux risk burning you out for good over a few lousy diamonds?"

"I wasn't in *that* bad of shape, was I?"

He looked her in the eye. "Worse. You're doing worlds better now, mind you, but I've never seen anyone that close to a crack-up who didn't end up coming apart completely."

She reached across the table to squeeze his hand briefly. There was no need for words. She was sitting here today because of his care and concern.

Taylor asked, "When you got your initial briefing on this case from Harry Trumpman, what did he say? Were you only supposed to track down the gemstones popping up around Marina?"

Holy cow. "No," she breathed. "That didn't come until later. I was told Devereaux got wind of some big illegal diamond deal going down. His information was that whomever was going to move the stones was attached to Marina Subova's entourage."

Taylor nodded. "Maybe we haven't been so far off track all along. Four Eyes—Brodin—trails along behind Marina, waiting to do some big diamond deal. In the meantime, he does a few side deals for the Russian Mafia while he waits for the right signal from the Russian government."

"Except now he's gone off her itinerary and is coming to Caracas," she said quietly.

Which meant it was time for the big deal to go down. They stared at each other in silence for several moments.

"Now what?" Taylor asked.

"I've got my father's journal in my purse. Everything else we left in the hotel is replaceable. I say let's blow this joint and hole up somewhere else until Joe Pees-his-pants calls us with Brodin's arrival time."

Taylor nodded crisply. They left the café and retraced their steps to the alley. They found their friendly, local gang still crawling all over the plush car. Amanda hastened to reassure the boys as hackles went up at the sight of her and Taylor. "Gentlemen," she said pleasantly, "you were so helpful before, I wondered if we might prevail upon you to transact a bit of business."

The youths were more than happy to hook her up with the local black market electronics suppliers, weapons dealers and even private lodgings when she peeled a fistful of bolivars off her wad of cash. She suspected she and Taylor were staying in the home of one of the kids' parents, but she didn't care. If the poverty of their bare room and lumpy mattress on the floor was any indication, the amount they were paying their hostess, a middle-aged woman, was a good year's income for her. It was money well spent. The lady fed them three square meals a day, brought them bottled water to drink and left them alone.

To pass the time while they waited for the call, Taylor pored over her father's journal. On the third evening, he closed the tattered book and rubbed his eyes.

"Any revelations?" she asked.

"He stole something. I've heard similar language from convicts time and time again when they've nabbed something and are dying to tell someone about it."

She frowned. "What do you think he nicked?"

"He keeps referring to turquoise in here, but I get the impression he's talking about a person, not the gemstone. Whatever it was, he believed it was tremendously valuable."

"At the end, he ranted a lot about how rich we were and I just didn't know it. I thought he was talking about having a roof over our heads and a family. That sort of stuff."

"What do you know about Udarsky?" he asked. That comes up a couple times in conjunction with whatever he stole."

She nodded. "We know Brodin's from there, and my father no doubt was familiar with it. Clearly there's a connection, but I just don't see the link."

Taylor pulled out his cell phone with its wireless Internet connection. "Let me run it through the Internet and see what I get." He fiddled with his phone and looked up at her, frowning. "It's an old Russian army town in the northwestern mountains of Kyrgyzstan."

"Do you suppose my father was flashing back to a place he spent time as a kid?"

Taylor sighed. "Who knows? Your father really was loopy by the end."

She laughed, but broke off when her cell phone rang. It was

almost midnight and nobody had this number except her answering service. She picked it up and put it to her ear.

A voice-mail message of a male voice played, recognizable as that of Joe Pees-his-pants. It said tersely, "Caracas International Airport tomorrow—10:45 a.m., private charter parking at the Avinco hangar." The phone clicked off.

Well, either the guy had kept his word, or they'd just been set up like lambs for the slaughter. And there was only one way to find out.

Chapter 15

Harry Trumpman's telephone buzzed, and he reached across his desk to pick it up. The East Coast tones of his CIA contact's voice made him sit up straight in his chair. "Harry. How are you? I know you're busy, so I won't take much of your time. I'm just checking in to see what Miss McClintock and Mr. Roberts have been up to recently."

Bull. But he played along to see where the guy was going. "At Devereaux's request, they put a small-time drug dealer in Mexico out of business. And for the record, they didn't kill the guy. They just suggested that he retire. Why do you ask?"

"And they stopped pursuing the other case?"

Harry snapped, "If you mean did they lay off your mole, yeah, they did."

"Any idea what they're doing in Venezuela at the moment?"

Venezuela? Jeez. The place was a political hornet's nest. No place for an American and a Brit these days. "Vacation?" he replied lightly.

The CIA man sighed. "What's the status of your agents? Are they currently active or not?"

"Why do you want to know?" Harry asked stubbornly. He wasn't fingering Amanda and Taylor for this jackass if he could help it.

Another long-suffering sigh. "My people in Caracas may have spotted your agents. I happen to have another operation that we've been setting up for months coming to a head down there. I can't have your people jeopardize it in any way."

Harry leaned back, thinking hard. There was no doubt in his mind that Amanda and Taylor were still working the diamond case. What were the odds that the CIA would have yet another totally unrelated operation running that Amanda and Taylor had just happened to stumble across? Whatever was going on with the CIA in Caracas was tied to the diamond smuggling for damn sure.

Harry sighed himself. "Look. My agents know to leave well enough alone. I'm sure it's purely a coincidence that they've bumped into some of your people. It's a nice time of year in that part of the world, and Amanda and Taylor are probably there to enjoy the tropical weather."

A harrumph disguised as a cough. "Just a heads-up, old friend. If your people get in the way this time, my agents are going to take them down."

Harry said casually, "If my team checks in, I'll be sure to pass the word to steer clear."

"You do that."

Harry hung up the phone. Asshole. He muttered under his breath, "Go get 'em, Amanda."

Max handed a tissue to the young nurse sitting beside him. She wasn't half-bad looking, even with red, puffy eyes. Another victim of his boss's vicious mood. Ever since Biryayev had been shot two days ago, he'd been a raging lunatic. Something had snapped inside old Nikko's noggin. The guy'd been radically pissed off when the gassing at the monastery hadn't bagged the McClintock girl, but now his rage was in another class altogether. To be standing in front of his quarry and not only fail to catch her, but also get shot in the process seemed to have broken Nikko.

Max would be amused at the way the old guy's nemesis kept slipping through the net, except it was no laughing matter that Biryayev was well on the way to losing his marbles. Too bad the McClintock girl's bullet had only grazed the bone and passed on through Biryayev's leg. The guy could use a couple months cooling his jets in a hospital to get his head back together.

A bellow from inside Biryayev's room, and yet another nurse came bolting out. Max shook his head. If only Nikko knew how many women he was sending his junior partner's way to comfort, he was sure the old guy would clam up and behave. Too bad Biryayev was only going to be in here for one more day. Meanwhile, Max pulled out another tissue and patted the next nurse's shoulder. Best to get while the getting was good.

Amanda had Taylor park the van in front of the international terminal in the wee hours of the morning. Both of them needed to get into place before the various security teams that would no doubt be observing and meeting today's flight arrived. The two of them had a long, boring wait ahead of them, but better that than trying to sneak past layer upon layer of thugs and security personnel just before Brodin's plane arrived.

The night was thick and dark, but lights on high poles illuminated Caracas International Airport in pink halogen light. She and Taylor hiked past the long domestic terminal, skirted the edge of a broad fenced expanse of concrete and headed for the ramp that stretched east toward the ocean, where private hangars serviced corporate jets.

One of Amanda's credit cards under a fake name was duly charged and the keys to a Learjet 60 handed over to her along with a pair of laminated ramp passes. It had cost a pretty penny to get the ramp manager to open up at this time of night, not to mention making sure the plane was parked at the far western end of the ramp. But the unimpeded view of the entire Avinco ramp next door was well worth it.

Amanda unlocked the sleek jet, lifting the upper passenger door as the lower door folded down into steps. The salt smell of the nearby ocean blew in damp and cold tonight, and she could feel her hair going frizzy in the humidity. Taylor, wearing a pair of workman's overalls, slipped into the plane and squatted in the low-ceilinged aisle. He took the satchel out of Amanda's hands and flashed a brief, intimate smile at her. "Is it bad luck to wish you luck?"

She smiled warmly at him. "I don't think so."

"Good luck, then."

"You, too. Give me a half hour to get back to the terminal and in position, and then we'll do a radio check. Say, on the hour." She leaned forward and gave him a quick kiss. "Thanks for everything."

He caught the back of her neck, holding her close for a deep, drugging kiss. "My pleasure," he replied against her lips.

Oh, Lord, she could crawl inside his jumpsuit right now and spend a week or so alone with him in there. She sighed in regret. The mission, dammit. She backed out of the jet reluctantly.

Taylor glanced at his watch, all business. "I'll talk to you on the hour."

She latched the door, sealing him in. A voluminous cotton skirt favored by natives tangled between her legs as a chilly breeze caught it and whipped it around her. She hiked briskly back to the domestic terminal and went inside the long building. A sleepy security guard passed her through the metal detectors and did a cursory X ray of her shoulder bag. He apparently wasn't alarmed by her cover story that this was the only time she could get a ride to the airport. She stepped into the main terminal. It was deserted at this hour except for a janitor at the far end mopping the floor. She walked to the first bathroom she encountered, and after a brief look around, stepped into a stall.

Amanda took her time applying a skin-darkening foundation, brown contact lenses and makeup to accentuate her big, now dark eyes. Next, she tucked her chestnut hair into a sleek black wig with a small bun at the base of her neck. Then she took the radio out of her roomy canvas purse. She inserted a wireless earpiece into her left ear and clipped the radio receiver unit that went with it to the waistband of her skirt. She turned it on. Her ear filled with loud static, and she hastily adjusted the squelch, silencing the noise. There. Better. Next, she threaded a tiny microphone under the collar of her blouse and pulled its hair-thin wire down the front of her shirt to the radio. She blew out a couple puffs of air and the light sound carried clearly in her ear. She adjusted the volume slightly, then sat down on the edge of the toilet to wait. It wasn't a glorious place to wait, but it wasn't likely to be the first place a bunch of men came looking.

Promptly on the hour, Taylor's voice sounded in her ear. "Radio check. How do you copy?"

"Loud and clear. How me?" she replied.

"Loud and clear also. Any unusual activity in the terminal?"

"No. We got in before Brodin's people, or the police, or the Russians, or whoever else is after us set up a security perimeter. Have you checked the jet's emergency escape hatch?"

"Piece of cake," he replied confidently. "I've already practiced with it a couple times. I can have it unlatched and out of the way in five seconds."

"Good. Get comfortable and sit tight. We're doing fine."

"Thank you, Mother Hen McClintock."

"Hah! You didn't call me that last night! I'll call you back in an hour or when someone interesting arrives, whichever happens first."

"Yes, dear."

She scowled. He just loved to yank her chain. "Go take a nap," she grumbled.

She could hear the grin in his voice. "Where? It's like sitting in a damned drainpipe in here. There's no legroom."

"I'll trade you," she retorted. "I'm perched on the edge of a toilet, praying I don't doze off and fall in." He chuckled at that one. How she loved the sound of his laughter. "Talk to you in an hour," she retorted laughingly.

And so the waiting began. A few minutes before 6:00 a.m., she was startled to full alert when she heard the bathroom door swing open. She had just enough time to grab the top of the wall behind her stall's door, lift her legs up and plaster herself as flat as possible before the intruder walked down the row of stalls, checking for occupants. The door of her stall stood partially open, its toilet innocently unoccupied, while she clung to the wall behind it by her fingertips. She saw a man's shoes walk past. Thankfully, he strode out of the rest room seconds later and she dropped to the floor.

She whispered into her radio, "A man just walked through the women's rest room and checked it out. He smelled Russian."

"Roger," Taylor replied. A pause. "And how exactly does a Russian smell?"

"Like bad tobacco, sweat and borscht," she retorted.

Two hours later, she radioed again. "I'm going mobile, now. I'll call back when I can. Could be a while."

Taylor's voice caressed her ear. "Be safe, baby. I don't like the idea of you roaming around by yourself with Russians crawling all over the place."

She smiled, warmed by his concern. "It's not like I've never done this before. I worked alone for ten years before you came along."

He grumbled under his breath, "Ten years too long."

Still smiling, she took off the radio and stowed it in the canvas bag. She took out the pieces of the ceramic pistol she'd acquired for this job and assembled them into a usable weapon. She stood up carefully on the toilet seat and removed the ventilator grille from high on the wall behind her. She stuffed the bag into the metal shaft and replaced the grille, securing it loosely with only the top screws so it would swing open easily. Time to leave her hideout and scope the place out a bit. She didn't need to get caught with a weapon if someone got suspicious and checked her out more closely. The morning's travelers had arrived and were moving toward the first flights of the day.

As she'd expected, a man followed her when she walked to the lone coffee shop that was open this early. The guy contrived to bump into her, and she felt his hands briefly on her rib cage. She smiled to herself. He apologized and wandered off while she made a mental note of his face. Amanda found a seat out of the main traffic flow and hunkered down in it as if she planned to be there for a while. She couldn't draw any attention to herself for the next hour.

Amanda noticed a trickle of men who looked suspiciously like American intelligence agents start arriving at the airport. In fact, she recognized one as a CIA field agent she'd worked with briefly a couple years back. Now, what in the world were *they* doing at this party? There was no chance the CIA guy had gone civilian with that regulation haircut and suit he wore. The Americans scattered inside the terminal. And then another arrival captured her attention. What had to be a full-blown Russian security team practically marched through the double doors in the center of the terminal. As they spread out, she caught a glimpse of a blond guy carrying a green knapsack peeling away from the clump of men. He looked like a typical college student. *Her tail from LaGuardia.* Well, wasn't the gang all here today? The Russians fanned out across the cavernous space, as well.

Had she not been so intent on not being discovered herself, it might have been entertaining to watch the two groups play cat and mouse with each other over the next hour. But as it was, she kept her head down and bided her time, watching a big wall clock crawl slowly toward ten o'clock. On the hour, she stood up and stretched, looking around as if she was searching for something. Spotting it, she headed directly for the bathroom she'd hidden in earlier. Retrieving her bag, she quickly inserted her earpiece and rewired the microphone. She turned it on. "Taylor, it's me."

"Well, I hope nobody else is using this frequency," he quipped.

"Very funny. The Russians and the Americans are here in force. Brodin should arrive soon, and I'm going out to position myself. Let me know as soon as you spot his plane and I'll do my best to get eyes on target. Let's see who this bastard's here to do his big deal with." Given the cast of players at the airport right now, it could be practically anyone. There was no doubt something huge was about to go down.

Taylor replied, deadly serious, "You got it." Then he added lightly, "See ya later, alligator."

"Do I have to do that ridiculous crocodile response?" she mumbled.

He chuckled, but tension vibrated in his voice. "Be safe."

Amanda tucked the pistol in the cloth thigh holster she'd sewn for it a couple days ago. She put her hand into the skirt's pocket and through the slit she'd cut in it. Her hand wrapped easily around the butt of the pistol, which rested high on her thigh. She tilted the gun, still in its holster, leveling it at an imaginary target. If she had to use the thing, she'd take the shot from the hip, through the skirt. That way she'd never show the weapon in the open. She left the rest room, making her way to the ramp side of the terminal, to the big plate-glass windows that overlooked the airport's bustling activity. She put on a cheap pair of sunglasses she'd bought from a street vendor a few days ago, both to shield her from the sun's glare and to cover her face.

She was tempted to just shoot Brodin when he stepped off his jet. Her sense of kill or be killed was running high over this guy. He kept showing up every time someone nearly waxed them. And they couldn't keep running forever from whoever was trying to kill them. Except she wasn't a killer. And neither was Taylor.

At 10:42, according to the terminal clock, a sleek Gulfstream Six landed, rolling from west to east on the main runway. "Look sharp," she murmured.

"I see it," Taylor replied.

She lost sight of the plane on its landing roll out, and counted the tense seconds until it taxied into view again. She concentrated on breathing evenly and slowly as the jet made its way toward the Avinco ramp. And then it kept on going! Right past the hangar.

"Shit!" Taylor exclaimed.

"Stay with it," she muttered.

"Could be the wrong jet," Taylor said in her ear.

It was the right jet. She could feel it. She watched it taxi toward the domestic terminal out of the corner of her eye. She took off walking down the terminal as the plane paralleled the building. Thank God she and Taylor had split up to cover different sections of the airport just in case. The plane finally stopped about halfway down the terminal, a good hundred feet away from the building. A marshaler threw a pair of wooden chocks around the nose gear.

She took stock. This could still work. Brodin would still have to come inside to meet his client, or the client would have to go out to the plane to meet him. Either way, she'd get a look at whom the Russian mobster was here to deal with. The Gulfstream's left side and main exit faced roughly in Taylor's direction. With his telescopic rifle sight, he'd be able to see the comings and goings, too. If he had to take a shot he was still within his effective range. Although his shooting angle had just gotten worlds trickier, with the control tower partially blocking his line of sight.

"Can you see the jet's door?" she asked under her breath.

"I can see the bottom half of the steps, but not the top of the hatch. You're gonna have to cover the doorway," he bit out.

"Roger," she breathed.

The commuter jet beside the Gulfstream opened its doors,

and a stream of passengers came pouring out of it. Two dozen milling men, women and children collecting bags and making their way sloppily toward the terminal. The Gulfstream's stairs started down. She rested her finger softly on the trigger of her gun. The bulk of the commuters were moving toward the terminal now. The ramp cleared slightly. *There he was.* Poised on the top step of the Gulfstream behind a bulky bodyguard was Brodin, in his distinctive wire spectacles.

"It's our guy," she murmured without moving her lips. C'mon. Move, you big lug. Lemme see your boss, she mentally exhorted the guard. She glanced up quickly to gauge Taylor's line of sight. He wouldn't be able to see Brodin yet. And then a movement out of the corner of her eye sent subliminal alarm bells ringing in her head. She turned her head slightly and looked at the reflection in her sunglasses. A man walking behind her with a limp and a cane. *Biryayev.* He didn't seem to be looking at her. Good Lord willing, he hadn't made her. But the way he'd stopped a moment ago, it could've been a jolt of recognition that caught her attention in the first place.

Should she abort the surveillance? But when would they ever get another shot like this at finding out what the elusive Brodin was up to? Just a few more seconds, and she'd know who the bastard was climbing into bed with. No way would their terrified contact finger the bastard a second time. She slid to her right, behind a large family exchanging enthusiastic greetings with one another.

Taylor spoke into her ear. "I've got Brodin in sight. Now let's see who comes to him."

Biryayev walked on past, leaning heavily on his cane.

She moved to the end of a broad observation deck that jutted about thirty feet out into the ramp. Although a dozen of the commuter passengers still milled around on the ramp collecting luggage and kids, she had a relatively clear view of Brodin. A couple of his guards peeled away to supervise luggage. Amanda gripped her pistol more tightly. She maneuvered the last few steps to the window past the family, who were still busy hugging and chattering. Brodin was in plain sight now. *A sharp movement out of the corner of her eye.* Biryayev was pivoting around, raising the cane toward her. Like a weapon! One of the bodyguards outside jumped and opened his mouth as if to shout something. In slow motion, she dived for cover, flinging herself toward a row of chairs.

The huge plate-glass window beside her shattered as a shot rang out. It hung suspended for an instant, then crashed to the ground outside with a tremendous explosion of glass and sound. Men all over the tarmac pulled out guns as she rolled behind a heavy trash can. A barrage of answering shots rained around her. People screamed and dived to the floor while glass and lead flew. Shots came from every direction now, some coming from in front of her, others flying over her shoulder from behind. She couldn't tell who was shooting at whom. Muzzles flashed from a dozen positions within the terminal, and at least that many more returned fire outside.

Biryayev advanced in her direction, a pistol in his hand now, close enough so she could see his face contorted in a rictus of rage. She looked around frantically. Nowhere was out of the line of fire as men shot wildly, everywhere. Police came sprinting down the terminal, blowing piercing whistles and adding to the chaos. Apparently, the street exits had been locked, because a swell of screaming passengers came surging back in her direction like a wave rebounding off a sea wall.

A shot zinged past her, clipping her left shoulder. It burned like a skinned knee. She glanced down quickly. Just a graze. Quickly, she calculated the direction it must have come from. Her instinct was to drop and fire back. Except there were civilians all over the place. She couldn't take the chance of hitting them. She *had* to choose the more difficult option of not shooting back. To get the hell out of here. Fleeing went against everything she'd ever learned. But she *could not* in good conscience lift a weapon among all these innocent people.

"What the hell's going on over there?" Taylor shouted in her ear.

She jumped up and took four leaping strides toward the window. She dived through the jagged opening, falling and rolling in one movement. She slammed to the concrete ten feet below. God, that hurt her shot shoulder. Maybe more than a graze, after all. Brodin's men trained weapons on her, but apparently saw only a local woman escaping and yanked their aims away. She dived toward an airplane tug, crouching behind the piece of heavy machinery. Someone fired out the terminal window toward the ramp. Probably Biryayev. The guy looked absolutely crazed.

Brodin's bodyguards lay on top of their charge while the rest of his people returned fire wildly. Good Lord. What a mess! More men fired toward Brodin's position out several windows. People screamed and ran in every direction, while the staccato sounds of gunfire rat-a-tatted and bullets whizzed through the air. She ducked behind the tug's big engine once more.

More gunfire from inside. Jeez, it was a free-for-all! Brodin's shooters turned away from the windows. Amanda took advantage of the momentary lull in the rain of lead and the utter chaos to make her crouching way around the far side of the tug. She saw Brodin try to stand up only a few yards from her, but one of his men yanked him roughly back down to the ground.

Brodin dropped something. A cloth pouch. A half-dozen shiny, flat, round objects fell out of the bag, and one of them rolled practically to her feet. She snatched it up and stuffed it in her left pocket. She backed around the corner as Brodin scrambled on his hands and knees, chasing after the rolling wafers. His men bodily tackled him, jerking him back under cover. She lost sight of him.

Slowly, the gunfire ceased. A few more sporadic bursts of fire, and then an eerie silence fell, broken by the screams and moans of the victims. At least a dozen people were hit, most writhing in pain, but a few lay motionless where they'd dropped.

Dull with shock, she made her way to the window she'd leaped out of. She climbed up on a stack of cargo to lever herself inside. Most of the family she'd been standing behind when the firefight broke out was down. Numb, she climbed through the window. She let go of her pistol. Unfired, it hung slackly against her leg.

Miraculously, she was unscathed except for the minor wound to her shoulder. She watched as Brodin's remaining security hustled him onto the Gulfstream, half carrying, half dragging him. The plane taxied away, gathering speed, as someone struggled to close its door.

A motion out of the corner of her eye caused Amanda to turn and stare.

A bloody man lay on the ground a few yards away from her. He rolled over and raised his arm to point a pistol at her. She sidestepped instinctively, and the arm fell back down to the ground. She rushed over to kneel beside him, looking carefully at the face. Dead eyes stared back at her. Her former CIA collaborator. She looked up. There. And there. Two more downed American faces. She widened her search. There. Over there, too. *Oh, Lord, the carnage.* Her stomach revolted. She tried to set aside her reaction. Reached for a state of emotionless calm. And failed. Utterly. Damn Taylor and his awakening of her conscience. Think, Amanda! Keep your brain engaged or you'll die out here!

The faces lay in a wide circle around—what? What had been at the center of their surveillance bull's-eye? It couldn't have been Brodin. They weren't arranged correctly to target him outside on the ramp. She drew a mental circle from body to body. The center of it had been…

It couldn't be. She staggered to her feet in disbelief. She began to back toward the exit slowly, the macabre scene burning into her memory like a hot coal. The center of the bull's-eye was where she'd been standing when the shooting broke out.

Had all this erupted because of *her?* Biryayev had fired in

her direction. It could've been at her or at Brodin, given where
she'd been standing. Had he recognized her? Her disguise had
only changed her coloring, not her basic facial features. If
somebody knew her well enough, they could've spotted her.
And he did lurch in recognition a few seconds before he fired.
Lord knew, Biryayev had certainly tried to kill her on that quiet
residential street nearly a week ago.

So Biryayev shot at her. Brodin's people had panicked and
fired back, thinking their man was the target. Then the Russians
fired on everyone, and the Americans joined in. Clearly the CIA
had a green light to take her out, or else that downed agent
wouldn't have just raised his gun at her as his last living act.
But why, for God's sake? Why did the CIA want her dead?

Her gaze swept around the terminal once more. Twenty,
maybe twenty-five victims in here in addition to the thirty or
so outside. Fifty-plus innocent men, women, and children, oh
God. She'd been the catalyst that started this whole massacre.

A policeman brushed past her, snapping at her to get out of
the way. Looking at the scene around her, Amanda's stomach
filled with bile and she headed for the front of the terminal. Police and ambulance personnel raced past, jostling her.

A hand on her arm detained her just as she reached the
doors. She whipped around violently, hands flying up to protect herself. It was a woman speaking rapidly in Spanish.
Amanda stopped her hands abruptly, halting the killing blow
only inches away from the woman's larynx. Amanda stared
blankly until the Spanish phrases untangled themselves and
comprehension came. The woman was pointing to the patch of
blood staining Amanda's left shoulder and asking if she was all
right. Amanda nodded and moved away from the woman.

She stepped across the street, avoiding the fire trucks and
police cars parked haphazardly in front of the terminal. Stag-
gering in shock, she zigzagged among the cars, moving generally to her right. She tripped over an unseen curb and finally
broke into a stumbling run. Her feet felt heavy and wouldn't

obey her properly. She plucked at the skirt as it twisted around her legs, tangling stickily where someone had bled on it. She wiped her hand on the front of her blouse as she ran, leaving a red blotch against the white cotton.

The sound of a commotion behind her roused her enough to glance over her shoulder. A half-dozen men pouring out of the terminal. With short hair and conservative suits. Americans. She ran faster, heading for the dark shape of their van in the back of the parking lot. Tears began to flow, blurring her vision. She gasped for air in sobbing, irregular breaths. A tall shape loomed beside the van motioning for her to hurry. Taylor. She staggered the last few yards to the powerful motorcycle he'd pulled from the back of the van. He shoved a satchel into her hand and pushed her onto the machine, then climbed on in front of her and jumped savagely on the kick starter. The engine roared to life and he gunned the throttle.

They bumped over a curb and across a strip of grass, bouncing onto an access road. Taylor turned his head and shouted, "How bad are you hit?"

"Not bad!" she shouted back in his ear.

"Then hang on. We're getting the hell out of here before those bastards come after us!"

Chapter 16

Geneva. Perched at the westernmost point of Switzerland at the tip of a territorial peninsula that juts like a finger poking into the ribs of France. The graceful city nestled in the mountains at the westernmost end of the crescent that is Lake Geneva, or Lake Leman, as the French call it.

Amanda stood under the stars and breathed the clean pine scent of the mountains. The frigid air burned her lungs, but it was invigorating. A stiff breeze blew off the lake tonight, reddening her cheeks and the tip of her nose. She huddled deeper into the turned-up collar of her coat. For the first time in days, she felt half alive. After the disaster in Caracas, it was as if a dense fog had enveloped her, muffling sound and sense and reducing events around her to a slow-motion crawl.

"Why Geneva?" she asked Taylor. He looked out over the black lake beside her, stalwart and controlled, completely in command of the situation. The irony was not lost on her. They'd reversed roles, with her the voice of conscience and moderation after the horror of the Caracas massacre, and him focused fiercely on completing the mission and saving her life.

"Marina Subova is here," he said succinctly.

"Ah." Something she should have remembered. Thank God he was operating on all cylinders. She'd be lying dead in a ditch or rotting in a Venezuelan jail were it not for him the past two days. He'd orchestrated their anonymous escape to Switzerland with a smooth precision she could be proud of. They walked another block along the lakeshore in silence. The moon bathed them in silvery, cold light, and distant mountain peaks flanking the lake glittered white. There would be good skiing already at the higher elevations.

"I got the report back from Devereaux on that wafer you picked up," he said quietly.

His words jarred her back to the case at hand. "What is it?"

"Diamond. Just as I suspected. But synthetic."

She frowned. That was significant, somehow. God, she wished her mind would get in gear. "I didn't know diamonds came in shapes like that." The wafer was nearly the size of her palm and roughly a millimeter thick. Polished smooth, it shone with crystalline purity.

"They don't. Somebody grew a diamond crystal in a lab and then ground it to that shape. The Swiss jeweler who examined it was impressed with its exact precision of manufacture."

She fought through more tendrils of fog in her brain and asked, "Why did Brodin have it?"

"The more pertinent question is, what is it for?" They walked a bit farther and then he turned to face her. He answered his own question. "Devereaux says it's a blank computer chip."

That startled her. A few more cobwebs tore away. "A computer chip? Made of diamond?"

"One of the biggest limitations on the speed of computer chips is heat. Silicon can only take so much before its performance degrades. But diamond can stand a great deal more heat."

"Which means," she said slowly, "that a diamond chip is faster than a silicon one?"

"Up to a hundred times faster."

She blinked. Every computer could be a hundred times faster than it currently was? Whoa.

"Diamond computer chips also will revolutionize the nano-chip industry. Medicine with robots the size of red blood cells will be possible."

"And why did Brodin have a pouch full of these diamond computer chips?"

"He was going to deliver them to someone in Caracas," Taylor replied.

She flinched at the mental images that single word conjured. She frowned up at him. "To whom? The American government, the Russian government and the Russian Mob were there."

He shrugged. "Good question."

She turned over the three possibilities. Finally. Her brain felt like it was coming to life. "We know Brodin's got access to synthetic diamonds, and the way he's been throwing around gemstone rocks this past year, I'd say the odds are excellent he's been using synthetic diamonds in all those arms trades he's doing. And we think those arms trades are being set up by the Russian government and signaled to him via Marina's music. My bet's on the Russian government."

"So the Russian Mob was there only to act as Brodin's security, and the Americans were there because they got wind of the deal with him and Russia and wanted to stop it?"

The second part didn't ring true in her gut. "The Russian economy is a free-for-all these days. So why wouldn't the Americans just approach Brodin and/or his supplier and buy some for themselves?" she asked.

Taylor frowned. "Let's ask Marina."

"You think she knows something about the wafers?" Amanda asked in surprise.

"Only one way to find out."

"Nobody else has been with her entourage nonstop for the past eighteen months. Kriskin's gone, Brodin's gone…*she's* the only unbroken thread." Hard to believe her old friend was tangled up in something like this. But then, look at her own life. Lord knew, Marina would have no moral compunction about dabbling in smuggling.

Amanda resumed walking, more briskly this time. Taylor's long strides kept up with hers easily. They retraced their steps along the shore and crossed the Quai du Mont Blanc, which spanned the Rhone River where it joined the lake. Black, forbidding water swirled under the bridge.

This time it was Taylor who broke the silence. "Can you arrange for us to see her?"

"How private do you want our conversation to be?"

"One hundred percent."

"Hmm. That means we'll have to get her away from her bodyguard, and probably out of her room wherever she's staying. I imagine somebody has it bugged. When do you want this meeting?"

"As soon as possible."

"Tomorrow night?"

"That'd be fine. Can you do it?"

"Of course. I'll appeal to her sense of adventure. She always did love to break the rules."

They walked a little while longer before turning away from the waterfront. They headed for their accommodations in a lower-profile section of town. Taylor unlocked the door to their plain but spotless hotel room and ushered her inside. For the first time since they fled Venezuela, she felt like her old self. She had completely unraveled after the massacre. It had been all she could do to keep moving and let Taylor herd her out of the country. An all-nighter on the motorcycle had put them in Cali, Colombia, where they had boarded a flight for Paris on their fake IDs. The train ride to Geneva had been simple enough for Taylor to arrange, even with all the antiterrorism security these days.

While it had not been difficult to sneak across the border into Switzerland, they by no means underestimated the efficiency of the Swiss police. The less the two of them exposed themselves, the better. They stayed inside all the next day, eating a picnic of sausage, cheese, apples and crusty rolls he purchased just around the corner.

In the early afternoon, Amanda placed a phone call to the auditorium where Marina would be performing for two more nights. She introduced herself as a florist with a large flower arrangement to deliver to Miss Subova. Would the theater prefer that it be delivered to the pianist's dressing room, or perhaps to her hotel instead?

She hung up and smiled triumphantly at Taylor. "Thirty-nine Rue St. Berges."

She placed a call to the home. "Hello. May I please speak with Miss Subova?" A pause. "I understand that she wishes to have privacy. I am a very old, very dear friend of hers. Please ask her if she'd like to take a call from Amanda McClintock."

Another pause.

"You bitch! Waking me up from my beauty rest!"

Amanda laughed. "Marina? Is that you? You sound like hell. And it's after noon."

"Don't talk so loud. I'm hungover."

"Hungover! You sound recently raised from the dead. I'm passing through town, and I thought you might slip away from your prison guards for an hour or two of freedom. Maybe tonight? I thought we might check out the local talent. Can I entice you?"

"Done. Where shall we meet?"

Amanda grinned and named a small nightclub she and Taylor had walked past the night before that was perfect for their purposes. Dark, reasonably crowded and next to one of the many small parks dotting Geneva. She hung up the phone.

"Well?" Taylor demanded.

She grinned, feeling more and more like her old self. "I had her as soon as I mentioned slipping her prison guards."

* * *

Max Ebhardt shifted his weight yet again. His rear end was going numb. The Mercedes he was sitting in was comfortable enough, but after six hours it was getting old. God, he hated surveillance. The dull ache in his posterior turned into tingling. How did Biryayev do it? His partner hadn't moved a muscle in over an hour. The man seemed completely oblivious to his surroundings. He ignored food except for what Max shoved under his nose. Hardly slept. Hell, hardly even spoke anymore. The older man had dark circles under his eyes, and his sagging skin held a sickly gray pallor. He hadn't shaved in days, and his clothes were unkempt. Biryayev forgot to bathe more than he remembered to, and Max wrinkled his nose at the results.

There was an unholy glow in Biryayev's eyes that made Max's flesh crawl. Rasputin, the mad priest who'd dominated czars and helped bring down the Russian monarchy, must have had this same obsessed look about him. Max seriously considered the idea that his boss might be going mad.

Biryayev handed the binoculars to him and ripped open yet another pack of cigarettes. Max cringed. The reeking blue haze from the last pack still lingered in the car's confined space. He cracked open his window and shifted his face closer to the opening. He lifted the binoculars and stared at the stage door of the concert hall where Marina Subova was performing. Biryayev had a hunch, so here they sat. Funny how everything had come full circle. They'd started by watching the pianist to pick up the McClintock woman's trail, and here they were, doing it all again.

Marina followed her new bodyguard out of the dressing room. This one was good-looking, but a stolid family man. Too bad. He opened the exit and held it for her. As she stepped outside, Marina noticed a black Mercedes parked across the street. Hadn't it been there last night, too? She frowned. She was getting too damn paranoid. Maybe she ought to see a psychiatrist.

As she stepped out of the car in front of her host's home, she cast a surreptitious look around. No sign of the black Mercedes. She really had to get a grip on herself.

The bodyguard waited outside her bedroom until she was settled down for the night before he went to his own room across the hall. Marina gave him a half hour to fall asleep before she got out of bed. She grabbed a coat and tiptoed out of her room. The taxi she'd ordered while still in her dressing room pulled up outside exactly on time, and dropped her off in front of Chez Madeline. Marina sighed. She should've known Amanda would choose a boring little bistro with no action. With a sigh, she stepped into the dim interior.

A slight figure detached itself from the counter and turned toward her. Marina reached out and gave her old friend a hug. "Good grief, Mashka. Did you have to pick someplace so...dull? I'm out of my cage! Let's go have some fun!"

Amanda laughed. "Okay. Let's get out of here." They stepped outside.

Marina said brightly, "I know a great bar across town where a bunch of ski instructors hang out. You ought to see the bodies on these Swiss guys! They may act dull in public, but they're not so bad in the sack."

Amanda laughed. "I've got a better idea. Let's take a little walk before we go there."

Marina peered closely at her. "What's wrong?"

"Let's walk."

Marina linked her arm through Amanda's as she had when they were girls. "Talk to me."

Amanda led her into the Jardin Anglais, the English Garden, a park on the banks of Lake Geneva. It must be beautiful in the summer. Even dried and brown, it was lovely. The two women walked for some minutes in silence. They neared the lake and passed into a long arched arbor. A shadow detached itself from the dark and glided forward. Marina gave a little shriek.

Amanda squeezed her friend's arm. "It's all right. It's my friend, Taylor."

"Hello, Miss Subova."

"Taylor? It is you?"

"Yes. I'm sorry if I frightened you. I asked Amanda to arrange this meeting. I need to speak with you in private."

Marina glanced uncertainly at Amanda. "I don't steal men from my best friend."

Amanda chuckled. "It's nothing like that. He has a few questions he'd like to ask you. Please don't be afraid to answer him honestly. I trust him completely."

Taylor peered into the dark shadows hiding Amanda's face. Did she really? He was inordinately pleased to hear her say it.

His attention snapped back to Marina as she demanded, "What questions could be so serious that you have to drag me to a secluded park in the middle of the night to speak of it?"

He looked directly into Marina's eyes. "Diamonds."

The Russian woman gasped. She swayed slightly and clutched Amanda's arm before she recovered herself. "What are you talking about?"

"You know perfectly well what I'm talking about."

"No. I know nothing about any diamonds."

Taylor schooled his voice to a gentle tone. "I'm not the police. And I don't work with or for the authorities. I have no intention of turning you in to anyone, Marina. But Amanda's in danger and I need some information if I'm going to help her."

"What kind of information?" Suspicion overlaid the fear in her voice. He wished this place was better lit. He could read her body language better if he could see her clearly. "We know about the diamonds. The big gemstones you've been selling. We also know about the musical messages encoded into your improvisations. Your government is making you play those, aren't they?"

Marina staggered. "How…when…what do you want from me?" she stuttered.

He reached out to take her arm and she backed away from him. He let his arm fall. No need to frighten her further. "I mean you no harm," he reiterated soothingly. "I just need to know where you're getting the diamonds from that you're selling to your patrons."

"Why?" she spit.

"Because whoever's supplying you is trying to kill Amanda."

Marina lurched at that one. And then laughed. Loudly. Like a braying donkey. "That's ridiculous," she guffawed. "He'd never hurt Amanda!"

"Who'd never hurt her?" Taylor pressed. "Tell me!"

She opened her mouth to speak.

"Max, wake up."

Foul breath wafted across Max's face. He turned his head away from the rotten smell and roused himself. "What is it, Comrade Biryayev?" His boss had gotten violently angry at Max the day before for accidentally dropping the Communist title.

"The little piano whore is sneaking out of the house."

Max groaned and sat up behind the wheel of the car. Why couldn't she stay in her room for once? It was after midnight, and Marina Subova was just heading out on the prowl. It was going to be another long night. He waited for the taxi to pull away before starting the Mercedes's powerful engine and steering quietly out of the shadows. "Twenty rubles says she picks up a blond tonight."

Biryayev growled. "She can fuck a Mongolian for all I care. Just don't lose her. The McClintock woman has got to come to the bait soon. I can feel the bitch getting close." Biryayev lifted his nose and sniffed the air like a dog. "I can smell her."

More likely he smells himself. Max drove on in grim silence, staying well behind the taxi. It was late and there wasn't much traffic to camouflage them. He was surprised when Marina got out at a quiet little club. This was certainly a departure from her usual style. He parked halfway down the block. Max was just making himself comfortable when their quarry emerged again from the café. And she wasn't alone. He leaned forward, squinting at her companion.

Biryayev, using the binoculars, hissed, "It's her. Amanda McClintock. She's taken the bait!"

The women crossed the street quickly and headed for the wooded park on the opposite side.

"I knew it! I knew she was here. Let's go, Comrade." Biryayev leaped out the car in barely contained excitement.

Max followed with less enthusiasm. He slid into the plentiful shadows behind his boss and followed Amanda and Marina as they walked rapidly across the lovely gardens. The pair of women ducked down winding paths, circled back twice and stuck to the darkest shadows, but he and Biryayev were better at surveillance than that. The women's clumsy attempts to lose them failed. Of course, if the McClintock girl had been by herself, it could've been more of a challenge. But with an amateur like Subova in tow, there was only so much McClintock could do. The women neared the lake and disappeared into yet another long, covered pathway.

Biryayev stopped and hand signaled that they'd separate and tail the women down each side of the arbor. He signaled that he'd shoot the McClintock woman before they exited the far end and Max should shoot Subova.

Max rolled his eyes and signaled back emphatically in the negative.

Biryayev scowled and repeated the signal to kill.

Max whispered urgently, "We have no permission to kill anyone. We're in Switzerland, for God's sake. It's neutral ground."

"Bullshit!" came an explosive whisper in reply.

"But…"

"Silence. I order you to kill Subova if you get the chance."

Max rose from his crouch without another word. Arguing with Biryayev was useless. The guy was completely unhinged.

He turned away. A strong hand gripped his arm, spinning him around. Biryayev snarled, "Don't forget, Comrade. McClintock's daughter is *mine*."

"Fine already." Jeez.

"Go."

Max ran silently along the wooden arches, encased in dead leaves. He heard the muted sound of voices and halted abruptly. He bent over low from the waist and continued forward carefully. He neared the dense foliage and dropped to his knees. There they were, just ahead. McClintock's boyfriend, Taylor Roberts, had joined the two women. Why this clandestine meeting? It felt like more than a simple escape from Subova's bodyguards to go party.

Max rose to his feet and eased forward once more. He was only a few meters from them now. Another step. And another. He could practically touch the McClintock girl. Had a clear shot at Subova over her shoulder. He raised his pistol. And hesitated. He wasn't a cold-blooded murderer. Did he dare disobey Biryayev's order? Would the sick bastard turn on him?

With a quick flip of his wrist, Max reversed the pistol in his hand, grasping it by the barrel. He brought the butt of his gun down sharply on the back of Amanda's head. And heard the spit of a silenced pistol.

Chapter 17

He was sandwiched in softness and warmth. Pain shot through his skull. Dim light shone behind his eyelids. The sound of quiet breathing. A thud and a muffled groan. This finally was reason enough for Taylor to crack open his eyes painfully. Bare white walls. The sounds had come from his right. He turned his head. And screwed his eyes shut against the hot knife of pain that shot through his left temple. He lifted his hand to his head. A bandage circled it. Carefully, he opened his eyes once more. Amanda sat on the floor, leaning wearily against a wall. She looked almost as bad as he felt.

"Hey." His voice came out a hoarse whisper.

Her eyes opened and she smiled wanly at him. She looked beyond exhausted as she stood up and came over to sit down gently on the side of the bed. "How do you feel?" she murmured.

"Rotten. What happened?"

Amanda hesitated. He knew her too well. She was thinking about what to filter out. "Tell me everything," he demanded.

"How much do you remember?"

Taylor frowned. "I remember…" He paused. "I remember asking Marina where she was getting her diamonds from. She started to answer me and then something hit me in the head."

He remembered the smell of wet grass beneath his cheek. It had been ice-cold against his face. A voice. Well, not a voice exactly, but a sound. Crying. The sound of someone stifling sobs. Amanda. He looked up at her in the dim room. She stared back at him patiently. It was coming back to him now. He'd opened his eyes and seen Marina crumpled on the ground, her ruined throat spouting blood like a fountain. Amanda was kneeling over him, begging him frantically not to die. She'd been wrapping something around his head. He vaguely recollected her hauling him to his feet and him stumbling drunkenly out of the park practically draped over her shoulder.

He said aloud, "Marina's dead, isn't she?"

Amanda nodded.

"Who did it?"

"I don't know."

"Any guesses?" he asked.

"No."

"What hit me?"

"The bullet that killed Marina grazed you in the left temple. There was a lot of blood. You gave me a bit of a fright."

A *bit* of a fright? He remembered stark terror on Amanda's face as she bent over him. "You're not looking so hot yourself, babe."

Amanda grimaced. "I've got a concussion. Somebody clocked me in the back of the head. Didn't want to risk sleeping until you came around. I'll need to be woken up every couple hours. Wouldn't do to slip into a coma."

"What time is it?"

"About 5:00 a.m." she replied.

"Where are we?"

"In a youth hostel. No one will bother us. They're all sleeping off a pot party."

Taylor stared at her in amazement. She was teetering on the edge of a complete mental breakdown, but when the shit hit the fan, she'd found reserves of strength he'd never have guessed she had. She pulled herself together and got him out of the park alive. He'd never met anyone, male or female, as courageous as this slender woman. He slid over to one side of the sagging bed. "Why don't you lie down? You look like you could use the rest."

Amanda didn't argue. She felt like death warmed over. She set her wrist alarm for two hours, stretched out beside Taylor with a grateful sigh and listened to his breathing settle into the even rhythm of sleep. She was too tired, too wired, to sleep. She replayed the details of the moments leading up to the shooting yet again, trying to glean any new detail she'd overlooked. Marina had laughed at the idea of her source killing Amanda. That meant the source was either nonviolent in the extreme...or— good Lord, it was so obvious she'd missed it before—her source knew Amanda! Not only knew her, but liked her. Enough not to kill her. Who around Marina fit that bill? Her mind raced. The *only* person it could be was Marina's father.

What did Anton Subov have to do with all this? He'd been KGB until the Soviet regime collapsed, and then he'd retired. Or had he? Had he jumped ship with so many other KGB officers and helped form the Russian Mafia? It made sense. Marina and Brodin were getting their diamonds from the same source. She was using them to raise cash, and he was using them to buy weapons. Son of a gun.

The train trip to Odessa took nearly two days. She and Taylor both slept almost nonstop, rousing only to eat and take care of their most basic needs. They were filthy, exhausted and only partially healed when they arrived. However, Taylor's Russian held up well enough to find them a room in a once elegant, but now shabby, hotel. A lot like the rest of the city.

Amanda woke up early the next morning. Her headache still

throbbed, although it had subsided to human proportions. Thankfully, the goose egg on the back of her head—probably from a pistol butt—was getting smaller, too. At least she wasn't dead, like Marina…. Amanda took deep, slow breaths until the nausea passed. Even the thought of bloodshed was enough to make her sick.

She forced her thoughts elsewhere. Anton Subov. He was the key to it all. He had to be.

They headed for the Crimean seashore resort where he lived with only a vague idea of where to find him. It turned out to be shockingly easy. They stopped a mailman riding by on his bicycle, and for twenty bucks U.S., he gave them not only the address but detailed directions on how to get there. In a matter of minutes, they stood at the end of a long driveway that wound away into a copse of young birch trees, their spindly white trunks reaching hungrily sunward.

She asked Taylor, "Any suggestions on how to approach this interview, Doctor?"

"Tell him the truth. I doubt anything less will work."

Amanda nodded. And shivered. She looked up to see if the sun had gone behind a cloud, for the air had taken on a sudden chill. But it shone down brightly on her upturned face. It was a long walk down Subov's driveway. Long enough for her to think about her life. She'd been dealt crummy cards in parents, but she'd survived. She knew only one way of living—paranoia and violence. So she'd compromised, finding a niche in the covert-operations community, where her lifestyle was acceptable—channeled and controlled—but acceptable.

She'd managed quite nicely until Taylor had barged into her orderly little world. He'd turned her life upside down with his wide-eyed innocence and moral certitude. He'd forced her to examine her values and finally to face the reality of her life. She was a criminal, playing an endless game of cat and mouse with other criminals. No matter what patina of higher good she'd claimed to serve, the plain fact was that Anton Subov's daughter was dead because of her. She'd led murderers straight to Marina and they'd killed her. If she survived beyond the next half hour, she was going to have to learn to live with that fact. She didn't know how she'd make peace with herself, but she'd find it or go mad trying. Like father, like daughter.

When they reached the front porch, she hung back. This was Taylor's gig. He was the trained psychologist with years of experience extracting information out of uncooperative subjects.

Taylor knocked on the heavy wooden door. A man answered, his back bent and his shoulders sagging. His head was mostly bald, its pink flesh mottled with liver spots above a bright blue gaze, incongruously alive in the weathered face. The impact of those eyes was almost physical. The keen intelligence that shone from them was palpable in its intensity, and gave him an overall sense of vitality that was impressive. "*Dobrii dyen. Menya zovut Taylor Roberts.*"

Subov answered in flawless English, "Good day, Taylor Roberts. What brings you to my humble doorstep?"

He replied quietly, "I've come to convey my condolences at the loss of your daughter."

Subov's eyes were instantly hooded, and Taylor sensed the deceptive relaxation in the man's stance. Perfect, lethal balance underlay the man's exaggeratedly stooped posture. Taylor packed his voice with all the genuine sincerity he could, "Mr. Subov, I mean you no harm. We work for no government, and we carry no weapons. If you would like to search us, that would be fine."

Subov stared hard at him for a long moment, then nodded. "You tell the truth." He looked back and forth between Taylor and Amanda, who still hung back in the shadows. "But neither of you need a weapon. You both can kill with your bare hands."

Taylor blinked at the man's directness and met it with his own. "That is true. But I hope it will not prevent you from speaking with us. I'd wager you, too, are capable of killing bare-handed."

Subov chuckled, a rusty sound. "That is also true, my observant young guest. And who have you brought with you?"

Taylor stepped aside to reveal Amanda fully to Subov. The man frowned for a moment, half recognizing her. And then his face lit up. "Amanda McClintock! My daughter's school chum."

Amanda stepped up to the old man and embraced him in a spontaneous gesture of comfort. Taylor blinked. Since when had she started hugging people in demonstrations of compassion?

Subov returned the hug briefly, patting her awkwardly on the back. "Enough. You'll embarrass me." He turned and led them into the house, Amanda's hand tucked safely under his arm.

Taylor followed the pair into a frighteningly formal drawing room. Faded Aubusson rugs covered hardwood floors, elaborately carved mahogany chairs boasted brocade seats and a pair of magnificent tapestries depicting hunting scenes flanked a long gilt mirror over the pink marble fireplace. The ceiling soared some fifteen feet over their heads, and frescoed cherubs cavorted around the crystal chandelier. It looked like something straight out of the czar's Winter Palace.

Taylor was relieved when they passed through the salon and into a much cozier room. A fire crackled in the brick fireplace, overstuffed club chairs beckoned and the mellow tones of the wood paneling were soothing. Subov took a seat and turned that saber-sharp gaze of his on Taylor. "What do you wish to speak with me about?"

"Amanda and I were present when Marina was killed. I would like to think that she didn't die in vain, and that with your help, something good might come out of her death. She and I were discussing something highly sensitive at the time she died that may be related to her murder."

"Her what?" Subov snapped.

Taylor blinked. "I beg your pardon?"

The man was white with rage. He half rose out of his chair. "My baby was *murdered?*"

Taylor stared, stunned. He'd assumed Subov knew. Christ,

the Swiss government—no, more likely the Russian government—must have covered up the incident. He stumbled through answering, "Yes, that's correct."

"Impossible. She was in a car accident."

Taylor touched the long scab on his left temple. "I was grazed by the same bullet that killed her. It struck her in the throat."

Subov subsided into his chair, aghast. "You lie."

"I'm sorry, sir. I do not." Taylor described in excruciating detail exactly what had happened in the park. At least as best as he and Amanda could piece it together. He spared Subov nothing. The guy *had* to believe them. Hell, he deserved to know the truth.

At the end of his recitation, Subov was silent. His hands shook violently, but he gave no other outward sign of reaction to the tale. Taylor hesitated, unsure of what to do. A lie by the Russian government he had not foreseen. Slowly, Subov's shock coalesced into muttering fury. Taylor silently translated the Russian invective. *Those bastards. Those murdering, lying bastards.*

He and Amanda waited a long time while Subov visibly sorted through his jumbled thoughts. Finally, he looked up. His voice was hard. "Tell me everything. From the beginning this time."

Taylor sketched the details of their investigation into the diamond smuggling for their host, starting with Grigorii Kriskin's suicide in Carnegie Hall and ending on Subov's doorstep. "I wish I could tell you who's behind all this, Mr. Subov, but I don't know. Nor do I know who pulled the trigger that killed your daughter."

"I do." Subov jumped up out of his chair, and paced, agitated.

It was Taylor's turn to be shocked. "You can't possibly know…."

"I have a pretty good idea." The man pivoted sharply and stalked back across the room.

"But how?"

"Do you forget who I am? For decades, I was one of the most powerful men in the world. I still have connections. I've heard rumors, innuendos, tidbits here and there, but I didn't put them together until now." His rage flared and he buried his fist in his other palm. "By God, they'll pay for this. If it's the last thing I do, I'll see to it they pay."

Taylor leaned forward. "We believe the same people who killed your daughter have been trying to kill Amanda over the last couple months. We need to know who it is. Was it the CIA?"

Subov stopped pacing for a moment and glared at him. "Lord, no. It wasn't the Americans. It was *Russians.*" He spit the word out with disgust.

Taylor leaned back, digesting that bit of information. "Government or Mob?"

Subov headed for the telephone on the console table behind the sofa. He snarled, "Let us find out."

He placed a call, speaking in rapid Russian that Taylor was only able to catch snatches of. Subov made several more calls in quick succession. Even if Taylor hadn't understood a word of Russian, it was clear that Subov was contacting people who owed him favors within both the Russian government and Mob.

Subov put down the phone and collapsed into an armchair, abruptly looking like an exhausted old man. "Now we wait."

Taylor looked away tactfully as a tear rolled down the guy's cheek. Silently, Amanda got up and brought him a box of tissues from the desk on the other side of the room. The wave of grief eventually passed. Subov's shoulders stopped shaking and he looked up, his eyes red rimmed. His voice rough, he ordered them, "Tell me again what happened."

He questioned Taylor and Amanda closely about Marina's murder, and Taylor was duly impressed by the guy's interrogation skills. Worthy of the best the FBI had to offer. And then the Russian asked the sixty-four-thousand-dollar question. "Who do you to work for?"

Taylor looked over at Amanda and she nodded. He duly replied, "We work for a man called Devereaux."

Subov sucked in his breath. "Indeed? And why would someone of his stature be interested in my daughter's passing off a few diamonds here and there to support her aging father?"

Amanda fielded that one. "Look where those few diamonds here and there have led us. I'd say Devereaux's instincts were right on target, wouldn't you?"

Subov nodded slowly. "My mistake. I never anticipated that my little stash of diamonds would draw the attention of someone like him."

Taylor couldn't resist. "What can you tell us about Devereaux?"

"You work for him. You tell me," Subov retorted.

Taylor stared the older man down, waiting him out. Subov sighed. "I've heard rumors. No more. Of a man, or a small group of men, called Devereaux, who has grown frustrated with the old ways of dealing with certain international forces. Devereaux has taken matters into his own hands and pursues his own brand of justice."

Taylor pressed, "What do your contacts say about Devereaux?"

"Everyone who knows of his existence fears drawing his attention. He is said to be ruthless in the extreme against anyone who crosses the line of his moral standards. A rich, powerful and dangerous vigilante. But a vigilante, nonetheless."

"You say that like you don't approve of him," Taylor remarked.

Subov shrugged. "Who's going to control the vigilante when he crosses the line himself?"

Taylor nodded, conceding the point. A discussion for another time.

He and Amanda allowed Subov to pick their brains at will, but the Russian, too, grew frustrated at the lack of conclusive evidence as to who killed Marina. The conversation trailed off. Subov closed his eyes to rest for a few minutes. Taylor and Amanda sat with him in silence, each lost in their own troubled thoughts.

The fire popped loudly, and Subov jumped. His eyes flew open and he levered himself out of the chair. "Are you hungry? I'll make lunch for us if you dare try my cooking." He walked slowly out of the room, like an old man who'd borne one blow too many in his lifetime.

Their wait for a return phone call turned into an overnight visit. Subov insisted they stay with him until he heard back from his contacts. In yet another surprising show of kindness, Amanda sat with Subov for hours after supper, reminiscing about Marina's childhood. She told dozens of funny and whimsical anecdotes about their school days together. Subov's laughter rang out through the evening over his wild daughter's heretofore unknown antics.

As Taylor climbed under the fluffy down comforter that night, he rolled toward Amanda, taking her gently into his arms. "That was a decent thing you did for him tonight. You brought an old man joy in the midst of his sorrow."

She sighed. "I think I needed it as much as he did."

"Do you feel better?"

"Yes. But I still can't escape the fact that I'm responsible for her death."

Taylor frowned. "Amanda, if anyone's responsible, I am. If I hadn't insisted on seeing her, she'd never have been killed."

Amanda reached up to smooth her palm over Taylor's cheek. "We all do what we have to. Rule number sixty-seven, or whatever number I'm up to—never look back."

"Never?"

"Not if you can help it."

"You don't sound entirely convinced. Isn't there a reckoning at the end of the line? When you're old and tired, won't you have to think about it then?"

Amanda whispered painfully. "I'm going to Hell."

"Hey. Weren't you the one who told me that if you didn't do the jobs, someone else would? You were given a unique set of skills that you use for the greater good. Yeah, it's dirty work, but don't the ends justify the means?"

"I've gotten innocent victims killed. First Grigorii Kriskin, then all the people in Caracas and now Marina. How am I going to live with that?"

He hugged her close. Lord, he was proud of her. She was completing the journey back to humanity before his very eyes. And she'd made it on her own. He smoothed her hair back from her tormented brow. "There are people, like me, who can help you learn to deal with it. But in the meantime, remember you're not alone. I love you, you know."

Amanda's shoulders began to shake. "I know. I don't understand why, but I know."

Taylor felt tears sliding off her cheek onto his arm. He rocked her slowly and let her cry.

Her whispered voice came out of the darkness. "I love you, too."

He dropped a gentle kiss on the top of her head, smiling into her hair. "I know." Finally. He'd found the tender, loving woman beneath the cold, calculating operative. Or, rather, she'd found herself.

Subov's answer came the next morning in a phone call from Switzerland. The bullet dug out of Marina's neck was fired from a 5.45 mm PRI pistol, the kind issued to officers of the Russian intelligence directorate. Subov hung up the phone, visibly shaken. He paced the large kitchen, agitated. "My own government killed her. They took away my career, exiled me in disgrace, stripped my wealth and now they've murdered my only child."

He spun in abrupt decision and faced Taylor and Amanda, who were seated at the kitchen table. "You want to know where Marina got those diamonds? I'll tell you. She got them from me." He headed for the back door, grabbing a coat. "Come. Let me show you something."

Taylor and Amanda hurried after him, snatching their coats off the pegs by the door. Subov strode quickly through the new snow that had fallen overnight, heading off through the trees. They raced after him down a slippery footpath that twisted and turned and finally emerged into a small clearing. A rude hut stood in the center of it. Subov leaned over a lock, fumbling with a key. He pushed the plank door open. "Come," he called impatiently.

Taylor hauled wood in through the low doorway, and Amanda helped Subov light a fire in the big iron stove that stood in the corner, next to a barrel of water and a big box of fist-size rocks. A sauna. The flame caught, and Subov fed tinder into the belly of the stove. After a few minutes, he added several logs and closed the oven door. He moved to the opposite corner of the room and, using a screwdriver he pulled out of his coat pocket, pried at the flooring. Taylor leaned down to help. He hooked his fingers under the board and lifted it the rest of the way free. Amanda coughed as a cloud of dust rose up from the long, narrow space.

Subov bent a creaky knee and reached down into the dark slot that was revealed. He handed up a large, brown envelope, then reached into the hole again. He drew out a dirty sack about the size of a pillow case. Taylor helped Subov to his feet, then followed the man to a bench by the tiny table in the opposite corner. Amanda sat down on the opposite side of the table with Taylor. Subov unwrapped a string from around the top of the sack. He pulled out a small, cloth bag. The Russian cleared the table with a sweep of his sleeve and gently poured out the contents of the bag. Dozens of small, folded squares of tissue paper. She sucked in her breath. One by one, Subov unfolded the papers and dumped out a series of magnificent diamonds onto the table.

She picked up one of the stones and shards of brilliantly colored light leaped and danced on the walls of the cabin. "It this real or synthetic?"

"Very good, young lady. It is both."

She frowned. "What do you mean?"

"It's a real enough diamond, all right. Except it was manufactured in a laboratory a number of years ago."

Taylor and Amanda stared at him.

Subov continued. "The Russian government perfected the technology to make gemstone-quality diamonds decades ago. They sent a sample of their finest work to the Politburo for approval. In my capacity with the KGB, I was responsible for storing the stones afterward." He swept his hand over the table to encompass the cache of stones. "These came into my care at a time when the Soviet regime was failing, and it was clear that I was to become obsolete. I decided to take out a little…insurance policy."

She examined another, even larger stone. It sure as heck looked real. "How are they made?"

"Basically, pure carbon is subjected to extreme heat and pressure. It's not that complicated a process. An American company demonstrated the technology fifty years ago. It was the Japanese who perfected the process. However, they used argon gas to fill the crystallization chamber, and this made the stones bright yellow. It took Russian scientists to figure out how to complete the process in a vacuum so the stones would be white."

Taylor let out a low whistle.

Subov continued, "The process was prohibitively expensive in the West. Your scientists concluded that making laboratory diamonds on a commercial scale was not economically feasible. But that is not the case for us. Stalin built a number of large dams and hydroelectric stations in remote parts of the Soviet Union back in the fifties. He hoped to draw settlers to the hinterlands. It didn't work, of course. But Russia and its former republics have huge amounts of surplus electrical energy going to waste for lack of power lines to carry it to the major urban centers."

"Kyrgyzstan," Amanda breathed.

Subov looked up at her in surprise. "You two have done your homework. Yes. Udarsky. It's a Russian military base near one of the great hydroelectric dams in Kyrgyzstan. Home of a secret diamond-manufacturing facility."

"Has Russia controlled and operated it all this time?" she asked.

"Production was shut down in the late 1980s. It's only with Mother Russia's recent economic woes that a deal was made with Kyrgyzstan and the Udarsky plant was reactivated by Russian scientists. That, and a new technology came along that made artificial diamonds extremely valuable again."

It was Taylor's turn to interrupt. "Computer chips! In a laboratory, the size, shape and purity of a diamond can be controlled and large diamond wafers can be made."

The Russian swore softly under his breath. "I could have used you two working for me when I was in the KGB. If you will forgive me for saying so, Amanda, your father was never half so clever as you."

Amanda gaped, stunned. It felt like the floor had just dropped out from under her feet. She jumped up, pacing the tiny room in agitation. "My father worked for *you?*"

Subov laughed. "Indirectly. He was much further down the food chain than I. But his reports came across my desk, yes."

She looked down at the stolen diamonds winking on the table in the firelight. "Is this the Udarsky cache? Was my father innocent of the charges your government made against him? Did he go crazy for nothing?"

"Oh, no," Subov retorted. "These stones are a drop in the bucket compared to the Udarsky cache. I never saw any proof of it, but some people remain convinced your father stole the entire output of the Udarsky diamond facility for thirteen years of its operation. *That* is the Udarsky cache."

She shook her head in denial. "My father never had anything like that. He was perennially broke, in fact. If he'd had the diamonds, he'd have sold them for cash. He was addicted to living expensively."

Subov shrugged. "The Udarsky cache was not shaped into gemstones as these are. They were made for industrial purposes, and as such only valuable to a few select buyers worldwide. Liquidating them would have been…difficult. Most within the KGB were absolutely convinced Christopher had the stones. Your father's control officer for one. The shadow of suspicion cast over your father ruined his control officer's career, as well."

"Who was that?" Amanda asked, voracious for any scraps of information that might shed light on the enigma that had been her father.

Subov frowned. "It has been a long time. Let me see. The fellow was rather forgettable. Middle-level bureaucrat with no real talent. His code name was Biryuz."

Taylor jolted. "'Turquoise'? Have I translated that correctly?"

Amanda stared. The references in her father's journal.

Subov nodded. "Yes. Turquoise. When he was in England, he went by another name, Nicky Somerset. Real name was Nikolai. Nikko Something."

A sick feeling tickled Amanda's gut. "Nikko Biryayev," she said with sinking certainty.

"Yes! That was it. He was your father's control officer. Last I heard he was still in the business. Trains new field officers. Mundane work for a mediocre man."

"What do you know of his latest protégé?" she asked urgently.

"Nothing. But I could make another phone call."

"Please do. It's urgent that I know what Biryayev's current student looks like."

Subov pulled out his cell phone. His request took no more than a minute to fulfill. He repeated over the mouth of the receiver. "Name's Max Ebhardt. Blond hair, blue eyes, one meter eighty centimeters tall, late twenties. Computer specialist. Poses frequently as a—"

"—college student," Amanda finished for him. She sat down heavily on the bench. That's why Devereaux gave her father's journal to her. Because he knew Biryayev might come after her when she kicked this hornet's nest.

Subov reached into the sack as he spoke and pulled out a stack of yellowed papers. "Udarsky has been turning out artificial diamonds again for several years now. And, in the last few years, Russia has boosted its overall diamond output by upwards of thirty percent."

Taylor was incredulous. "You're saying that a third of all of Russia's diamonds are artificial?"

"Potentially. Check out the major diamond retailers' reports for the last ten years or so. Even they're speculating on how Russia's doing it. Did you know geologists are phenomenally accurate in forecasting the quality and quantity of diamonds a mine will produce throughout its entire life, and that they assay every single diamond mine in the world? A few years back, Russia stopped letting foreign geologists into its mines. And suddenly, Russian diamond output soared."

Amanda's head whirled with the implications. The pieces had been in front of them all along. The strange conversation between Taylor and Brodin in Mexico. Brodin must have made a deal with the American government to get his hands on a shipment of diamond computer chips in return for protection and a new identity. He thought Taylor was the American government liaison.

It explained the American government's obsession with keeping her and Taylor away from Brodin. It also explained the Americans' presence in Caracas. They were there to complete the deal with Brodin and take delivery of the diamond wafers that could be etched into computer chips. That was why the dying American agent had tried to shoot her. He was no doubt under orders to protect the Brodin deal at all costs.

The Russian government's attempt to stop her and Taylor's investigation by force abruptly made sense, as well. They were protecting their cash cow in Udarsky, not to mention the hot new computer-chip technology their scientists there had mastered. No wonder Biryayev shot in her direction in Caracas. He'd probably been under orders to stop Brodin from delivering the diamond chips to the Americans. She wasn't Biryayev's target at all. Brodin was. The simultaneous attack on Brodin by the Russians plus the American net to surround and stop her had triggered the firefight in Caracas. Oh, yes. It was all becoming clear. As clear as a flawless white diamond.

Subov shrugged. "I imagine Devereaux suspects the truth, but without proof, he cannot make any accusations."

Ah, but Devereaux could put his best operative on it and rock the boat to see who fell out. Even if that operative was on the verge of a breakdown. She looked up and saw the same thought pass through Taylor's harsh gaze.

Subov's rusty voice went on relentlessly. "How the world has changed. Now, it's not even a concern that Russia is flooding the market with cheap, plentiful diamonds and ruining the global diamond market. There are not even any more simple arms races. Now we have a technology race."

"They're one and the same. Technology is the weapon of the future," she replied grimly.

The old man stared at her for several long seconds and then nodded slowly.

She waved a hand at the table's contents. "Why are you telling all of this to us?"

Subov's words lashed her. "Because I want you to destroy Udarsky."

"You can't be serious!" she exclaimed.

"I am."

She protested, "I don't even know where the Udarsky facility is, how it's laid out, how it's built…I couldn't possibly go in blind and expect to succeed. The amounts of explosives needed to blow up an entire factory would be prohibitive. How would I, a foreign, private operative, procure any of the equipment or supplies I'd need for the job?"

Subov chopped his hand across the air. "You forget to whom you speak. And where."

She raised her eyebrows questioningly.

"This is free Georgia. Not Russia. This country is engaged in a low-intensity civil war. It's not readily visible on the surface, but it is there nonetheless. Army units all over Georgia have gone renegade and taken their supplies with them. Explosives will be the least of your problems. As for destroying Udarsky—" Subov pushed several of the yellowed papers across the table "—here is a copy of the factory's blueprints."

Subov sorted out the remaining documents into two piles. "This stack is a detailed description of the production process. It has enough of the fine points of making the computer chips for another laboratory to repeat and refine the process without too much trouble. This pile is the production records for the first thirteen years of the plant's operation. I don't have access to updates of these documents since my retirement. But it is, in essence, an inventory of the Udarsky cache."

"How much is this supposed cache worth?" she asked.

"In today's dollars, I'd guess around ten billion."

"Ten *billion?*" she repeated in shock.

"That would explain why so many people were so hot to find it," Taylor commented dryly. "Not to mention why a man in a fragile emotional state might lose it completely if he was sitting on something that big that he couldn't turn into cash."

Amanda stared at Taylor. Why was it she was only coming to understand her father now, years after his tragic death? If only he'd talked to her about any of this before he passed away!

Taylor commented to Subov, "We saw a Russian Mafia member trading gemstone diamonds for weapons early on in this investigation. Do you know anything about that?"

Subov nodded. "The Russian government is too poor to pay in cash, so it pays in diamonds. A middleman, in the form of a mobster, injects the stones into the diamond market in a way where they are not likely to be examined under a microscope. It is possible to tell synthetic diamonds from natural ones under proper magnification or refractive testing. But use the Mafia, and Russia cannot be caught."

Shifting topic, Taylor asked, "Why should we blow up Udarsky? What's in it for us?"

Subov didn't answer. Rather, he reached into the sack one more time and pulled out a dirty yellow ribbon. The wide, grosgrain kind little girls might put in their hair. He fingered the length of ribbon and looked Amanda straight in the eye. "Your father put this in a safe-deposit box for you shortly before he died. We suspected he'd left you directions to the Udarsky cache in that box, so we took the liberty of obtaining its contents. It is only fair to give it to you now."

He held out the bedraggled ribbon, and Amanda reached for it numbly. "My father left this in a safe-deposit box for me?"

Subov nodded. "His will stated that the contents of the safe-deposit box constituted your primary inheritance."

"How do you know what my father's will said?"

Subov merely raised an eyebrow. Well, that explained her father's crazy last will and testament. The estate lawyer had put down the reference to a safe-deposit box that didn't exist as yet another incident of Christopher's madness. Her father was looking more sane by the second.

Subov's piercing gaze captured her attention once more. The Russian leaned forward and said intensely, "Blow up Udarsky for your father. Complete Christopher McClintock's legacy."

She said flatly, "I beg your pardon?"

His words whipped at her. "What do you think the Udarsky cache was? We didn't mess around with making pretty baubles for rich, capitalist women at that factory. The entire output of the facility for thirteen years, with the exception of these demonstration stones—" he waved at the diamonds on the table "—was crystals for use in computer chips."

He leaned forward, propping himself on the edge of the table. "Your father single-handedly halted the development of diamond computer chips for twenty years by stealing every last one of those wafers."

"Why didn't the Russians just duplicate the work?"

"Your father stole the blueprints to the process, as well, and a couple weeks after the theft, the scientist who invented the process died in an avalanche while skiing. The key knowledge of the process was lost and never could be duplicated." He snorted in disgust. "The price we paid for our paranoia. We thought if only one man knew the secret it would be safe. We didn't anticipate that he would take it to his grave." Subov paused, looking them both in the eye before continuing. "And now you can see to it that everybody in the world has a fair shot at this technology. Don't let it become a weapon by one country to use in economic war or a technological arms race against another."

She stared at Subov. His gaze cut through her like a diamond-edged saw. He was telling the truth. She could feel it in her bones. Along with something else. Profound relief. Her father hadn't been a traitorous madman. He'd been a hero. He sacrificed everything he had and was to keep his secret. And his journal had been a last-ditch attempt to explain himself to her. So many of his ramblings made perfect sense now. All the talk about robbing the dragon, stopping the clawing beasts, preventing chaos and economic imbalance with his work, the vast riches in his possession.

Taylor leaned forward to face Subov. "What's in it for you if we blow up the Udarsky diamond factory?"

"Revenge."

Chapter 18

Their white outer garments blended in perfectly with the frozen landscape. They crouched on top of a rise and took turns peering into the distance through a pair of powerful field glasses. The Udarsky industrial production facility came into focus, squat and gray, tucked into a gentle valley. A huge electrical transformer hovered, spiderlike, just north of the factory, spreading its wire tentacles protectively over the facility. Four giant power lines fed it from the nearby Toktogul Dam, which harnessed the energy of the Naryn River and created the immense Toktogul Reservoir. A storage yard lay on the south side of the building, stacked high with barrels proclaiming it a chemical production plant. Even thorough examination with the binoculars did not reveal the hidden laboratories housed beneath the fertilizer plant.

Double fences surrounded the complex, and guard towers opposed each other in the northwest and southeast corners of the security perimeter. Although they couldn't see them,

Subov's information indicated that 20 mm machine guns were mounted and manned continuously in those towers by pairs of soldiers. Supposedly, there were no roving guards outside the facility. No surprise, Amanda thought wryly. The temperature today was a balmy five degrees Fahrenheit at midafternoon.

She looked briefly at her watch. Three o'clock. The sun was sinking rapidly behind them in the west. It would set in another hour. They slid back off the top of the ridge so their silhouettes would not be visible against the setting sun. It was a relief to stand up, to get away from the insidious cold of the frozen tundra soaking through her heavily insulated clothing as she lay on the ground. They had seen enough. It was time to make their move.

"What do you mean you can't find the car?" roared Nikko Biryayev. "How in the hell do you lose a Mercedes 560 out here? It's the only one for hundreds of kilometers around!"

The police chief shrugged. "Nonetheless, it has disappeared."

"So find it!"

"My men did their best."

"Damn, damn and double damn." Biryayev paced the length of the Kyrgyzstani policeman's dingy office. He spun and growled, "Max, call the army base again. Those troops I ordered should be here by now."

Ebhardt stepped out of the office. He placed a phone call, but not to the Udarsky army post. He murmured into the receiver, "Look, Devereaux. I can't control him anymore. He's demanded five hundred Russian army soldiers from the Udarsky military base be released into his command to conduct a manhunt for the McClintock girl. What are your instructions?"

Ebhardt listened intently. "Yes, sir. I understand. I will do my best to keep him calm, but you'd better hurry up and pull some of those strings you're so famous for holding. I can't run interference on him much longer. He's completely insane."

* * *

Subov slowed the big Mercedes and steered carefully off the frozen track. He drove into a small copse of spruce trees nestled in the lee of a steep rise. The factory was a kilometer away on the other side of that ridge. Subov would wait for them here.

Amanda regretted having to step out of the car's warmth. She shrugged into overwhites—insulated, waterproof, white nylon pants—and a hooded jacket that zipped over her heavy clothing. She and Taylor obliterated the car tracks quickly and moved into position to observe the road. She looked at her watch—11:30 p.m. The truck bearing the next shift of guards should be along anytime now. Taylor lifted his head abruptly beside her. She held her breath, listening. The faint rumble of a vehicle was growing louder. She released the safety on the Uzi submachine gun cradled in her arms, and Taylor did the same.

Headlights flashed into view. They pressed themselves deeper into the snow. Cold seeped through the insulated jumpsuit to grip her. The truck drew even with them. It slowed slightly, swerving around a large pothole. The headlights swung in their direction. Amanda didn't breathe. She didn't even blink. The engine surged, and the driver swung back the other way, continuing down the track. She exhaled slowly. The red taillights receded rapidly.

Taylor handed her a grenade launcher and two gold and two silver canisters. She loaded a gold one and pocketed the remaining three. Taylor did the same and stuffed his three extra canisters into pockets in his white suit. He shouldered the ungainly weapon. "Ready?" he asked.

She nodded resolutely. This one was for her father. "Ready."

Taylor swept his free arm around her shoulder, pulling her close. He was a shapeless lump, but she still felt his strength and silent support through the layers of protective clothing. His breath formed a white cloud around them as he said, "One last mission. After tonight you won't ever have to do anything like this again. I promise."

She leaned her head briefly against his reassuringly solid chest and squeezed her eyes tightly shut. She mustn't cry. The tears would freeze on her cheeks. Taylor released her, and she pulled the drawstring of her parka hood closed, creating a narrow fur-lined tunnel in front of her face. The visibility was awful, but the outside temperature was approaching thirty below zero and still dropping. Besides, if the guards spotted her out on the open tundra, she was a dead duck, anyway. Seeing the guards coming wouldn't do her any good. Camouflage was her only hope.

Taylor's muffled voice came from her left. "Let's move. We've got one hour and fifteen minutes to be in place. We launch at 1:00 a.m."

They strapped on snowshoes and started the half-mile hike to the factory. A deceptively long walk in this kind of weather. She settled the grenade launcher more comfortably across her shoulder and strode after Taylor's tall white back. They moved quickly until they reached the top of the ridge, where they separated. Taylor veered off to the right while Amanda tracked to her left. She moved into position parallel with the northernmost tower. She pulled out her night-vision goggles, put them on and crested the ridge on her belly. It took a couple minutes, but eventually she was able to pick out the moving shadow that was Taylor as he eased down the south ridge. He was very good, moving fluidly, without a noticeable rhythm.

He would circle around to the far side and then cut in close. Time for her to go. She flipped over on her back and eased headfirst down the hill. Moving on her back kept snow out of her hood. It also provided an unconventional silhouette for a human. She was careful not to rip her clothing on any sharp protrusions as she slid down the incline. The cold would kill an unprotected person in a matter of minutes out here.

A stretch of open tundra lay between her and her target. The flat expanse was deceptive, riddled with small gullies and tufts of vegetation frozen under the thin layer of snow. This part of the world was a cold desert and didn't get much more than a foot or two of snow each winter. Her progress was painfully slow, but the alternative was detection and death.

Move. Stop. Count to three. Move. Move. Stop. Any repetitive movement could catch the eye of a guard. It took her almost an hour to reach a point she judged to be a hundred yards from the guard tower. She rolled over onto her stomach and engaged the telephoto function of her NVGs, searching for her target. There it was. A small metal grate at the base of the tower. The inlet vent for the furnace that heated the two-story concrete structure.

She checked her watch. Ten minutes to spare. She distracted herself from the encroaching numbness by pondering which tropical island she was going to visit when this was over. She was going to lie on a beach until she was positively baked. *Time to fire.* Very slowly, she eased the grenade launcher in front of her and into firing position. She checked her watch one more time. Cold seeped all the way up to her elbow as she pulled back the cuff of her mitten to look at the luminescent face.

She unzipped the slit in her right mitten. *Three…* Her gloved index finger poked through the slit and wrapped around the cold metal trigger of the grenade launcher. There was no wind at all. Firing conditions were perfect. *Two…* She took careful aim. *One…* And fired. A gentle whump sounded in her ear. The canister soared high into the sky in an arcing trajectory. It sailed clear of the first fence and landed in the snow five yards short of the guard tower.

She'd missed! Did the guards hear her fire? Were they training their weapons on her right now? As long as she was perfectly still, they probably couldn't see her. But she had to reload and try again. Soon. She lay frozen in indecision, her instinct to survive warring with her responsibility to take out this tower within the next few seconds.

If Taylor succeeded and she failed, her guards would quickly know something was amiss when the ones in his tower failed to report in. Alarms would be triggered, and Taylor would be caught and killed before he could get away from the factory. Fighting down panic, she eased the backup canister out of her pocket. Checking to be sure she had the gold one, she opened the chamber of the grenade launcher and slid in the canister loaded with the first component of a binary nerve agent. She corrected her aim and fired again. The canister soared high, pausing for a moment at the top of its arc, then dived for the ground, picking up speed. It landed directly underneath the tower, rolling to a stop against the concrete wall and splitting open. Thank God.

She loaded the second agent into the weapon quickly and fired. She had the range now. The silver canister rolled to a stop beside the first one. The containers released their loads of colorless, odorless gasses simultaneously. The two chemicals, harmless by themselves, would mix in the furnace vents and emerge as an incapacitating gas that would render the guards unconscious in a single breath.

Amanda lay motionless and counted to one hundred. Time enough for any remaining gas outside the furnace vents to dissipate so she wouldn't be knocked out if she got downwind of the canisters. If the gas had worked, the guards were neutralized now. She felt worse than naked, lying in this exposed position. She could stay here and freeze to death, or she could take her chances with being shot. Some choice. She eased backward, watching for any signs of movement in the tower. Nothing. She rose to a crouch and continued to move away slowly. Another hundred yards between herself and the compound. She couldn't stand it any longer. She turned and ran for the ridge. She collapsed beyond the crest, panting. God, that had been stupid. If the guards had been awake or only partially incapacitated, they would have seen her for sure. What had possessed her? She'd certainly lost the feel for this type of work.

The night air burned fiercely in her lungs. How could something so cold feel so hot? Time to go get Anton and the car and head into the plant itself. She pushed to her feet and continued toward the trees and warmth. Subov greeted her when she opened the car door and slid inside.

She panted, "Where's Taylor?"

"He's not back yet. Drink this. You must be chilled."

Now there was an understatement. He pressed a cup of hot coffee into her half-frozen fingers.

"Did you succeed?" Subov asked tersely.

Amanda nodded.

He smiled. "I must admit, I didn't think you were up to it. That was a difficult shot."

She smiled back. "It was two difficult shots. I missed with the first canister. I had to use the backup. It's a good thing you insisted we take the spares."

Subov smiled grimly. "I wasn't the Director of Plans for the KGB for nothing. No plan ever works in execution as smoothly as it does on paper."

She sipped the bitter coffee, tasting the bite of whiskey. She generally hated the malt liquor, but tonight, she needed its heat to warm her all the way to her belly. A dark shadow slid past her window, and the passenger door flew open.

Subov jumped. "Taylor, you startled me. You are very quiet. Or maybe I am getting old."

Taylor slid gratefully into the front seat, swigging from the flask Subov passed to him

"Well?" the old man demanded.

"No problem. How'd your shots go, Amanda?"

"Fine."

"Good girl."

She retorted testily, "You don't have to sound so surprised. Who taught *you* how to fire a grenade launcher, anyway?"

Taylor grinned.

They warmed themselves for a few minutes before Subov spoke. "Ready for phase two?"

* * *

A thin, blond woman poked her head in the door. "Mr. Trumpman?"

"Hmm?" Harry looked up from the pad of paper he'd been doodling on. The CIA was kind enough to provide pen and paper for his entertainment while he cooled his heels in their conference room. They would probably have some psychologist analyze his scribbles after he left.

The blonde stepped in and closed the door. "I was asked to give you an update. We just intercepted a phone call in which two Russians were discussing a possible manhunt for Miss McClintock."

Trumpman lurched. "Where did it originate?"

"Kyrgyzstan."

"Where the hell's that?" he growled.

"South of Kazakhstan, north of Tadzhikistan, east of Turkistan and west of nowhere."

What on earth were Amanda and Taylor doing there? He asked more calmly than he felt, "What are you guys going to do about it?"

"A message has already gone out. All available field agents who can reach the Udarsky district in the next few hours have been sent there immediately. Their orders are to find your people and neutralize them."

He jumped to his feet, shouting, but the blonde backed out quickly and closed the door behind her. The lock clicked.

The Mercedes purred to a stop at the main gate to the Udarsky facility. They waited a good minute for any response from the guard towers. Each structure contained controls to open the automatic gates. Nothing happened. The gas had worked. Taylor stepped out of the idling car in his Russian army general's uniform, hefting a large bolt cutter. He hacked through the thick links of the fencing where the lock was attached. He slid the heavy gate open on its oiled track. He did the same to the second gate, then climbed back into the driver's seat.

Subov leaned forward as the car rolled forward once more. "Remember. Don't open your mouth. You'll give yourself away instantly."

Taylor grinned. *"Ponyatno."* Literally translated, it meant "understood." It was the equivalent of a crisp "Yes, sir!"

Subov grunted and tugged on his old uniform, decked out to the nines with ribbons and medals. Enough to intimidate anyone in this backwater, Taylor expected. Hell, the man himself was plenty intimidating. Taylor helped Amanda out of the car. She had to be freezing in that skirt. But it was in keeping with her cover as Subov's personal assistant. The trio passed by the main doors leading to the chemical plant and made its way to a smaller set of doors beyond. Subov's blueprints indicated this was the entrance to the diamond-production lab.

Taylor opened the door and held it while Subov and Amanda stepped through into a small vestibule. They passed through a second doorway into a large lobby. Lockers lined both walls. A single door stood at the far end of the room, and beside it, a mesh cage. A guard inside it stared at them in slack-jawed surprise.

Subov strode forward aggressively. "I am Anton Subov. The general and I have just arrived in town to have a look at this place. We want to inspect the laboratories right away."

As luck would have it, the guard was an old-timer. The way he spilled coffee all over himself as he leaped to his feet made it clear he recognized the former number-two man in the KGB. His jaw sagged even farther open.

Subov strode over to the cage. "Are you dumb, man? Can you not speak?"

"I…I am honored to meet you," the guard stammered. He stood up off his stool behind the counter, coming to a rough approximation of attention.

"My pleasure." Subov held out his hand. The man opened the small window to grasp it. Subov whipped out a silenced pistol and put three slugs in the guard's chest. The man dropped to the floor, out of sight behind the high counter.

"Durak," Subov mumbled. "Fool." He tucked the pistol back under his coat while Taylor blinked at Subov's casual violence. Taylor reached across the counter inside the cage and felt under its edge. He found a button and pressed it. So far the blueprints were holding up perfectly. The door beside the cage slid open. He pulled the little window shut.

"Come on. Let's go."

They walked through the opening and down the stairs. The door slid shut behind them.

Amanda murmured, "Well, we're in."

Taylor murmured back sotto voce, "Yeah. Now's let's make a firecracker of this joint."

They walked calmly down the corridors, opening each door they came to. The night-shift technicians inside the rooms looked up in surprise at the interruption, but said nothing when they glimpsed Taylor's and Subov's uniforms and rank insignia. Thankfully, no solicitous supervisors appeared to be on duty at this late hour, and the three of them moved around the facility unhindered. Taylor couldn't believe it was this easy. They turned out of the main hallway into a narrow corridor leading to a maintenance area for the huge steam generators. He murmured under the low rumble of sound, "Are you getting the shots?"

Amanda nodded fractionally. "Yes. I just hope this thing works."

Subov snorted. "It's Japanese, not Russian. It will work."

Taylor grinned. Amanda's briefcase concealed a camera and wide-angle lens. She'd recorded on film each of the rooms they'd glanced into. Quickly, they moved through a rabbit warren of storage rooms and maintenance bays, leaving bricks of plastic explosives in each. The devices were equipped with remote-activated detonators. When they were clear of the facility, they would call in a bomb threat and empty the place, then they'd blow it up. Anton had been violently opposed to giving the employees any warning, but it was the only way Amanda and Taylor would agree to help him. There had been far too much blood spilled, innocent and otherwise, over the Udarsky diamonds. They placated Anton by offering him the chance to push the button that would make the whole plant go up in smoke.

They'd marked on the plans several key structures that must be destroyed to bring down the whole building. Most of them were in obscure places where the structural supports were located. One by one, they booby-trapped the critical locations.

It took them almost an hour to plant the explosives. Amanda watched Taylor climb down nimbly off one of the main steam generators. "That's the last one," she announced.

Subov muttered, *"Davai poshli."*

"What does that mean?" she asked.

Taylor translated with a grin, "Let's be gone."

"Amen," she agreed fervently.

They began to retrace their steps toward the lone exit from the facility. They'd made it back to the long main corridor when a loud Klaxon sounded. Somebody'd discovered something. The unconscious guards in the towers, or maybe the downed guard in the security cage. Not that it really mattered. The three of them looked at each other grimly and started to run. People began to pour out into the hallway. Subov waved his arms and shouted, *"Syrr, Syrr!"* *Fire! Fire!*

The crowd surged for the stairs, taking up the cry. With a fertilizer factory overhead, chock-full of volatile, dangerous chemicals, the threat of fire was highly effective in causing an all-out stampede. A lone armed guard stood at the top of the broad stairway, pistol in hand. He bellowed at the mob to stop, to no avail. He pointed the gun at the ceiling and fired once. The crowd jumped collectively, and the front ranks of technicians cringed, pushing back. But those in the rear continued to rush forward, fleeing the supposed fire. Milling, shoving confusion was the result. The crowd's fear escalated into panic.

The first people shoved the guard. He spread his arms, barring the doorway. Amanda couldn't see exactly what happened to the guy, but he went down under the stampeding crowd. She grabbed Taylor's sleeve and hung on for dear life as the wild jumble of bodies pushed and jostled around her. She lost sight of Subov.

The first people were streaming through the lobby when the sirens started wailing outside. She winced. Reinforcements. Not good. Taylor used his size and strength to plow through the crowd, pulling her in his wake. She helped him shed the army greatcoat and uniform jacket on his way up the stairs. They'd made it about halfway up the long stairway when uniformed soldiers began to pour into the lobby ahead. A volley of shots was fired into the pandemonium, and the crowd panicked afresh. With a roar, they surged forward, pushing the soldiers outside before them.

She stumbled and screamed, "Taylor!" The crowd would trample her if she went down.

Taylor paused and turned, dragging her upright by main force. "Keep moving. Stay on your feet at all costs," he urged.

The first wave of people burst through the lobby and outside like water shot from a cannon. Guards tried ineffectually to corral the mass of humanity. Amanda and Taylor stuck together, caught in the lobby, searching frantically for Subov. He had the detonator. Without it, they would not be able to destroy the plant. The flow of the crowd drew them closer to the exit. Finally, a determined phalanx of army guards managed to block the exterior exit from the diamond lab, drawing the rush of people down to a single line. Each face that passed by the soldiers was being carefully examined.

She exchanged a glance with Taylor. They were dead meat. They were swept along toward the armed men, helpless to escape the crush of sweating bodies pressing them relentlessly forward. They squeezed each other's hand tightly, saying a silent farewell as their demise loomed a few yards ahead.

They were perhaps a dozen feet from the exit when a commotion erupted in the doorway. Someone was jerked roughly out of the departing line, and shouted words were exchanged. Amanda heard the meaty thud of a fist connecting on flesh. Someone groaned. Other fists connected.

A struggle broke out as she and Taylor drew abreast of the cluster of soldiers. Amanda caught a brief glimpse of a battered and bloody face going down beneath the guards. Frantic blue eyes met hers. Amanda froze. My God. *It was Subov.* He gestured once with his head toward the parking lot. The line stopped for a moment as the bystanders gawked at the sight of the brutalized man.

A soldier barked, "Move along!"

Amanda was pushed hard by the woman behind her. She lurched forward. And they were clear. The guards hadn't stopped them. She pulled on Taylor's sleeve and stopped to look over her shoulder at their companion. "That was Anton. We've got to help him!" she cried.

"There's nothing we can do. We can't take on two dozen armed soldiers."

"But…" She looked back over her shoulder. She glimpsed Subov being hauled to his feet. He wobbled, but remained upright. His eyes searched the crowd, finding her. His right hand stole into the pocket of his coat. Amanda's gaze met his in stunned comprehension.

"Run, Taylor! Run!" she screamed.

She sprinted as fast as her legs would carry her away from the building. Taylor set out after her and raced along beside her. They made it to the far side of the parking lot before the first explosion rocked them, knocking them off their feet. Taylor rolled and covered her as a second blast wave tore past them, searing hot, exploding car windows all around them. They scrambled to their feet, crouching low as another explosion rocked the air. Terrible screams erupted as flying shrapnel shredded everything in its path. Taylor snagged a blanket out of the back seat of a car, and then they ran for the gates with the rest of the fleeing workers. Everyone within fifty feet of the building was prostrate on the ground. Subov had sacrificed himself for them. She staggered, and Taylor pulled her along mercilessly.

"We've got to keep going, Amanda. Come on!"

The terrified mob ran out of energy about a quarter mile away from the factory, where they turned around to watch the inferno. Further explosions continued to rip through the fire-enshrouded building, sending barrels and pieces of concrete flying up into the orange sky. The pyrotechnics were spectacular. Even this far away, heat baked their faces, illuminating them in the bright glow of the flames. Sparks whirled high into the night sky, spiraling upward in the hot vortex rising from the blaze.

Resolutely, Taylor turned his back on the sight. "We've got to get away from here."

He was right. She turned and followed him. They walked along the road toward town. The heat of the fire faded, and she was shivering violently in just a few seconds. Taylor must be half frozen with just that blanket around him.

An eternity later, they drew level with the spruce grove and ducked into the trees. The cold was even more intense as dark shadows wrapped around them. They headed for the hollow where they'd stashed their emergency gear. Taylor passed her a parka, which she pulled on gratefully. He donned a second one. He'd just reached into the hole again for the overwhites when abruptly, something cold and hard pressed against the back of Amanda's neck.

"Freeze!"

She obeyed in stunned shock. She saw Taylor raise his hands slowly away from his body and stand up. Someone must be behind him, too.

Eerie, maniacal laughter echoed around the clearing, and icy shivers ran up and down her spine. The sound reminded her an awful lot of her father. The man behind Taylor spoke in a gravelly voice. "Step apart. Slowly. The girl to the left, you to the right."

Amanda and Taylor obeyed. And something hit her. *She recognized that voice.* From where? She racked her brains frantically. A dark street in Caracas. Telling his name to a police officer. Nikko Biryayev. Oh, Lord. Not her father's control officer!

The one behind her shoved her farther into the woods with the barrel of his weapon. "This way. Move." Her unseen captor backed off and followed at a safe distance. Damn. No chance to turn and attack him. "That's far enough," the guy said. "Stop." An American voice. Young. That must be Max What's-his-name. The blond guy she'd jumped in New York.

Taylor spoke over his shoulder to his captor. "Who are you?"

"I'm your destiny, Taylor Roberts. You two have escaped for the last time. Tonight I will watch you die. You thought you were so good, but I caught you both. The KGB has triumphed against the insidious forces of capitalist imperialism once again."

Amanda spoke up derisively. No way was she showing this lunatic fear. "The KGB is dead and gone, Biryayev."

"I will kill you!" Nikko screamed. "Your father ruined me, and now I shall ruin you!"

She sneered. "The way I hear it, you were a mediocre, mid-level bureaucrat who killed your own career by losing the Udarsky Cache." Amanda started toward Biryayev. If she could get him mad enough, he might hit her rather than shoot her. And then she could take him down. She'd worry about the other agent after that.

An arm went around her neck and a gun pressed against the middle of her back. "Hold still," Ebhardt murmured in her ear. She stopped, arrested by the curious lack of malice in the guy's voice.

Biryayev ranted, "Like your sham of a legal system, Soviet justice demands a trial before sentencing. You will confess your crimes before I pass judgment on you." Biryayev rattled off a half-dozen Russian high crimes and then turned to Taylor. "How do you plead?"

Taylor shrugged. "You caught me. Guilty as charged."

Amanda choked. What was he doing? *He was trying to get Biryayev to kill him instead of her.* But Biryayev was going to kill her, anyway, for being her father's daughter. No way was she letting Taylor go down on her behalf. "Stop it," she snapped at Taylor. "I'm done, anyway. Nikko, you fool. Taylor's not an operative. He's nothing more than my cover. What kind of numbskull are you to mistake him for a trained agent?"

"A pathetic try to save your lover, you bitch. I'll kill you both, once and for all, tonight."

Amanda suppressed a sob. This was a nightmare. *Think.* There had to be something she could do. But what?

Biryayev stepped behind Taylor and lifted a heavy pistol to the back of his head. She lurched against the arm around her neck, and it went slack. Surprised and more than a little confused, she eased away from Ebhardt.

Taylor lifted his head and looked across the short distance that separated them. He smiled quietly into her eyes and mouthed the words, "I love you."

She flung herself forward. It was too far, but she was determined to take the bullet for him. *"Nooo!"* she screamed.

A single shot rang out.

Chapter 19

Amanda raced toward the two bodies lying on the ground in a heap. *"Oh, God. Taylor. No,"* she moaned. She saw red. She'd tear Biryayev's head off with her bare hands.

One of the bodies moved. Rolled clear. She staggered and came to a stumbling halt as Taylor pushed to his feet. Using his foot, he rolled over the body of Nikko Biryayev in disgust. A neat hole gleamed black in the center of the man's forehead. She flung herself at Taylor, clutching him fiercely.

For just an instant Taylor's arms tightened around her, but then he let go. "Step back, Amanda." His voice was cold, devoid of emotion. Her arms fell away from him. She took one step back. Then another.

He looked over her shoulder. "You there. Drop your gun."

Ebhardt complied, tossing it a couple yards away from him.

"On your knees. Hands locked behind your neck."

Ebhardt did as he was told.

Taylor's gaze turned to Amanda. So cold, his eyes. A trained operative at work. "You all right?" he bit out.

She nodded, tears beginning to flow.

"Er, pardon me." Ebhardt cleared his throat, and Amanda turned toward him in surprise. "Mind if I get up? It's a bit nippy down here on the ground."

Taylor gestured at Nikko's sprawled body. "Why did you shoot him?"

Amanda's jaw dropped. She'd been so relieved that Taylor was alive, she hadn't stopped to consider where the shot had come from that killed Biryayev.

The blond agent shrugged. "He lost it. Had to be stopped."

Taylor looked briefly over his shoulder. "Nice shot. Thanks."

Amanda took a tentative step toward Taylor. His silver-blue gaze was luminescent in the scant moonlight as he turned it on her. And then a click sounded off to their right. The distinctive click of a hammer being pulled back on a weapon. She froze. Taylor did the same.

A voice out of the dark. "Miss McClintock, Mr. Roberts, you are under arrest for tampering with a United States federal investigation."

Sheesh. What else could go wrong in their lives? She was tempted to make a run for it and go out in a blaze of glory. But faint amusement gleamed in Taylor's eyes. He asked casually, "Don't you think you're a little far from home for a line like that to work?"

Man, he'd become a cool customer.

Four men stepped out into the clearing. One of them snapped, "You two have been a bona fide pain in the ass for the last time. Do you have any idea what you've just done?" He jerked his head toward the orange glow in the distance.

Taylor chuckled. "Yeah, we blew up a lot of shit. That fertilizer plant was about to corner the world market on it."

Ebhardt grinned, but the Americans didn't seem to find it funny.

"Down on your knees. Both of you."

Taylor turned around slowly to face the talker, and Amanda followed suit, not obeying the order. "What are you going to do? Execute us with a couple shots to the back of the head?"

"Go ahead. Give me an excuse to do it," the guy snarled.

Taylor still was unruffled. "Didn't you get the memo, you asshole? Stunts like that were outlawed back in the seventies."

"Get down!" the guy roared. His pistol swung up to eye level, and it wavered slightly in the guy's agitation.

A rippled of clicks sounded from across the clearing. Everyone froze. A new voice from behind her. "Ladies and gentlemen, stay where you are." A quick order in Russian, and a line of a dozen soldiers advanced, machine guns poised at their hips.

Max grinned. "Gotta love that cavalry. You got here in the nick of time, sir."

The Russian officer nodded at Ebhardt, then turned and spoke to his American counterpart. "Before you make up an excuse to execute these criminals, Yankee, perhaps we should speak to them. I am given to understand that this pair should not be underestimated."

The American agent scowled at the Russian military officer.

Amanda watched in disbelief as the Russian grinned back. "Never fear, my hasty friend. We shall be happy to help you execute them. We would simply like to extract a bit of information, first."

Would this nightmare never end?

The Russian turned to her and Taylor. "Please answer the American's question. Do you have any idea what you just destroyed?"

The guy, in good Russian chauvinist fashion, was looking at Taylor. She needed to deflect some of the attention to herself or Taylor would never stand a chance of getting out of here alive. When they made their break for it, all the force would come to bear against him.

She spoke up brashly, startling the Russian. "Of course we

know what we just destroyed. Why else would we be here? We don't give a flip for the price of shit in Kyrgyzstan."

That put the guy back on his heels.

She continued, "In fact, not only do we know what was buried under that factory, but the whole world's about to know, too."

Everyone lurched at that announcement, American and Russian alike.

She pressed on. "Do you really think we'd be dumb enough or amateur enough to barge into a situation like this without a dead man's switch in place?"

"Shit." The American agent swore viciously off to her right.

The Russian's eyes merely narrowed. "Go on," he said curtly.

She glared back at the officer. She spoke with careful precision. "We have, locked in a number of safe-deposit boxes far, far away from here, complete blueprints for this factory, sample diamonds that it produced and a detailed description of the diamond-computer-chip-making process. If my friend and I fail to check in with any of our banks within the next twenty-four hours, and once weekly thereafter for the rest of our natural lives, copies of the contents of those security boxes will be sent to every major government in the world electronically and in hard copy. *Ponyatno?*"

The Russian glared long and hard at her and finally snarled, "Yes, I understand."

She took a step toward the American. "Do I make myself clear?"

He spit out, "Crystal clear, you bitch."

She threw a hard look all around the clearing. "The two of us walk out of here, unharmed. And nobody—*nobody*—harms either one of us. Ever. In fact, it would behoove both your governments to see to it actively that Taylor and I live long, healthy lives."

"Or else what?" the Russian snarled.

She answered coolly, "Or else your precious computer-chip

technology will fall into the hands of every government in the world with a capacity to produce them."

A thick, charged silence settled over the copse of trees. Nobody moved for a long time. A puff of breeze whisked through, lowering the temperature another couple degrees.

Into the void, Taylor said quietly, "C'mon, Amanda. Let's blow this Popsicle stand." He took her by the elbow. They turned and walked out from between the two lines of armed men.

Taylor calmly commandeered one of the American's cars and slid behind the wheel. He drove in silence for a long time. He glanced over from time to time, but Amanda huddled in the seat beside him, saying nothing. The aftermath of the night's work visibly rolled over her, taking its cleansing toll.

He felt nothing.

And that scared him worse than anything he'd ever experienced in his life, up to and including that moment when Biryayev put that pistol to the back of his head. Was this what it was like to finally lose one's soul? To burn out completely? *Was he going insane like Amanda's father and Biryayev had?*

Amanda jerked awake as the car phone rang by her left elbow some time later. She picked up the receiver and put it to her ear, but said nothing.

"Amanda, is that you?" It was a male voice, but she couldn't tell much beyond that. It sounded almost metallic, maybe altered by some sort of machine.

"Who's this?" she asked shortly.

"Devereaux."

Her eyebrows shot up. How in the hell did her boss know she and Taylor were in Kyrgyzstan, let alone in this car, with this phone number? A sudden certainty rushed through her and she asked abruptly, "Did you engineer that Mexican standoff back at Udarsky?"

"I did," the voice answered evenly. "Nice work getting out of there. The dead man's switch was inspired."

"Thanks. It was Taylor's idea."

"You trained him well," Devereaux replied dryly. "How's he doing?"

She glanced over at her partner. "With time, I think he'll be all right."

"And how are you?"

"I'm fine." And she realized she meant it. She'd walked through fire and come out intact. Thanks to Taylor.

"Then congratulate your partner on a job well done for me," Devereaux replied.

So. That had been Taylor's job, after all. To get her through this mission in one piece. "I'll pass him the message," she said dryly.

There was a short pause. Then Devereaux asked quietly, "Are you satisfied with the outcome of this case?"

"The one thing we didn't find is the Udarsky cache," she replied.

"Don't worry about it. Those early diamond chips are outdated and too small for today's computer applications. The cache is worthless now. But for the sake of appeasing your curiosity, I believe your father hid it inside the oak tree on the cliff behind your house."

She reeled from that casual revelation. Of course. The picture in her father's journal of the day they'd planted the oak tree. Her father's late-night visits to it whenever he returned from his mysterious disappearances. The yellow ribbon in the safe-deposit box—her father had hummed an American tune about tying a yellow ribbon around an oak tree incessantly in his latter years. She asked, "So, if the Russians find out the Udarsky cache is worthless, does that mean they'll stop chasing me over it?"

"I should think so. I can arrange for that information to become known in the right circles."

"Thank you, sir."

"My pleasure. One word of caution, however. Your dead man's switch will only protect you for as long as diamond-computer-chip technology remains relevant. Then all bets are off."

"Taylor and I will cross that bridge when we come to it."

"Call me when you approach that bridge."

"I'll keep that offer in mind, sir."

"Please do." A pause. Then, "Did you find what you were looking for on this case?"

She frowned, considering the question. Devereaux wasn't talking about diamond smuggling or even about high-tech computer chips. He was talking about her father's legacy. "Is that why you put me on this case?" she asked suddenly. "To make my peace with my father?"

"It seemed the least I could do for you after all your years of loyal service to me."

She laughed in genuine amusement. "You sure know how to pick your retirement gifts."

"One does one's best," Devereaux replied wryly. "Speaking of retirement, your severance pay, in the sum of ten million dollars, has been wired to your Swiss bank account. Have a nice life. And do enjoy Taylor. I picked him out especially for you."

She gaped at the phone. Sometimes the reach of this mysterious man was downright frightening. She mumbled a goodbye, abjectly grateful that she'd worked for Devereaux and not against him.

Sunlight peeked over the eastern horizon before Taylor finally pulled the car over to the side of a deserted mountainous road. She was glad to get out and stretch her back. Taylor joined her in looking out over the stark, jagged mountains before them. She felt him studying her in that analytical way he did when he was trying to suss out her mental state. She gazed back at him, assessing herself, as well.

For the first time she could ever remember, she was calm. At peace, even. All the way down to her soul. She smiled up at him, letting it show in her eyes.

He shook his head briefly. "I didn't think you had it in you."

Her smile widened into a grin. "With a shrink like you on the case, how could I not come out okay?"

The beginnings of a smile impinged upon his serious expression. "I'd have bet a million bucks that first night I met you that you'd go up like a supernova before this case was solved."

"I wouldn't have taken that bet before I met you. I think you saved my soul."

"You did that yourself. I just showed you the way."

Together, they watched a thin sliver of sun crest over the mountains. Daylight burst forth in a blaze of glory all around them.

"Taylor?"

"Hmm?"

"Will you let me show you the way back? Out of the darkness inside you? The way you did for me?"

She looked up into his beautiful blue eyes and saw the moment when the hard shell he'd surrounded himself with these last few weeks cracked. Not a lot, but it was an opening.

And in that moment she knew. *He was going to be okay.* Together, they'd find their way to lasting peace. To forgiveness of self. To hope. And most important, to life—and love— everlasting.

* * * * *

Books by Cindy Dees

Silhouette Bombshell

Killer Instinct #16

Silhouette Intimate Moments

Behind Enemy Lines #1176
Line of Fire #1253
A Gentleman and a Soldier #1307

If you enjoyed what you just read,
then we've got an offer you can't resist!

Take 2 bestselling love stories FREE!

Plus get a FREE surprise gift!